Once in a Blue Moon Lodge

Also by Lorna Landvik

Patty Jane's House of Curl
Your Oasis on Flame Lake
The Tall Pine Polka
Welcome to the Great Mysterious
Angry Housewives Eating Bon Bons
Oh My Stars
The View from Mount Joy
'Tis the Season
Mayor of the Universe
Best to Laugh

ONCE IN A
BLUE MOON
LODGE

A NOVEL

LORNA LANDVIK

University of Minnesota Press

Minneapolis

London

Published by the University of Minnesota Press
111 Third Avenue South, Suite 290
Minneapolis, MN 55401-2520
http://www.upress.umn.edu

ISBN 978-1-5179-0269-8 (hc)
ISBN 978-1-5179-0270-4 (pb)
A Cataloging-in-Publication record for this book is available from the Library of Congress.

Printed in the United States of America on acid-free paper

The University of Minnesota is an equal-opportunity educator and employer.

22 21 20 19 18   10 9 8 7 6 5 4 3 2 1

For Harleigh Gem and Kinga Paige
my lovely and beloved daughters

PROLOGUE

O N THE DAY MY GRANDMOTHER GOT ARRESTED, I found out I was pregnant.

With triplets.

Yikes.

Knowing there was no way to alter its pass/fail grade with extra credit, I was light-headed and sweaty taking the home pregnancy test, and when the wand's little plus sign glowed, indicating my passing mark, I sat slumped on the edge of the tub, feeling a roiling mixture of terror and glee. I had long wanted to start a family, but I wanted one the old-fashioned way: married to the dad, the two of us united in love for each other as well as our upcoming bundle of joy. As it was, the baby's father and I had been united, but only once, in a sleeping bag that smelled of fried trout and wood smoke.

Two days after my home test result, I visited the gynecologist who breathed in a little gasp as she looked at the fuzzy sonogram screen. No matter the size, a gasp is generally not something you want to hear coming out of the mouth of your health care professional. When she described the blurry shadows, *I* gasped; turns out that that bundle of joy was plural.

"Hey, Nora, meet the jailbird," said Patty Jane as I staggered into the kitchen, the rug, the floor, the earth itself having just been yanked out from under me.

"Jailbird," scoffed my grandmother. "We weren't behind bars— they just had us in a little room."

"Ione says Crabby's only regret was that the arresting officer didn't frisk her."

"Ja, she said he reminded her of the first boy she ever kissed!"

Shaking her head, my mother said, "Imagine the damage inflicted on that poor guy."

Their conversation was not helping my rising discombobulation, and I reached for the most used appliance in our household, the coffeepot. After pouring myself a cup, I sat down at the table and asked them to kindly give me a clue as to what they were talking about.

"Nora, today was the gun shop sit-in, remember?" said Grandma, in the light Norwegian accent that turned her sentences into little songs. "And we got arrested for trespassing!"

Not content to be a master grandmother, Ione was a founder of OBFC (Old Bags for Change), a group of seniors whose goals were no less lofty than worldwide peace and justice for all. Still, she found time in her rabble-rousing to bake, and it was a plate of her most recent offering—thin-as-brittle sugar cookies—that she pushed in my direction.

"Nora, what's wrong?" asked Patty Jane, when I failed to help myself to that which I usually found irresistible.

I stared into my cup with the intensity of a tea leaf reader, but no answers were revealed, as it was filled with coffee. Knowing there was no other way to say what I had to say than to say it, I sighed as heavily as a convict at another denied-parole meeting.

"I'm expecting triplets."

"Triplets of what?" said Patty Jane, helping herself to a cookie.

"Triplets of babies."

There was an odd flurry in the air, as if the molecules and atoms had been stirred up, and for a brief moment we were taken outside of that cheerful kitchen and into another dimension, where time stood still and space swirled.

"Whose babies?" asked Patty Jane, the hand that had taken a cookie frozen in air.

"Mine," I said. "I'm pregnant. With triplets."

Palm splayed across her chest, my grandmother whispered a fervent, "Uffda mayda."

There's no real translation for her favorite phrase; depending on its emphasis, it could be as mild as "Oh my" or as explicit as any curse word. Ione never swore, but in this case the inference was there.

Patty Jane, however, never bothered with inference: "Holy shit, Nora!"

Remembering that long-ago day, I write, *Family stories shouldn't be treated like heirloom china or antique ornaments, carefully wrapped in tissue paper to be brought out only for holiday display. They're meant for everyday use, like favorite recipes or faded patchwork quilts. Stained or torn, they offer sustenance and comfort.* I drum my pencil furiously on the paper, pockmarking it with graphite. My goal is to compile a book of family stories for my girls' eighteenth birthday, but I've crossed out as many words as I've left in. Recalling the thrilling and scary day the gynecologist told me I was carrying a trio has made me wonder: how much do I leave in and how much of the story do I leave out?

Sena would prefer the unabridged version, complete with interviews, footnotes, and graphics. Grace would like only those tales featuring love and truth and harmony, but I'd like to offer them something a little bigger than a brochure. Ulla would encourage me to mine for the jokes or, failing that, to "Sex it up!"

I read what I've just written to my mother.

"Very nice," she says, looking at me through her sunglasses. "But I don't get it."

"What do you mean you don't get it?"

"Well, we've never treated our family stories like heirloom china or old ornaments—"

"—antique. *Antique* ornaments," I say, miffed, because I know she's right.

"And it isn't as if you've hidden much from the girls, just as I hope I never hid much from you."

"Just as Grandma never hid . . . oh, wait," I say, and we both laugh. It's a beautiful June afternoon and we're out on the deck, facing the Ocean, which glitters with sunshine. Lounging beside me on a chaise longue, my mother looks like a cover girl, and I tell her so.

"Yeah, right. For AARP, maybe." She adjusts her sun hat; in the battle against gray, Patty Jane is a soldier who has never fallen, and I know she wants to protect her latest dye job.

Looking back at the words on my legal pad, I sigh, and write: *In our family, strangeness, while not necessarily the rule, is not necessarily the exception either.*

When I share this insight with my mother, she hoots. "Well, what do you expect? You're telling stories about a family!"

"It'd just be easier if ours were a little more *normal*."

"Well, you know what Tolstoy said: all normal families are alike; each abnormal family is nuts in its own way."

"Good one, Ma. I'm sure he'd appreciate the new translation."

She shrugs. "I never really understood the original quote. Why does he think that all happy families are alike but unhappy ones are unique in their unhappiness? Isn't it all sort of fluid? A happy family on a Wednesday can be miserable as hell by the weekend."

"So you think I should write about everything? Uncensored?"

Pushing down her sunglasses, my mother raises one eyebrow.

"Right," I say. "You're the *last* person I should ask about censoring oneself."

"Just tell whatever you want to tell in whatever way you want to tell it."

"But how do I start?" I ask, my voice skipping back a few decades to reclaim an attractive prepubescent whine.

Tapping her chin, Patty Jane looks out at the sparkling water. "Hmm, how about . . . 'Last night I dreamt I went to Manderley again'?" Hearing my sigh, she adds, "Okay, then, what about, 'It was the best of times, it was the worst of times—'?"

"Thanks a lot, Mom."

"You know me," she says, leaning back on the chaise longue and offering herself up to the afternoon sun. "Always happy to help."

I drum my pencil on the legal pad once, twice, three thousand times. Leave it to Dickens to have already used a line that perfectly summed up practically anyone's story, including ours.

It really was the best of times and the worst of times.

꿈 Part One

Winter 1988

PATTY JANE ROLVAAG WAS MIDDLE-AGED, and though she had lived through enough drama to fuel a hit Broadway show, she was lovely, without the qualifiers "still" or "for her age." The swaggering cohost of *Babs & Boyd in the Morning!* certainly thought so, putting moves on her more appropriate at a singles bar than in a television studio. That Boyd Burrows was a former football player and sportscaster out of his element when interviewing anyone who didn't wear a helmet or jockstrap was immaterial: bad manners were bad manners.

"There'll be a lot of sniffles when this beloved neighborhood institution closes its doors at the end of the year," he said, reading the teleprompter copy. "Yes, it'll soon be the end of both pin curls and programs at Patty Jane's House of Curl, Etc., the unique salon within a salon, a place where the client's interior gets as much attention as her exterior!"

The hulking man, whose brawn tested the seams of his Italian-made suit, turned away from the camera and aimed his killer white smile at his guest. "I have no idea what a 'salon within a salon' is, but let's meet its proprietor, who I have to say has taken pretty good care of *her* exterior." Punctuating his words with a little wink, he added, "Welcome to the show, Patty Jane."

Returning his wink, Patty Jane said, "Thanks, Boyd," and in her head she added, *You big ape!*

To her staff and clientele tuning in to the show's popular Neighborhood Legends segment, the announcement of the closing of the House of Curl, Etc. was no surprise, having been advised of it by Patty

Jane weeks earlier. They had reacted with tears, pleas to reconsider, and, in Crabby Bultram's case, threats to sabotage its sale by telling any prospective buyers that (a) the smell of permanent wave solution was indeed permanent, embedded in the walls and especially noticeable on hot summer days; (b) the property was one termite bite away from collapse; or (c) the place was cursed.

There was no truth to A and B, and Patty Jane had been quick to correct C: "Had been."

The always prepared and professional half of *Babs & Boyd*, felled by a sudden flu, had called in sick that morning, leaving Patty Jane to deal with the half whose preference was to wing it. As usual, Boyd Burrows hadn't read his prep sheet, and as Patty Jane tried to tell the story of the House of Curl, Etc., he constantly interrupted her.

"What!? It all started when your husband, Thor, went missing?"

"Yes, and with him gone, I had to figure out a way to make money. So I opened Patty Jane's House of Curl and operated it out of my home—"

"—I thought it was Patty Jane's House of Curl, *Etc.*," said Boyd, in a tone suggesting his guest was confused.

"We added 'Etc.' to the name when we had the opportunity, many years later, to move the salon into a much bigger place."

Knowing that she would need a lot longer than her five-minute allotment to explain the admittedly strange and complicated history of her salon, Patty Jane instead changed tack and began listing some of the events the Etc. had hosted.

"We've had musical and dance recitals, talks given by everyone from an astronaut to a zoologist—"

"—what? An astronaut gave a talk in your beauty parlor?"

"Our lecture and performance series has attracted a wide range of interesting people—"

"—yeah, but wouldn't that sort of be a comedown for an astronaut to speak in front of a bunch of ladies getting their hair done?"

"We don't hold the events in the actual beauty salon," said Patty

Jane, keeping her voice light and forcing her eyeballs not to roll. "The House of Curl, Etc. has different rooms for those."

Finally, Boyd Burrows gave up, deciding to focus on that which he knew he understood: seduction, proceeding to make suggestive comments about "beauty *operators*" and wanting to "be swiveled in *your* chair," but when he leaned into Patty Jane, asking if she'd like to run her fingers through his hair, she said, "No, thanks. But I wouldn't mind putting my hands around your neck."

"That was priceless," said Paige Larkin, who'd watched the live broadcast that morning. "The look on his face!"

Patty Jane shook her head. "And get this—off the air, he still asks me out to dinner."

"No! What did you say?"

"I said I make it a point to never dine with patronizing, pinstriped TV show dumbasses who give lousy, unprepared interviews and then try to pick up their guests!"

The cold air turned Paige's chortle into a stutter of vaporous clouds.

"At least you're laughing," said Patty Jane, taking her friend's arm. "That's good."

A gust of icy wind blew Paige's thin cashmere coat against her legs. Even in freezing weather, she saw no reason to abandon style, and, besides, both menopause and the rage she felt toward her philandering husband were a combination that worked to keep her body temperature set on high.

"I thought I had learned how to live with humiliation," Paige said. "But when he got together with this one, it was just too much." *He* was her husband, Spencer Larkin, and *this one* was a twenty-four-year-old employee at their country club. "She wasn't even that good a waitress—she would always get my order wrong—and yet there Spence'd be, tipping her 30 percent!"

The two women walked up to Lake Street, crossed the bridge to St. Paul, and followed the river south, and by the time they'd gone over the Ford Bridge back to Minneapolis, Paige, whose monologue had been punctuated by everything from tears to vitriol, felt as if she'd been in a deep and productive therapy session. Patty Jane felt in need of a strong cup of coffee, with a brownie chaser.

Back home, on a November afternoon whose gloom had settled in as both color and mood, Patty Jane stood leaning against a door frame, not seeing the forest of birdhouses displayed in the rectangular space but what had filled the room years ago: the rinse sinks, the hair dryers, her sister's harp. Harriet had been dead for nearly twenty years, but there were still moments when an aching loneliness spread through Patty Jane like an emotional rheumatism. It had been Paige's parting remarks that had ignited a memory triggering this flare-up of sadness: "And now to find out Spence and his girlfriend have been using our family's cabin as their love nest; how could they? That was my refuge!"

Tens of thousands of Minnesotans own these refuges, with many of them passed down through generations, but there was no deed to a lakeside cabin in Patty Jane's family. Her parents' worldly possessions were few at their deaths (both related to decades-long alcoholism), and their orphaned daughters had had the sad task of picking through the Dobbins' meager estate.

"If empties were money," Patty Jane said as they cleaned up the tiny kitchen, "we'd be zillionaires." Anna had outlived Elmo by only four months, and by the vast collection of beer and gin bottles, it appeared she had been drinking with the goal of joining him as fast as she could.

"Poor Ma," said Harriet.

"Poor is right." The sympathy coloring her sister's voice was not present in her own.

Patty Jane was not coldhearted; she had loved her parents but knew they had willingly taken up the shovels that dug their own ditches and used others' sympathy as an excuse to keep digging rather than as a ladder to help themselves climb out. Years later, when Harriet fell into her own alcoholic morass, experience had taught Patty Jane that while she could extend a helping hand, she couldn't force her sister to grab hold of it.

Family vacations had been few and far between; parents who like to escape in drunken fogs rarely have the impetus or energy to take trips that involve more planning than figuring out whose turn it is to go to the liquor store. But one summer the Dobbins had managed to make the drive up to a small family-owned resort on Lake Osakis. For two days of bliss, Patty Jane and Harriet were regular kids with regular parents, who dove off an old wooden dock and paddled around in a dented aluminum canoe and batted a birdie over a sagging badminton net. The first night they went into town for drive-in hamburgers; the second night, after the sun settled into its pink and red blanket, they roasted marshmallows (although the girls, impatient, blistered them black) and sang songs around the campfire.

The voices of Patty Jane and Elmo were serviceable, but it was obvious that Harriet's musical genius was fruit plucked from her mother's side of the family tree. When the two of them began singing "Home on the Range," Patty Jane thought, *There's no family I'd rather be in than this one.*

It was an unfamiliar sentiment, but its truth filled her with a calm and complete happiness. Leaning against her father's shoulder, she looked across the campfire, watching the leaping stalagmites of flame light her mother's and sister's faces. Anna and Harriet played with the harmony, tossing it back and forth as if it were a toy. The long light of summer had waned into darkness, and the lake behind them was invisible to the eye but not to the nose, smelling pine-tinged and fishy.

"How about 'You Are My Sunshine'?" called out a voice from a nearby cabin.

"They've already got a fan club," whispered Elmo to Patty Jane as the singers honored the stranger's request.

When they were done, another voice called out, "How about 'Sentimental Journey'?" and after they'd sung that, another voice asked for "The Man I Love." After a whispered conference, Anna called out, "My daughter doesn't know the lyrics to that one, but here's one for you," and the two launched into the campfire classic "Red River Valley."

Hours later, the sound of breaking glass was an ugly coda to the evening of music.

"Good one," said Anna, her lovely singing voice now thick and coarsened with drink.

"Shut up," said Elmo. "Shut up and gimme another one."

"Patty Jane?" whispered Harriet, fear ripping away the gauze of sleep. "Patty Jane, are they—"

"—yes," she answered, and in the narrow log-framed bed they shared in the dark rental cabin, the sisters held each other, their puny armor against what raged outside.

More interior sulk-and-ruminate drunks, the girls' parents rarely fought. But that night had them screaming and yelling, and people in the other cabins—those who hours earlier had thanked Anna and Harriet for the lovely concert—were now screaming and yelling back.

"Shut up!"

"Go to bed and sleep it off!"

"What's the matter with you? These are family cabins!"

Elmo, who sober had the soul of a gentle man, got into a fistfight with a vacationing pipe fitter from Eau Claire, a fight he lost, which left him with a bloody nose and a shiner that would swell so that his eye was a mere slit in a ripe purple plum.

The resort owner broke up the fight, and the family Dobbin was forced to leave the next morning—Anna and Elmo hungover and miserable, Patty Jane and Harriet just miserable.

"Mom?"

"Jesus Christ!" said Patty Jane. "Don't sneak up on me."

"Ma, it's not like I tiptoed in." Nora gestured to the clogs she was wearing. "Anyway, sorry." Copying her mother's pose, she leaned against the other side of the door frame and folded her arms across her chest. "So, Neighborhood Legend, I taped your segment. You want to watch it?"

"No! I'm in a lousy enough mood as it is."

"Aw, Ma, of course you are. You announced on national—well, local—TV that we're closing down. That makes it official."

"Yeah, I guess."

"Are you having second thoughts?"

"Maybe third or fourth thoughts," said Patty Jane, her mouth lifting in more a shrug than a smile. "But, no. It's the right time."

"So you're in a bad mood because . . ."

"Oh, it was just something Paige said about her family cabin being her refuge. It made me think about the one time our parents took Harriet and me to this little resort."

Aware of her mother's fractious childhood, Nora said, "Well, that sounds . . . nice."

"Hansen's Haven!" said Patty Jane, brightening as she remembered the resort's name. "And it was nice . . . 'til it wasn't. And then, you know how it is, one thought leads to another and suddenly . . ." Patty Jane nodded to a corner of the room. "I'm seeing Harriet sitting over there, playing 'The Beer Barrel Polka' for Gudrun's birthday request."

"Oh, I remember those. She played 'Last Train to Clarksville' for my twelfth birthday. I doubt there're many harpists who play the Monkees."

"Or 'The Beer Barrel Polka.'" Patty Jane's chest lifted and fell in a deep sigh, but it signaled a finale to her gloom, not its continuation. She was equipped with an internal alarm that sounded when emotions threatened to get out of control or, in this case, when sadness needed to be turned off before it soured into moping.

"Say, did you see this?" Taking her daughter's hand, Patty Jane led her into the maze of birdhouses. "Your dad just brought it up. It's a replica of the IDS Tower—and look, it's even got a lobby!"

Nora traced the lines of the miniature bird skyscraper. "Incredible." The word—along with other adjectives like *amazing* or *exquisite*— was often used to describe the craftsmanship and imagination of Thor Rolvaag's birdhouses.

"I know, he just keeps getting better and better."

If the look mother and daughter exchanged were a fragrance, it would have a top note of wonder, a middle note of love, and a base note of sorrow.

"Hey," said Patty Jane, "I was so busy fending off that ignorant lecher on TV, I can't even remember if I mentioned what's happening tonight."

"You didn't," said Nora. "But we've already got about fifty people coming."

"Good. Are you?"

"I wasn't planning to. I thought I'd—"

"—oh, come on," said Patty Jane. "It'll be fun."

➤➤ 2

"THE TANGO—AH, THE TANGO. It is all about desire, it is all about passion, it is all about control," said the man whose oily black hair was serrated with comb marks.

"But whose control?" asked his partner, whose sharp angular eyebrows gave her an unwavering look of disdain. "Is it the man or the woman who is in control?"

"I woood have to say," whispered Patty Jane, imitating the dancers' accent, "that een their case, eet ees dayfinitely thee wooomon."

At the couple's nod, Inky Kolstat punched the play button, and the dancers began to follow the tape's slow and slinky music. In the calendar of events, it had been listed as *A Night of Tango!* and all comers were urged to "help us welcome Franco and Vilma Sergovia, international Tango Stars, as they finish their world tour by heating up the floor at Patty Jane's House of Curl, Etc.!" It didn't matter to anyone in the audience that the Sergovias' "world tour" had only consisted of stops in Fargo, Billings, Boise, and Bozeman. What counted was that the thirty-eight women and eleven men in attendance were being transported to a world of steamy Argentinian sex and intrigue.

Near the end of their performance, when the couple recruited volunteers, cheers rose as Thor took the hand Vilma extended to him.

Oh boy, thought Nora, watching her father.

Uffda mayda, thought Ione, watching her son.

Mother of God, thought Patty Jane, watching her husband-in-name-only.

Franco and Vilma Sergovia knew this was a crowd favorite, plucking from the audience willing dance partners, and they had formulated a winning strategy: Franco, after appearing to carefully deliberate, would choose a woman who most likely spent her high school dances wilting against the wall, while Vilma would zero in on the most attractive man in the audience.

Sitting together was a contingent of women who had been clients of Patty Jane's House of Curl since its inception, and while they still came to get their (now grayer and thinner) hair styled at the Etc., they considered the true salon to be the one that extended pampering to their minds and souls. For years, women having their hair cut or curled in the day might return in the evening and give their attention to hobbyists, enthusiasts, and the occasional expert who offered insights into Puccini's operas or Icelandic folk art or the easiest way to butterfly a butt roast.

Inky, a dedicated fan of Hollywood, had been one of the first to take the leap from customer to instructor and had held lectures on subjects ranging from "Ronald Reagan's Oeuvre" to "Female Second Bananas in Comedy: From Patsy Kelly to Vivian Vance." Growing up, Nora had been privy to many of Inky's lectures, and she returned home after her stay in Los Angeles to the woman's wrath.

"Nora, you were in Hollywood! You were living everyone's dream!"

"Inky, I was drawing up contracts about ancillary rights and production credits. It wasn't like I was a movie star."

"But you could have been!" said Inky, who told anyone willing to listen that Nora Rolvaag was in a league with her favorite leading ladies, Rita Hayworth and Debbie Reynolds.

The Hollywood expert sat next to Dixie Anderson, who that morning had dyed Inky's wispy hair a "Rhonda Fleming red," as per her client's instruction. Dixie had been one of the first to stand behind a beautician's chair with Patty Jane, and she still styled hair, albeit on a shortened schedule due to arthritis that had squatted, uninvited, in her knees and fingers. Next to her was Crabby Bultram, a woman still cranky enough to be deserving of her nickname.

"A man can say anything and he's respected for his honesty," she had said long ago. "If I were a man, you can bet they never would have called me Crabby."

"No," Patty Jane demurred, "I'm pretty sure they would have."

Paige Larkin sat next to her friend Marvel Stang. Marvel wondered what Paige (whose children were as slim and blond and elegant as their mother) thought about her own daughter Elise, who Marvel had dragged along to the dance exhibition with the unspoken admonition that it "sure beats sitting around eating me out of house and home!" Elise and her two children had moved back home after a divorce, and even though Marvel was enamored of her grandkids, she couldn't wait for the day when cartoons didn't blast the morning quiet to smithereens, couldn't wait *not* to break up fights based on whether Jacob got a smear more peanut butter on his toast than Katelyn or whether Katelyn had indeed flushed one of Jacob's Legos down the toilet, couldn't wait for what she and Earl had rightfully thought they had earned: a little peace and quiet.

Still, it hurt her deeply to hear Elise crying behind the closed door of her old bedroom (still decorated with her high school gymnastics trophies, her cheerleading pom-poms and Shaun Cassidy posters); to see her attack the contents of the refrigerator and pantry as if she were not only famished but angry; to overhear anguished phone calls to her best friend in which she bemoaned, "Thirty-one years old and my life is over!"

Now, when the tango dancer with the five (darkening into six) o'clock shadow held out his hand, Elise wanted to shut her eyes and will him away, but her mother was poking her so hard that she was willing to risk public humiliation just to escape that spleen-bruising elbow. Tugging at the ribbed hem of her sweatshirt, Elise blushed furiously as Franco led her to the front of the room; she still hadn't lost her baby weight (never mind that her "baby" had just started kindergarten) and in fact had compounded interest on it.

On the small platform that served as a stage, the professional couple demonstrated a few steps before holding their arms out to the amateurs. Elise flushed again and Thor, watching Franco, adjusted his posture, cocking his elbow higher.

"Very good," said Vilma. She had been prepared to flirt outrageously with this handsome man, but up close, she could see in his blue eyes an odd blankness. If eyes indeed were the window to the soul, this hombre had pulled down the shades.

I'm dancing with an imbecile, she thought. *Franco's got a whale in his arms and I've got an imbecile.*

"Again," Franco said, and together he and Vilma, leading their partners, instructed them to step "slow, slow—quick, quick—slow." They rehearsed their steps several times and Franco would later tell Vilma that at first he felt he was pushing around a tree stump, but after he cued the old woman with the flaming red hair to start the music, something loosened in his heavy, resistant partner. "I am telling you, Vilma, I could feel the change instantly, and I thought, *Dios mío—I could really teach this one something!*"

It was true, when Inky started the music and Elise felt the pressure of Franco's hand on her back, she thought, *What the hell; I've got rhythm, I used to be a gymnast, I'm not how I look!* Her eyes met her teacher's and returned their intense stare, and the couple began moving around the stage in sensuous syncopation.

You could have hit Marvel over the head with a tap shoe. She stared at her daughter, seeing the beauty and grace Elise kept hidden under all that fat and hurt. "Mercy," she whispered.

For these demonstrations, it was easier if Vilma took over the man's role and led, and Thor too easily followed his partner. His jaunty movement was more suitable for the foxtrot than the tango, but he never once stepped on Vilma's toe, a rare and much-appreciated gift to a dance teacher. Feeling guilty that she had misjudged him, Vilma whispered into his ear words of instruction and encouragement.

When the exposition was over, both couples curtsied and bowed, and the audience rose in a standing ovation.

Thor grinned and bowed again, and when the audience laughed, he bowed a third time.

"Thank you, thank you very much," said Franco, subtly directing Thor and Elise off the stage. It was he and Vilma, after all, who were the stars of the show, and they preferred to take their final bows alone.

"Thank you," he said, as Vilma threw a kiss to the crowd, "thank you for letting us bring to you the beauty of the dance!"

* * *

Any worthwhile cookbook compiled by a PTA or church circle has its Seven-Layer Bars recipe, but Ione was never one to submit to the authority of written instructions and had upped the ante, adding an extra layer to her bars. A small crowd had gathered near the coffee urn, eager to dig into them and, when they ran out, the store-bought ladyfingers Inky had supplied. Refreshments were always served after a lecture or performance, which inclined people to stay around and talk about what they had seen or heard. Now wistfulness colored the discussions, knowing that nights like the one they'd just experienced were coming to an end. A knot of women stood reminiscing about the time a magician had asked for a volunteer to saw in half, and the audience, in loud unison, had elected Crabby.

Brushing past them, Nora said, "Elise, you were wonderful!"

"Thanks," said Elise, eying the square bar perched on a napkin in Nora's palm and filled with everything she loved—chocolate! caramel! coconut! Usually she would have been the first in line, the first to have seconds, and the first to have thirds, but she happened to shift her gaze to see Vilma slip, with the same sinewy grace she had shown on the dance floor, into the coat Franco held open for her.

I'd like to slip into a coat like that, she thought, *a coat held open by a man who wants me.* For the first time in recent memory, Elise Stang MacIntyre declined an offered dessert and instead just had coffee.

Back home, Nora marveled at her father's star turn on the dance floor.

"Really," she said, setting the flat white box in the middle of the table. "Who knew you were so smooth on your feet, Dad?"

"I knew he could dance," said Patty Jane. "We cut up the floor a few times, remember, Thor?" A puzzled smile answered her question; no, he did not. Both the idiom and the memory escaped him.

Nora chuckled as she served her dad a slice of cold pizza. "Tonight will go down as an Etc. classic."

Ione nodded. "Ja, watching Thor tango . . . oh my, it was better than hearing Millie yodel."

Patty Jane laughed, remembering Gudrun's cousin visiting from Austria, who long ago had given a roomful of women a lesson in the art of Alpine yodeling. "Well, if you're going to go that far back, how about when we had that yoga demonstration and Crabby got stuck in Downward Dog?"

"I am *so* glad I wasn't there to see that," said Nora.

"She said her knees locked up," said Ione. "It took three of us to get her out of it."

Having bitten into his pizza, Thor chewed for a moment and swallowed, staring up at the ceiling. He wiped his mouth with one hand, and with the pizza slice drooping in his other he said, "*El tango no está en los pies. Está en el corazón.*"

Nora looked to her mother, who looked to her mother-in-law. Ever since Thor's return many years ago, these exchanged looks of surprise had been commonplace.

"Did you hear that?" asked Patty Jane. "Did he just speak Spanish?"

"It surely wasn't Norwegian," said Ione.

"What'd he say, Nora?" asked Patty Jane.

Her high school and college Spanish had gotten much better after having lived in L.A., thanks to a friendship Nora developed with her next-door neighbor, who was originally from Oaxaca. The two walked early every morning in nearby Bronson Canyon Park, and María Elena was happy to oblige her friend's request to "*habla español, por favor.*"

Wanting to be sure she had heard her father correctly, Nora asked Thor to repeat what he said and after he complied, she smiled. "He said, 'Tango is not in the feet. It is in the heart.'"

⇶ 3

H ER ENERGY DRAINED after taping up a box of legal files, Nora sagged into her leather swivel chair, and the bad mood that had been nipping at her heels jumped up and flopped its mangy self square onto her lap. She had been taught by example that the best antidote to brooding was action, but rather than boosting her spirits, the act of packing up her Etc. office was only deflating them.

Buyer interest had increased tenfold after Patty Jane's television appearance, and after weighing several offers, she had accepted one, with plans to be out by the new year. Change was in the air, but Nora's impulse was to open a window and let it out. Pieces of mail fanned across her desk—the day's delivery had included three letters from Etc. clients expressing everything from gratitude ("The class I took on flower arranging started my career!") to petulance ("Now where I am supposed to get my highlights done?") to hyperbole ("From enlightenment and engagement to . . . emptiness!"), but it was her law school's biannual newsletter and a wedding invitation that had further stirred the stew of her discontent.

Her old roommate, Pam Gregory, having recently won an acquittal for a hedge fund manager in a sensational, televised trial ("He even bilked his doorman!") was featured on the front page of the newsletter. Under a photograph of Pam wearing a designer business suit and a severe but flattering chignon was a quote in boldface type: "I'm Not Paid to Lose."

Nora's old boyfriend, Curt, with whom she had worked at the Hollywood firm of Jasperson, Oakes, and Beltzer, was featured on the wedding invitation as the groom-to-be, and she recognized the name of his future bride as the actress in the prime-time soap opera *Hawk Ridge*.

She crumpled up the newsletter and with the nail of her middle finger scraped at the embossed names on the invitation before tossing them both into the old dental spit sink that now served as a receptacle for pens and pencils and, occasionally, a wastebasket. It's not that Nora had wanted a career like Pam's, representing millionaire swindlers and billionaire cheats, and Curt's obsession with his celebrity clientele ("One day I'll be known as Lawyer to the Stars!") had seemed so childish, but at least they were going after—with a vengeance—what they had always wanted. And now Curt was getting married (to a celebrity: bonus points!) whereas Nora's calendar didn't even deserve the modifier *social*, its last entry a coffee date three weeks ago.

She used to be as much a go-getter as they were. Hadn't she sped through college, raced through law school, earning high grades, prizes, and recommendations? Her current office apparel consisted of faded jeans, a Minnesota North Stars sweatshirt, and a ponytail, but hadn't she once worn designer business suits and severe but flattering chignons? Hadn't she been described as a dynamo, a force, a force to be—

"*Bonjour, Nora!*" said Karen Spaeth, after a quick knock announced her presence. "*Ça va?*"

"Okay," said Nora, who in her teens had taken one of Karen's classes and remembered enough to answer a simple "How are you?"

"*Je sais que tu es occupée . . . ,*" began Karen who employed the immersion method in her classroom and sometimes forgot that French was not the lingua franca outside of it. "*Excusez-moi,* I know you're busy packing up, but do you have time to see my mother?" Along with handling the business concerns of the Etc., Nora's law career also included advising many of the salon's staff and clients on legal matters.

"Sure. What's the problem?"

"Well, she's been getting all these harassing phone calls about magazines she says she didn't order and—"

"*Certainement,*" said Nora, wondering what Pam Gregory would think of her thrilling caseload. "Bring her in tomorrow."

She left the office early, fairly certain her absence wouldn't tip the scales of justice one way or the other. As she drove home, sleet began to fall, splattering against the windshield in tiny explosions. Nora turned on the wipers and in their side-to-side rhythm she heard *Loser, loser, loser,* and when she pulled up in front of the original House of Curl on Nawadaha Boulevard, her childhood—as well as her adult—home, she turned off the car's ignition. Even though the windshield wipers were stilled, the *loser* refrain was not.

The house was quiet. It wasn't yet three o'clock, but she turned on the kitchen light, and a yawn of silence answered her query, "Anyone home?" She wandered into the living room with no motive other than deciding where to nap, but a faint tapping redirected her across the room, back through the kitchen, and down the basement steps.

"Hey, Dad," she said, dragging a stool over to the workbench and settling herself next to Thor, who was doing what he most often did—building birdhouses.

Her father interrupted the simple hum that accompanied his carpentry work and smiled. "Hi, Nora."

"Looks like an airplane hangar, Dad."

"Yeah," said Thor. "'Cept for birds." He resumed hammering a corner of the roof.

Sitting next to her father, Nora felt her whole body exhale a sigh of relief, the tension that was a storm inside her evaporating like steam. He hadn't always had this effect on her; when she first met Thor at the age of fourteen, she could barely look at him without feeling sick, scared, or enraged.

His story was sad and strange, and it began several days before Nora's birth, when Thor Rolvaag disappeared. The handsome architecture student had decided it was finally time to RSVP yes to some of the many sexual invitations women offered him. Not all—that would have taken him weeks, months!—but he thought diving into the beds of two different women might help him forget his impending paternal responsibilities. It did, briefly, but afterwards he hadn't reckoned on the guilt that cut through the exuberant taboo of it all, and early dawn found him running home along a snowy River Road, toward the woman he had betrayed, the woman he loved more than anything—his pregnant wife, Patty Jane.

It was fear more than anything that had driven him into these women's beds; he was afraid of the weight of love and its flip side, loss. His own father, Olaf, a Norwegian immigrant, had died when Thor was only six years old, and his death had cast a long shadow across his heart. Running home, he vowed to explain all this to Patty Jane and beg for her forgiveness, and if she wasn't willing to grant it, he'd work hour by hour, day by day to earn her trust again, and he'd be a wonderful father, unafraid to love. The promise made to his bride would never be delivered, because at that moment Thor leaped over a snowbank. He was an athlete and had no problem clearing it, but he landed on an ice-slicked sidewalk and from there the athlete was powerless to stop his trajectory. A massive oak tree, however, was not, and Thor made crunching contact with it, headfirst.

He was rescued, in a manner of speaking, by a woman named Temple Curry, an oral surgeon whose career had long been shuttered by her mental illness. A near hermit who kept strange hours (once, a neighbor rushing his laboring wife to the hospital at 2 a.m. had seen Dr. Curry weeding her garden in the moonlight), she had been out sledding in the quiet pink of daybreak and, witnessing Thor's accident, had loaded the prostrate man on her toboggan and towed him to her house across the street. There, in squalor hidden by the home's stately exterior, she kept him prisoner for years. Granted, he was a prisoner who enjoyed occasional field trips (his crazy warden always at his side), and when Temple noticed him taking an interest in the basement wood shop of her deceased father's, she supplied him with enough tools and material to create the birdhouses he seemed compelled to build.

Nearly fifteen years later, when he was rescued and back at home, Patty Jane had taken him to specialists, but they could not conclude one way or another if the brain injury he had sustained would have been less traumatic had he been treated immediately—or differently—after his accident. That the House of Curl salon moved into the large home that Temple Curry bequeathed them after her death was another bizarre (but practical—they did need more room) twist to a story that Nora had learned to synopsize: "My dad was gone throughout my childhood, but he came back."

It had taken her years to say—and mean—"I love you" to her father, but now being in the presence of the gentle man was a tonic, and she was granted the luxury of being no one but herself, knowing Thor loved whatever that self was.

"So, Dad," she said, watching as he placed the hammer on the worktable and surveyed the hangar as carefully as if he were Mr. Boeing inspecting a new facility. "I've been in sort of a funk lately. I mean, it's just so weird. No more Patty Jane's House of Curl, Etc.! Sure, you can build your birdhouses anywhere, but what am I supposed to do? Open a law office in the dining room? Although now I won't even be booking acts—because there won't be any more acts to book!"

Continuing his inspection, Thor ran his fingers along the roofline.

"I mean, I know I should look at this as a new beginning, but a new beginning to what? I don't know what to do. I feel like I'm stuck—stuck in a trap I set for myself."

Her father folded his hands in his lap and cocked his head as he looked at her.

"I know what you're thinking," said Nora. "If you set the trap, unset it, right? But what if I don't know how? What if I've lost the key? It seems like everyone has the key except for me!"

"No, you have keys," said Thor, his usually placid brow furrowing. "Maybe in your purse."

Nora smiled. "You're right, Dad. They're probably in my purse."

Satisfied with his counsel, Thor picked up a block of sandpaper and rubbed it against the roof's edge. Behind the furnace, a load of clothes tumbled in the dryer, and Nora tucked her hand in the crook of her father's elbow. A feeling of calm—not a signature emotion of late—settled in her chest, and as she sat watching him work in a basement that smelled of wood shavings and laundry, she knew what she would do, at least what she would do in the upcoming weekend.

➤➤ 4

THE APPEARANCE OF THE FOUR ELDERLY BOWLERS was a source of amusement to the truant high school kids in the next lane, who rolled their eyes and whispered, "This oughta be good," and "I'm surprised they can even lift the ball," and "Oooh, looks like someone took their Geritol." Their smirks and derisive comments had vanished by the time Ione rolled her second spare, and when she added a little victory dance after it, they applauded.

Ione blew on her fingernails and polishing them on her chest said, "I guess I did take my Geritol."

"You tell 'em," whispered Crabby fiercely as Ione sat next to her on the varnished wood bench.

"Ione, that brings you up to 180 with two frames to go," said Evelyn Bright, scribbling on the paper score pad.

Minna Czelski was up next and had been walking toward the ball rack when she stopped abruptly, as if meeting an invisible door. When she turned around, her friends could see the confusion on her face.

"Can I go home now?"

"Don't you want to finish the game?" asked Crabby.

Minna looked as if the question had been asked in a language she didn't speak. She stood frozen as a dark stain blossomed on both sides of her pant legs.

"Oh, my god, she's peeing herself!" squealed one of the girls in the next lane.

While Ione and Evelyn attended to Minna, Crabby strode over to the high schoolers, grabbing a ball from the rack.

"Why don't you brats pretend you're the pins," she said, hefting the bowling ball and slapping it with her free hand, "and I'll see if I can roll a strike."

At the Etc., there had been a recent trio of lectures on aging. It had peeved Ione to realize the audience had been entirely composed of senior citizens. "After all," she groused to Patty Jane, "from the time we're born, *everybody's* aging."

The first lecture "Humor Counts!" had been given by a chirpy blond woman whose gray roots were almost hidden in her champagne-colored hair, and whose jokes Evelyn Bright vaguely remembered from *Reader's Digest* columns. "Move Your Body!" was the topic of the second lecture, given by a presenter who wore a shiny black tracksuit that matched his lopsided toupee and who proclaimed that thirty daily squats guaranteed a person ten extra years.

A retired engineer running for city council ("I want to build a different kind of bridge!") gave the third lecture, and he urged his audience of senior citizens to get active, get involved: "You've got to make your voices heard!"

Raising her hand, Crabby asked, "Even if we do, who wants to listen to a bunch of old bags?" Still, it was the lecture that most inspired Ione and her friends, and resolving that they had hopes for the future even as their own were running out, they formed a group dedicated to social action and change and gave themselves the name Old Bags for Change, or OBFC, because, after all, Humor Counts! Their first planning meeting was to take place in a coffee shop, after they'd bowled a few games (Move Your Body!), but because of Minna's accident, they decided to reschedule the meeting, date to be determined.

And probably won't be, thought Ione, so disheartened that once she had gotten home safely (Evelyn drove as if she were trying to qualify for the Indy 500), she had collected her mail off the hall table, waved off a Scrabble invitation from Patty Jane, and taken to her room, where she sat on her bed, the contents of her Treasure Box strewn in front of her. She opened the box once or twice a week to add a letter to a fat re-ribboned stack and only occasionally inspected its other items—sometimes when needing aid and comfort, sometimes when desiring a prop to assist her in a walk down Memory Lane. *Or sometimes,* she thought, picking up a small bundle, *when I want to make a sad mood sadder.*

Tied inside the blue ribbon was the official documentation of her life and how much loss had occurred in it. Included was her Norwegian birth certificate and her son Thor's American one; her citizenship papers and her marriage license; her husband's death certificate (seeing the number thirty-four under "Age at Death" still made her gasp). But it was the part of her life that wasn't, couldn't be included in that documentation that always made her heart pound, made tears leak out of her blue eyes, and today made her think of the snotty kids at the bowling alley who only saw her as an old lady. Flushing with anger, she whispered, "You have no idea!"

After she'd calmed her breath, she thumbed through the rest of the bundle: the newspaper obituaries of those she had loved—family members back home, assorted friends from her church circle and the salon, and Harriet and her fiancé, Avel Ames.

The thin stack of flattened cereal boxes tied in a wider ribbon also represented sadness, for the man posing on them was her vibrant and impossibly handsome son, Thor, when he was still Thor. He had been talked into product modeling only once, by his brother-in-law-to-be, Avel Ames. Heir to a grain fortune, Avel thought a picture of Thor on an Ames Grains' cereal box might appeal to housewives at the supermarket. Certainly, Avel had seen in person the effect Thor had on women. It was a savvy business move; the company received many letters ranging from questions like, "Who is that beautiful hunk of manhood?" to promises of brand loyalty, "From now on, Mighty Bites is my cereal of choice!" Hoarding, let alone wasting, was anathema to Ione's economic way of living, but for the brief time that her missing son's picture was displayed in grocery stores, she couldn't resist buying a box of Mighty Bites every time she shopped, forcing herself to eat the cereal even though she much preferred Wheaties.

The fattest beribboned bundle comprised letters, and the feelings they might inspire depended on which letter she chose to read. Some, from back home, were more than fifty years old. Added to the bundle would be the most recent one, the letter she'd received from her grandson.

Once Alva Bundt had pointed out that, of course, because Clyde Chuka was Harry's father, the boy was technically not Ione's grandson. Alva had not been prepared for Ione telling her in no uncertain terms what she could do with her technicalities. Just as Ione had been a constant presence in her granddaughter Nora's life, so was she in Harry's, until he had left to go to boarding school. Thankfully, Harry liked to write letters, and he and Ione enjoyed a prolific correspondence. She reread the letter that had been waiting for her on the hall table.

Dear Grandma,

I was kind of down today—maybe because I talked to Nora last night and her bad mood spread, making me wonder why I thought it was so important to go to Braddock. Like, why aren't I at home with all of you, helping you close down the Etc., why aren't I going to a normal school with all my old friends, why aren't I playing hockey with guys I've played with for years, why did I leave Rebecca Olson (not that she was my girlfriend — but she might have been if I stayed).

Why, why, why? (Existential crisis, much?)

But today in band class a really cool thing happened. There's this guy Ethan. (There are like twenty Ethans here, and even though Harry is kind of a weird name, at least there aren't twenty more of 'em!) Anyway, Ethan's like a majorly good musician but also a real jerk. There's also this guy Caleb (only three Calebs around!) who's just as good but in a different way. He can't read music, but he can play anything by ear—like, if he hears a song once, he sits down at the piano and plays it!

But Ethan says he's not a real musician, that he's lazy and cheating, and this guy Caleb, oh man, that really hurts him.

Anyway, the band teacher, Mr. Archer, is pretty cool, and he knew all this stuff was going on between them, and so today he says he has some Beatles sheet music and asks Ethan to play it, which he did. And he played it great. Then he hands the music to Caleb and Caleb sits there at the piano and says, "You know I can't read music," and

Mr. Archer says, "Yeah, but can you play it?" and Caleb says, "Sure," and plays "Hey Jude" like he wrote the song himself. I mean it was like, "wow."

Then Mr. Archer asks if either of them knows the Rolling Stones song "Lady Jane," and both of them say no (although I did, Grandma, musical historian that I am). So he's got the song cued up in his tape deck and plays it for the class and afterwards asks Ethan to play it, and he says, "Sure, where's the music?" and Mr. Archer says he doesn't have it and Ethan says, "Well, then I can't play it."

But Caleb could. And Grandma, it was sweet. He only heard the song once, but it's like it went from his ears into his fingers. I'm not bad at playing by ear, but, man, I could never do what Caleb did— it's just so weird, like those people who can do really complicated math equations in their heads, kind of like a gift, you know?

Speaking of gifts, Dad sent me some great Clash (a great, unfortunately disbanded band) T-shirts from London and like everybody in school wants to buy them. I could make some serious cash, but they're so cool, I'd never sell them.

All for now. Love you,
Harry

P.S. Ava (almost as cute as Rebecca Olson) said she'd go to Winter Snow Dance with me!!

Her long-standing habit had been to answer a letter the day she received it, as it seemed more of a conversation. But with the emotions of the day swaddling her in torpor, what would she write? *Ja, I too am down today, wondering what I am doing . . . if I have any value anymore . . . if I'll ever get over not being what I wanted to be . . . (Existential crisis, much?)*

Oh, stoppe det, she scolded herself, getting up to fetch some stationery. She couldn't let her mood get in the way of the business at hand. First she'd peel the potatoes for dinner, and while they were boiling she'd sit down and write Harry a good grandmotherly letter, one that wouldn't scare him.

⇶ 5

S TUDYING A MAP OF STATE PARKS, Nora debated between one
near the North Shore or another near Brainerd and chose the
latter, preferring, especially in winter weather, the much closer
drive. Ione had given her a sack of freshly baked gingerbread cookies
for the road, and Nora had set off excited, but a wrong turn around
a big lake had put her on a road that forced her around a bigger lake.
Instead of backtracking, she continued on, hoping that by sheer force
of will she would find the right county road sign. "Why didn't I leave
earlier?" she muttered. Being lost in daylight was one thing, but
being lost in the waning light of a December afternoon was another
thing entirely.

Passing the hump of a deer carcass on the side of the road, Nora's
body tensed, expecting that at any moment another leaping antlered
animal would choose the wrong time to cross the road. She punched
the radio buttons, but within seconds an energetic refrain of an old
Doobie Brothers song gurgled into static. Beyond the tall pines on the
left loomed the lake with the apparently unending circumference, and
from the tall pines on the right something sprang out. Nora gasped
and braked hard, and it took her a moment to realize that what she
had almost turned into roadkill was not a deer but a human being.
Covered up as it was, it was hard to discern the sex of the small figure
waving its arms, and when the small figure opened the passenger door,
Nora's first thought was that a man was hijacking her car, or worse.

"Give me a lift!" It was an order rather than a request, but Nora
was relieved the voice giving it was more a soprano than a bass.
Before she could answer, "Sure, hop in," the woman had.

"Dang boots!"

Stumped for a response, Nora sat for a long moment until her passenger, after setting her canvas Musette bag at her side and clicking her seat belt buckle, said, "Well, come on, then. Let's go!"

On the drive, the woman, who had a pronounced New York accent and whose face under her fluorescent orange stocking cap was lined with frowns, explained that she was walking home after "doing business in town."

"Town?" asked Nora.

"Charleyville!" Jerking her mittened thumb over her shoulder, she added, "About three miles that-a-way."

"You walked there?"

"No, I skipped. Then I cartwheeled!"

"You seem sort of upset."

"Well, aren't you perceptive!" said the woman. Shaking her head, she made a dismissive "tuh" sound and muttered something about only wanting a ride and not the third degree. Nora was tempted to mutter words of her own but took the high road, literally if not figuratively, when the woman shouted, "Turn up here!"

"Take a right!" was the next directive, and Nora turned off the road lined with a sentry of fir trees and into a long driveway.

"Stop here!" said the woman. "Or do you plan to plow into the garage?" Unbuckling her seat belt, she opened the door and plunged out of the car, with the instructions, "Bring in my bag!"

Watching her demanding passenger limp across the snow-dusted lawn and up several wooden stairs to the log home, Nora was tempted to toss said bag out the window and floor it, but she knew she couldn't leave a person so obviously in distress. Her innate good scout tendencies also made her retrieve, from the small cooler in the backseat, the paper sack of Ione's cookies. With both bags, she made her wary but curious way up the steps.

Whoa, she said to herself, impressed by the expanse of the railed deck as well as the hot tub in the corner. She opened the sliding glass door into a mudroom and, after wiping her feet on the mat, entered the kitchen. The woman, who'd taken her stocking cap off to reveal curly gray hair, was seated at a massive oak table. "I thought I had broken these in," she said, chucking a boot in Nora's direction. "I swear, my feet are nothing but blisters!" Peeling off a thin wool sock, she draped it over a chair and began to inspect her toes with the unabashed and unapologetic fervor of a monkey.

Coming in the side entrance, Nora had no idea the cabin was so big. The light was dim, but she could see that the spacious kitchen opened up into a room big enough to host a party for a really popular person.

"What . . . what is this place?" asked Nora, setting the bags on the table.

"It's Our Lodge, what do you think it is?" said the woman, wincing as she patted her blistered heel. "Now soap up a washrag at the sink there and get me a box of bandages from that cupboard above it."

After following orders, Nora handed the woman the requested items and introduced herself, adding, "Would you like a cookie?"

"Cookie? I don't have any cookies!"

"Well, I do," said Nora, nodding at the bag on the table. "They're gingerbread."

It was as if an inner balm spread through the woman, and she sat back in her chair, a smile softening the face that had been clenched in anger. "You'd better put on the teakettle, then, and take off your coat. And I'm Nellie. Nellie Freeburg."

While her mood might have improved, her bossiness hadn't, and as she watched Nora scoop out cocoa powder from an old-fashioned tin, Nellie, with her loud, nasal voice, said, "A level teaspoon! That's all you need, a level teaspoon."

"Are you going to tell me how to drink it, too?"

"If it looks like you need instruction in that area, then sure." She broke a cookie in half and chewed for a moment, her eyes widening. "What you don't need instruction in is how to bake a good gingersnap."

"I didn't make them. My grandma did. And they're gingerbread cookies, not gingersnaps. Gingersnaps tend to be more brittle and—"

"—thank you, Miss Cookie Expert," said Nellie. "Whatever they are, I need the recipe." Rummaging in her Musette bag, she withdrew an apple, an opened carton of cigarillos, a faded clump of plastic flowers, a stack of checkbook registers rubber-banded together, a whisk broom, a wool scarf, and finally, with an "Aha," a pen and a steno pad, which she shoved toward Nora. "And of course I'll have to give my compliments to your grandmother. Believe it or not, I do have *some* manners. Give me her address and phone number."

"It's the same as mine. We live together." After writing down the information, she slid the pad back to Nellie, who glanced at it and said, "Oh, Minneapolis. What are you doing up here?"

"I . . . I'm on a retreat."

"A retreat from what?"

Nora shrugged, and instead of giving an answer she herself wasn't sure of, she surveyed the detritus on the table and said, "You sure carry a lot of interesting things in your bag."

"What, I should carry around rouge, perfume, perhaps adult diapers?"

Feeling herself flush at the woman's retort, Nora muttered an apology but couldn't help adding, "Sheesh."

Nellie let out a raspy laugh, which was not the reaction Nora anticipated, even as she knew the woman's reactions were beyond anticipating.

"These," said Nellie, snapping the rubber band around the checkbook registers, "I needed for a *delightful* meeting with my banker." She held up the plastic flowers. "And these are from a rendezvous with my husband."

"Oh, is he—"

"—*was* he," Nelle corrected. "My Walter is no longer of this earth. My rendezvous with him now occurs at the Charleyville cemetery, where every month I replace his flowers—he's got mistletoe and holly now—sweep snow off his stone, and lay his favorite cigarillo next to it." She held up the whisk broom and cigar packet in her show-and-tell.

"And the apple?"

"In case I got hungry."

Nora could have muttered another "Sheesh," but instead she laughed and was surprised again when tears sparked in Nellie's eyes.

"I'm sorry," Nora said, reaching across to give her a sympathetic pat, but in an evasive move Nellie lifted her mug in both hands and took a loud slurp of cocoa.

"Do you ever watch the Macy's Thanksgiving Parade on TV?"

If Nellie's conversation were a carnival ride, Nora would have been dizzy.

"Uh . . . yeah."

"That's where my Walter and I met: in the middle of Thirty-fourth Street and in the crowd, I somehow got pushed into him, right into his arms, which he took as a sign. He said he always expected good things at the parade—although once he almost got clipped by a giant Bullwinkle balloon—but never had a beautiful woman fallen right into his arms!"

Nellie's face and voice got softer, and Nora leaned in to hear her story.

"My Walter was probably the only man to ever think I was beautiful, but, then, that one opinion is the only one you need, right?"

He was short and older by ten years, and although Nellie, even shorter, preferred tall men her own age, she did like the cut of his suit and his polished wingtips. ("They were so shiny you could see the Chrysler Building in their reflection!") Walter was an adman, whose catchy slogans aided cigarette and toilet paper sales. Nellie was a secretary for the vice president of Pierre Chastain, a knockoff clothing designer in the fashion district. ("Hard to believe," she said, fondling her ragged sweater neckline, "that I used to dress in counterfeit Dior and Givenchy, huh?")

Their courtship was brief, and they married five weeks to the day they'd met on the parade route. "I loved our life in Manhattan, being a wife *and* a career woman in my fake designer duds, but Walter was getting restless. He felt he had gone as far as he could in his profession. 'Nell,' he used to say, 'how many more cigarettes or rolls of toilet paper do I have to help sell?' When one of his clients—a cereal manufacturer, I think—invited him to his Minnesota lake home, well, that was all the sign Walter needed. He said he'd lived in the Asphalt Jungle long enough: now it was time to settle in Paradise."

He took an early retirement; with his stock options, the couple was able to afford a lot facing the lake and built a log cabin for the eight or so children Walter thought they should have.

"But it didn't happen. Turns out I was barren as the Dead Sea—or Walter was. That's life, or in our case, it wasn't . . . anyway! With the cabin already built but no kids to fill it, well, Walter decides to open it as a lodge. Sure, it was easy for him—he was Mr. Gregarious—he oozed charm; he loved people." Nellie shook her head as if she were describing his faults. "Me, I was chief cook/bottlewasher/handywoman, much happier to be in the kitchen or replacing a broken window pane than out with Mr. Sociable in the great room, hosting Happy Hour while someone's untalented genius banged out "Heart and Soul" on the piano, and some yahoo lying about the twenty-pound bass he caught. You know what two words I came to despise? *Tourist season.*

"Unfortunately—and what an understated word that is, huh?— Walter only got to run our lodge for four years before he died of a heart attack, right out there on Palm Avenue, after we'd stuffed ourselves at the Lake Inn's All-You-Can-Eat fish dinner. I shut down our lodge pronto and—"

An oven buzzer went off, startling them both, and Nora was even more startled when Nellie clapped her hands together. "Listen, it's been a pleasure chatting, but *Jeopardy!* is on, and you would not believe the luck the returning champion is having with the Daily Doubles. Bye-bye!"

"But I . . ."

She watched as Nellie stood up and began to hobble away from the table.

"But . . . can you at least tell me how to get to Meridian State Park?"

"Oy, you *were* lost!" said Nellie, turning to her. "That's about ten miles back." She shouted out directions and when she was finished, added, "Nice meeting you!"

*   *   *

"Clyde, I thought you were coming home tomorrow!" If there were an Olympic event for dashing out of a house and into the arms of one's beloved, the speed and finesse in which Patty Jane completed this challenge would have earned her Gold.

"I got an earlier flight," said Clyde Chuka, earning a Silver by dropping his suitcase on the front walk and catching her in his arms while remaining standing. His bobble, and the possibility for a moment that they both might go down, cost him his own Gold.

Their mouths and arms clamped on to one another's, and Wally Neirbo, their next-door neighbor, was glad the wife had nagged him to check on the rosebushes just so he could witness a spectacle of passion that had long ago flown from his own personal coop. He had lived next door for more than thirty years, and his crush on Patty Jane was a steady flame. He thought she was one of the prettiest gals he'd ever seen, plus she had personality, traits that the wife seemed to have lost long ago, along with her interest in him.

It bothered Wally a little that an Indian was the recipient of affection from such a fine specimen of womanhood. But his ten-year-old granddaughter's recent failure to laugh at his jokes and instead claim they were racist had cut him to the core, causing Wally to take a surprising path toward self-examination. *We were taught that the white man was the good guy,* he mused in silent debates, *but what if we weren't always taught right?* Standing behind the leafless crab apple tree, he watched the kissing, hugging couple until arm in arm they entered their house. Sighing, Wally continued his backyard inspection. He'd covered the rosebushes in burlap weeks earlier before the first frost, and when he reported back that, "Yes, dear, all is secure," he wondered what his wife would do if he grabbed her and laid on her mouth the kind of kisses he had just seen.

"She'd smack me back a-course," he muttered, "only with the back of her hand."

He understood this not to be an overstatement but a fact, and he chuckled, even as he shook his head.

"So Nora's off in the wilds, huh?" said Clyde, after Patty Jane had filled him in on the goings-on of the family. "Good for her."

"She left just after lunch. Honestly, Clyde, I think she's going through a midlife crisis."

"Nora's too young to be going through a midlife crisis."

Patty Jane laughed. "Well, a *pre*-midlife crisis. She said she's a little lost, what with the Etc. closing and all, as to which direction she's supposed to take."

"It appears she took north," said Clyde, and they both smiled at his little joke.

"Anyway, she thought a little retreat might help her clear her head. A winter camping retreat—that'll clear her head all right." She watched as Clyde unscrewed the bottle of nail polish. "No, that's too red."

"I don't think it's red enough," said Clyde Chuka, flattening with the nail brush a bright bead of color on Patty Jane's pinky. In the 1960s, when he was a starving—or at least hungry—artist, he'd been hired as the House of Curl's manicurist. "I get inspiration holding women's hands," he had semi-joked, and he still occasionally treated old clients to a free manicure. The couples' own ritual called for him to do Patty Jane's nails whenever he returned from a trip.

Now there was an international demand for Clyde's art; he had spent the past three weeks working in London's Regent Park installing four sculptures of Native American heroes in today's world. Cochise, Crazy Horse, Sitting Bull, and the lesser-known Modoc woman Kaitchkona Winema were made of metal and posed on piles of garbage. Cochise looked down at the mountain of plastic laundry, pop and water bottles his horse waded through; Winema was falling back onto a pile of disposable diapers and razors.

The newspaper reviews Patty Jane demanded Clyde bring home for her scrapbook were on the table, and she read her favorite part aloud for the third or fourth time. "'Mr. Chuka isn't ashamed to wallop viewers over the head with his message that the waste and consumption of today are destroying the natural world of his ancestors, but his rendering—the sorrow on Crazy Horse's face made this reviewer gasp—is so precise, so detailed, that one cannot walk away from one of his sculptures unmoved.'"

"They were awfully nice to me there," said Clyde. He pursed his lips and blew softly on Patty Jane's wet nails. "Although if I never have to eat another serving of mushy peas, it'll be fine with me. Give me your other hand."

With a wave of her fingers, Patty Jane obliged.

"Now let's talk some more about Harry," said Clyde.

There is nothing so delicious to parents as talking about a child who's doing well—and their fifteen-year-old son, Harry, was doing well. He, like his namesake Aunt Harriet, was a gifted musician who played guitar and piano well and the drums exceptionally well. He was also a talented hockey player, and it was in this capacity that he had accepted a scholarship to a boarding school in southern Minnesota whose alumni included a long list of NHL players as well as two senators and an actor that *People* magazine had determined was the Sexiest Man Alive. On his hockey team, Harry played right wing on the second line and anchored the school's jazz band with his precise yet wild percussion. He was close enough so that his family could attend both his home games and concerts, and he was able to visit on occasional weekends.

"Well," said Patty Jane, "he got a goal and two assists in his last game, wrote a song for his girlfriend, Ava, that he played for me over the phone—and Clyde, it was good—and here's the bonus: he said he got an A on his paper on the history of the Supreme Court!"

"Who do you suppose he takes after?" Clyde asked, and Patty Jane said, "Some unknown superhero ancestor," and Clyde said, "Maybe my great-grandfather, He Who's Skilled with Sticks," and they laughed.

It had been a mirthful manicure, and after Clyde set down her hand, he returned the brush to the bottle and twirled it closed. "Now let those dry for a minute or two," he said, standing up. "Then I'll meet you in the bedroom."

"Ooh, did you bring me a present?"

"I hope you'll think so."

⇛ 6

I T WAS NEARLY DARK, and although the sign signifying Balsam
Road was obscured by—what else?—a balsam, Nora made the
correct turn. She would have liked to mull over the monologue
of the strange and eccentric woman she'd just met, but she needed
to repeat Nellie's directions aloud and watch for road signs and deer.
Her posture was rigid, her knuckles under her gloves were white,
and when her headlights finally illuminated the sign to the state
park, she hooted. After driving a short bumpy distance down a gravel
road, she angled her car next to one of the parked vehicles in the dirt
lot. Once outside, she turned on her flashlight and headed toward
a long narrow clearing where several tents had been pitched and a
campfire blazed.

"Welcome," said a man as she approached the small group of people huddled around the fire. "Tonight's beverage is the ever-popular
Lake Water Wowie."

Nora had been around a fair number of campfires in her day. With
fellow nine-year-olds she had sung what they thought were hilarious
versions of old rounds—"Throw, Throw, Throw Your Bra, Gently
Down the Stream" and "Michael, Oh, You Are a Bore, Hallelujah."
When she lived in L.A., she'd taken trips with friends to Baja or
Yosemite, roasting marshmallows while debating the quality of milk
chocolate versus dark, the existence of God, and how if men wore
high heels for one day, they would understand that the world must
change. But hunching around a campfire with complete strangers

drinking something called Lake Water Wowie was something of a first.

Introductions were made. Gus and Jeannie were from Tuscaloosa, Sheldon and Saffron were from San Francisco, Clint and Mitchell were from Omaha. Guy was Canadian.

Accepting a plastic glass of the liquid Saffron poured from a thermos, Nora asked, "Is this some kind of reunion?"

"Nah, we're just leftovers from the Stummit Meeting," said Gus.

"*Stummit* Meeting?"

"We're Stanitors—followers of Stan," said Sheldon. "Stan Eisenberg?"

Taking her shrug as a cue, the assemblage jumped to their feet and with arms lifted to the darkening sky howled and yipped and gyrated, and Nora wished she hadn't been in such a hurry to get out of her car. Fortunately, the group's stamina couldn't hold up to its strangeness, and the bizarre wolf calls and Pentecostal dance moves quickly ended.

"Oh, now we've scared her," said Jeannie in a little drawl as the group members sat back on the logs arranged around the fire. "It's just that we get so excited to spread the word of Stan Eisenberg. His movement—Stanitization—is what will bring this world back to Stanity." Gus reached behind a cooler for a pair of bongo drums and began beating out a rhythm. Again, Nora thought longingly of her car's interior.

"Stanitization," said Mitchell, stressing his syllables to the bongo beat, "is about prospering financially while challenging ourselves physically. 'Money in the bank and firing up the tank.'"

"Yes, Stan believes life inside office towers weakens the wolf in all of us," said Sheldon as Gus thrummed and pounded the drums. "And when the inner wolf ails, other things—including your finances— fail." The group lifted their chins and offered another round of howls to the darkening heavens, and Gus's hands must have blistered, so frenzied was his bongo beating. When he abruptly stopped, so did the howling and the two thermoses were cordially passed around the circle.

"This year Stan thought we should test our physical mettle by camping out in the winter," said Mitchell, prodding the fire with a stick. "Which is probably why there were only about thirty people here. Last year, when the Stummit's theme was Triumphing over Temptation, over two hundred people showed up in Maui." Nora pictured a crowd of people, dressed in muumuus and leis instead of parkas and earmuffs, testifying to the power of the free market while resisting the urge to hula.

"You think we're part of a nutty cult, don't you?" Startled by the mind reader's words, Nora had no time to censure herself and nodded at the handsome man who asked them.

"Well, it is a little bit nutty," said Clint, "but aren't most good ideas? And sure, there are definitely some Stanitors who could be called cult members, but we're not that far gone, are we?"

Everyone except for Nora and the Canadian averred that they were not.

"Heck, we just like the outdoor retreats," said Gus. "And the financial advice, of course. Stan is a former Wall Street bigwig, and I swear with his advice my portfolio's grown like a son of a gun."

"It's not like we're the Hare Krishnas or anything," said Saffron. "We don't have to give up our worldly possessions or ridiculous things like that."

"There isn't a guru in the world who could make me give up those," said Jeannie, fondling the fur muffler around her neck. "I've got too much nice stuff."

Nora allowed herself a chuckle; her new acquaintances were weird, but it didn't seem as if they were sneak-away-and-alert-the-authorities weird.

"What about you?" she asked the compactly built Canadian who'd been using his mouth for drinking but not for howling or chanting. "Do you have a lot of nice stuff, too?"

A shy grin revealed a chipped front tooth. "I . . . not." He shook his head, a dark blush spilling over his fine features. "I am not good English. French, *oui*. English, *non*."

"Do you *parlez-vous français*?" Jeannie asked Nora. "'Cause none of us does."

"*Un petit,* but not really," said Nora, whose one class with Karen Spaeth was years ago.

"All we know about him is that he's a really good ice-fisherman," said Saffron. "Which is a totally new concept to me."

"He treated us all to lunch," said Sheldon. "And while my allegiance is to saltwater fish—Have you ever had mahimahi?—the trout he fried up was campfire gourmet." He held up his plastic cup. "To new friends!"

"*Les amis!*" agreed the Canadian, raising his glass in a salute.

"You haven't slipped anything in this, have you?" asked Nora as she sipped the tasty and potent Lake Water Wowie. "This won't make me get Stanitized, will it?"

"Its only power is to make you drunk," said Clint. "But only if *you* make that choice."

Most of Stan's followers chose to, and as the winter evening settled in, the party got commensurately worse. An accordion might have nicely accompanied the song "Edelweiss," but Gus only had bongos, and so he patted out a jerky beat as he sang—while choking up—the Austrian song. His sniff was phlegmy. "It's the song that inspired me to write about my favorite flower. It's called 'Camellia, My Camellia.'" Clearing his throat, he began to sing a song whose tune mirrored "Edelweiss," but whose lyrics included painful rhymes like "Camellia, oh, how you make me feelia."

"He submitted it to the governor's office," said Jeannie, "for consideration to replace 'Alabama' as our state song." She tucked her chin into her fur muffler and shivered. "He never heard back."

After the serenade, and more Lake Water Wowie refills, Sheldon and Saffron began educating the group as to what exactly was wrong with marriage in general and theirs in particular.

"It's not that I'm bored with Sheldon," said Saffron. "I'm just bored by the idea of him."

"Would it help if I changed my name like you did, Debbie? Would I be a little less boring if I answered to Thyme or Oregano?"

"Ha," said Saffron. "You don't have the flair to be called Oregano. Maybe Salt. Certainly not Pepper."

When Clint began to brag about his looks ("I can't tell you how many times I've been asked if I'm a professional model") and Mitchell began to sniffle about how hard it was to be the partner of such a handsome man ("Next to him, everyone's a troll!"), Nora decided that for her the party was over. It seemed the Canadian was thinking along the same lines, because he wobbled up a moment before she did.

"What?" said Jeannie. "You're leaving? But we haven't even told you about Stan's Platinum-Plus Plan." Her words were slurred so that she put an *h* on the end of *Plus*.

"Uh, I'm already pretty committed to Amway," lied Nora.

Gus appropriated the bongos, and the capitalist beatniks began chanting, "Stan's Platinum-Plus Plan, man! Stan's Platinum-Plus Plan!"

Turning from the group in the direction she thought she'd find her car, she stumbled, but the Canadian's reflexes were quick and he reached out a hand to steady her. His hand remained on her arm as they staggered into the blackness. Giggling the way escapees will, the couple quickened their pace as the group cried after them, "Be wild—be free—be rich!"

"I . . . I now for glad I no speak good English," said the Canadian.

"I now for wish I didn't," said Nora. "*Stanitization*—can you believe it?"

"All I know . . . crazy."

Yips and howls from the drunken wolf worshippers bleated through the night air.

"Amen, brother." Nora turned on her flashlight and its beam was a slash of yellow light against the darkness. "Do you think you could help me set up my tent? It's in my car . . . wherever that is."

"Yes. I you help."

"Oh, thanks. What's your name again—Guy?" She pronounced it as she had heard it, the French way, rhyming with *he*.

"*Oui*. And the name you . . . Norma?"

"Nora."

"Ah. More pretty. Like you."

A frozen explosion of stars decorated the night sky and Nora breathed in the frosty air, filling her chest with the scent of winter. When she exhaled, it was with laughter.

"What? What now funny?"

The voices of the party they had left were faint, like a radio playing in another room.

"Nothing," said Nora, the word tumbling out in a visible vapor. "I'm just happy, I guess."

"I . . . too," said Guy, and they practically clanged together, so strong was the magnetic flux between them.

For several moments, Nora stared at a domed nylon ceiling, wondering where she was. The rosiness of light let her know it was morning, but it took some replaying of the prior evening's events before she was able to understand she was in a tent and that it wasn't hers. She sat up, the throb in her head a reminder of the potency of last night's Lake Water Wowies. Her clothes were in a pile next to the sleeping bag, and gasping in the cold air she pulled them on and unzipped the tent door, the arc of fabric folding down on itself. The morning was bright and cold, and a light snow had fallen, powdering the ground with white. A campfire snapped in a circle of stones about ten feet from the tent. Next to the fire was a covered skillet.

Out of the cramped quarters, Nora stretched and did a slow 360 turn, surveying her surroundings. There were no other tents at the end of the clearing; the Stan clan had apparently taken their money-loving wildness back to civilization. A note scrawled on the back of a grocery receipt had been tucked up in the pinched edges of aluminum foil covering the skillet: *Merci, belle Norha! I more fish! For lunch! I you enjoy!*

"Well, I you enjoy, too," said Nora under her breath. She was touched by the thoughtfulness of a one-night stand who not only left her a nice note but a campfire breakfast of fried trout, two sunny-side-up eggs, and a thermos of coffee. A fork and knife rested in a speckled blue cup. She was not touched enough, however, to stick around for what couldn't help but be an awkward reunion, fish lunch or not, so after gulping down her breakfast, she doused the fire and hightailed it to her car, whistling a slightly sharp "Edelweiss."

Her drive was punctuated with sniggers of laughter as she thought back on what had been one strange and oddball encounter after another: Nellie, the Stanitizors, Guy.

When the images of what had occurred in the French Canadian's tent blipped on her mental screen, she giggled, flushed, and giggled again. How could she? Nora had never had a one-night stand, preferring the simmer of a slow cooker rather than the quick flash of a sauté pan. She laughed at her dumb analogy and thought maybe she was thinking of cooking metaphors because of the tasty breakfast Guy had left her. What had he seasoned the fish with? Cayenne pepper? Paprika? Something had given it an unexpected bite. She laughed again at her choice of words, recalling how she'd bit the Canadian's earlobe and he'd bit hers back.

Ooh la la, she thought but her saucy remembrance was shoved aside by a rude and unwelcome question: what if she got pregnant? Not possible; Guy had used a condom; she remembered him opening up his wallet and ripping open the foil packet he'd tucked inside. Still, hadn't she grown up hearing the story of her mother's absolute knowledge of Nora's wedding night conception, even with contraception?

"I knew it the moment it happened," Patty Jane had said. "The precise moment sperm met egg."

I sure don't feel that way, thought Nora, and deciding she was as instinctual as her mother, at least as far as the state of her uterus was concerned, she relaxed.

The state of her whereabouts was another thing entirely. She had intended to spend two nights in the state park, but now with no Plan B she drove aimlessly around a maze of roads circling lakes and doubling back on them. A gentle shake of snowflakes had become a flurry, and the windshield wipers, turned to high, worked in steady sweeping arcs. It might be a good time, Nora thought, to revisit Nellie and persuade the former lodge owner to open her doors to a paying customer.

As if that would ever happen, she thought, the idea of finding Nellie's log cabin as well as being welcomed into it unlikely, and when she saw the arrow sign with the numbered freeway that would take her back to the Twin Cities, she followed it, deciding it was time to retreat from her retreat.

≫ 7

TAKING DOWN THE CHRISTMAS TREE was an event bound by certain rituals in the Rolvaag/Chuka household. Tradition called for it to occur on the afternoon of New Year's Eve so that the year would begin fresh. A reserve tin of Ione's best Christmas cookies (krumkake, spritz, and almond crescents) was brought out, and Thor always supervised the ornament storage, assigning each wooden reindeer or Santa Claus bauble to its own particular spot in one of four boxes.

Since the age of ten, Harry had been in charge of all holiday music (a self-appointed position, but one nobody disputed), and he had brought home several mixtapes of music that included classics by Nat King Cole, Elvis Presley, and Bing Crosby as well as newer takes on holiday songs by artists like Bruce Springsteen and David Bowie. A recent musical discovery of his was Pepe Pizzoli, an Italian tenor who sang songs like "Rudolph the Red-Nosed Reindeer" with the emotional intensity (and pitch) of a teenaged girl discovering she's gotten her first period.

"I don't get a lot of chances to use the word *caterwauling*," said Clyde, "but that's *definitely* caterwauling."

Thor, bobbing his head and shimmying his shoulders, said, "I like it."

"Me, too," said Harry. "The guy's totally unique."

"Uffda," said Ione, as the singer's reedy, heavily accented voice squealed about Rudolph going down in history.

"Mail call," said Nora, who had stepped away from the music debate when she'd seen the postman trudging through the snow and up the front sidewalk. "I asked Vince to come in for some coffee and cookies, but he said it's only momentum that keeps him going in weather like this." She leveled a look at her brother. "Harry, please. Enough. That guy's giving me a headache."

"Buncha Philistines," muttered Harry as he turned down—but not off—the stereo.

"More cards?" asked Thor, who loved opening the Christmas mail sent to the family.

"Sorry, Dad, the season's about over for that." Nora rifled through the stack of mail and distributed the bills and business letters to Patty Jane and Clyde Chuka. "And here's a letter for you, Grandma. The postmark's from *Norge*."

As Ione studied the thin blue envelope, her cheeks and the tip of her nose flushed pink.

"Excuse me," she said quietly, leaving the room.

Eyebrows were raised and raised again when she returned minutes later, her eyes red.

"*Hvem var brevet fra?*" asked Thor, whose brain damage had left unscathed the part that understood his first language.

"*En gammel venn.*"

"Okay," said Patty Jane, wiping on a napkin a residue of butter that clung to her fingers after she ate a spritz cookie. "Translation, please."

Ione reclaimed her chair, the floral wingback that was the sole survivor of a living room set Patty Jane had bought decades ago, when the beauty salon was finally making enough money to indulge in luxuries like furniture not from the Salvation Army. It was positioned next to the window, from which behind its sheer curtain displayed a driving snow.

It was a picture that seared into Nora's brain and one she could bring up years later: her grandmother sitting, her naturally straight posture unbowed by age, holding the pale blue envelope in her hands and saying to the tree detrimming assemblage, "I must go back . . . back home to Norway." As if her grandmother's words were a game of Tag and she were It, Nora said, "I'll go with you."

The room quieted—even the infernal voice of Pepe Pizzoli singing

"A Chipmunk's Christmas" seemed muted, distant—as Ione stared at Nora, who stared back.

"It's not a pleasure trip," said Ione. "I have business to take care of."

Nora shrugged. "I won't get in the way. It's not like I've got anything going on here. And besides, it's about time I see Norway."

"Me, too, Ma!" said Thor, but his eager expression was not long lasting, his face crumpling like a boy who'd been given a toy by someone who a moment later jerked it from his hands. He bowed his head. "Too far." Countless times, Ione had twirled the living room globe and shown Thor the country of his parents' birth, shown him the ocean and landmasses that separated their home from her original one.

Thor lifted his head. "Ma. Take Nora."

Ione had the heart of an explorer, but it was a heart whose beat was tempered by responsibility and circumstance. As a girl, she'd been crushed to learn that she couldn't join the Merchant Marines when she grew up.

"Why do you even think of silly things like that?" her mother had scolded her. "Girls don't sail around the world!"

I will, Ione thought but didn't say. She was a Viking, after all. Her heroes were Erik the Red and Leif Erikson, and the modern-day Viking Roald Amundsen. Of course she'd explore Antarctica like Roald Amundsen!

The older she got, the more she conceded her dreams. When luck—via her marriage—allowed her to move to America, she was excited to discover her new country, but her dreams of motoring with her young family to the exotic wilds of New Mexico, Florida, or Maine ended when her husband Olaf's life did, and for a long time the responsibility of raising Thor as well as making a living trumped adventure. Booking passage to Pago Pago or volunteering with a church group teaching Nepali women how to quilt were two of her travel considerations once her son had married, but then his years-long disappearance shoved those dreams aside, and she stayed home, honoring again duty and responsibility.

Once Thor had returned and the household had settled into its own strange normalcy, Ione had vigorously and joyously accepted the invitation of her friends the Fitches to join them on a road trip through the United States. Through the years, they had been a merry traveling threesome. "At first they claimed I was their referee," Ione explained to Patty Jane. "But honestly, they never fight. None of us does. But Norman's interests have narrowed—uffda, all he wants to visit are war museums, war monuments, or war cemeteries. So now I have an even more important role: Ruth has someone to explore things with that don't have to do with war!" Travel with the Fitches, unfortunately, was now in the past tense after Norman's increasing struggles with macular degeneration and complications that befell Ruth after hip replacement surgery.

Within thirty-six hours of the mysterious letter's delivery, Ione and Nora were buckling their seat belts. Although Ione had been on an airplane several times, she was no jaded passenger.

"I just can't believe you can wake up in one continent and go to bed in another!" she said for the second or third time.

Her grandmother's mood was effervescent and its bubbles wafted over to Nora, lessening the irritation she felt being crammed between Ione and a man who had apparent dibs on their shared armrest and who constantly sucked air through his teeth. It was as if she were seated next to a dog playing with a squeak toy; her impulse was to roll up her seat pocket's airline magazine and swat him on the nose with it.

When the airplane taxied, Ione gripped her granddaughter's hand, her mouth an *O* of awe, and when the wheels left the ground and the airplane slanted upward in its takeoff, Ione pressed her forehead against the window. She stared out at the changing view, watched as the runway gave way to roofs and treetops, watched as those became a board game, a facsimile of a city filled with neat rectangles filled with squares. Rivers and lakes were nothing but gray lines and blots, and it wasn't until the plane leveled off above a fluffed-up carpet of white clouds that Ione, tears glittering in the blue eyes that had just seen so much, turned to Nora and said, "Uffda."

Everything—from the pilot's announcements of geographical landmarks to the flight attendants' initial walk down the aisle offering peanuts and beverages ("Doesn't that blond one look like Florence Henderson?") and their later service of dinner ("Isn't it something, Nora? Hot meals on an airplane!") to minor turbulence—was met with delight by Ione. But after they'd passed over New York City and the Atlantic stretched out below them, when the man next to Nora had thankfully replaced his squeaks with subdued snores, a serious expression settled on Ione's face as she stared at her empty coffee cup.

"Penny for your thoughts," said Nora.

For a long time, Ione failed to cash in the offer. Finally, she whispered, "I'm sorry I haven't been forthcoming with you, but I just needed time to process some news." Her sigh was long. "There's a lot you don't know about me."

Taken aback, Nora laughed at the odd little joke she thought her grandmother was making.

"There's a lot that *most* people don't know about me."

"Grandma, you're scaring me," said Nora, trying to hide the truth of her statement with a lightness of tone.

The two women were leaning into one another, their foreheads nearly touching.

"You'll be meeting people who were very important to me," said Ione. "People who broke my heart in ways I didn't know it could be broken."

Nora swallowed.

Both she and Patty Jane had assumed the reasons for this trip had something to do with Ione's relatives—the reading of a will, the sale of old farm property—but when Ione refused to offer any details to her initial statement that she had business to take care of, they began to make up their own reasons, privately surmising that Ione was returning to ski in a Septuagenarian Invitational or was a retired spy being called back to solve the Lapp Lander Reindeer Heist or Homicide by Lutefisk—crimes that had long baffled Norwegian Intelligence. Now Nora felt ashamed of those dumb jokes, and she busied herself arranging over their laps the thin airplane blanket whose fabric content contained nothing of the natural world.

"I was in love a long time ago," whispered Ione. "Mad in love, as you say."

The man next to her snorted in his sleep, startling Nora but not more than Ione's words had.

"With Grandpa?" Even as she asked the question, her heart pounding, Nora knew the answer would be no.

"With a man named Edon. He was the man I was meant for, and I was the woman meant for him."

The overhead light was dimmed, but in it Nora could see the dreamy look in her grandmother's eyes.

"*Whirlwinds* is too slow a word to describe our courtship."

"Whirl*wind*," said Nora reflexively.

Ione nodded, after all these years still grateful to better her English. "*Takk. Ja,* I could not be in Edon's presence without feeling breathless, as if I'd just won a race, the most important race of my life." Ione had always spoken of her long-dead husband, Nora's grandfather, Olaf, with love and affection, and Nora was torn between the desire to beg her grandmother to stop and to beg her not to.

"That's who we're going to see, Edon." After a moment, she added, "And Berit."

"Who's Berit?"

Ione's voice was dark, as if her throat were filled with phlegm. "My cousin. My best friend. My worst enemy. Edon's wife."

Why didn't the oxygen masks drop down? Why didn't the captain's voice come over the PA system, telling everyone in a calm but terse voice to assume crash positions? What was going on? When had Nora ever, *ever* heard her grandmother describe someone as "the man I was meant for" and another as her "worst enemy"? Were they flying over the aeronautical-metaphysical version of the Bermuda Triangle, where ships don't disappear but sense and reason do?

Ione had always been Nora's ballast, the person she could count on to remain steady and constant, despite the height of the tsunami's waves, the hurricane's winds. But now she knew that the bright blue eyes of her beloved grandmother's were also the bright blue eyes of a woman she didn't know.

8

1927

"O H, IONE! What will your mother say?"

"Who cares?" said the seventeen-year-old girl, even though a part of her cared very much indeed. She ran a hand through her hair, which minutes earlier was a half-meter longer.

"But I'm supposed to be looking after you!"

Understanding the looseness with which eighteen-year-old Berit took that responsibility, Ione laughed.

In front of the mirror, the cousins stared at their slightly stunned reflections. Standing, Berit held a pair of scissors. Seated, Ione held BoBo, the stuffed bear that had kept watch over her since she was a baby kicking away crib covers, BoBo who had made the trip to Oslo with her and to whom she still clung whenever she was scared, nervous, or uncertain. And she was now all three, even though it had been her suggestion that she and Berit bob their hair. Her cousin seemed to give her the courage to do what she was afraid to do alone.

"Okay, it's your turn," said Ione, stepping on a blond swirl of her fallen hair as she got out of the chair.

From a young age, Ione had known that a traditional life of early marriage and motherhood was not for her; the world—and not just the little plot of farmland she'd been raised on—was her oyster! The quest for more was something the cousins shared and honored in one another. The plan that spring had been for Ione to spend a month in Oslo with Berit, to sit in on a few classes and decide if nursing might be a career for her as well. Ione already knew the answer to that (nei!), but she made a *show of paying close attention when auditing classes, even as she knew the trip's real purpose was fun and adventure. Both were easy to come by with her cousin.*

Ione was used to male attention, but when she was with Berit it cranked up to a silly—and sometimes dangerous—degree; on the street, men desirous of a second look might walk into a lamppost or trip on their own neatly tied shoes. Now when the two vibrant women sashayed into the parlor of Guri Peterson's house, the posture of the young men gathered there changed; there was a straightening of spines, a smoothing of hair, a puffing up of chests.

"Berit's here," muttered Viola Ramstad to Agnes Bakke. Like Guri, both girls attended nursing school with Berit and were tired of what they perceived as her grand entrances, jealous of the ease with which she bewitched men.

"And her cousin," Agnes muttered back. About to offer her comparison on Berit's and Ione's looks, she instead, like the others, gasped when the two women took off their hats. The whispers that flitted and buzzed across the room like pollinating bees were full of equal parts approval and disapproval, and all contained the words: "Their hair!"

"Berit—what have you done? I love it! And it's Ione, ja? I love yours, too! I'm going to bob mine tomorrow—or I would if I had your courage! Come and get some punch!"

Guri Peterson preferred paragraphs to sentences, and she spoke with a speed that allowed her to get ten words out to most everyone else's three. She was Berit's study partner at school—a fortuitous pairing for which Guri was grateful, convinced that Berit's quick mind and patient drills had kept her from flunking out, especially in anatomy.

With her hands on the women's bowed sashes, the hostess pushed/led them to the table stocked with smørbrød, cakes, and punch. Greeting the other partygoers with waves and hearty "Hallos!" Berit asked, "Who is that in the corner with Lars and Johann?"

"All the girls have been asking about him," said Guri, ladling fruit punch into a crystal cup and handing it to Ione. "This is what I know: his name is Edon. Edon . . . oh, I can't think of his last name. He's not *from here—Molde, maybe?—and he's taking an economics seminar at university. Johann met him at a library lecture this afternoon and invited him along."*

"Han er så kjekk," said Berit, her words riding along with Ione's, who was saying the same thing. *He is so handsome.* The look the cousins gave one another held their usual regard for each other's good (that is, matching) taste, but sprinkled in, like pepper, was competition.

"I saw him first," said Berit.

"Says who?" said Ione with a laugh, and as if a starting pistol had been fired, they set off toward the finish line.

It was an evening full of young people celebrating their youth, jousting for position as they joked, flirted, showed off (Lars Bjork demonstrating his talents as a ventriloquist, giving the dummy—his brother Hans—a high-pitched voice whose laugh was an eerie loon's warble), and played games (there were still citizens outraged by the name change Christiania had undergone, and Guri suggested they all come up with names better than Oslo. Johann's "City of Blonds!" was deemed the winner).

Both Ione and Berit managed to flank Edon as the group gathered around the piano Alf Amundsen pounded on, his repertoire vast, his technique not. Berit leaned close to Edon so that he'd smell the rosewater she'd spritzed on her neck, and Ione leaned close to Edon so that he could hear that she knew all the English words to "Yes Sir, That's My Baby." Viola was thrilled that both women had narrowed their focus to one man and were too busy to notice Selmer Fremstad, whose affections it was her goal that night to capture.

When Guri produced the records her diplomat father had brought from a trip to America, they rolled back the rug and cranked up the Victrola, and Edon asked Ione for the first dance. Berit shrugged at Ione's triumphant smile, knowing that he had to ask someone for the first dance, and why wouldn't it be Ione, seeing she'd practically thrown herself in his arms? But when the song ended, Edon and Ione didn't let go of one another, and when the second song began and they waltzed right out of the room and onto the terrace, Berit was so rattled that she stepped on her partner's foot and then hissed at him for his clumsiness.

It made absolutely no sense to her: sure, Ione was pretty, but she was beautiful.

When Ione told her cousin that she and Edon were going for a walk, she was unprepared for the flash of anger that darkened Berit's eyes or her snide response, "What did you promise him—everything?"

"What's that supposed—" she began, but Berit had pivoted as neatly as a windup toy, and grabbing the willing arm of Selmer Fremstad, headed toward the door.

"Tell me something about yourself I don't know," said Edon as they strolled, hand in hand, down Fredricks Gate alongside Palace Park.

"That would be just about everything," said Ione, "seeing as we've only just met."

"How can someone you've just met feel like someone you've always known?"

"Ja," said Ione, drawing in the word with a gasp of air in that peculiar Norwegian way. She felt exactly the same.

He squeezed her hand.

"Well, I'm from Stavanger."

"You already told me that," he said. "How about you tell me about something a little more personal, something about when you were a child."

Ione stared ahead, squinting as if to better see the past. "All right, here's one. When the minister's wife died, the ladies of the church made cookies and cakes for the funeral reception. Tables and chair were set up outside behind the church—it was a beautiful summer's day—when suddenly the minister stood up and barked in his gruff voice, 'Who made these sandbakkels?'

"I had, but I wasn't about to admit it to that man, who was just as scary away from the pulpit as he was from behind it! There was a long silence until my mother chirped up, 'Pastor Sundstrom, Ione did!'

"I couldn't believe my own mother had betrayed me and I was ready to bolt into the cemetery and run home, but then the pastor smiled and wiped a tear from his eye and said, 'I didn't think anyone could bake as good a sandbakkel as my dear Alma could, but here a little eight-year-old has!'

"As relieved as I was over the compliment, I wasn't about to correct the pastor and tell him I was eleven."

"I love sandbakkels," said Edon. "They're my favorite cookies."

"Until you taste my krumkake," said Ione, feeling almost Swedish in her bravado.

"So, is that your favorite thing? To bake?"

Ione considered the question, not asked out of anything other than curiosity, from what she could hear.

"I do love to bake, but I love to do a lot of things."

"Like what?"

Entering the park, she said, "It would take too long to list. And besides, it's your turn. Your turn to tell me something about yourself when you were young. Something you've never told anyone."

He whistled low.

"I cried the first time I saw Munch's The Scream."

He could have told Ione anything: "I wet the bed until last year" or "I like to dress up in my grandmother's corset," and the same rush of feeling would have flooded her heart. *I love you.* Aloud she asked, "When was that?"

"I was seven. Every year my Aunt Bessie—the bohemian of the family—would take me on the train for a 'cultural excursion' in Oslo. That year she took me to the National Gallery."

"I'm sure you're not the only one who's been scared by that painting."

"I was not just scared by it, I was thrilled. It was as if all the fears and monsters inside my little boy's head were understood, and for the first time I saw the power of art, the power of expression."

"And how do you express yourself?"

"I'm still trying to figure that out. The plan is to finish out university in London—I'm studying economics, or I might tuck myself away in a garret and paint . . . or write . . . or learn how to play the fiddle."

Still holding hands, Ione laughed as Edon raised hers high, and they walked for several minutes, arms swinging back and forth.

"Look!" said Ione, pointing with her free hand. "A light just went on in the castle. In that window there!"

"It's probably King Haakon signaling us to come up for some aquavit," said Edon.

"Or Queen Maud summoning us for tea."

They walked and walked, all around the palace grounds, to Frogner

Park and outlying neighborhoods, down alongside the fjord, past the
Akershus Castle, and into the city center. They traded stories and laughed
until the eastern sky blushed pink, and was it any wonder that when they
reached the doorstep of Berit's rooming house that Ione melted without
question into the curve of Edon's arms and offered her lips as eagerly as
he offered his?

"I cannot believe you're just coming in," said Berit, sitting at the kitchen
table, her arms folded across her chest. "I was worried sick."

"Oh, you were not," said Ione pleasantly. "You knew I was with Edon."
She sighed as she sank into the chair across the table. "Oh Berit, I'm in
love!"

Berit's impulse was to fling her coffee at her cousin, to burn off that
simpering smile, but instead, with great deliberation, she dropped two
sugar cubes into her cup.

"Ione," she said, twirling her spoon so that it clinked and clanked
against the china. "Be serious—you just met him!"

"Berit, I think I was in love the moment I saw him."

Anger manifested itself as an electric heat that prickled up the length
of Berit's spine and into the back of her neck. How was this possible? It
was she who knew when she first saw him that Edon was hers.

Swallowing hard against the tight knot of outrage that rose in her
throat, she forced herself to laugh.

"Love," she said. "Oh, Ione, what do you know about love?"

A chauffeur stood at their airport gate with a sign reading "Ione
Rolvaag."

"Well, this is fancy," said Ione as they walked toward him.

On the drive to Telemark County, both women planted themselves at windows on opposite sides of the wide, leather backseat,
Ione uncharacteristically quiet, murmuring, "Ja" or "Uh-huh" as Nora
exclaimed over the beauty of the snowy mountainous landscape, the
bright-colored houses and stave churches, the many blonds in the
small cars that passed them.

When the chauffeur pulled up to a red wooden house with white shutters, Ione whispered, "*Herregud, hva har jeg gjort?*" Nora spoke little Norwegian, but she didn't need a translator to understand the expression on her grandmother's pale face that asked, *Dear God, what have I done?*

The chauffeur insisted on carrying their bags to the door, leaving Nora free to hold up Ione, who seemed as if she had forgotten how to stand, let alone walk. The door opened and the white-haired man standing in its threshold was tall and rangy.

"Ione," he said, and in his rusty voice Nora heard an amalgam of emotions, the predominant ones being excitement, wonder, and sadness.

"Edon," said Ione, her voice an echo of the same sentiments.

The man leaned toward Ione, but she leaned back, pushing Nora between them.

"My granddaughter," she said. "Nora."

"I am so pleased to meet you," said Edon, and Nora did what Ione did not; she opened her arms to hug this man who seemed to mean the words he'd just spoken. He wasn't reticent in returning her embrace, and Nora found herself blinking back tears.

"I look forward to making your acquaintance," he said, after they'd let go of one another. "And my wife, too, will be happy to meet you. But for now, if you don't mind . . . could I have a private moment with your grandmother?"

"Of course," said Nora, taken by the man's courtliness. "Please."

The small parlor she waited in could have been the reception area of a folk arts museum. Blue and red wooden trunks and cabinets were painted with flowers and scrollwork in the swirling, symmetrical style called rosemaling. The windows' white linen curtains were ornamented with the elaborate Hardanger embroidery as were doilies covering tabletops. *Whoa*, thought Nora, examining an intricate piece quilt that was folded in a rectangle and draped over the sofa. *Grandma's got a rival.* It was a thought that merely recognized artistic talents similar to Ione's, but of course she now understood the words' deeper implications.

"The thing about my cousin Berit," Ione had said on the plane, "is that as many gifts as she had—and believe me, Berit had plenty—it was never enough. She wanted yours, too."

On the airplane, after Ione had finished telling her story, she and Nora had sat in a long silence, unmoving, as if the thin blanket covering them had absorbed the weight of her words and they were pinned under it. Finally, Nora asked why Ione had consented to have her come along.

"You were the one who insisted, remember? And then . . . I suppose I wanted a witness."

In the span of a plane ride, Nora's grandmother had become a woman of mystery, a woman with a past, and sitting in the pretty parlor of a pretty red house whose front windows displayed picture-postcard views of Lake Tinnsjø, hearing an occasional cry or shout from behind the closed door down the hallway, Nora wondered what was going to happen, now that the past had met the present.

The knocking on the door was persistent, but Ione ignored it, not sure if it was real or a part of her dreams. If it is real, she thought, Berit will answer it. Having stayed out late again with Edon, she had only been asleep for several hours and didn't want to get out of bed.

"Ione? Ione? Berit?" The knocking grew louder. "Anyone home?"

Her eyes widening as she recognized the voice, Ione scrambled up from the daybed and raced to the door.

"Mama!" she said, flinging it open.

"Ione!"

The unexpected happiness of seeing her mother was quickly darkened by fear.

"Mama, why are you here?" she said, pulling away from their embrace. "Is Papa all right?"

"Oh, Papa's fine," said Hannah Kittleson, stepping inside the small apartment. "Goodness, Ione, what did you do to your hair?"

Ione palmed the sides of her hair, which was much shorter than when she last saw her mother. "We . . . uh, Berit and I gave each other bobs."

Hannah laughed. "It suits you. Does Berit's?" She raised her voice and called her niece's name.

"She's at school," said Ione, seeing the time on the wall clock. She rubbed sleep from her eyes. "Mama—mama, why are you here?"

Her mother's features broadened into an expression of glee.

"Oh, Ione, I got a wire from Jens! Hildegard is in labor. Who knows, by now she may have had them—ja, the doctor says two! The train doesn't leave until ten-thirty, and I want you to come with me! Come with me to see the babies and to help your brother and Hildy!"

"Two?" said Ione. Excitement zipped through her. She was going to be an aunt of twins! "Oh Mama, I'd love to go, but—"

"—but what? Ione, Hildy asked for you. I'll be there at least two weeks, but you don't have to stay that long. Just for a couple of days. Oh, Ione, I want you to be there with me. And how many times have you said you wanted to visit Germany?"

Many, thought Ione, nodding.

"But I've . . . I've met this man, Mama."

"A man? You didn't mention any man in your last letter."

"Well, I've only been seeing him for a little while and—"

"—and he'll be here when you get back."

"But . . . if the train leaves at ten-thirty, I won't have time to tell him I'm leaving. And we've got plans tonight!"

Hannah leveled her serious-mother gaze at Ione.

"Write him a note, Ione. Berit can give it to him."

"But—"

"—Ione, no buts. Now pack a bag. I'll help."

The excitement of travel—the slight sway and clickety-clack of the train, the observation of fellow passengers (Wasn't there something shifty in the eyes of that sweaty gentlemen with the handlebar mustache, and what was in that leather-tooled valise that long-faced woman wouldn't let go of?), the passing views of town and country—soon made Ione's reluctance over leaving Edon seem girlish and silly.

She was going to a place she'd never been!

Hildegard was a local girl whom Ione had claimed as a playmate long before Jens claimed her as a bride. Her father was a German whose relations had owned and operated a hotel in Bavaria for more than a century, and after the Great War, Hildy and her new husband honeymooned there. Two more visits followed, after which they accepted an invitation from the elderly aunt and uncle to help run the place.

Ione had been to Sweden and Denmark but never Germany, and now at the end of her travels, she'd get the bonus of meeting not just one but two nieces or nephews or a combination of both!

9

I T WAS AN ODD SENSATION to be on one's feet one moment and
then, with no effort of one's own, to be prone in the snow the
next.

"*Oh, beklager!*" said a woman, but she wasn't sorry enough to stop.
"*Bashi! Bashi, kom! Kom hit!*" The woman chased the Rottweiler who
had broken free of his leash and had, in his crazed race to freedom,
clipped the back of Nora's right leg, sending her sprawling. After a
moment of stillness, Nora pushed herself up to her forearms and
gulped, finally finding the breath that had been knocked out of her.
She didn't think she was hurt, at least she hadn't heard anything snap
and—

"—*Er alt i orden?*"

Staring at pant legs, Nora tilted her head back to expand her view.
A man in a navy wool coat loomed over her.

"I . . . *jeg snakke ikke norske*," she said, and as she struggled to
rise—lying on one's stomach in a snowbank was not a posture conducive to conversation—the man reached for her hand and helped
her to her feet. She bobbled a little, as if she had spent the morning
at a breakfast bar that didn't serve breakfast, at least not in solid form.

"*Uffda,*" she said, appropriating her grandmother's favorite
expression.

"Well, you speak *some*," said the man, with just a trace of a Norwegian accent. He swatted away snow from the sleeves of her jacket.
"Now, can you walk to that bench there?"

"Yes, sure," said Nora. The path was icy and clutching the man's
arm seemed a prudent thing to do.

Seated at the bench, the man sat close to her and said, "Are you sure you're fine?" He looked into her eyes as if he were on a hunt for something. "You feel dizzy? Confused? Is there pain anywhere?"

"I'm fine, thanks." Feeling both silly and touched at his concern, she added, "*Doctor.*"

"It was lucky the snow cushioned your fall. That was a pretty big dog. And you're welcome."

There was a graciousness in his voice that made Nora ask, "Wait a second, are you a doctor?"

"Ja." The man held out a gloved hand. "Dr. Thomas Strand, at your service. My field is endocrinology, but my guess is that you suffered no glandular damage."

She returned his smile.

"I'm glad your head was protected by that hat—a very nice hat, by the way—"

"—*takk.* My grandmother knitted it."

"Still, I'd like to make sure you're not concussive. Will you answer a few questions?"

At her nod, he asked, "Name?"

"Nora Rolvaag."

"Are you from Minnesota?"

"Yes," she said, surprised. "Are you psychic, too?"

He grinned. "Hardly, but I like to think I can recognize someone from my home state."

"What? You're from Minnesota?"

"I was born there. My father had a year's fellowship at Carleton College in Northfield. I was only two months old when we came back to Norway, but I've got dual citizenship." Further explaining that he had gone to medical school at the University of Wisconsin at Madison, he added, "When I heard your accent, I knew right away you were from the Midwest, and you look so Nordic, well, I took a guess you were from Minnesota."

"I'm impressed."

"I am, too," he said, looking at her for a long moment. "So what brings you to Oslo?"

"I'm on a trip with my grandmother. She's visiting her cousin . . . who's dying."

"I'm sorry to hear that."

Nora shrugged. "My grandmother's feeling a lot of emotions besides sadness. It was sort of a . . . tumultuous relationship."

"Where are you staying?"

"At her cousin's house. In Telemark. On Lake Tinnsjø. I took the train up here this morning."

Posing no threat to pedestrians, a slow-moving beagle waddled by, tethered by a leash to its owner.

"Well, fortunately, Miss Rolvaag, I see no signs of head trauma. Excuse my presumption: is it 'Miss'?"

Nora smiled. "I prefer 'Ms.'"

"Yes, of course," said Thomas and looked at his watch. "In any case, Ms. Rolvaag, I think it would be prudent if I monitor you for a while. Do you have plans for lunch?"

"Not yet. I was going to visit Frogner Park and eat afterward."

"I couldn't have prescribed better." He rose, offering a crooked elbow.

She took it.

Clumps of snow covered thighs, buttocks, penises, breasts.

"You really should see this in the summer," said Thomas as they walked Frogner Park's promenade, past sculptures of nude bodies hugging, dancing, frolicking, wrestling, doing gymnastics, sitting in repose, or, in the case of *The Angry Boy*, throwing a tantrum. "When your view is unobstructed."

"It's not *that* obstructed," said Nora, and it was true; there were plenty of naked body parts free of snow.

Still holding on to his arm—Had she ever let go, on their long walk to the park and into it?—they approached the centerpiece of Vigeland's sculpture garden, the *Monolitten*, a tower of nudes rising up to the cold gray sky.

"I've got to take my grandmother here," said Nora. "When she was in Oslo, this was just a regular park." She tilted her head, studying a sculpture of a child getting a piggyback ride. "And Clyde Chuka, too. He'd love it."

"Is he your . . . is Mr. Chuka your boyfriend?"

Nora laughed. "No, my mother's. Well, way more than her boyfriend—her life partner, I'd say. Father of my brother, Harry. A real father to me, too, when my dad wasn't . . . and even when he was. Is."

Thomas looked both determined and unable to understand. "They sound . . . interesting."

Nora laughed again as a gust of wind blew gauzy swirls of snow off the sculpture of two broad-shouldered gymnasts.

"That they are."

"Then let's go eat," said Thomas. "Let's join the living—and the clothed—and you can tell me all about yourself and your interesting family."

Berit hated to turn down Guri's supper invitation—the family had an in-house cook and the food was always good—but a little headache had grown into a throbbing one that took away her appetite for both food and companionship. It was no surprise that her cousin wasn't home; the surprise lately was when Ione was home, and as Berit hung her straw hat on a hook, she said aloud, in a sour voice, "I wonder what the two lovebirds are up to now?"

Spring temperatures were mild outside, but since Ione had been seeing Edon, a frost had taken root in the two rooms the women shared, getting icier with each passing day. Oh, sometimes Berit pretended to listen as Ione prattled on about the romantic/clever/poetic thing Edon had said or done, or the museum they'd visited, or the concert they'd heard. On rare occasions Berit accepted one of the invitations Ione continued to proffer, but only to events that involved lots of people, like a dance or party. She had no stomach for spending time alone with Romeo and Juliet.

Putting the kettle on the stove and sitting down at the small table, Berit pressed her fingers into her aching scalp. She leaned forward, massaging her forehead and her temples, the sound coming out of her halfway between a sigh and a groan. When she opened her eyes, she fixed them in a stare for a long moment before shifting aside the pain of her headache to allow for the question, "What's that?" Picking up one of two envelopes she hadn't noticed lying on the woven white placemat, she quickly tore open the one with her name on it.

> *Berit!*
> *Mama came to fetch me to go to Germany with her. Hildy is having twins! I'll be staying several days and plan to be back next Tuesday or Wednesday. Please give Edon his letter when he comes to pick me up tonight!*
> *Love,*
> *Your Cousin Ione*

The envelope marked "Edon" was underlined with a swish, and Berit studied the exuberant flourish for a moment before slicing open the side of the envelope with her thumbnail. Ione's handwriting was pretty—they had both been taught the importance of penmanship by Fru Dokken—but it was rushed and so filled with pet names and mewling exclamations of love that Berit's headache deepened. In the last paragraph, the purple poet really poured it on:

> *Know, darling, that nothing is more important to me now than our love. But I couldn't deny my mother, or my brother and sister-in-law. Or those two babies coming! Still, when I'm not changing diapers or wiping spit-up off my shoulder, know that I'll be thinking of you and counting the hours until I'm back in your arms. So keep them open!*
> *Look for me next week—if I'm not home Tuesday, come back Wednesday, and if I'm not back Wednesday, come back Thursday! Remember, absence makes the heart grow fonder . . . although I doubt a heart so filled with love as mine could grow any bigger!*
> *Yours Always, and Always Yours,*
> *Ione*

Fury coursed through Berit's body, and she clenched her hands, crumpling the letter. Startled for a moment by the passion of her action, she tried to smooth out the creases before realizing it didn't matter; she was never going to give it to Edon anyway. At least not that letter. Berit smiled, and as she went to the desk drawer to get the stationery, she realized her headache was gone.

Edon shifted uncomfortably, his long legs crammed under the small kitchen table. He hadn't liked the disappointment he felt when Berit instead of Ione opened the door—seeing Ione, after any absence, made his heart flip. And he hadn't liked that Berit grabbed the small bouquet of irises he had brought and rushed to the sink, all the while telling him to, "Sit! sit!" And he most definitely did not like when she set the glass of flowers in the center of the table and sat across from him, her face wearing a discomfiting expression of pity and concern.

"So, is Ione down the hall?" he asked, voicing aloud his desire that she was only freshening up in the communal bathroom.

Berit continued staring at him with that damned look on her face, and Edon swallowed a cold tickle in his throat.

"What is it? Where's Ione?"

Bowing her blond head, Berit stared at her hands and Edon wondered briefly if she were praying.

"Berit! What is it?"

Her eyes brimming with tears, Berit looked up and whispered, "Oh, Edon. Ione's gone."

"Gone?" He pushed himself back, his knees banging on the table edge. "What do you mean, gone?"

Pressing her lips together, Berit took a moment to compose herself. "She . . . she never told you about Alf?"

"Alf?" A flush of heat rushed through Edon's body; he felt as if his hairline were on fire. "Who's Alf?"

"Here," said Berit, reaching into the pocket of her apron. "She left this for you."

Edon tore open the envelope, his face tense as his eyes scanned the words.

"She wrote me one, too, and if—"

He didn't wait for her to finish, stumbling out of the chair and lurching across the room.

It wasn't until she heard the slam of the rooming house's front door that Berit leaned forward, and putting her hands to her face, burst out laughing.

Dear Edon,

I know this letter will come as a surprise and for that I am sorry. But remember when you told me how real happiness can only come from following one's heart? Well, that's what I have to do, Edon.

I was certain things between Alf and me were over, and that is why I never mentioned him to you. But he came to Oslo several days ago and when I haven't been seeing you, I've been seeing him. And I realize, Edon, that my first love, Alf, is my real love.

I am sorry I didn't give you the courtesy of telling you this in person. By the time you get this, I will be on a train with Alf. To where he hasn't told me, but I am sure it will be an adventure!

Know that I am very fond of you,

Ione

His heart hammering, he leaned against the millinery shop window and read the letter again. Why would Ione write such lies? Was she testing him in some way? He read it a third time, looking for clues that might reveal its true meaning, the big joke of it all.

Not finding any, his knees turned to rubber and he slumped against the store window displaying women's cloches, toques, and turbans positioned on oval stands that even without faces, seemed to stare at him.

Ione had made it so easy! Relaying news to Berit like a cub reporter—"Edon said this, I said that, we did this," mooning over his simplistic sayings about true happiness, about following one's heart, about love. She wasn't worried about the handwriting—she didn't know if Ione had written anything to Edon, but even if she had, the cousins both had a pride in artistic penmanship hammered into them and freely used loops and flourishes.

Alf, Berit thought, wiping away the tears of laughter that had leaked out of her eyes. Oh, Edon's face when I told him about Alf! It was an inspired pick for a name, Alf being the boathouse drunk back home who blew sloppy kisses to any young woman who had the misfortune of passing by.

She realized, as she got up to make a cup of tea, that she was hungry, and grabbing her light spring coat she raced out the door, hoping to get to Guri's in time for supper or at least in time for dessert.

Laughing and joking with the three other nursing students about exams and the body odor of Fru Malberg, Berit maintained her festive spirit through the pot roast and boiled potatoes, through dessert. When they sipped glasses of port, she graciously accepted Guri's toast: "For all the help you've given me, Berit, you let me put the dunce cap down!"

But as she walked home, the enormity of what she had done fell on her like a fog. Berit didn't go directly to the rooming house; she cased the streets of Oslo like a detective, looking around corners, into recessed doorways, searching for Edon. If she found him, she didn't know how she'd explain what she'd done, but she'd have to. Her hope was that after he killed her, he'd forgive her.

When she saw a tall, dark-haired man come out of a café, her heart pounded with relief, but it wasn't Edon, and by the time she got home and into bed, she was jittery and short-winded, not from the strong coffee Guri had served or the cook's famous gold cake but from the reckoning of her great misdeed.

Lying under the covers shivering, she thought of Edon's face, leeched of color; she thought of him lurching out her door, phony letter in his hands. Her own were clasped to her chest, as if she were trying to contain a bird, and the bird was her conscience, flapping its wings, clawing at her innards as it squawked over and over: What have I done?

10

T HE TEMPERATURE OF THE WATER WAS PERFECT, hot but
tolerable, and rose-scented bubbles covered her in a cloud
of floral foam. Luxury wasn't anywhere near the top of Patty
Jane's list of what she held sacred (love, curiosity, peanut brittle),
but she did appreciate when she was in the lap of it, as she was now,
wearing an eye mask, her head resting on a rolled-up towel, classical
music playing on the plastic portable radio perched on the toilet lid,
and the hallway telephone placed on the floor within reach.

After the sisters saw the movie *Pillow Talk,* Harriet had opined
that a bathtub phone conversation represented the pinnacle of high
living. "It's just so sophisticated!" she had said. "Imagine being in a
tub like Doris Day and talking on the telephone to Rock Hudson!"

Patty Jane wasn't imagining any such thing, but she smiled at the
memory; she'd brought the phone in purely for convenience. Clyde
had taken Thor to the bakery (a poor substitute for his mother's
baking) and she didn't want to miss any calls, especially any from
her daughter, especially after the last one, in which Nora had told
her about Ione's heretofore secret life.

Sinking into the hot water, she was just about to plug her nose
when her relaxing soak was interrupted by the jangle of the ringing
telephone, and, startled, Patty Jane bolted up in a splash of water.
Yanking her eye mask off (as if she needed to see to hear), she picked
up the receiver and eagerly said, "Hello?"

"Nora? Nora Rolvaag?"

"No," said Patty Jane, disappointed to hear her daughter's name rather than her voice. "This is her mother. May I take a message for her?"

The finale of Ravel's "Bolero" crescendoed and water dripped on the tile as Patty Jane stretched over the tub to switch off the radio.

"Yes, I'd like her to phone me as soon as possible, please."

"Hmm, that might not be all that soon. She's out of the country."

The efficiency of the woman's voice flagged in a disappointing, "Oh."

Crossing her feet on top of the faucet and admiring the pedicure Clyde had given her, Patty Jane said, "Like I said, I'd be happy to take a message."

"Well," said the woman, "it's rather time-sensitive. Do you have a fax machine?"

"Wowie," said Thor, standing at the driveway's entrance.

"You can say that again," said Clyde Chuka.

"Wowie," said Thor.

"It sort of looks like a Swiss chalet," said Patty Jane. "A Swiss chalet built by a lumberjack."

Brenda Vick, the woman whom Thor had greeted with an exclamatory, "You're *tall*," nodded. "It's all that detailed millwork on the shutters and around the eaves."

"Are the logs white or yellow pine?" asked Clyde.

Brenda Vick laughed. "I'm a lawyer, not a realtor, but I did do a little homework." She cleared her throat. "The logs are all native white pine and the roof's shingles are cedar, replaced just last year."

As they walked, a cold wind blew, and pulling tighter the collar of her puffy down coat, Brenda said, "It's a little hard to imagine this is the summer, but on the other side of this driveway is a big garden, and all those bushes by that shed over there are lilacs. Lilac bushes also hide the septic tank." The driveway ended, turning into a double garage. In a single file, the trio followed the woman down a gradual slope.

"Sorry the path's so narrow," she said. "I shoveled it this morning so you could get an idea of the property from a couple different angles."

At the end of the gradually descending path, by a cottonwood tree, Brenda invited them to look up at the cabin perched on top of the rise and note the size of the wraparound deck.

"The perfect place to sit and view the ocean."

Confusion silenced the visitors; even Thor knew something didn't make sense.

"It's a joke that never gets old," said Brenda with a smile. She gestured to the frozen body of water behind them. "That's the name of the lake."

"The *Ocean?*" asked Patty Jane.

"Charleyville is surrounded by five lakes," said Brenda. "And it has its share of eccentrics—including a mayor who once mounted a campaign to rename all the lakes. He was only successful in changing Lake Marion—this lake—to the Ocean."

"The Ocean," said Thor. "Wowie."

"One hundred and seventy feet from door to shore," said Brenda, leading them back up the shoveled path and onto the deck. "There's the side entrance," she said pointing, "and the one that probably is used most. But let's go in this way."

Patty Jane hadn't known what to expect—everything had happened so fast, from Brenda Vick's strange phone call that morning, to reading the faxed material, to the what-the-hell executive decision she'd made to take a road trip and see what, exactly, was what. But she couldn't help her gasp as they stepped through the front door, and Brenda said, "Now this of course is the great room."

"It looks like a lodge out of an old movie," said Patty Jane. "Except in color."

The varnished log walls and pine floors gleamed. A fire snapped in the floor-to-ceiling stone fireplace that was centered in the far wall, and a railed pine staircase led up to the second floor. A baby grand piano was between two windows on the right side, and a massive oak table and chairs were arranged on the left, in the partially visible kitchen. Burnished copper sconces were installed on the walls, and there were several arrangements of pine-framed chairs and sofas, their cushions covered in leather, corduroy, or a hunter-green-and-gold plaid.

"Damn-a-lama-ding-damn," whispered Patty Jane.

"Wait'll you see the rest," said Brenda.

They toured the kitchen, the two bathrooms, and four bedrooms on the main floor and climbed the staircase to look at another bathroom and two bedrooms, one of which was three times the size of the other. "The owner sold all the furniture that was upstairs and in the basement," said Brenda. "But she wasn't ready to sell the main floor's yet. She liked that it looked as it had when her husband was alive." The finished basement featured a laundry room, another bathroom, two small rooms, and a large room, empty save for a foosball table.

Twirling a handle on the foosball table, Thor asked Clyde, "Wanna play?"

While Clyde took Thor up on his offer (eventually losing three games), the women convened in the kitchen.

"I'll make some tea," the attorney offered, "although it looks like you could use something a little stronger."

"Where's the owner now?" Patty Jane asked. "I'd like to meet her."

"Nellie's at my place. She'd planned on coming, but she got a little nervous at the idea of people poking around the place." Brenda turned on the burner under the kettle. "As you may have gathered, she's a little eccentric."

"A *little*?"

Brenda smiled. "Like I told you, we breed them up here."

"Maybe there's something in the water," said Patty Jane.

"Something in the *Ocean* water."

"Geez, Nellie," said Brenda, surprised, as a small woman, hand extended, walked in from the mudroom and toward the table.

"I'd like to meet you, too. I'm Nellie. I'm a little eccentric."

Patty Jane rearranged her gaping mouth to a smile and said, "I'm Patty Jane. And aren't we all."

"You're lucky I didn't say what I really think of you," Brenda teased as the older woman sat down. "How long have you been lurking about? How'd you get here anyway?"

"I hitched a ride with Marge Severson. And I'll have some tea, too, thanks for asking." She squinted at Patty Jane. "I see the similarity between you and your daughter, who Brenda tells me is in Norway."

"Yes, with her grandmother."

"Ahh, the famous cookie maker. Did you bring any?"

"Cookies? No. That's Ione's specialty, not mine."

"Oh," said Nellie disappointed, and when Brenda served tea, she took a slurpy sip.

"So your daughter has given you permission to say yay or nay to my offer?"

The question surprising her, Patty Jane swallowed a big glug of tea and had to wait a moment while it worked its way down her throat.

"Actually, no. I just spoke to Brenda this morning—I was in the bathtub." She flushed, wondering why she needed to include this bit of information. "After I read what she faxed me, we drove right up here."

"We being you and the gentlemen I saw in the game room?"

Brenda shook her head. "So you really *were* lurking about."

"Yes. Thor and Clyde. My husband and . . ." Patty Jane shrugged. "Oh, it's a long story."

"Aren't they all," said Nellie. "What do you know of mine?"

"Other than the little Nora told me about meeting you and what you said in your letter, not much."

"Well, here's the rest of it."

She proceeded to tell the same story she had told Nora, but no oven timer went off alerting her to *Jeopardy!* and she was able to finish it. "So I shut down Our Lodge pronto, and the day after Walter's funeral I had Kent Harug come out and dig up our big wooden sign and I burned it that night in the fireplace."

"She said she didn't want any yahoos thinking they were still open for business," said Brenda.

"What was on that sign?" asked Patty Jane.

"The lodge's name," said Nellie, her tone asking, *What did you think?*

"Which was?"

"*Our Lodge*," said Nellie. "That's what it was, and that's what we called it." She rattled her empty teacup, and Brenda got up to get the kettle. "Even without the sign, though, that's what it's always been to me."

"But why did you stay?" asked Patty Jane. "I mean, wasn't it hard keeping up this place all by yourself?"

"She's had help," said Brenda, filling Nellie's cup. "Girls from the community college have boarded here, and she hires out—mostly kids—to do lawn maintenance and snow removal, but mostly—"

"—mostly I do it myself," said Nellie, throwing Brenda a dirty look and Patty Jane another. "Because Walter loved Our Lodge and I loved Walter."

"And it's all because of Grandma's *cookies*?" said Nora. "And *Jeopardy!*"

The voice over the phone chuckled.

"Will you read me it again?"

Lifting up her reading glasses, Patty Jane rubbed her eyes. They had gotten home from the lodge just after eight, but aware of the time difference, she had waited until midnight to call.

"Okay," she said, smoothing the letter Brenda Vick had faxed to her. She cleared her throat.

Dear Nora,

Do you believe in serendipity? You should, because it exists. My Walter was a true believer in signs, and he taught me to be open to life's little winks and nudges, your gingerbread cookies being one of them. They were my Walter's very favorite.

Here's the thing: over the years people have pestered and badgered me to sell Our Lodge, but knowing how much it meant to my Walter, I have ignored all those pests and badgers. However! In case you didn't notice, I am no spring chicken—not even a summer hen, ha ha. And I'm tired. My plan was to just keel over in a couple years, preferably on the deck, listening to the loons out on the Ocean. But having seen my evil banker again yesterday, he reminded me ever forcefully of my dwindling funds and the need to sell pronto.

Walking home, the bile kept rising in my throat at the thought of selling, of all sorts of yahoos and looky loos tromping through my home . . . and then, a little bell in this belfry of mine rang. I remembered the young lady on some kind of retreat who several weeks ago was not just kind enough to pick me up on this very road, but who gave me GINGERBREAD COOKIES *on the same day I'd visited both my evil banker and my dear Walter! And here's the kicker, the sign that didn't reveal itself as a wink or a nudge but outright clobbered me: today on* Jeopardy! *there was a category of Jane Fonda movies, and this was the Daily Double clue: "She was the unhappy wife of a banker living in* A Doll's House.*" And the answer was* NORA!

Of course I have no idea if you're in the market for a quality lakeside log cabin such as this, but why wouldn't you be? What I'm saying is I'd like to give you the first opportunity to buy it. The whole kit and caboodle. Walter would not just approve, he'd practically insist.

My trusted attorney (who's nothing like my evil banker) is Brenda Vick, and she will be handling the sale. However! As I said, I believe in signs and serendipity, and if I can act on this crazy whim, it's only fair that you do the same. Therefore, I ask to hear your answer by 12:00 (yes, high noon!—why not?) Friday afternoon. That gives you time to drive up here and take a good look at the place. (And if you want to bring more of your grandmother's gingerbread cookies, all the better!) If you're not ready to grab that which is being thrust at you, I'll rescind the offer while you see a psychiatrist. Brenda will then be advised to sell it to a saner yahoo at a whim-less price far higher than the one I offer you.

To every season, turn, turn, turn,
Nellie

There was a pause long enough for Patty Jane to wonder if the line had disconnected.

"Nora?"

In their long conversation, she had related everything she could remember about the meeting with Nellie as well as her impressions of the lodge.

"Still here, Ma . . . I just . . . it's just so crazy. I don't know what to say."

"Well, like the letter says, you've got 'til high noon, which is 7 p.m. your time. Brenda doesn't think Nellie would absolutely hold you to that time frame—she says it's just Nellie being dramatic, but she also says, 'With Nellie, you never know.'"

"And you say it's a steal?"

"Nora, everything's included. The furniture, the linens, the dishes—*everything*. As Clyde said, 'It's the steal of the century.'"

Sitting at the painted kitchen table for a long time, Nora stared at the cup of coffee Ione had set in front of her. She'd been excited to spend the morning as well as the train ride back to Oslo filling her mind with thoughts of Thomas, the man she'd met just yesterday and the man she was going back to spend more time with today. Now she was supposed to make a major real estate decision about a property she'd barely seen that overlooked a lake called the Ocean?

"I'm just sort of . . . *floored*," Nora said, and Ione translated the idiom for Edon, who nodded. When Nora relayed what her mother had told her over the phone, they had listened intently, Ione occasionally whispering an "uffda," as she refilled their coffee. "I mean, what would I do with a lodge? Life—whew! It's one thing after another."

Both Edon and Ione nodded their agreement.

His last patient of the day kept Thomas from meeting Nora's train on time, and that she had to wait twenty minutes for him made her even more nervous and jittery.

"How far is it to your apartment?" she said, after he'd greeted her with a hug and an apology for tardiness, and when he told her about ten blocks, she said, "Perfect. Do you mind if we walk?"

"If you don't mind a little snow," said Thomas, taking her bag. "I don't."

They hadn't gotten out of the terminal before Nora told him that she was on a deadline, that she had—she pushed down her mitten to looked at her watch—two hours and seven minutes to make a decision that would be life-altering.

He was taken aback by the drama in Nora's statement, but calm was reflexive in his nature and he merely replied, "We alter our lives every day by our decisions."

Like air out of a balloon, a spritz of anxiety rushed out of her and she laughed.

"Thank you, Doctor. But this could be *life-altering* life-altering."

Snow was falling hard and wind pushed away their words so that they had to lean into each other to hear them, and by the time they'd reached his apartment, they were both sodden and cold. Nora's shivers, however, as she told Thomas of the strange offer, were more emotion than weather induced.

Listening to her carefully, Thomas occasionally asked questions, including the obvious one, "Could you afford it?"

Nora nodded. "I have savings from when I lived in L.A.; plus, when I sold my house there, I invested all that money."

It was another question that helped her make her decision: "If you took the leap, and it didn't work out, how hard would you fall?"

In lieu of the champagne he didn't have, Thomas put a bottle of Chardonnay on ice as Nora called her mother to tell her she was saying yes to Nellie's offer.

While Thomas was at work, Nora explored Oslo, happily recounting, as they dined in the evening, her visits to the Kon-Tiki Museum, the Old Akes Church, and the Nobel Peace Center. She spent the first night in the guest room of her host's apartment, but on the second night the sleeping arrangements changed.

"What's this?" said Nora, when Thomas passed her a slip of paper over the table.

"A prescription."

"To be quiet?" she joked, knowing she'd monopolized the conversation by telling him about what she'd seen at the Resistance Museum.

They were eating at an Indian restaurant on St. Olavs Gate, and the smell of curry hung like vaporous drapery.

"I can't read it," she said, unfolding the square. "It's in Norwegian."

Their waiter, a man whose skeletal frame put into question whether or not he ate any of the food he served, took their dessert plates and asked if there was anything else they needed.

"Why, yes," said Nora, handing him the paper. "Could you translate this, please?"

The waiter bowed. He could speak five languages and in West Bengal he had taught Latin at a boy's school; to have someone ask him to translate filled his scrawny chest with memories of classrooms, of languages, of the divine act of communication.

He cleared his throat, as if in benediction: "A change of sleeping quarters is recommended for optimum health and pleasure of both patient and physician."

The waiter, whose fallen arches hurt, offered a professional, neutral smile. It was getting late—most customers had gone home and he was nearly finished cleaning his section—and the man only wanted to go home and resume the two-day chess game with his wife, who was smart and skillful and never clucked at his bad moves.

Outside the restaurant, Nora told the doctor she would take his advice and when they first kissed, she felt a little light-headed, as if she'd been knocked over by Bashi the dog all over again.

11

O N THE LONG JOURNEY HOME, Ione was filled with a fizzy excitement
of new love multiplied by three: the big wild love she felt for
Edon and the tender baby-love she had for her two new nephews. She couldn't wait to tell Edon all about them; how even down to
the single blond curl that sprouted up from the middle of their foreheads
they were so identical that Hildy tied a string around Dann's wrist to
distinguish him from Dag. She wanted to tell him how holding a baby
(and in a few joyful and slightly scary moments, two) in your arms filled
you with a sense of awe and responsibility—and besides that, it was
fun!—and how lucky she felt to be related to the two most adorable,
interesting, and fascinating babies in the world. She had a lot to do before
having her own babies, what with their world travel (when they spoke
of their individual dreams, they now included each other in them), but
any ambivalence about having them at all had evaporated by the sight,
scent, touch of her beautiful nephews.

During the ferry crossing, she sat next to a plump woman with cheeks
pink as summer roses. They chatted amiably in a mishmash of German,
Norwegian, and English (the Frau's eyes wide and her pretty mouth
pursed as Ione told her of the twins), and when they entered the Port of
Rodby, Ione opened her eyes, realizing she had fallen asleep, her head
resting against the pillowy softness of her seatmate's shoulder.

She would have wired Edon her return date and time, but not knowing
the address of his guesthouse, she'd wired her cousin instead, hoping
Berit would be able to relay the message to Edon, who'd greet her at the

station with open arms. As the train made its way up into Norway, she fantasized about running to him (she hoped he'd be wearing the homburg that made him look so dashing) and the long kiss they'd share, and how they'd laugh when she presented the silly gift she'd gotten him—a beer stein with a cupid on the handle.

Upon disembarking, she stood on the platform for a long time, waiting to be pleasantly surprised, but when she wasn't, she half-ran, half-walked all the way to the rooming house.

Racing up the stairs, her suitcase bumping on the steps, she hollered, "Berit? Berit?"

Her cousin was seated at the small table, her hands wrapped around a cup of tea, and wearing such a morose expression that all the excitement and exuberance that had fueled Ione's long racewalk from the train station had suddenly drained.

"Berit," she said, a matchstick of fear lighting, "Berit, was is it? Is Edon all right?"

Her cousin's eyes closed as she slowly shook her head.

"What!" said Ione, her voice shrill. "What is it?"

"Ione," said Berit. "Ione, Edon's gone."

"Gone? Gone where?"

"He . . . he left you a letter. It's in the bedroom—"

Ione ran toward the bedroom as Berit added, "on the dresser."

After a wail that seemed to shudder the apartment walls, Ione ran back to the kitchen.

"What does this mean!" she shouted, flapping the paper as if it were on fire. "When did he give it to you? What did he say? Where did he go?"

Her voice was an assault and Berit pressed her back against the slats of the chair, her hands clenched around the edge of the seat. Ione looked wild—undone—her eyebrows crooked like checkmarks, her skin so pink it looked parboiled.

"I . . . I . . . uh—"

"—why didn't you make him wait for me?" The scream of Ione's voice veered off into a moan, and with a choked cry she sank into the other kitchen chair as if she'd been shot.

Watching her soundlessly sob, Berit felt afraid, afraid for her cousin. She was unhinged!

"Oh, Ione," *she whispered, not intentionally but because her mouth was dry of saliva.* "He came to the apartment and—" *For a wild moment, Berit felt on the verge of confession, but she quickly stepped back from what would be a perilous precipice.* "And . . . and he said he was leaving Oslo. He said to tell you sorry, and then he handed me the note. What did it say? Is it so awful?"

Ione's head lolled in one direction and the other as if a tendon in her neck had snapped, and another flash of fear pulsed through Berit.

"Ione?"

Her head fell forward, but with great effort Ione lifted it, and Berit nearly gasped, seeing the pain in her cousin's eyes.

"He's left me," *she said, her voice flat.* "He's left me and I don't know how to find him so I can change his mind."

"Ione, you only knew him for . . . what? Not even two weeks! Maybe it's better you found out early what kind of man he was, that his promises . . ."

A wave of shame rolled over Berit, and she closed her mouth, unable to listen to her own lies.

"The last night we were together," *said Ione, her voice still flat, almost a drone,* "we were in the park. It was so hard finding places where we could be together, alone. And we almost . . . but we didn't. I had never, never felt such excitement. I wanted . . . I wanted him so badly—I was ready—but then a group of drunks came along, and we decided that wasn't the best place to . . . to love each other the way we wanted to. I told Edon I'd ask Guri if we could use her apartment . . . but then the next morning I left for Germany. Why did I leave for Germany?"

Ione slumped in her chair like a boxer who'd been drubbed in the first round. But at the knock on the door, she bolted up as if she'd been electrically jolted.

"Edon!" *cried Ione, scrambling toward the door.*

Berit was half-lifted out of her chair, but another jolt—this one of panic—pushed her back. What if it was Edon? How would she explain what she'd done? Would they accept a plea of temporary insanity? Would they—

A gale of relief blew through her body when she heard the voice of Fru Eggert, their landlady, informing Ione that tomorrow men would be coming to replace the roof shingles and not to be alarmed by the noise.

"Takk!" said Berit, going to the door, hoping to distract the woman from the bereft figure that was Ione. Placing her hand on her cousin's shoulder and gently pushing her aside, she thanked the landlady again.

"I think she's come down with something," Berit whispered, and before Fru Eggert could offer to bring her cure-all fish soup, Berit had shut the door.

"Explain it to me again," said Thomas. "Berit gave Ione a letter supposedly from Edon? That *she* wrote? What did it say?"

The train they were riding chugged around a curve and Nora pressed her shoulder into Thomas's and closed her eyes, hoping to better recall her grandmother's recitation. "Something like, 'I enjoyed our time together and wish you a wonderful life, but it's over. I'm leaving Oslo. Good-bye.'" Opening her eyes, she said, "You look so shocked."

"I can't believe one person could be so diabolical." Thomas shook his head slowly, as if the action might make sense of what he had heard. "But how could she forge his handwriting?"

"Grandma says it was typewritten."

"Diabolical," said Thomas again.

A little girl turned around in the seat in front of theirs, smiling shyly as she held up her doll for their admiration. Thomas said something to her in Norwegian, which made her giggle and answer, "Pippi."

"I'm sorry for the circumstances that brought your grandmother here," Thomas told Nora after the girl turned around, uninterested in further conversation. "But I'm so glad you came with her."

When Nora impulsively invited Thomas to meet Ione over the weekend and he just as impulsively said yes, they both laughed at the astonished look the other one wore.

"But only if you're sure I won't be in the way."

"*I'm* in the way," said Nora with a shrug. "I could use an ally. And besides, you're a doctor. Doctors are never in the way, especially in the house of someone who's sick."

Now tucking her hand in the crook of Thomas's elbow, she looked out the train window and the passing landscape composed of tall firs, their boughs frosted with snow. "You smell like the view," she said, nuzzling her face into the soft wool of his neck scarf to better inhale his woodsy cologne.

"*Min kjaere,*" he murmured and these words she recognized: *my love.*

Happiness felt like light in her chest, and she thought that however the world was for her grandmother, for anyone, her own right now was a planet perfectly aligned.

Pressing her face against Thomas's scarf and his woodsy wooly goodness, she giggled.

"What are you laughing at, my dear?"

Nora squeezed his bicep and lifted her face to bring her lips in kissing proximity to his, keeping to herself her thoughts on planetary alignments and his woodsy wooly goodness and the old-fashioned way he called her "my dear."

⇶ 12

ERIT HEARD A CRASH—*later she would have to sweep up broken chards of a beer stein scattered across the floor—and moments later her cousin shambled like a hypnotist's subject into the kitchen, carrying the suitcase she hadn't had time to unpack.*

"Ione, no."

Making no indication that she'd heard her, Ione continued her trance-like walk to the door.

"But where are you going?" asked Berit, her voice cloaked with an urgent sadness.

"I don't know," said Ione. "Back home, I guess."

Guilt and remorse rose in Berit, but not to the level of confession. She had been living in a state of unease seasoned with panic, afraid of getting caught in her lies with every knock on the door. How had she failed to figure out the ramifications of what she'd done? And yet if Ione went away, she'd be given a reprieve, time to think about how to repair—or further cover up—the terrible damage she'd caused.

"I'm so sorry for you," said Berit, which wasn't a total lie. "Will you write to me?"

"Ja, sure," said Ione, drooping under her cousin's hug. "Although what I'll write about, I can't say . . . now that my life is over."

Berit stepped back and forced a laugh.

"Don't be so dramatic, Ione. It's better to be hurt by a man early on, before you put a lot of time into him, before you really know him."

Ione's eyes were swollen from crying, but there was a glint of something hard as she looked at her cousin. "I did really know him, Berit. I really knew him and I really loved him and I was really sure he felt the same way."

Planning to go back home to Stavanger, Ione surprised herself at the ticket agent's kiosk when she requested a ticket to Garmisch-Partenkirchen. After informing her of ferry times and train changes, the agent issued the tickets, and in the early evening Ione found herself embarking on the southern route of the northern one from which she disembarked that morning.

Her family's delight at seeing her outweighed their surprise, especially as one of the twins was suffering from a case of colic that manifested in a piercing scream, frazzling all in the household. "Please, you take him," said Hildy, passing her Dann (or Dag? She'd forgotten which one wore the string bracelet) whose high-pitched wail made Ione's ears ring.

"There, there," she said patting the infant's back. Turning away to walk with him, she whispered, "I know just how you feel."

A week and a half later when her mother left to return to Norway, Ione didn't go with her.

"If it's all right with you," she'd asked Hildy, "I wouldn't mind staying here awhile."

"Are you serious? Oh, Ione, I'd love that! Sometimes I feel so . . . so overwhelmed, and you've been such a help . . . oh, takk!"

Jens was just as happy, although after seeing their mother off at the station, he asked his sister why she'd wanted to stay.

"To help Hildy," Ione said. "And I love being around the babies."

"You're a seventeen-year-old girl," Jens said.

"What do you mean by that?"

"I mean, a seventeen-year-old girl usually wants to do more than babysit her brother's babies."

"Hildy's only nineteen!"

"Ja, but all she's ever wanted is to be married to me and have babies." Jens couldn't help his self-satisfied smile. "And from what Mother told us, you'd met a man in Oslo you were taken with."

Lilac bushes flowered along Bahnhofstrasse, and Ione stopped, burying her nose in a cluster of tiny fragrant petals.

"Ione, you don't have to hide from me. I know you're hurting."

Hannah had pressed her daughter for details about the man she'd been so sad to leave and so anxious to get back to, but a curt, "It's over" had stopped further conversation on the topic. Jens, however, was a protective older brother, and it was apparent his sister was in need of counseling, counsel he was happy to provide.

Ione breathed in one more lungful of the sweet melancholic perfume. When she faced her brother, he nearly flinched at the depth of sadness expressed on her face.

"Oh, Jens, I met the man for me. And I was the one for him." She smiled gamely as tears welled in her eyes. "Or so I thought. But it's over and I need to be away from everything that reminds me of him." She took his arm and nudged him to begin walking. "And besides, I'm the only one who can soothe Dann when he's colicky, ja?"

In the hotel her brother and sister-in-law managed, Ione's days were filled with watching the twins, helping clean rooms when the maid was sick, helping the cook chop vegetables or bake bread, signing in guests at the reception table, and serving wine and schnapps at the late-afternoon gatherings held in the hotel library in cold weather and al fresco in the back garden when the weather was warm. There were plenty of hotel guests who flirted with her and some bold enough to ask the pretty young Norwegian for a date, but Ione always refused, choosing to spend her nights piecing a quilt with Hildy or playing checkers with Hildy's elderly uncle, Heinrich.

She wasn't exactly happy, but she was busy, and being busy gave her less time to wonder why Edon had left her. Since she was a child, she had gone to bed every night whispering a simple prayer, and now this habit was accompanied by another ritual, of hugging BoBo, her old stuffed bear to her chest and crying herself to sleep.

On a warm spring day, when the alpine flowers carpeted the mountains in pastels, nearly a year to the day she had arrived, Ione decided she was strong enough to get out on her own, to do what she had always wanted: to explore the world. She didn't get very far: studying the globe in her small attic room, she was interrupted by a staccato rap on her door.

"It's Papa," said Jens, his face ashen. "He's had a stroke."

And so instead of wandering through the maze of a Casbah bazaar or exploring Roman ruins, instead of swaying atop a camel in the Gobi Desert or on a rickshaw in Shanghai, instead of eating mangoes in New Delhi or nuts in Madagascar, Ione found herself back in Stavanger, doing for her father what she had done for her nephews: wiping drool from his chin, soothing him, distracting him, bathing him. Ivar Kittleson never had much call for hugging and kissing, expressing love for his family by providing for them, and it gave Ione a tender pleasure to have so much physical contact with her father. She couldn't say how long she might have cheerfully attended to him, relaying the local gossip or serenading him with nonsensical songs: "Oh, Papa, I'm going to wipe your whiskery chin, Oh, Papa, would you like some bathtub gin?"

She couldn't say, because he died a week later, in the bed he'd been born in. His death turned his vital and fun-loving wife into a stunned widow, incapable of doing much of anything but sitting with a shawl draped around her shoulders, staring out the front room window. So Ione's duties as a daughter/nurse continued, except with a different parent.

Ione's other brother, Ivar, lived nearby, but even though he was his father's namesake, he didn't feel a responsibility to help Ione other than keeping up his habit of coming over every Sunday for the supper Ione now cooked instead of Hannah.

Aunt Lena gave Ione some relief, coming over to tend to her sister-in-law; as Hannah napped, she would have cake and coffee with Ione, filling her in on Berit's exciting life in Oslo, her new job in the hospital and how she had to fight off all the doctors asking for a date. Ione craved this information since her cousin provided none. Berit had answered two or three of the letters Ione had written her while in Germany, but always with one-page responses that gave updates on the weather, a new café she'd visited, or a film she had seen, but absolutely no word about Edon.

"Ione," she'd written in the first letter, "all I know is he's left Oslo; at least no one has seen him. For your sake, forget about him."

Finally, after receiving no replies to nearly a dozen letters, Ione stopped writing to Berit. The hurt and confusion over her cousin's snubs rose again when Berit failed to return for Ivar's funeral.

Aunt Lena made excuses for her. "She so busy, she couldn't take the time off from her work." Berit did write a condolence letter, but it was addressed to "Aunt Hannah and Family" and there was not a paragraph or a sentence directed solely to Ione.

Another year passed, and Ione could feel the idea she had of herself as a bold and daring adventurer fading into the reality of herself as a spinster. She was modern enough to believe that a woman should not be defined by her marital status; for her the word spinsterhood meant a loneliness of spirit and a door closed on possibility.

It was at the christening of the baby of her cousin Paul and his wife, Kirsten, that Ione saw for the first time in over two years the baby's godmother, Berit.

Late to the church, Ione tucked herself into the back pew and nearly cried out with pleasure when she saw her standing by the baptismal basin. She was more beautiful than ever, wearing a chic cloche hat and the kind of dress that reminded Ione that homemade clothes like her own never had the panache of something store-bought.

In the receiving line after the ceremony, Berit accepted her hug but returned it halfheartedly. When Ione said, "Oh, Berit, I've missed you so much!" her cousin smiled and nodded, but expressed no similar sentiment.

Outside the church, she heard her name called with the kind of enthusiasm Berit had failed to summon.

"Ione! Ione!"

She barely had time to register the voice's owner before she was enveloped in arms.

"Guri!" she said, catching her breath as the two stood happily looking over one another. "Guri!"

"Ione, your hair's grown so long!" The young woman laughed. "I saw you when you snuck in the back—"

"—uffda, my mother had come down with the grippe, and it was such a struggle convincing her not to come, and then getting out of the house myself . . ."

As the church lawn filled with celebrants dressed in their summer *finery, Guri hugged her again. Ione appreciated her friendliness, especially in contrast to her cousin's lack thereof.*

"So you're a nurse now, too?"

Guri nodded, a flush of pleasure tinting her features.

"Thanks to Berit's tutoring. We work at the same hospital." *She hugged Ione for a third time.* "It's just so good to see you!"

"And good to see you," *said Ione, feeling young and fresh and alive for the first time in a long while.*

Aunt Lena hosted a reception at her house, insisting that Ione take home a piece of cake and some smørbrød for Hannah.

"We're having another party later this evening," *Guri told her.* "Make sure your mother's all right and make sure you come back!"

Because the invitation hadn't come from her cousin, Ione was hesitant, after putting her mother to bed, to do anything but crawl into her own with a book. But it was too early, not even nine o'clock, and besides, maybe now that Berit was undistracted by all her godmotherly duties, she and Ione could finally have the reunion they deserved.

It was still light out on this summer's night as Ione made the short walk to her Aunt Lena's house; when she rapped on the back door, it opened quickly.

"Ione!" *said her aunt.* "We didn't think you were coming! How's Hannah?"

"In bed, sleeping. Is the party over?"

Aunt Lena nodded, but after a moment the sad face she put on turned mischievous. "But some young people have gathered in the barn. They'll be happy to see you."

Small but high, the barn wasn't the size of those on bigger farms, but it did house two horses and a dairy cow, which lowed softly when Ione climbed the ladder to the hayloft, squinting to adjust her eyes to the dusky, dusty light.

"Ione!" *said Guri.* "You're here!"

Sitting on hay bales in front of the opened loft door, two young men and a woman greeted Ione with similar good cheer. Berit, however, looked at Ione as if she were an unwanted chaperone, arriving to stop all fun and games and tattle to the authorities. Instead of cowing Ione, this inflamed her, and she purposefully plopped down next to Berit and said, "How's my favorite cousin?"

"Nei, she's my favorite cousin," said Helge, his words slurred. At sixteen, he was the youngest in the group and therefore drinking the most, wanting to prove he could keep up. "Here." He passed her a bottle of aquavit.

Ione took a swig, shivered, and took another.

"It's good, ja?"

Fanning her mouth, her eyes watering, Ione nodded.

"Berit's aunt made it," said Robert.

"My mother," said Helge, and to Ione, he added, "who wouldn't be your aunt, since we're not related." He looked up at Berit, confused. "How can you be our cousin and yet," he gestured toward Ione, "we're not cousins?"

"It's not that hard, Helge. I'm related to Ione on my mother's side. I'm related to you on my father's side."

"My deepest pardon," said the boy, who then burped.

Ione smiled at the hapless Helge and took another swig from the bottle.

"So all of you went to school with one another?" said Guri, knowing the answer because introductions had been made earlier, but wanting to fill in the conversational pause.

"Except me," said Helge. "I live up in Tromsø. It takes someone dying or being born to get us this far south."

Thinking this was rather clever of himself, he chuckled.

"Ja, we were all schoolmates," said Anna, "In fact, the first torch Robert carried was not for me but for Ione!"

"Nei, it's you I've always loved," said Robert, wrapping his arms around her and pulling her closer.

Pushing him away with a laugh, Anna patted her hair, done up in the old-fashioned coronet braids she had worn since childhood.

"It's true—if all the boys weren't in love with Ione, they were in love with Berit."

"I can see why!" said Helge, his enthusiasm knocking him off his hay bale. "Oof."

He laughed with the others, but as he boosted himself up, a wave of nausea washed over him.

"I don't like that look on your face," said Berit. "You'd better not do it in here!"

He staggered a few feet before losing the contents of his stomach in a pile of hay.

"Sorry," he said, wiping his mouth with his sleeve. As he zigzagged toward the trapdoor, Robert went to help him.

"Don't let him fall down the ladder," said Berit. "My aunt would kill me!"

The women waited, but there was no thump, thump, thump, no crash, and when Robert returned, he kicked a mound of hay over the vomit.

"Anna, how about we say good night as well?"

"Nei!" said Berit. "The party's just starting."

"Whoo," Anna said, swaying as she stood. She brushed bits of straw off her skirt. "I think for me it should have ended a couple of sips ago."

At the couple's departure, the bottle was passed around again, and while Ione wasn't drunk, the belt holding in her manners and reserve had definitely been loosened. Wanting more physical distance from her cousin as she confronted her, she situated herself on the hay bale vacated by Robert and Anna, and said, "So, Berit. Are you finally going to tell me what this is all about?"

Berit crossed her arms and leaned back, but as there was no wall behind her, she almost tumbled backward. "I don't know what you mean," she said, righting herself.

"I mean, why have you ignored me these past two years? Why do you never write me?"

"I wrote you."

"When I was in Germany, ja. Three times. Since then, nothing. This is the first time I've seen you since I left Oslo, and you, you treat me like a stranger. No, you'd probably be kinder to a stranger!"

Hearing her own words, Ione began to cry and cried harder when it was Guri and not her cousin who put her arm around her.

"Honestly, Berit," said Guri. "Why don't you just tell her?"

"Shut your mouth, Guri."

Startled, Ione looked up, the harshness of Berit's words acting like a tap turning off her tears, and drawing in a ragged sigh she wiped her face with her fingers. The tension in the loft was palpable, some of it seeping down into the barn below. A horse whinnied.

Berit sat very still, a furious stare fixed on her friend. Like most people, Guri acquiesced to the moods and desires of Berit Merdahl, but not this time, and returning her stare, she said, "Tell her why you've been afraid to see her."

"Afraid to see me?" said Ione, confused. "Why would Berit be afraid to see me?"

"Because of what she did to you."

"Guri, I said shut your mouth!"

"No, I won't, Berit. For once I will not!" Turning to Ione, she said in a rush of words, "Edon didn't write that good-bye letter to you—Berit did! And she wrote a letter to him, pretending it was from you! Edon thought you had left him for a man named Alf!"

"Alf?" said Ione dumbly, as the heat in her body rose, as her heart beat against her chest wall like a fist trying to punch through.

"Alf, the old boathouse pervert!" said Berit, her laughter lasting a few notes before it turned into a keen that propelled her off the hay bale. She lunged toward her cousin. "Ione, I'm so sorry! I don't know why I did it!" On her knees, she took Ione's hands. "I was just so—so jealous! Almost crazy with jealousy! At first, at first the letters seemed like a little joke I could fix, but then I never did!" Her voice rose in a wail, and a whinny from below answered. Like a penitent child, Berit dropped her head into Ione's lap and sobbed into it.

Guri swallowed down bile, wondering if she were going to add a pile to the one Helge had earlier left. Of the many emotions she felt, the dominant one was fear, not for Berit but for Ione, who sat so still, whose face was ghostly white.

"Ione," she whispered. "I'm so sorry, I . . . Berit swore me to secrecy! She only told me a few weeks ago; we'd been celebrating my birthday, and I suppose we may have had too much champagne—Father got a whole case sent to him from the French ambassador and—"

"—Edon," said Ione, staring straight ahead. "What happened to Edon?"

"No one ever saw him again, just like none of us saw you again," said

Guri, desperately wanting to be helpful. "Some of the gang wondered if you two had run off together—"

At this Ione gasped.

"—but Johann—remember Johann? He was the one who'd met Edon and invited him to my party?"

"Yes, I remember," whispered Ione.

"Well, here's the funny thing. Right before Christmas, Johann's brother met up with him in, of all places, Portugal!"

"Portugal!" said Ione. Struggling to rise, she pushed Berit away. "I'll go to Portugal!"

"No, no, he's not there anymore."

Ione sank back down on the hay bale.

"It was the strangest thing," continued Guri. "Johann's brother . . . Erik, maybe? . . . was reading a newspaper in the hotel lobby, and this man asks him—in English, because it's a British paper—if he might borrow a section, and Johann's brother . . . Milo? . . . anyway, he hears the accent and asks the man, 'Er du Norsk?' and the man says yes, he is!"

"And it was Edon?"

"Ja!" *Guri couldn't help her delighted laugh over the coincidence, but knowing the rest of the story she had to tell, it quickly faded. She cleared her throat.* "And so they introduce themselves to one another and hearing the man's last name, Edon says he knew for a short time in Oslo a Fosse, a Johann Fosse, and the man gapes at Edon and says, 'That's my brother!' Of course they exchange more information, just to make sure it's the same Johann Fosse, and it was! Johann's brother . . . Marcus! That's his name, I think—he works for the government in trade or something and travels a lot, mostly to Spain and Portugal but—"

"—Guri! I don't care about Marcus or Milo or whatever his name is—what did he say about Edon?"

"Oh, Ione . . ."

"What did he say?"

Berit had propped herself up against a hay bale, her knees hugged to her chest. She had been silent, save for the occasional quiet flutter of a sob that rose from her chest, but now she knew as much as it pained her—and she knew she deserved to have it pain her—she had to finish the story.

"He said Edon was on his way to Venezuela, Ione." Berit's voice was low. "He was going there to be married."

Ione's hands flew to her face, cupping her mouth.

"They'd met in London, about a year earlier—they were both studying there . . . isn't that what Johann told us, Guri?"

The woman's head bobbed as if the bones in her neck were a spring.

"They were going to live in Caracas, her hometown and—"

"—stop," said Ione, rising. She was still for a long moment, her hands held up as if she were trying to push away any more words. There was light beyond the open loft door, but inside Ione stood in a shadow.

"I don't want to hear another word," she said, lowering her arms and clasping her hands at her waist. It was as if the effort physically hurt her, but Ione forced herself to look at her cousin. "I don't want to hear another word about Edon, about anything, ever again, from you, Berit. More important, I never want to see you again. Ever."

She turned and walked across the scattered hay to the trapdoor, her steps as straight and sure as if she'd had nothing to drink all evening but black coffee.

⇒ 13

I ONE HUGGED HER GRANDDAUGHTER as if she were a stranded mountain climber and Nora was the sherpa who'd come with supplies.

"Grandma!" said Nora, when their embrace finally ended and she looked into her tear-sparkled eyes. "Are you all right?"

"I'm just so happy to see you! And you," she said, turning to Thomas. "I'm so glad that you're here, too!"

She launched herself into the arms of a man she'd never before met, and Nora could only stand back, wide-eyed. Her grandmother was generous with physical affection in the close circle of her family, but outside of it she believed a nod—or if she wanted to get really personal, a handshake—was as warm a greeting as needed.

"I'm sorry," she said, pulling away from Thomas. "I'm just so glad to have young people in the house!" To Nora she added, "And I'm really glad you've met a nice Norwegian."

"Well, sure he's Norwegian. But remember, I told you he's American, too."

Ione said something to Thomas in their native tongue and they laughed before Thomas translated, "She's not going to hold that against me."

Stepping inside the house, Nora inhaled deeply, smelling two of her favorite aromas: brewing coffee and something baking.

"Gold cake," said Ione, with a grin.

At the table, they toasted Nora's announcement that she had agreed to buy the lodge.

"Although it might be one of the dumbest things I've ever done," she said, clinking her coffee mug against the others.

"Will you open it for business?" asked Edon.

"No," said Nora, and her head seemed to shiver rather than shake. "Actually, I don't know what I'll do, but my mother—she's seen the whole place—convinced me it was sort of a deal I couldn't refuse."

"Well, if you ever do open it," said Edon, "maybe I'll come and rent a room."

Nora couldn't help but notice her grandmother's eyes light up as she said, "Å, det ville vaere hyggelig."

Understanding the gist, Nora agreed that yes, that would be nice, and said, "Whatever I do with it, you're welcome anytime."

She and Thomas took a walk after the coffee party, and when they returned, Nora had barely unwound her scarf and taken off her coat when her grandmother had her by the arm and was leading her in one direction, while Edon, suddenly appearing like a sentry at the parlor doorway, motioned Thomas inside. She managed to shrug at Thomas before she was hurried down the hallway toward the room where both Ione and Edon had spent so much time.

"Sorry to pull you away like this," whispered Ione, "but she's awake now and finally wants to meet you."

Nora had been perfectly happy *not* meeting the woman who'd caused her grandmother so much pain, but as Ione pressed down the handle and opened the door, she could do nothing but follow her in. The curtains were drawn and the room was dim, and under the medicinal smell there was one of perfumed decay. The room's decor continued the folk art theme. The bedposts and headboard were rosemaled and bright rectangular rag rugs covered the painted wood floors, but there was no clutter; even the dozen or so pill bottles were arranged on a wooden tray, looking almost sculptural.

Nora's instinct was to back away from rather than go toward the tiny, sallow figure buried under the white pillowy duvet, but Ione's firm hand at the small of her back pushed her forward to a bedside chair.

"You're lovely," said the old woman, reaching out her clawlike hand. "And I apologize that I haven't invited you into the death chamber until now."

Her words were so surprising that Nora half-gasped, half-laughed.

"*Death chamber,*" said Ione with a tsk. "Uffda, Berit."

"Uffda, yourself."

The woman's face was ravaged by disease and age, but her high, wide cheekbones and delicate features hinted at its original beauty, especially when she smiled as she did now. Nora felt a slight pressure on her hand, a faint pulse as Berit squeezed it.

"But you. Ione tells me you're an *advokat.* She is so proud of you."

"And I am so proud of her," said Nora, and as her nostrils flared, she pressed her lips together, holding back the many emotions that made her want to cry.

Seating herself on the chair on the opposite side of the bed, Ione said, "Nora, did you know Berit had a son?"

Nora's breath rose forcefully in her throat, almost like a hiccup. "What?"

"Ja, Per," whispered Berit. "Both your MorMor and I have sons— hers almost died and mine did."

"In an avalanche," Ione said, shaking her head. "He was just nineteen."

"He was on the national team," said Berit, the pride in her voice making it stronger, louder. "Certain to head for the Olympics, world championships. But skiing with friends in Switzerland—at the end of May, of all times!—well, he died." She stared ahead at the curtained window. "Per was a sweet boy, too. As kindhearted as I was not."

Ione patted part of the blanketed bony hump. "Oh, you could be kind, Berit . . . if it helped you somehow."

Nora's eyes widened, first at the cruelty of her grandmother's statement and then as both women laughed; her emotions were getting what felt like an aerobic workout.

The few raspy huh-huh-huhs were an effort for Berit and she closed her eyes.

"You see, Nora, she always falls asleep when she doesn't want to talk about something. "Don't you, Berit?"

A ghost of a smile softened the masklike face, and after a moment Berit opened her eyes.

"Ja, that's one good thing of dying. Bad manners are excused."

She turned her head toward Nora.

"And you are allowed your deathbed confessions . . . and apologies. I made mine finally to Edon, finally to your grandmother. What I did to them has been my great burden . . . my burden of shame. I tried to ease it by being a good mother, a good wife . . ." There was another pulse, an attempt at a squeeze, from the claw hand that still held Nora's. "And that Ione came here, that she would do this for me . . . for Edon . . ."

Her voice trailed off and the room held a heavy silence of the words just spoken. After a time, there was the sound of raspy but regular intervals of inhales and exhales.

"That's what she'll do," whispered Ione. "She gets everything off her chest in these short blurts and then she goes to sleep."

Gently sliding her hand out of Berit's relaxed grip, Nora smiled at her grandmother. "Bursts," she said. "She gets things off her chest in short bursts."

Ione, usually so accommodating when it came to a correction of her grammar, paused for a moment, frowning. "Nei, I meant what I said. She *does* blurt."

The next morning, after a breakfast of rømmegrøt, a rich cream porridge, Nora declared a need to burn off "about ten thousand calories" and asked who'd like to join her for a walk to the lake.

"You all go," said Ione. "I'll stay here with Berit."

Edon led the way down a path whitened with newly fallen snow. Although he carried a walking stick, there was nothing slow or timorous about his pace.

After they had walked a half-mile or so, he stopped and pointed. "Over there. Over there was the facility the Nazis used, hoping to build a nuclear bomb."

"Operation Gunnerside," said Thomas, his voice reverent.

"Oh, my god," said Nora, feeling like a student who'd prepared for a sudden pop quiz. "I just read about this at the Resistance Museum!"

"Ja, it was one of the greatest acts of sabotage against the Nazis," said Edon. "Birger Stromsheim and his crew blew up the plant and then skied 250 miles to safety in Sweden." They stood in silence in the winter morning, looking out past ice and snow and mountains and into the far distance of history.

"There was even a movie made about it," said Edon presently. "*The Heroes of Telemark.* Starring your Kirk Douglas."

Nora smiled, wondering if Kirk Douglas knew he was *her* Kirk Douglas.

"Were you one of the heroes of Telemark?" she asked.

"Nei. I worked for the Resistance but did nothing so dramatic as Birger Stromsheim. Most of my work was in a supply office in Oslo."

"When did you come back from Venezuela?" asked Nora. The last she had heard of Edon's story was that he'd married and gone to live in Caracas.

"In 1939. Clara had left me for another man several years earlier."

"Oh, Edon," said Nora. "I'm sorry."

The man's wide shoulders lifted in a shrug.

"It was for the better, I think. I didn't love her the way she deserved to be loved. I did love Caracas, though. It was so different from what I knew, but when the war began, I left my job at university—I was teaching economics—and came home. And it was in Oslo that I met, or re-met, Berit. In 1940. The Germans had just occupied the country, and there was—I don't know how to describe it—a need to grab what was there, because it seemed so much was being taken away. And so we grabbed on to one another. And when she became pregnant—in such times, a new life!—we married."

"Even after what she did to you and Grandma?" said Nora, her voice incredulous.

"Ja, but remember, I didn't know any of this until . . . until Berit understood she was not going to live much longer."

"She kept it from you all those years?" asked Thomas, who found it difficult keeping all the subterfuge straight.

Edon nodded sadly.

"But didn't you wonder what happened to Ione?" said Nora. "Didn't you wonder why she and Berit—who were so close—never kept in touch?"

"She told me Ione had married and moved to America. She told me they had a falling-out over something silly. To tell you the truth, it helped *not* to hear of Ione."

In his long sigh, his posture changed, stooping him a little.

"We should go back," he said, turning around. "It's getting cold."

They walked for a long time in silence. In the distance, smoke uncurled from the chimney of the pretty red house with the white shutters.

"*Og så levde vi våre liv,*" said Edon softly. "And so we lived our lives."

"Were you happy?" asked Nora.

The old man's smile was rueful. "I knew great happiness as a father. As a husband, I was . . . content. I grew to love Berit—she has many wonderful qualities—just as I had grown to love Clara."

"*Grown* to love Clara?" asked Nora. "You didn't love her right away?"

"I only loved Ione right away. It seems this heart of mine was too small to—" He conferred with Thomas until he got the English word he was looking for. "To *muster* up that same kind of love for anyone else."

Nora looped her arm through his. "Your heart seems plenty big to me."

Late that afternoon, they called Thomas in, even though Ione and Edon hadn't needed his expert medical opinion to tell them what they already knew.

"*Ja,*" the doctor had said. "She's gone." He looked at his watch. "5:54 p.m. For the death certificate."

Ione nodded, Edon nodded, and after Thomas nodded, he left the room, leaving the two to sit quietly on opposite sides of the bed, holding the hands of the woman who had meant so much—in so many ways—to them.

Presently, in the soft gray light, Edon let go of the lifeless hand of his wife and moved his chair to sit next to Ione and took her life-filled hand in his own. Neither could avert their gaze from Berit. The sharp angles and corners made by pain and emaciation had softened, and she wore an uncharacteristic expression of peacefulness.

"Death becomes her," Ione said, and they couldn't help it—they laughed. Then they cried. Hard.

⋙ 14

T HOR, ON HIS NEW FAVORITE TOY—the riding snowblower they had found stored in the garage—had cleared off the ice in a rectangle whose dimensions approximated a hockey rink, as well as a separate oval for skaters not interested in chasing down and shooting pucks. The sun was bright in a blue sky and the snow sparkled, as if a glittery thread had been woven into its soft white contours. That the thermometer outside the lodge registered minus seven couldn't detract from the dazzling central Minnesota day; the three people skating on the frozen lake were as much in their element as surfers on a wave or skiers on a slope.

Thor and Harry had been playing a game of one-on-one hockey, impressing each other with their stick handling and sneaky moves while Nora spun and jumped, pretending to be Dorothy Hamill. She felt happy and free, and who wouldn't in air that felt so cold and bright? Who wouldn't feel happy and free while gliding across the ice backward, movement she did with grace and speed, movement that surfers or skiers couldn't do? Was there any other sport where one could go backward as effortlessly as they went forward?

Well, of course there's swimming, she thought magnanimously, but unlike those who practiced their sport in unfrozen water, she wasn't splashing all over herself.

It had been two weeks since her return from Norway and the third visit up to the lodge, which because of yesterday's closing was now officially hers. Doubt and anxiety had nagged at her like persistent flu symptoms, and there were times when she had taken to bed (she had her choice of many but most often collapsed on the one in the largest main floor guest room), wondering how she was going to manage everything that ownership of a big drafty log cabin entailed.

"Actually," she admitted to Thomas in one of their long conversations that stuffed dollars and kroner into the coffers of their respective telephone companies, "it's not drafty at all. Brenda says its construction is A-1."

"Like yours," said Thomas.

Their flirtation was a cherry on top of the sundae that made up the rest of their hours-long talks, in which they shared dreams, counsel, gossip, support, and laughter, listening to one another as if their ears to the receiver were the most important connection in the known world. Every time Nora (reluctantly) hung up, the phlegmy doubt/anxiety symptoms cleared a little.

She felt she could officially declare herself flu-free in Brenda's office, when after signing the papers, she asked the woman responsible for her new property, the woman she hadn't seen since her camping trip more than a month ago, what she was going to do next.

With a scowl, Nellie said, "Anything I want!"

After having done her spins and her figure eights, Nora raced around the oval's perimeter like a speed skater, hunched over, hands clasped behind her, her thoughts wandering to her favorite subject: Thomas.

"I think of you all the time," she had confessed to him on the phone.

"I think of you more," he had answered and those words were a refrain in her head as she skated faster and faster, her blades on the ice making the sound of a chef sharpening knives.

The whole family had been invited to celebrate Nora's official ownership, and as Patty Jane watched the skaters from the window, she was filled with a contentment that were she a cat would have had her purring. Harry had a rare weekend off from school so that everyone she loved most in the world was either outside within her view or inside the lodge within her reach.

"You should put on your skates and join them," said Clyde Chuka.

"With those just out of the oven?" Patty Jane turned away from the window as Ione set a pan of caramel raisin rolls on a rack to cool. "No way."

Helping herself to a cup of coffee, she sat at the table, a big grin on her face.

"Ione, you should see the effect your rolls are having on Patty Jane," said Clyde. "She looks almost gleeful."

"Then looks are deceiving. I'm not almost gleeful. I am gleeful."

"They're still too hot to eat," said Ione, joining them at the table.

"And do you know why?" said Patty Jane.

Confusion fluttered across the older woman's face. "Because I just took them out of the oven?"

"No. I mean, why I am gleeful."

"Okay, I'll take the bait," said Clyde. "Why, my darling, are you filled with glee?"

"For so many reasons, but mostly, I'm just so glad we're all together here in this beautiful place." Patty Jane took her mother-in-law's hand. "I'm glad you and Nora got safely home . . . and I'm glad you're finally in the mood to bake something."

Ione nodded before bowing her head to study her folded hands. "Eight days," she said softly. She had stayed in Norway longer than Nora, wanting to help Edon with Berit's funeral arrangements. "Eight days since I've been back, and it's only today that I woke up without feeling all . . . all wiry."

"Wiry?" asked Clyde.

"Ja, as if my nerves were wires and all those wires were shorting out."

"Well, you've been through a lot," said Patty Jane.

"Ja."

"Did your talk with Edon last night help? My God, you were on the phone long enough."

"It helped a lot," said Ione, unsuccessful in containing her smile.

"Look at you!" said Clyde. "You look just like Harry when he talks about his girlfriend, Ava."

Ione wiggled her sparse eyebrows in a lascivious expression, or at least a fairly good attempt at one.

It was a wonderful day in what Nora deemed their "inaugural weekend," until Thor found himself trapped in an icehouse with two women whose interest in catching walleyes was a far second to their interest in getting drunk on Hamm's beer. Two jigging rods leaned against the wall over the empty bait bucket, and Thor was the only one paying attention to the hole augered in the ice, having gotten down on all fours to get a closer look.

"Don't fall in," said the woman named Sal as Thor peered into the twelve-inch hole.

The woman named Marie topped off her laugh with a belch.

"Yeah, you don't want to swim with the fishes."

"Yeah," said Sal, "'cause that'd mean you were dead."

Thor got up and sat on one of the portable stools whose seat was a canvas sling. There was a click of a lighter, and the sharp smell of butane and burning tobacco filled the small shack.

Thor smiled politely at the women.

"I should go," he said, and not for the first time.

"Oh, come on," said Sal. "You're not going to find a better party than the one we've got going on in here!"

"Yeah," said Marie, draping herself over Thor as if he were a coatrack and she were a mink. "Now quit playing dumb and let's have some fun!"

Her mouth on his tasted like beer and cigarettes and, Thor thought, buttermilk, and he turned his head, not liking those three particular tastes at all.

"Have you seen Thor?" Harry asked his sister. "I want to see if he wants to get another game in before the sun goes down." Shaking her head, Nora stretched luxuriously, having been reading a little and dozing a lot in front of the fireplace.

"I've been looking for him, too," said Ione, coming in from the kitchen, wiping her hands on a dish towel. "He said he'd help me with supper."

No one worried about Thor roaming his neighborhood in Minneapolis, because it *was* his neighborhood. He walked to the ice rink at Lake Hiawatha during the winter for pickup hockey games, and in the summer to the same lake to swim. No one felt any reservations sending him on errands—to Dokken's or the Red Owl to pick up a loaf of bread or a dozen eggs, to Nokomis Shoe Shop on Thirty-fourth Avenue to retrieve a mended purse or resoled loafers, and he easily made his way to the Riverview Theater for the buttered popcorn he loved when he wanted to see a movie that didn't interest anyone else. (The movie itself didn't matter to him; he considered the buttered popcorn the main attraction.) He in fact had a fairly astute sense of direction, but even so, he was in strange territory now, with no familiar landmarks.

He certainly hadn't planned on being held hostage in an icehouse; he had only planned a walk along the road.

"Hey, handsome," the woman, Sal, had called, slamming the door of a rusty Oldsmobile Omega with her foot. "Got time to help a damsel in distress?"

Thor wasn't sure what a damsel in distress was, but he understood the word *help*.

"Follow me," she said, and after she handed him a case of beer, he did, across the road, down a gradual slope, and onto the frozen lake.

"We're over here," she said, nodding at a little shack in a small colony of other shacks.

"You live here?" asked Thor.

"Yeah, right," said Sal with a strangled sort of sound that Thor thought might be a laugh.

"What took you so long?" asked the woman inside. "And hubba, hubba, who's the silver fox?"

"I found him outside. What's your name, anyway?"

"Thor."

"Thor," said Marie, sitting on the canvas stool. "Are you like a Swedish god or something?"

Smiling politely, Thor said, "Norwegian."

When the sun set on the winter afternoon and there was still no sign of Thor, Clyde Chuka and Patty Jane headed north looking for him, and Nora and Harry went south. But it was neither search party that rescued Thor but a ten-year-old boy named Lewis.

"Mom," he said, entering the icehouse. "Who's this guy?"

"His name is Thor," said Sal. "And what the hell are you doing here?"

"I'm hungry. Did you catch any fish?"

"Shit," said Marie, her arms still around Thor. "Go check the line."

"There's no line to check," said Lewis, looking at the hole in the ice. "Mom, come on, we should go home."

"I'm not ready to go home," said Sal, and there was a short pfsst! as she pulled the tab of her fourth can of beer.

"Me neither," said Marie, her head cradled on the shelf of Thor's big shoulder.

Lewis was nothing if not perceptive, and he saw in the man's eyes a look that suggested he might not be having as good a time as his mother and Marie.

"Are you okay?" Lewis asked the man.

Thor's head trembled in a spastic shake.

"Mom," said the boy, putting his hand on his mother's shoulder, "who *is* this guy?"

"I told you. Thor."

"He's a Swedish—no, a *Norwegian*—god," said Marie, lifting up her head. "A silver fox." Her voice was slurred.

"Where're you from?" asked Lewis.

"Minneapolis," said the man, looking like he might cry. "From Minneapolis."

Lewis had noticed what the women had not or didn't care to— that something wasn't quite right with the man.

"Are you staying somewhere nearby?"

Thor nodded his head.

"Umm," said Marie, tightening her grip around Thor, "you smell good."

"Would you like me to take you back there?" asked Lewis.

Thor's nod was so vigorous that Marie, jostled, asked, "What the hell?"

The boy was used to taking charge. He took the woman's hand and pulled it, until she was dislodged from the man's lap.

"Hey, hey, hey!" said Marie, staggering to the floor. "What the fuck?"

"I'll take you home," Lewis said.

"Okay," said Thor, standing.

In less than fifteen minutes, the two had climbed up the stairs of the lodge's deck and were knocking on the sliding glass door.

"Thor!" said Ione, opening her arms so wide that her back cracked.

She hugged her son, and a millisecond before all the air was squeezed out of him, she relaxed her grip and said to the boy standing on the kitchen mat like a soldier at ease, "And who are you?"

"Lewis. And he—uh, Mr. Thor—was with my mom and her friend. In Marie's icehouse. Fishing, I guess." He knew no effort had been made to catch a single fish but saw no reason to implicate his mother or this strange man.

"How," asked Ione, "how did you know where to bring him?"

"Well, I kind of figured it was Nellie's place 'cause I knew she'd moved out," said Lewis. "I used to shovel for her. But really, I didn't bring him so much as walk with him. Once we got to the road, he seemed to know where he was going."

"Went one way there," said Thor, bobbing his head. "Other way back."

Ione laughed, dispersing all remnants of worry that had settled in her chest. Turning to thank Thor's escort, she saw the look of naked longing on the boy's face.

"Are you hungry?" she asked as he averted his gaze from the meatloaf she'd just taken out of the oven. "We'll be eating as soon as everyone gets back."

"He is, Ma," said Thor as Lewis shook his head. "He said so."

"Then you'll join us," said Ione.

An hour and a half later, Clyde Chuka and the boy stopped at the cluster of icehouses, but the dark one Lewis led Clyde to was littered with beer cans and empty of people.

"They probably went into town," said the boy simply, and as they walked back over the ice to the van, Clyde let the boy carry the flashlight, remembering how kids liked to be in charge of tasks like that. A short time later, they reached a small trailer hunkered alongside a rutted path.

"You can drop me off here," said Lewis.

"How about I come in with you?" said Clyde, pulling the van up next to a dented mailbox, nesting on a pole. "And make sure someone's home."

"My grandma's home," said the boy. "And the light's on. So thanks."

Lewis slipped out of the van, slamming the door shut, but if he thought Clyde would drive off, he was mistaken. The man was fast, almost beating him to the trailer steps.

"Like I said, my—" began the boy, and as Clyde nodded toward the door, he shrugged and pushed it open.

"See," he whispered. "She's right there. But don't wake her up or she'll be mad."

The lump on the couch was buried under a patchwork quilt missing some patches, a graying tangled ponytail fanning out over a bed pillow without a case. The lump stirred and then snored.

The scene depressed Clyde; he knew that the chances of the grandmother providing any conscious company for the boy that night were probably slim.

"Are you sure you'll be all right?" he asked.

Lewis nodded, his hand on the door's grimy knob.

"Thanks again for the ride," he said. "And thanks for the dinner. It was really good."

Clyde ruffled the boy's dark hair and turned, slipping a little on the icy metal grating of the steps.

There was no cloud cover to obscure the winter sky, but Clyde Chuka was oblivious to its starry beauty, thumping the heel of his hand on the steering wheel as he drove home. He knew the boy was responsible—probably the most responsible one in the household—

but Clyde hated the idea of leaving Lewis in that trailer home, listening to his snoring grandmother as he waited for his mom to come home. Or maybe he didn't wait anymore; maybe Lewis had learned what Clyde had learned as a little boy—that sometimes your mother came home and other times she didn't, and it didn't matter whether or not you stayed up to find out.

Part Two

THE SOYBEAN FARMER who founded Charleyville was known for his practical jokes, the first one being to name the town after his pet squirrel, who'd perch itself on the farmer's shoulder to be hand-fed raisins and peanuts (proving this was an old sepia-tinted photograph hanging in the town hall).

During a winter that blew in ten-foot snowdrifts, the farmer, dreaming of more temperate climes, decided to officially name the town's main street Palm Avenue. Streets ran in tidy, numerical order, but as the town grew, other avenues were named after trees not seen or grown anywhere near the great north, including Avocado, Guava, Banana, Lychee, and Carambola. Throughout the years, there were movements started by more staid citizens to change the avenue names to ones honoring the area's many indigenous trees, but these were always voted down by the majority who liked that Guava Avenue was lined with crab apple trees, that silver maples graced Jackfruit Avenue, and that the only nut-bearing trees on Lychee Avenue were bur and white oaks. Fifty years after the founder's death and inspired by his whimsy, another bold new leader informed his constituents at a town hall meeting that by mayoral decree he was changing the names of the small lakes that surround Charleyville.

"You can't change the names of the lakes by mayoral decree!" griped the postmistress, who was considered an expert on all things government.

"Then I *can* suggest we vote on it," said the mayor, who was the rare big talker who backed up his bravado with research. "And we'll take that vote to the county board, to the DNR, all the way up to the federal board if we need to!" His grin was wide; he had dimples and smiled just as often to show them off as he did to express pleasure. "Now our avenues set a particularly alluring tropical tone. Why not our lakes? Why not be surrounded by the Atlantic, the Pacific, the Indian, and the Arctic?" His grin remained but his jaw muscles tightened when the postmistress pointed out that the Atlantic and the Arctic weren't exactly tropical.

The vote dictated that four lakes keep their original names, but Lake Marion, on which the mayor lived, officially became Ocean Lake (ever after known as the Ocean), and with these five lakes in close proximity to the town center, Palm Avenue flourished, featuring shops and services catering to both the locals and a thriving tourist trade. Tucked among the post office, a medical clinic, a drugstore, the bank, and several two-storied office buildings, including Brenda Vick's law office, were boutiques offering clothing, handcrafted jewelry, and big-city prices, two stores that sold used furniture, clothing, and miscellanea (the difference being that Juniper's called itself an antique store while the Ladies' Aid sold "consignments"), a husband-and-wife-run barber and beauty shop called Hair by Mac & Marlys, restaurants (Ma's was worn and homey, the Lake Inn was buffed and polished, and the available toppings listed on the Pizza Palace menu included herring), two bars (Skippy's and the Beacon), Candy Town (the store in which all kids wanted to claim citizenship), Gladdy's Floral Arts, an arcade, the Charleyville Cinema, and a bookstore named Bob's.

The Food Village grocery store, several gas stations, Lundvall's Liquors, the Frostee Freeze drive-in, a laundromat, more bars, and a bowling alley called the Ten Pin dotted the divided highway leading in and out of town.

It was Nora's fifth visit to her cabin and the second to Ma's for breakfast, although this time she was less interested in the omelet of the day (wild rice sausage) than in who might have been part of the restaurant's clientele.

"He was Canadian," said Nora, her hands curled around a thick ceramic cup of tea. "French Canadian. A little guy. Dark-haired?

He was at Winner Lake—he was a fisherman—the same time those Stanitizers were?"

"Oh, I remember those idiots," said Jo, the waitress. "They papered Palm Avenue with flyers announcing their strange little cult meeting, but Marge Severson—FYI, she's our mayor—took them all down. Bud Dryer asked whether she was interfering with their First Amendment rights, and Marge said no, she was just cleaning up litter. Her sister's daughter became one of those Martians or Moonies or whatever they call themselves, so I think Marge is a little sensitive about brainwashing."

The bell on the door tinkled as a couple entered the diner; after they hung up their overcoats, they made their way to the counter.

"Kent," said Jo. "Ellen! This is Nora—she bought Nellie's place."

"Welcome," the couple said in unison, with Ellen adding, "You sure got yourself a beautiful property!"

"More like a shrine to old Walter," said Kent. He tucked a paper napkin into his flannel shirt collar. "Are you going to turn it back into a lodge or keep it as a shrine?"

"Honestly," said Ellen, and jabbing her husband with her elbow, she rolled her eyes at Nora.

"Uh, right now," said Nora, "right now, the plans are to use it as a vacation home."

Setting up the duo with coffee, Jo said, "Good news. The wild rice sausage came in."

"That's what we're hoping," said Kent.

"A family up on the reservation makes it and brings it down," Jo informed her newer customer. "If I were you, I'd try some with a couple scrambled eggs and toast."

"Just tea today," said Nora, the idea of wild rice sausage—along with other ideas—making her queasy.

"Hey, Nora here is asking about a little French Canadian fisherman who was here a couple months back along with those crazy Stanitizers. Either of you know him?"

Pondering the question, the couple at the counter pushed out their lower lips and squinted.

"Nope, doesn't ring a bell," said Ellen.

"Nope," said Kent. "Although I was helping Carl at his store, and I remember one of them nuts coming in and buying near about a case of gin."

For the Lake Water Wowies, thought Nora and reflexively touched her temple, recalling the hangover the Stanitors' libation had given her.

"He asked me if I'd like to triple my income in thirty days. I told him, 'Sorry, pal, I ain't got no income, being retired four years ago!'"

Those at the counter shared a chuckle before Ellen asked, "Why're you looking for him anyway? Did that fisherman run off with some money of yours?"

"No," said Kent, "some walleye!"

Nora pretended to join in the laughter the little joke generated, but to herself she was practically screaming: *He didn't run off with anything. What I'm worried about is what he left behind!*

For a while, there were ways in which Nora could make excuses for her mood swings (My life has been crazy lately!), the nausea (A nascent ulcer?), her newfound distaste of coffee (A sudden caffeine allergy?), even the tenderness of her breasts (Bras just didn't have the proper support these days!). But when no top button of any pair of jeans could be fastened and she felt odd little whirrs and flutters in her belly, she could no longer ignore the most likely reason for three months of missed periods.

It was on a blustery March day, when all thoughts of spring were pushed aside by a brutal wind, that she sat stunned on the toilet, watching the wand of a pregnancy test perform its magic. Two days later, her gynecologist confirmed the wand's diagnosis and with a sonogram showed what it couldn't measure: she was carrying triplets.

"What puzzles me," the doctor said, after handing her patient another tissue, "is that you haven't had a period since December, and it took you this long to think you might be pregnant."

"Well, you know, I don't have the most regular cycle in the world," said Nora defensively. She swiped at another batch of tears in her eyes. "I feel so stupid. It's just that *so much* has happened lately! I was traveling—and international travel can delay a period!"

The doctor's expression suggested Nora try again.

"And then I've been stressed out about a lot of things. Like I said, a lot has been happening—and stress can delay a period!"

"Yes, it can, Nora," said the doctor kindly, understanding how strong a force denial can be when it comes to pregnancy, let alone three pregnancies. The last thing her patient needed now was a lecture.

In a state that went past numbness and neared catatonia, Nora had driven home to the house on Nawadaha, where at the kitchen table, Patty Jane and Ione were discussing the day's big drama—or what they thought was the day's big drama—the trespassing arrests of the Old Bags for Change for protesting inside a gun shop.

After a long and confused conversation wherein Nora announced she was expecting triplets and Patty Jane, asked, "Triplets of what?" after disbelief, tears, and the random "Holy shit!" from Patty Jane and "Uffda!" from Ione, Nora made her mother and grandmother swear to secrecy, wanting to wait until Clyde Chuka was home from a show in St. Louis and Harry from school to tell them in person.

"And don't tell Dad yet," Nora said of Thor. "Maybe he'll understand more when I start showing."

There was someone else to whom she needed to tell her news face-to-face, and fortunately—or unfortunately—she was going to soon get the opportunity.

Shooting to the top of the IDS Tower in downtown Minneapolis made some passengers feel as if their stomachs were a free-floating entity, but Nora couldn't blame her persistent vague nausea on the elevator car's speedy ascent.

"I thought we were celebrating," said Thomas, after changing his order of a bottle of champagne to a lone glass for himself. They were seated in the Orion Room, at a table next to floor-to-ceiling windows that overlooked the lights of Minneapolis and, across the river, St. Paul. It was a romantic locale, and Nora had made reservations as soon as Thomas had given her the dates of his visit. When she got the doctor's report, she hadn't the heart—or courage—to cancel their reunion.

When the waiter departed, Thomas's hand reached for hers just as Nora's reached for his. Since her time in Norway, they had kept up a correspondence that had letters flying between the two countries, and they spoke to each other in bi- and tri-weekly telephone calls. Letters were signed, "All my love," or "*Hjertelig hilsen,* and whispers of "I love you" and "*Jeg elsker deg*" ended their phone conversations.

"How did I get so lucky," said Thomas, his thumb stroking hers, "to be with the most beautiful woman in the world? No, beautiful is too small a word. You're glowing."

Hormones'll do that, thought Nora.

The conversation accompanying the salads concerned Ione and Edon and their own planned reunion in Mexico.

"I helped her shop for a swimsuit!" said Nora. "She's seventy-nine!"

During their entrée course they talked about Nora's decoration of the lodge ("Nellie left behind a lot of furniture, but I just ordered a *huge* sectional couch to go in front of the fireplace, and I've put a couple of dad's birdhouses around") and Thomas's work ("I had a patient claim that she cured her hypothyroidism by gargling with vinegar and jumping rope, and the thing is, her numbers are completely normal now"). Dessert had them staring into one another's eyes and trying not to leap over the table and into one another's arms.

Her confession would have to wait until she took him to a popular tourist spot, when they stood by a stone fence, looking at the ice curtain that was the frozen Minnehaha Falls.

"We read that poem in school," said Thomas. "On the shores of Gitche Gumee, / Of the shining Big-Sea-Water . . ."

Nora would have happily listened to the poem's full recitation, but her courage was a candle flame that had sputtered all evening, and before it went out for good, before Thomas could get to the part about the shining big-sea-water and where the wigwam stood, she cried out, "Thomas, I'm pregnant."

"*Hva?* What?"

A winter's moon shone on her face as she looked up at him, nodding.

His confusion was not long lasting, and his mouth split open in a wide grin.

"You're pregnant?" His hands at her waist, he boosted her off the ground and kissed her, hard. "Nora, that's wonderful!"

She couldn't help but echo his laughter—Why not join in the delight, as fleeting as she knew it would be?—but it took only seconds before her laughter had turned a corner into tears.

"With triplets!"

"*Hva?*"

Nose to nose, they stared at one another, and in a voice that tumbled out in a frosty wail, Nora cried, "And they're not yours!"

Thomas's arms slackened and Nora slid in slow motion against his body until her boots touched the ground. The look on his face filled her with shame.

"I'm so sorry! I wanted them to be! More than anything I wanted you to be their father!"

"And you . . . you're sure I am not?" he said, a frantic yearning in his voice.

"I . . . the timing doesn't work out. Oh, Thomas, you don't know how I wish that it did!"

A gust of wind fluttered the fringe of Nora's wool scarf, and against its sharp cold rebuke they turned away from it, and from one another.

The laughter and chatter from Patty Jane's coffee party didn't disturb Nora, but hearing her name (once, then twice) did, and she jerked awake, blinking hard. She wiped the bottom half of her face with her fingers; she didn't think she had drooled, but she didn't think she'd fallen asleep either.

"Elise, hi," she said, sitting up straighter on the couch.

"Hey. Sorry to disturb you, but I just dropped my mom off and Patty Jane said you were in here, so I thought I'd say hi." Marvel

Stang's daughter Elise looked around the living room. "I haven't been in this room since I was a kid waiting for my mom's permanent to set."

"And now everybody's back in the kitchen," said Nora, stifling a yawn.

She was zapped into full consciousness when Elise took off her coat and she got a good look at her visitor. "Wow, you look great!"

"Thanks," she said, a tinge of pleasure blooming on her cheeks. "I've lost a little weight."

"I'll say!" said Nora and, embarrassed over her exuberance, added, "Sorry, I meant—"

"—don't worry about it, I'm getting used to strong reactions. Crabby actually said, 'Why, the whale's turning into a minnow!'"

"No," said Nora, patting the couch.

Accepting the invitation, Elise sat down.

"I think she meant it as a compliment. And Inky said, 'Lose fifteen more pounds and you'll start looking like a leading lady!'"

Both women laughed.

"If the Etc. was still running, I'd hire someone to teach a class in how to give a compliment," said Nora. "And I'd make sure both Crabby and Inky signed up for it."

"If the Etc. was still running, maybe I'd teach a dance class."

Noting Nora's surprised expression, Elise said, "That's how I started losing weight. Remember that tango performance? Well, I had so much fun dancing with that guy, I thought, 'I want to do more of this!' So I started taking lessons downtown at Arthur Murray's." Looking at her hands folded on her lap, Elise said softly, "My parents paid for them. I felt like such a failure—I couldn't even pay for my own dance lessons!—but Dad said, 'This is an investment in your life, kiddo.'"

Nora's eyes filled in an instant, and she took out a tissue from the wad in her sweater pocket.

"Sorry," she said, with a shrug. "But that's just such a nice story."

Elise's grin was broad. "*And* your hormones are probably going wild."

"So you heard, huh?"

"It's the talk of the town. Well, that and me—the former beluga—losing forty-six pounds."

Nora responded to her joke by bursting into tears.

Scooting closer, Elise draped her arm around Nora's shoulders.

"I just miss him so much!" said Nora. "I meet the man I'm supposed to be with, and then I blow everything by having gotten pregnant with a one-night stand!"

"Oh," said Elise quietly. "I didn't hear that part."

Nora slumped forward, her hands dragging down her face. "I can't believe I just said that part."

"I won't tell a soul," said Elise. Her hand, rubbing Nora's back, made a swishing sound against the wool.

"I know that's a pretty big secret not to tell, but if you could keep it, well, I'd sure appreciate it. My family knows, but . . . but I don't need Crabby or Inky speculating on my loose morals and the babies' paternity."

"Everyone . . . as far as I know thinks it's the Norwegian guy. That's at least what I heard. Have you . . . have you heard from him since he was here?"

Nora nodded. The reason one of her sweater pockets was full of damp tissues was the letter in the other pocket. She took it out and handed it to Elise.

"Go ahead. Read it. Read it out loud."

Elise did.

My dearest Nora,

You know I love you. I do. I love you!

But the question I am trying to figure out is, do I love you when you're pregnant with three babies who aren't mine? Time will tell, and time is what I am taking to think all this through. However, I don't want to offer you false hope, Nora. Solving the problem of our physical distance seems a lot easier than solving this problem. I am still . . . stunned.

No doubt less than you, though. I hope you're feeling fine and taking excellent care of yourself.

For now, I am a bit lost,

Thomas

"Oh, Nora," said Elise, when she was finished reading. "Have you heard from him since?"

The date scrawled in the corner was three weeks earlier.

Nora shook her head. "And he hasn't called either."

"Is there anything I can do for you?"

Ready to politely decline, Nora surprised herself. "I'm supposed to get some furniture this weekend up at the lodge. Want to help me boss around the delivery guys?"

⇉ 16

"I'M TRANSFORMED. I'm transported. I've transcended." These words were whispered by a tanned woman whose long white hair flowed down the back of her embroidered shawl and whose fingers, neck, earlobes, and one big toe were adorned in silver or turquoise or a mixture of the two. "Really, I feel as if the artist has not just molded clay and forged steel, but reshaped and soldered my very soul."

Everyone in the small cluster of people surrounding the oracle nodded and murmured their assent, except for Patty Jane, who rolled her eyes and wandered over to the cheese and wine table. In her years of attending Clyde's gallery or museum openings, she had heard adjectives ranging from *amazing* to *zoetic* and generally basked in and agreed with the praise (although she later had to look up the word *zoetic*). But she had no time for those art patrons whose taste was obviously so much more profound and deep than the plebeians surrounding them, for those who said things like "reshaped and soldered my very soul."

As she helped herself to a skewered cheese cube and a glass of white wine, Patty Jane heard a voice behind her ask, "So you're the artist's wife? I haven't seen you here before."

She turned to see a tanned man with a white pompadour whose white linen slacks and white linen shirt were accented by a belt whose silver buckle was studded with—what else—turquoise. "That'd be me," said Patty Jane. She and Clyde had long ago found it was easier to introduce themselves as husband and wife, even though legally Patty Jane had never divorced Thor.

"His work's sensational. You must be so proud of him."

"I agree with you. And I am."

"My name's Bryce," said the man, "like the canyon."

"Beg your pardon?"

"My parents spent their honeymoon camping in national parks. I was conceived in Bryce Canyon, so they named me after it."

"Good thing it wasn't the Badlands," said Patty Jane, "or Yellowstone."

The man's smile showed off gleaming white teeth that not only looked fake but vaguely menacing.

"You've got a cute sense of humor, I can see that. Tell me—"

"—Patty Jane."

"Cute name, too. So tell me, Patty Jean, do you and your artist like to swing?"

Taken aback, a moment passed before she said, "Like at the park?"

The tanned and turquoised Bryce stared at her as if she were daft, which only incited Patty Jane further. "We actually prefer to slide, although we can be persuaded to teeter-totter."

Crossing his arms, the tanned man said, "So now you're being *extra* cute."

Patty Jane took a sip of wine.

"No, I'm just trying to get out of an awkward situation. Excuse me."

"Back in the Saddle" was an obvious choice, considering their location, but one of Cher's hits was not, and as the singer with the deep baritone mournfully sang about "Gypsies, Tramps & Thieves," Clyde Chuka laughed, in response to both the serenade and to Patty Jane's recounting of the unwanted invitation she'd gotten at the gallery.

"Did you notice Charise, that woman in the serape with the long white hair?" Clyde asked.

"Charise?" said Patty Jane. "Figures. And yes, how could you not notice her? She was going on and on about your work. She claimed you did something to her soul with a soldering iron."

"Well, that Bryce guy who wanted to swing with us is Charise's ex-husband."

"She must have gotten most of the turquoise in the settlement. He only got enough for a belt buckle."

"Margaret says they're both filthy rich. In fact, she told me Charise bought *Missed Opportunity* and Bryce bought *You're Welcome*."

Patty Jane whistled low. "Damn. Imagine what they would have bought if we had swung—swang?—with them."

"Waltzing Matilda," sang the balladeer.

Chuckling, Clyde squeezed Patty Jane's hand and she returned the squeeze. They were side by side, lying on their backs, a familiar enough position, but one they'd never taken in a moving hay wagon.

"I feel like this is what they used to do for kings," said Clyde.

"You are a king to Margaret," said Patty Jane, of the woman who'd hosted Clyde at her gallery over the years and whose business relationship had grown into a friendship, one that now included accommodations at her ranch outside Santa Fe. Margaret had offered a night ride to Clyde and Patty Jane, but being on the back of a horse at night didn't appeal to them as much as it might to, say, Paul Revere.

"This is something I do for city slickers like you," Margaret said, hitching up the horse to the wagon. "And as an added bonus, I'm giving you Juan, my singing ranch hand."

A young man in a black cowboy hat and sheepskin jacket stepped forward.

"He'll honor any request, including silence, right, Juan?" The man bowed before jumping onto the hay wagon bench and Margaret flung herself on her own horse, adding, "Meet you back at the house in an hour for a nightcap."

It was a cool night, and Patty Jane and Clyde had snuggled on top of a bed of hay and under the woolen blanket Margaret provided. As they were serenaded and gently jostled in the wagon, they stared up at the cold blaze of stars in the western sky.

"This should be a medical treatment," Patty Jane said. "A guaranteed worry and stress reliever."

Clyde squeezed her hand again, knowing exactly what she, not a natural worrier, was worried about.

"We'll be there for Nora, honey. Whatever happens."

"I know. It's just that I want the man she loves to be with her, too."

"Of course you do."

"I don't want Nora to have the same bad luck I had in raising a kid—or in her case, three, *three!*—without a partner. I mean, I know I had Ione and Harriet to help me, but what I wanted was her dad. I just wanted Thor to be there with me."

"Of course you did."

"But then I got lucky, I found you—my real pilot light. Is it asking too much to want my own daughter to have the same kind of luck, the good not the bad, that I've had?"

"I don't believe there's such thing as asking too much. I believe in asking for what you want. If you get it—great. If you don't, well, at least you asked."

Not having anything to add to that good advice, Patty Jane rolled on her side, nestling up to Clyde, and it was in that position that they listened to the balladeer sing "Paper Roses" followed by "Psycho Killer" followed by "Vaya Con Dios."

"You've got some eclectic taste," said Clyde.

"What?" asked Juan, turning around in his seat.

Clyde repeated what he'd said, and both he and Patty Jane sat up, pulling the wool blanket around them as they leaned against the side board of the wagon.

"If that means I like all kinds of music," said Juan, "yes, I do." He clicked his tongue and the horse ambled in a wide arc at the turn-about in the road and headed back toward the ranch, as Juan sang "So Long, It's Been Good to Know You" and "The Lion Sleeps Tonight." Patty Jane and Clyde joined in, and they began to sing along with the Carpenters' song "Close to You," until they realized that the balladeer wasn't singing but crying.

Margaret Arlen, a gracious host and grateful businesswoman, had built (well, Luis, her houseman had) a roaring fire and had set out (well, Luis had) a bottle of champagne and glasses and a tray of her famous (well, her cook Paula's) cornbread taco mini-muffins and stuffed mushrooms and was looking forward to a relaxed and cozy evening exchanging stories of patrons, sales, and upcoming projects with her favorite artist and his partner.

She hadn't planned on the guest list expanding and was thus surprised when her tear-stained ranch hand, flanked by Clyde and Patty Jane, entered the room.

"Clyde," she said, pushing Matisse, her snippy Pomeranian, off her lap as she rose. "Juan. What's going on?"

Patty Jane beat both men to the explanation.

"Margaret, it's Juan's little sister. She needs help."

As the fire roared, the champagne was sipped, the snacks eaten, and Juan's sister's story was told. It was a sad but too familiar one that involved a man who claimed he loved his woman more than life itself but apparently not more than her own, seeing as he tried, with punches, kicks, and near-stranglings, to extinguish it.

"She's only eighteen! I'm afraid she won't see her next birthday!" said Juan.

"She broke up with him," said Patty Jane, who'd heard more details on the wagon ride home. "But of course that doesn't mean she's safe. He drives by their house—she lives with her mother—"

"—Estrella," offered Juan.

"Has she got a restraining order against him?" Margaret asked him.

"Yes, yes. But a piece of paper is not much protection."

Margaret looked at him for a long moment, long enough that Juan's face reddened and he bowed his head, looking at his folded hands.

"So are you telling me this in the hopes that I can do something?"

"She's down in Albuquerque," said Patty Jane. "Juan doesn't feel his mother is helping the situation—"

"—she, she is a wonderful woman," said Juan, his voice pained, "but she is not so helpful to my sister. She thinks she should go back to him—he makes a lot of money and—"

"—if he could just get Silvia up here, find her some work . . . ," said Patty Jane.

Margaret Arlen had regal bearing, and with her chin raised she resembled a queen looking down on her subjects. "I don't really have any position available, Juan," she said. "Either here at the ranch or at the gallery."

Juan slumped in his seat, and Clyde said, "Well, Margaret, you know a lot of people. Maybe you could ask some of your friends if they need any help?"

She restrained herself from sighing. She didn't like being put on the spot but would suffer it when a valued artist put her there. Forcing lips that wanted to scowl into a smile, she said, "What sort of work does your sister do, Juan?"

A smile broke the gloom of Juan's face.

"Silvia's a musician. She plays the guitar and she is a really good singer. She has the same warm voice as that Karen Carpenter, remember her? Everyone says so."

This time Margaret forced her eyes not to roll.

"That's all well and good, Juan, but I don't really know anyone who needs a really good singer. Does she have any office skills? Any—"

"—she just finished a beauty type of school, you know, to be a hairstylist."

Patty Jane coughed and patted her chest, helping the stuffed mushroom she'd just swallowed make its way down her throat.

"Did you say Silvia is a hairstylist? She sings *and* styles hair?"

"She was on work study," said Juan proudly. "Three months after she graduated high school, she graduated beauty school!"

Turning to Clyde, Patty Jane said, "I think we might have the perfect place for her, don't you, Clyde?"

"Patty Jane, you don't run a beauty shop anymore, remember?"

"Well, I know that. But I also know a lot of House of Curl clients looking for a new stylist."

NORA LAID IN BED, willing herself to calm down. She had woken from a funny dream about buying shoes (the store had stocked footwear made of unusual material—Astroturf loafers, cotton candy slippers), but any lingering amusement she might have felt remembering a pair of boots crafted from bottle caps was erased by a fear as cold and ferocious as an avalanche.

"You're okay," she whispered to herself, her hands covering her slope of belly. "You're fine."

Liar! Liar! Liar! her mind shouted back. *You're not fine at all!* She had been to the doctor that afternoon and despite her assurances that everything looked great, the panic that gripped her said otherwise. *Breathe,* she reminded herself as she felt choked for air. *Breathe.*

It wasn't the first time she had woken up seized by terror, but reminding herself she'd been through this before provided scant comfort. Her heart didn't beat so much as bang with a force that hurt her chest. Her nightgown was glued to her back in a cold sweat even as she felt fevered with heat. Worst of all, she had lost control of her thoughts. Her mind was the scary part of a carnival Fun House, the part with the distorting mirrors and the blasts of hot air and the spinning tunnel, and all the barkers and carneys standing outside shouted the same chorus: "Three babies! Three babies! Three babies!"

Flinging aside the blankets as if they were smoldering, Nora pushed herself up and staggered out of bed. The short hallway was lit by a nightlight and she raced down it, first to the bathroom to empty a bladder that needed constant emptying, and then to its end where she threw open a door and plunged herself into the room as if it were water and she was ready to ride a wave.

As her eyes adjusted to the dark, she was disconsolate to see that Patty Jane and Clyde's bed was empty. With a groan, she backed out of the room and was headed toward Ione's room upstairs when a door opened and a voice asked, "Nora?"

It was Silvia, the young woman Patty Jane and Clyde had brought back from New Mexico and whom she had just met that afternoon, after she'd returned from her weekend at the lodge.

"Nora, what is it? Are you all right?"

"Yes, I—no, I—I don't know! I'm just so scared!"

Silvia put her arm around her and nearly stumbled when Nora leaned into her, clung to her.

"It's . . . it's all right," said Silvia, trying to stay on her own two feet as she led Nora into her room and with a slight push positioned the distraught woman on her bed. Sitting next to her, Silvia took her hand and said, "Can I get you something? Some tea maybe?"

Frantic, Nora shook her head. "No. Don't leave. Please."

The digital clock on the bedside table read 9:18 p.m. when they sat down, and it read 9:22 p.m. when Nora stopped trembling and finally spoke. "Thanks," she said, patting Silvia's hand, which hadn't let go of Nora's other one. "Sometimes . . . sometimes I just get so scared." She shrugged elaborately. "Triplets."

Silvia didn't know much about Nora, but she did know she was expecting *tres bebés*. "I can only imagine," she said softly. "It must be so scary, so, I don't know . . . mind-blowing."

"*Exactly.* It's scary, mind-blowing, and everything in between." She exhaled a lungful of air. "So I didn't wake you up?" Nodding at the clock, she rolled her eyes. "Oh, probably not. I forget everyone else doesn't go to bed so early. I never used to."

"I was working on a song." A guitar leaned against the room's easy chair, a notebook on the floor.

"Oh, yeah, Mom said you've got a beautiful voice. Harriet would have liked that."

"That's just what your mother said."

Nora smiled. Where a frenzy of disquiet had stomped inside her chest, calm began to tiptoe in.

"Harriet was the most fabulous aunt. She could play just about any instrument you put in front of her—she taught me how to play the trumpet and always made me feel like I was a person who mattered and not just some kid, you know?" She smiled and moved the palm of her hand over the mound of her belly. "She would have been absolutely thrilled about these babies, although her mind would have been blown too."

Both women laughed softly, and Silvia, lifting her hand tentatively asked, "Do you mind?"

"Be my guest," said Nora, pushing out her already pushed-out belly, and Silvia rubbed her palm over it.

"Are they identical?"

"They can't really tell yet. It's pretty rare, though. Although any way they're formed is not exactly *common*."

"What do you mean?"

Lowering her chin and in a deep, authoritative announcer's voice, Nora said, "Things I've learned since becoming pregnant with triplets: sometimes one egg splits and then splits again—there's your identicals. And sometimes one egg will split in two while a totally separate egg is fertilized and *sometimes*—and whoa, consider these odds—three separate eggs are fertilized by three very serious sperm."

"What do you think yours are?"

"From the sonogram, I know they're girls. Three girls! But if they're identical or not, they have no idea. *I* have no idea. I still can't quite grasp *that* they happened, let alone *how* they formed." A big intake of air lifted her shoulders and her sigh dropped them; it seemed to Nora that every other breath was a sigh. "And then today I go and piss off my obstetrician . . . maybe that's why I got so scared tonight."

"How did you piss him off?"

"Her. By firing her."

"She was a bad doctor?"

"No, not at all. Maybe a little cautious, but I think all ob-gyns whose patients are expecting triplets are. No, I told her I decided I was going to have the babies up in Charleyville. I've got a little lodge there."

Silvia nodded. "Yes, I heard about this lodge."

"See, my doctor here—I've got one up in Charleyville, too—told me I had to stop traveling back and forth and stay in the city until the babies are born. And I told her I'd stop traveling back and forth, but I'd stay in Charleyville."

"And she didn't like that?"

"She thinks any doctor outside the metro area is a country bumpkin who accepts a bushel of corn or a side of beef for payment. But I like Dr. Everett—he's the doctor I'm seeing up north—and he took me on a tour of the nearby hospital, which actually has a really good neonatal reputation." She nodded, saying the words out loud helping to finalize her plans. "Plus it gives me a good excuse to do what I've wanted to do for a while."

"Which is?"

"To move to Charleyville permanently . . . or at least for the time being. It's just so peaceful there, and peacefulness is something I could use right now." Nora stifled the yawn her smile had opened into.

"Well, now that I've completely monopolized the conversation, tell me about yourself."

"Your mother didn't tell you?"

"A little bit. I mean, how your brother talked about what a great musician you are, how you've already got a beauty license, and that you—"

"—had a boyfriend—my first serious boyfriend—who beat me up?" said Silvia quietly. "And a mother who wanted me to stay with him? Who told me I'd be crazy to press charges?"

Their roles were switched immediately. Now Nora was the comforter rather than the comforted, reaching out to embrace the young woman who had begun to cry.

"I'm sorry . . . it's just all so . . . complicated." Using her hands as rags, Silvia mopped up her wet face. "My mother . . . ay, *mi mama* . . . is a woman who thinks the whole world's against her. I mean, sure, it was hard for her—she and my Papi came from Mexico and struggled for years, but my Papi never made it seem like a struggle, you know? If something was wrong, he'd find a way to make it right. He was as light as Mama was dark." She looked down at her hands. "And it seemed Papi was right, that all their hard work *was* paying off . . . and then he died. In a stupid factory accident. I was nine years old and we'd just moved into our very own house. He painted my bedroom a beautiful blue. 'It's called Sylvan Blue,' he told me, 'but I call it Silvia Blue.'"

The young woman took several deep breaths, collecting herself. "I'm sorry. I . . ."

"Please," said Nora. "Go on."

Silvia told how her mother, scared and intimidated, accepted the first offer the company lawyers gave her; how it wasn't enough to pay off the mortgage; how she worked for years cleaning other people's houses so the family could stay in their own. "So when I met this guy who not only was a college graduate but this super-successful realtor guy, my mother thinks I've hit the jackpot! Her daughter had been rescued by Superman—never mind I didn't need rescuing and never mind Superman had a hard time handling things like jealousy and anger! Never mind he was pretty good at slapping, hitting . . . choking."

"Oh, Silvia," whispered Nora.

"And the really bad part was that my mother didn't think it was all that bad! That maybe if I just was a little quieter, a littler nicer, a little more of whatever Garret wanted me to be, it would all work out. Because this was a guy who was making big money, this gringo could take care of me!"

Staring at Silvia, Nora's head was moving back and forth in barely imperceptible shakes.

"I didn't tell your mother much about my own mama. I mean, Garret was really messed up, but when I broke it off with him, he was already moving on to another girlfriend"—here Silvia crossed herself—"believe me, I pray for her. I can't tell you how happy I am to be away from that *estúpido,* but really, I needed to get away from my mother, too. She was just . . . not on my side." Silvia ran both hands through her long black hair. "I know it must be hard for you to imagine—it was hard for my brother Juan to imagine, because my mother is an entirely different mother to him." Resting her intertwined fingers on top of her head, she stared at the ceiling. "I don't know Patty Jane *that* well, but I can already tell she's the kind of mother who's on your side, the kind who doesn't try every day to put out your spark."

Tears beaded in Nora's eyes. "She *loves* to ignite sparks, not put them out."

"When she invited me to come up here, first of all, I thought, *Is she legit?* Second, I thought, *Minnesota! Isn't that by Canada?* And third, I thought, *I don't care where it is, if it'll get me away from my mother and Garret—and in that order—I'll go!*"

The smile she gave Nora contained apology and embarrassment. "Aren't you sorry you asked me to tell you about myself?"

"Not at all. I'm just sorry you've had to go through so much."

"At least it's given me plenty of song material."

Nodding toward Silvia's guitar, Nora asked, "Would you play something for me?"

Picking up her guitar and settling into the easy chair, Silvia said, "And I don't mean that all my music is sad and depressed. Sometimes when I feel really bad is when I write the lightest music." She plucked each string, tuning the A and D strings. "This is a lullaby. I wrote it for my cousin's baby, right after a big fight with my mother, who was crying about how all her brothers and sisters have grandchildren and she has none." Her laugh was rueful. "It doesn't matter to her that I'm only eighteen!"

She strummed a few chords and began singing, and had Nora heard Juan's appraisal, she would have agreed; his sister Silvia's voice did have the same honeyed warmth as Karen Carpenter's. If it were a fabric, it would have been a deep-ply velvet.

"That is so pretty," said Nora, leaning against the pillows propped on the headboard.

Silvia sang in English and in Spanish for a half-hour, ten minutes for which Nora was conscious, and when Patty Jane and Clyde returned from a crowded art museum fund-raiser, smelling of fellow patrons' cologne and the wine an overenthusiastic fan had sloshed all over Clyde's suit lapel, they peeked in the opened door to find two sleeping women, Nora slack-jawed and snoring on Harriet's old bed, and Silvia conked out on the easy chair, her guitar cradled in her arms like a baby.

⇛ 18

H EARING OF NORA'S DECISION to make the lodge her permanent residence ("for now"), Patty Jane asked as a favor
to her and her grandchildren-to-be that she always have
someone staying in the cabin with her.

"Someone like you?" teased Nora.

"Sure, if you insist," said Patty Jane. "But when I can't be here—
anyone. I just don't want you to be alone."

There came to be a revolving cast of regulars making sure that
Nora wasn't alone—Patty Jane and Clyde, Thor, Elise (with and
sometimes without her kids), Silvia, and Harry on school breaks.

Ione spent a lot of time at the lodge, even bringing her sewing
machine (on which she crafted three baby blankets made of varying
squares of pink floral, calico, and plaid fabrics), but she had recently
decided to fly all local coops. She was going to do it, to meet Edon
in a place neither had been and one that they felt held the kind of
romance and new beginnings they themselves were experiencing.

"Puerto Vallarta!" said Evelyn Bright. "Isn't that where the in
crowd goes?"

Ione laughed. "Ja, the in crowd. My crowd."

"You'd better not drink the water," said Crabby. "That dysentery'll
ruin your whole trip!"

"I like blueberry pie," said Minna, a segue that made her friends
laugh and that made her smile shyly.

Earlier, the four senior citizens had made a quick, giggly run out
of the cabin's kitchen and to the deck's hot tub, dropping their towels
and robes to reveal the suits—albeit altered—they were born in. As

they eased their way into the churning water, Crabby cupped her breasts, as droopy as deflating water balloons. "I have to be careful these don't get caught in the jets."

Inside the cabin, the others attending Nora's All-Girls' Weekend were engaged in a white-knuckle game of Scrabble. As Elise looked up a word she had challenged, Nora had to laugh. "What's wrong with this picture?" she said. "Grandma and her friends are out there partying in a hot tub and we're arguing about the word—"

"—quetzal," said Elise. "Dang. It's in here."

Silvia beamed. "And it's a double word score," she said, counting up her points.

"Hey," said Patty Jane, lounging in front of the fire. "Keep it down or I'll call the cops."

Evelyn asked what shots Ione had to get before she left for Mexico, and Crabby said she had a second cousin who'd gotten malaria in Mazatlan and suffered ill effects the rest of his life. After Ione assured her friends she'd be fully vaccinated, the four hot-tubbers settled back under the starry night sky, their heads resting against the padded vinyl edging.

"I feel small for saying this," said Evelyn, watching wisps of steam rise from the water's surface. "But I can't help it, Ione. I'm jealous. My love life is long over, but yours is just beginning."

"How long has it been since Corny died?" Crabby asked, her voice uncharacteristically soft.

"Eleven years. Married for twenty-nine." Evelyn sighed. "He was the luxury lover of the family—he ironed his undershorts *and* our sheets because he said he liked the crisp way they felt, but honestly I don't think he ever once stepped foot in a hot tub."

"I remember how he always used to wear a red carnation in his lapel," said Ione.

"That was my Corny. A red carnation in his lapel and a splash of Canoe cologne. He never left the house without either."

"Is he here?" asked Minna. "So I can see his red carnation?"

"No, Minna," said Crabby. "Cornelius is *dead*." She dragged her hand across her red and sweaty forehead. "At least you had twenty-nine years, Evelyn. I didn't even get to marry Bernie."

Through the steam, Evelyn and Ione exchanged looks. Crabby so rarely mentioned the fiancé who'd been killed in World War II that any time she did, it was as if for the first time.

"Tell us about Bernie," said Ione.

"He had naturally curly hair," said Crabby, as if that explained something. "Full of the dickens. Big fellow, loved to dance, but he was bad at it. Loved to sing, and he was pretty good at it. He used to serenade me with 'I'll See You in My Dreams.'" She shoved the bubbling water with her fist, nearly splashing Evelyn. "What the hell, it probably wouldn't have lasted anyway."

The April night was chilly. Light from inside spilled onto the deck through the sliding glass door, but in their corner it was dim. For a long time the women sat quietly in the churning water, until Minna spoke.

"Donald said marijuana was bad *and* illegal."

"Well, he's right," said Crabby sharply. She tried to be patient with Minna and her non sequiturs, but while patience might be a virtue, it wasn't hers.

"Dennis didn't think so," said Minna. "Dennis liked it. We liked it, remember?"

The smile she gave Ione was the smile of their mischievous, fun-loving friend so often absent these days. It was a signal that although Minna's brain was more and more addled in the present, she still had the capability of pulling out a long-ago memory and recollecting it as clearly as if it had happened yesterday.

"What do you mean, *we*?" asked Crabby.

Evelyn giggled.

"The three of us. Ione, Minna, and I. Dennis gave it to us."

"Dennis!" said Minna. "Dennis, my son!"

"I know who your son is," said Crabby, her tone of voice matching her nickname.

"That's right," said Ione, reaching across the steamy water to pat Minna's shoulder. "Dennis was our dealer."

"Good heavens!" said Crabby.

"It was fun," said Evelyn, "although we kept coughing up the smoke."

"In between laughing like crazy nuts," said Ione.

"I had no idea I was surrounded by a bunch of potheads!"

"Oh, Crabby," said Ione. "We only did it once—well, maybe twice, no more than three times —years and years ago."

"When Dennis was home, home from college," said Minna. "That boy was such a rascal! When I was putting away his laundry and found a bag of what looked like dried thyme in his underwear drawer, I pretty much knew what it was. And when I confronted him, he didn't lie or say it belonged to a friend; he just said, 'Ma, you should try it sometime.' And right then and there Dennis rolled me a big fat doobie. That's what they called them—doobies."

Minna's head had sunk so low in the water that the tip of her chin was submerged in it.

"I zipped up that doobie in my purse pocket and took it to the House of Curl, and when I showed it to Ione, she said she'd always wanted to try marijuana."

"I was there, too," said Evelyn. "I'd just gotten my hair done. So we snuck off to Ione's room and toked away." She mimed holding and inhaling a joint, cracking up everyone except Crabby, whose face looked steamed from both temperature and emotion.

"It was the times, Crabby," said Evelyn. "I remember Minna saying she was a lot more worried about Dennis being sent to Vietnam than smoking a little pot." She shrugged. "And he turned out all right."

"Not just all right," said Ione, a little huff to her voice. "He's a big shot at Mutual of Omaha, right, Minna?"

"I wanted Donald to try it with me. I thought it would help him feel . . . lighter. But he said it was bad and illegal."

Minna's voice trailed off as the memory that had brought her back faded, and she stared ahead, lost in a world of which they were no longer a part.

Finally, Evelyn, who felt her already-puckered skin had been puckered into oblivion, said she thought it was about time she got out. There was no disagreement, and both she and Ione flanked Minna, helping her to stand up. Crabby laughed.

"What?" said Ione.

"I was just thinking of how I could get a rise out of my sister-in-law, Fern. She's the one who every year sends me a Christmas card with a picture of her big happy smiling family on one side and Bible verses on the other. I'd like to take our picture now, and I'd send it with the caption 'Wishing you a Merry Christmas, Fern, and a Happy *Nude* Year.' Wouldn't that show her something!"

"That would show her a *lot*," agreed Ione.

After dinner they assembled in the great room, and Silvia had just begun playing a song she introduced as "the very first song I wrote in Minnesota" when the doorbell rang. Not seeing anyone on the deck behind the sliding glass, Patty Jane went to open the rarely used front door.

"Nellie!" she said, as a small woman barreled through it. The former owner was introduced to the others, as was Brenda, who had accompanied her and who shrugged at Nora, mouthing, "She just showed up at my door."

Hands on hips and looking pointedly at Nora's belly, Nellie said, "I see you've been busy!"

"Yes, I'm, uh . . . I'm having triplets."

"That's the word I heard. You don't mess around, do you?"

Patty Jane, remembering the hostessing manners Nora forgot, asked if the visitors would like some coffee.

"And we've got some coconut cake Ione made."

Nellie's hand shot up. "A big piece here!" and to Ione she said, "By the way, I'm still waiting for a certain cookie recipe from you."

In between bites of cake, and a request for a second piece—"But just a smidge"—Nellie held court, telling stories about the lodge and her husband. "My Walter would have loved seeing this room filled like this," she said, "although he might wonder where all the men are?"

Patty Jane laughed. "We made them stay home in Minneapolis."

"It's an All-Girls' Weekend," said Nora. "We're celebrating Ione's upcoming trip."

Licking the last trace of frosting off her fork, Nellie asked, "Where're you headed? The Pillsbury Bake-Off?"

"She's meeting up with her boyfriend in Mexico," said Crabby.

"Just came from the Southwest myself!" said Nellie. "Or at least close: San Diego. I have a sister there."

"You've been with her this whole time?" asked Nora. No one, not even Brenda, had known of Nellie's whereabouts after they'd signed the papers at the real estate closing.

"Yup. And would have stayed longer—oy, their ocean's a lot different than ours!—but Meryl and I can only take each other for so long. Next I'm off to Brooklyn, where I'll be staying in the brownstone my family's owned for over eighty years. I'll probably be moving into my old bedroom, that is, if my sister Sylvia will move out all her dolls. She collects them. It's a little spooky."

"We've got a Silvia here!" said Evelyn brightly.

"So I heard," said Nellie, and turning to the young woman she'd earlier been introduced to, she said, "You don't collect dolls, do you?"

Relieved when Silvia chose to laugh—it never was exactly clear when Nellie was joking or not—Nora said, "No. She's a musician. In fact, she'd just started playing for us when you came."

"Well, don't let me stop you!" said Nellie. An odd silence filled the air, as if there were a collective cessation of breath; the group didn't know how to interpret Nellie's tone of voice.

"She means it," said Brenda, who was most familiar with her friend and client's unintentionally brusque and off-putting manner. "Please."

Silvia obliged and after her first song, "A Strange Hopeful Place," Nellie applauded the loudest.

"I remember those feelings exactly! When my Walter brought me to Minnesota!" Settling back on the couch cushions, she said to Nora, "By the way, I *love* this sectional. I should have thought of something like this."

Silvia continued playing and Evelyn closed her eyes. As a music teacher, she was drawn into the House of Curl through Harriet, who had been her student/prodigy. Because of her contacts through the McKern School of Music, Evelyn was able to convince the composer

Bryce Nielsen to be one of the first performers in Patty Jane's living room. Perched behind his portable electric keyboard, Bryce had cracked his knuckles and smiled at the small group of women.

"The first song I'm going to play for you is one that came to me in a dream." As he began playing and singing, Evelyn had whispered to Harriet, "'Summer Wind.' It was a hit record for that husband-and-wife duo, Steve & Liz—remember them?"

In the question-and-answer section that followed the performance, Pauline Johnson had said, "Last night I dreamt about making popcorn for Lady Bird Johnson. Could I turn that into a song?"

The composer was used to laymen scoffing at the ways in which ideas came to him. "If you don't, maybe I will," he said, and as he played a few chords he sang, "Lady Bird, Lady Bird, you look so forlorn. / Let me cheer you up with some buttered popcorn."

"Oh, for cute," said Evelyn.

She wasn't the only one entertaining memories of past musical moments in the salon's history. As Silvia sang the Beatles song "In My Life," Patty Jane was reminded of the day Bev Beal's mother died and how Harriet had played "Let It Be" on the harp.

When Silvia launched into "A New Me," an up-tempo, bouncy song she'd just written, Nora thought of the Brady Boys, a barbershop quartet composed of impossibly cute teenaged brothers, the oldest of whom had asked the then-thirteen-year-old Nora if she wanted to go for a spin in their tour bus. Her mother, overhearing the invitation, had RSVPed, "Absolutely not."

Watching the poised and confident young girl play, Ione was reminded of a different kind of performer, the nervous male opera singer whose Adam's apple had seemed to warble in concert with his strained high notes.

After she introduced her song "Now That I'm on Fire," Silvia's fingers raced up and down the fretboard as if challenging her voice to keep up, which it did, in a buoyant declaration of independence and power. "So hard you tried to douse the flames, but it seems that you forgot. / All it takes is one tiny spark to get things really hot."

For a moment after the last notes were played, they seemed to dance around in the air like dust motes.

"Bravo!" said Nellie, struggling to jump up from the couch. "Bravo!"

"Oh . . . ," said Silvia, taken aback. "Thank you."

"My Walter loved music in this room! We'd host sing-alongs and take turns playing the piano."

What could they do but insist Nellie play, and she was happy to oblige them, rushing to the baby grand, sitting on the bench, and cracking her knuckles with comic flourish. All in the room were hushed, expectant, and Nellie teased the moment, wriggling her fingers over the keys. Finally, they struck their target and target it was, and the keys cried "Uncle!" as Nellie clumsily banged her way through "Moonlight Sonata." At least Patty Jane thought it was "Moonlight Sonata"; Nora thought she was listening to "Great Balls of Fire."

The pianist's face creased with pleasure when she finished, basking in the silence of an awestruck audience, a silence Nora felt obliged to end by clapping. The others joined her, lemmings too stunned to know what else to do. Getting off the piano bench, Nellie took an elaborate bow and, rising, cackled, "Ha! I had you all!"

The women erupted in relieved laughter.

"My Walter was the pianist, not me," said Nellie. "The only tension in our marriage was when I insisted on playing something."

Nora had gotten used to people considering her pregnant belly as something like merchandise, on display and ready to pat and touch, but she still was surprised when Nellie laid her freckled hands on it.

"I'm so thrilled for you," she said. "Thrilled that there'll *finally* be babies here! Our Lodge is in good hands." She gave a final pat to Nora's belly. "Have you named it yet?"

"Like I said, I'm having triplets."

Nellie hooted. "No, I meant Our Lodge! Now that it's your lodge, it should have a new name."

With that, she turned to Brenda, gave a short whistle, and said, "Let's go!"

In the fireplace, the undersides of charred logs glowed red but produced no flames. Everyone had gone to bed, except for the two women sprawled on the couch, watching the fire's final act. Any other night, Nora would have won a first-into-bed race, but this had not been any other night, the excitement she shared with her mother acting like a stimulant.

"Do you think I could really do it?"

"Why not?" said Patty Jane.

It had surprised and delighted them that witnessing Silvia's—and in a way, Nellie's—performance had given them the same idea.

Decades earlier, Patty Jane had proposed to Harriet, Ione, and a ten-year-old Nora the idea of bringing a salon into the salon, because most women "are looking for something more in their lives." Wanting to open up the world a bit for her customers, she initiated the Artists and Other Notables Lecture Series. Its debut had caused a near-riot by the small group who'd been offended by the black-and-white "art films" a friend of Clyde Chuka's had projected on a sheet in Patty Jane's living room; the only thing missing as they chased out the filmmaker were pitchforks and torches. Despite its rocky start, the non–beauty salon salon proved very popular, its classes, lectures, and exhibitions growing yearly, attended by House of Curl and then Etc. patrons and nonpatrons alike.

"Of course, I couldn't do anything until the babies are born," said Nora. "Or maybe I could? It would give me something to do other than gain weight and watch my feet swell."

"I just don't want you to overdo anything."

"Then would you help me?"

"Of course," said Patty Jane, reaching to take her daughter's hand.

"Still, you sold the Etc. Why would you want to do this again?"

"Because it's not the same thing. It's your place, not mine."

"So maybe it's not the end of an era," said Nora, repeating what so many clients had expressed.

"Maybe it's just the beginning of a new one."

⇥ 19

"EVERYTHING LOOKS AND SOUNDS GREAT," said Dr. Everett, after hopscotching his stethoscope across the acreage of Nora's belly. He took out the ear tips, and the stethoscope looped around his neck, hanging down the front of his white coat, the requisite physician's jewelry.

"You keep this up and we'll have you going to forty weeks."

"That's kind of an impossibility, isn't it?" asked Nora.

"It's extremely unlikely," said the doctor. "But I've seen enough in this office to know that anything's possible."

Gloating over her good report and the feeling that she just might break some mothers-of-triplets record, she strolled (in her mind—in reality, she *waddled*) down Palm Avenue, perusing the display cases at Candy Town and picking up the red hot jawbreakers Clyde liked, stopping in to say hello to Brenda in her law office, and browsing at Caroline's Boutique, rifling through the racks of fashionable clothes she might one day fit back into.

The afternoon had grown hot and sticky, and her bulk and hormones caused sweat to leave dark crescents under the armholes and along the neckline of the shapeless maternity shift she wore. By the time she returned to the cabin, Nora had begun to wilt. Two letters waiting for her on the kitchen counter were like sniffs of smelling salts, immediately reviving her and erasing all covetous thoughts of a cool shower. (Getting in and out of a tub was no longer an option.)

She read the letter from her grandmother first. Ione and Edon weren't satisfied with their original two-week-long Mexico vacation and had extended it, traveling through Guatemala and Nicaragua. Nora expected the letter to be like the others, a recounting of the wonders of seeing ancient sites, fauna, and flora: "Today we explored the pre-Columbian site of La Venta, Nora, and it made me feel small and big at the same time"; "the birds here, Nora—scarlet macaws"; "the passion flower, Nora, the Mexican frangipani! So many flowers that dazzle you with their colors and their perfumes!" And the wonders of traveling with Edon: "What he wants to see I'm excited to see, what sites I want to visit, he can hardly put on his walking shoes and sun hat fast enough!"

As she began reading, however, it was obvious this was a different letter entirely:

Dear Nora,

Of course, your mother and father and Clyde and everyone are taking good care of you, but still, I miss not rubbing your feet or back or whatever is sore, bringing you soup or tea or pickles with ice cream, if that's what you are craving.

On Wednesday, I was wishing I had someone to take care of me, because Nora, I was so frightened, seeing a side of Edon that I'd never seen and didn't like one bit. He was so angry, snapping at me, at the lovely couple who runs our hotel, at the bus driver, and finally, after he hollered at a woman selling flowers on the beach, I asked him, What on earth was the matter? (Honestly, this behavior was so not like him I thought maybe he was having some little mini strokes.)

I don't know what I was prepared for, but I wasn't prepared for Edon covering his face with his hands and sinking to the sand as if his knees had given out! Nora, he cried like a baby, and when he stopped, he apologized to me for his bad behavior and for not warning me about it.

This caused me to feel a little scared—had I so misjudged this man's easygoing personality? But nei . . . what he told me made me cry, too. He told me that every year for three or four days, he feels as if a black cloud falls down on him, almost suffocating him with sadness.

You see, Nora, it's the anniversary of his son Per's death.

"Of course, Berit mourned deeply," he said, "but as time went by, she seemed to be able to heal better. For me, every anniversary was a time to pick at the scab of my wound."

He told me he thought maybe it would be different this year, now that he was with me, that our love might be enough to make him forget.

I said I never wanted him to forget Per and that I wanted to be at his side as he remembered.

Seeing another flower seller, I called her over and bought a little bouquet and told him it was in honor of his dear son.

"When was his birthday?" I asked and after he told me (April 3), I asked what he did to celebrate that occasion.

"Usually cry," said Edon. "It's a day, too, that passes with much heaviness."

Well, Nora, I told him that had to change, that I could understand him feeling so low around the anniversary of Per's death, but not of his birth!

"Next April we are going to celebrate!" I said. "We will honor your son who meant so much to you, and I will make him a gold cake!"

Edon has thanked me a million times for helping him get through this terrible, sad time (imagine all those years, going for days in what he called his "May Misery"), and now that it is passed, he is back to being my wonderful travel partner, sharing his enthusiasm and knowledge, explaining that because San Juan was the first port of call for galleons entering the West Indies, Spain ordered that the city be protected by big fortresses and sandstone walls. Today we visited the El Morro fortress, the largest in the Caribbean and the one that stood guard over San Juan Bay for centuries. Always so interesting traveling with a man who's interested!

Now we are trying to decide whether to go to Cuba (there are ways of getting in when you don't enter through America) or fly over to South America. We're both interested in seeing the country that's divided by the equator—yes, Ecuador.

Jeg elsker deg,
Your Grandma

Poor Edon! thought Nora, sitting down at the oak table. *All the weights he bore all those years!* She was so glad he had Ione to help him lighten the loads he carried. But wasn't that the story of love, of not just celebrating and dancing your way through the good times, but of holding and comforting one another through bad times as well as the memories of bad times? Knowing she wasn't thinking just about her grandmother and Edon's love story but also her own, Nora stared for a long time at the other internationally stamped envelope, at her name and address written out in Thomas's scribbly handwriting, afraid to open it, afraid its contents might alter, or worse, *end* that story.

Since his visit, there had been a few letters—five to be exact; she was counting—and in them he had continued to speak of his confusion about what to do with their relationship. But the fact that he was still writing to her (there had been one telephone call, but it was so full of hesitant starts and stops, of talking over one another, that a second hadn't followed) gave her hope that in some small way, he was still in her life.

She carefully, fearfully eased the envelope flap open, Pandora lifting a box lid.

Dear Nora,

Thank you for your last letter. I too miss you; in fact, it seems as if absence does make the heart grow fonder. But the mind still struggles.

A patient of mine died yesterday, and his death has put me in a reflective mood. His name was Bent (a Norwegian name that doesn't seem too popular anywhere but Norway), and diabetes had ravaged him, but he never complained about the indignities and horrors he long suffered. In fact, he was my most cheerful patient ever.

"How is it that you're not more upset about this?" I had asked him several years ago when he was recovering from the amputation of his left foot.

"Take a look at the one I have left," he said pulling up the hospital blanket and wiggling his long and gnarled toes. "It's the foot of a troll! Lise said she almost didn't marry me because of my troll feet. I'm glad to be rid of one!"

The dialysis clinic is in the same building as my offices, and I'd occasionally stop by to say hello during his treatments. He always greeted me as if I were an honored guest and it didn't matter if he, the host, were hooked up to a dialysis machine—it was going to be a party.

How is it, Nora, that some people can make a party when they're sick and weak and their very organs are shutting down, and other people with vibrant health refuse to join in on the joy?

I think of you so often, Nora. I don't know where these thoughts will take me/us, but know they are frequent and loving.

Yours,

Thomas

Nora held the letter to her breast as if it were a blanket and she was cold. And then she read it again. And again.

"Oh, *Focus, Fred!*" said Elise, smoothing the cover of the paperback with her palm. "I love this book!"

"Have you read the others in the series?" asked Bob, the bookstore proprietor.

"Of course! I liked *Concentrate, Corine!* and *Breathe, Bryon!* but none as much as her first."

Bob noticed the look of feigned interest on Silvia's face and laughed. "The heroine is a pediatric psychiatrist who solves mysteries with the help of her young clients."

"Yeah," said Elise. "*Focus, Fred!* is about a kid with ADHD who helps Dr. Helen—she's the heroine—solve the murder of her apartment building's superintendent."

"The author really knows how to write both suspense and comedy," said Bob, but Silvia only offered a vague smile, unconvinced.

"Where's the music section?" she asked and Bob pointed.

"Last shelf on the left. We've got theory, biographies, and song books."

Nora had gravitated to the worn but comfortable couch that was the centerpiece of the bookstore's reading area. Late-morning sun shone through two mullioned windows, and she rested her feet on a tufted leather ottoman. Two smaller feet, in dirty tennis shoes and wriggling back and forth in boyish energy, shared the space with hers. They belonged to Lewis, the boy who had rescued Thor from the icehouse and who now spent as much time at the cabin as he did in his own home.

The two of them leaned companionably against one another, Nora occasionally sighing as she read *Saint Maybe* by Anne Tyler, and Lewis occasionally gasping as he read *Hatchet* by Gary Paulsen.

"That's the thing you never think of," said Lewis, finishing a chapter and resting the book on his scrawny chest.

"What's that?" asked Nora.

"Mosquitoes. You live through a plane crash, you're lost in the woods—no, not the woods—a whole *wilderness,* and you've got all sorts of things to worry about like, 'What am I going to eat?' or 'What's going to eat me?' but then what just about kills you are the fuc—" He stopped himself. "Are the mosquitoes!"

Smiling, Nora gave him a little nudge with her shoulder. Clyde Chuka had given the boy a firm but loving lecture (one Patty Jane had listened to with bemusement; Ione's insistence that Patty Jane add a quarter to a jar every time she swore had done a good job of limiting her own colorfully foul vocabulary) about how boys should not use language that will make others form unfair judgments about them, and Lewis was making a valiant effort to clean up his act.

"I think everyone should wear a watch that's like a walkie-talkie," said Lewis. "So if they live through a plane crash or something, they could get help no matter where they were!"

"Excellent idea," said Nora, and as the boy settled back against her shoulder, said shoulder rose with a sigh of contentment. She saw Silvia, tucking a hank of her long black hair behind her ear as she stood in front of a shelf, her finger running horizontally along the book spines. She saw Elise and Bob laughing and chatting as they rounded a corner and disappeared behind another.

Flyers had been posted around Charleyville, advertising an "Open House—Where You Might Learn a Thing or Two!" and forty-five curious people from town and its lakeside environs showed up. They were directed to the lodge's separate entrance into the basement game room, and after helping themselves to strong coffee and gingerbread cookies made from Ione's recipe (it was only fitting), Nora welcomed them and introduced Silvia, who provided a mini-concert.

Next Elise asked for a volunteer to take a quick lesson in the cha-cha. Both Thor and Bob had raised their hands, but Thor had flapped his so enthusiastically she could hardly ignore him, and besides, she liked the symmetry of bringing him up as her first volunteer, considering it was when they both were Franco and Vilma's partners at the Etc. that her life began to change. Silvia played "Oye Como Va" on her guitar as accompaniment, and Thor's natural rhythm and lack of self-consciousness made him an easy partner, and he milked the applause his demo generated. Elise next called Bob up and while he was clunky and tentative in his movements, she liked being in the bookseller's arms, liked looking into his earnest brown eyes, during the brief moments when he wasn't looking down at his feet.

It was a success—six people signed up for Silvia's Beginning Guitar, and eleven, including Bob, for Elise's ballroom dancing lessons.

Nora's book was positioned on the shelf of her belly, but she had stopped reading it, content to observe her friends in the bookstore. Knowing it would be fleeting, she basked in the momentary sense that all was well with the world, a feeling generated by her two new friends.

As her pregnancy progressed, Nora wrestled with small decisions: should she have an orange or tomato juice? Should she wash her hair or choose to believe its grease was a natural conditioner? Should she make her bed or leave it unmade, since she'd be napping in it in a couple of hours anyway? She was therefore extra proud of making the big decision of moving up to the lodge and starting her mini-version of the House of Curl, Etc., especially as it was having sweet and unintended consequences.

Because of their teaching commitments, both Elise and Silvia were at the lodge every weekend ("I haven't hosted this many slumber parties since I was a kid!" Nora told her mother), and the trio had become fast friends. Elise was several years younger than Nora, and Silvia was only eighteen, but their age differences were of no consequence as they confessed their secrets (they'd howled when Elise admitted to sending her ex-husband off to work with a laxative in his coffee thermos and her excuse, "It was right after I'd found out what he and his office dispatcher were dispatching!"), their fears ("I'm afraid I'm either going to die during labor or die right after, when I see what I'm up against," said Nora), and their dreams ("Sure I want to perform," said Silvia, "but I want to write songs that other people will be singing for years").

The three *amies* had spent the previous night in town, watching *Jules and Jim* at the Charleyville Cinema (its owner, Monsieur Mel, was a devoted Francophile who occasionally played one of his favorite French movies to combat what he called Hollywood's "commercial pap"). Her hormones, as well as the movie's plot and sound track, had Nora sobbing into her butter-stained napkin, at a level which couldn't help but make Elise and Silvia laugh, which couldn't help but make Nora switch gears and laugh, too.

With their friendship, Nora felt that her safety net, already held up by her family, had two additional spotters.

⇉ 20

I AM A BEACHED WHALE, thought Nora, reclining on a deck chair. *Only, I'm not a humpback whale, I'm a hump-fronted one.* Her summer dress had enough fabric to make a pup tent, and pulling at its neckline she fanned herself. The July morning was muggy and warm, on its way to getting hot.

"Here, Nora," said Thor, placing a glass of iced tea on the small table next to her. "With a straw."

"Thanks," said Nora, smiling at her father, who for weeks had been acting like her own personal valet. Sitting next to her, he nodded, pleasure filling his face, and repeated what he had said at least a dozen times since they'd gotten the phone call from Ione: "Ma's coming home."

"I know. I can't wait to see her."

"Three days!"

Nora laughed. "I know, Dad." She rubbed her huge belly. "Wait'll she sees how I've grown."

The Ocean was blue and sparkled from the sun's attention, and the two of them gazed out at it, watching the family of loons past the dock. Bracketing his mouth with his hands, Thor issued a call and the loon called back.

Nora laughed. "Good one, Dad."

Contentment as well as her semi-reclined position eased the discomfort in her body, which had settled in her pelvis, in her hips, in her legs.

Elise and Silvia had driven back to Minneapolis the previous night, their teaching obligations fulfilled, and Patty Jane and Clyde were leaving soon. Earlier that morning Patty Jane had inventoried the contents of the refrigerator.

"There are those walleye fillets Kent brought over," said Patty Jane. "And you should use up that fresh asparagus." Shutting the fridge door, she turned to her family seated at the kitchen table. "Maybe I should stay."

"Mom," said Nora, who'd been thrilled (*I can concentrate! My mind hasn't turned to mush!*) to fill in the final squares of the newspaper's crossword puzzle. "Please. Dad and Harry'll be with me, and I know Dr. Everett's number by heart."

"Yeah, Ma, don't worry," said Harry. "We'll take good care of her. Thor'll wait on her hand and foot like he does, and I'll get my strength training in, trying to get her in and out of chairs."

"Ha, ha," said Nora.

"We will take care of Nora," said Thor, his face serious.

Clyde Chuka lent his support, reminding the fretting matriarch that Harry now had his driver's license and could get his sister anywhere she needed to go.

"Oh, all right," said Patty Jane grudgingly. She and Clyde had several events scheduled in the Twin Cities, including a dinner party the following night at the home of a prominent arts patron and fan of Clyde's work. "But don't do anything stupid."

"Are you talking to me or her?" asked Harry, his voice wounded.

"All of you," said Patty Jane.

Before school let out, Harry had been crushed when his girlfriend, Ava, informed him that while he was really nice, "I'm just not ready to be with one guy exclusively," and that their relationship was over. He had planned to spend only a couple of days at the lodge before going home to the balm and camaraderie of his childhood friends, but a certain red-haired girl who worked at the Frostee Freeze was not only *really* cute but had happily given him her number when he asked.

"Are you two awake?" he asked now, coming out on the deck to find his sister and Thor basking in the sun.

"I am now," said Nora, tipping back the visor of her straw hat to look at him.

"Me, too," said Thor, sitting up straight like a student called to task by his teacher.

"Well, I was just wondering," said Harry, his voice casual, "if it'd be all right if I took the car into town. I wouldn't be gone long—an hour at the most."

"To see her?" asked Thor, who'd been with Harry the first time the red-haired girl had shoved open the little window at the Frostee Freeze and asked to take their order.

Nora laughed at the blush that colored Harry's ears.

"No secret is safe with Thor," she said. "What's her name?"

"Heidi," said Harry. "And I don't even know if she's working. I'm just in the mood for a cone."

"Go," said Nora with a wave of her hand. "And bring me back a strawberry malt."

Thor nodded. "Me, too. But chocolate."

Either she had dozed off (it seemed she couldn't blink without dozing off) and lost track of the time, or Heidi wasn't working because Harry returned much faster than Nora expected.

Hearing the car on the gravel driveway, followed by a door slamming, she said to Thor, "Oh, goodie. Our malts." She smiled, listening to her brother's footsteps and anticipating the ice-cream treat soon to be sliding down her gullet.

"Uh-uh, Nora," said Thor. "Not malts."

To protect her skin from the afternoon sun, she had perched her hat over her face. Lifting it off now, she squinted at the figure standing before her. Her gasp was so loud that Thor, frightened, reached over to take his daughter's hand.

There was a sudden flurry of sound and motion: names shouted, the scrape of her lawn chair as she tried to propel herself out of it, Thor's chair toppling as he leapt to his feet to help Nora up, and finally, the sensation of arms around her and her sway into them as they held her tight.

And at the sound of another car coming up the gravel drive, Thor said, "*Here's* our malts."

"I know I should have telephoned," said Thomas, after the hullabaloo of their reunion. "But even as I drove through town and onto the lake road, I wasn't sure if I was coming."

Nora blew her nose, again.

"I'm so glad you did," she said.

When Harry wasn't being an obtuse teenager, he could be a sensitive young man who understood when his sister needed privacy, so he had dragged Thor out for a swim as Thomas told Nora about how he had just happened to be in the neighborhood.

"Jack—we were roommates at Madison—called me three days ago, telling me he'd met the woman of his dreams and I *had* to be his best man. 'Couldn't you have given me a little notice?' I asked him and he said, 'I did—we just decided to get married this morning!' Normally, I would have said no—Jack's a lot of fun, but his spontaneity can get a little old, and I've already been to his first two weddings. But when I realized Fargo was fairly close to Charleyville, how could I say no? I know I should have given you some advance warning, but like I said, I didn't know if I'd have the courage to actually stop by." He rolled his eyes, mocking his mile-a-minute delivery, and smiled two seconds before his back heaved with a sob.

Nora's impulse was to rush to his side, but rushing to anyone's side was a physical impossibility, so she did what she was able, which was to sit there, unable even to stretch her arm across the patio table to touch him.

"I'm so sorry," he said, finally lifting his head from his cupped hands. "I just . . . it's just so hard to see you like this."

The words were ones usually directed toward people emaciated by cancer or stunned into unknowingness by dementia, but Nora knew exactly what he meant and forgave him his blunt—but truthful— assessment. "I know," she said quietly.

The fingers that had traveled down Thomas's cheekbones to his jawline now fanned upward to wipe away his tears, and he breathed in and breathed out like a worried scuba diver not quite at the water's surface and bearing an empty tank.

"Oh, Nora, forgive me. That . . . that was beneath me. Beneath you. Of course I knew that you'd be . . . showing your pregnancy. But as much as I thought it, seeing it is something different. It makes me realize it's really real."

Nora couldn't help reflexively patting her belly.

"Yes, it is, Thomas. It's really real."

They had managed to have a nice dinner, thanks to the fillets thawed in the refrigerator and Thomas's insistence that he knew his way around a grill, as well as the distraction of the others at the table, including Lewis, who had shown up, intuitively knowing when food was being served. "Whoa!" he said after hearing Thor and Thomas *snakker norsk.* "Teach me some of that!" and as the sun drifted below the trees on the western edge of the lake, everyone on the deck ate their grilled walleye as Thor pointed to the fish and Thomas said, "*Fisk,*" and Thomas pointed to the sky and Thor said, "*Himmelen,*" and Thor pointed to Nora's belly and Thomas said, "*Babyer.* Lots of *babyer!*"

It had been awkward for Nora, saying good night and watching Thomas climb the stairs instead of accompanying her down the hallway toward her first-floor bedroom, with its bathroom conveniently located just feet away.

⇛ 21

I T WAS TEN THIRTY BY THE TIME NORA, mug of tea in hand, made her waddling way out to the deck. Thomas and Thor had completed a full morning of activities, including a swim, breakfast, a walk down the road to check on a new cabin under construction, a tour of the outdoor shed that served as Thor's studio (where Thomas was rightly impressed by the current birdhouse-in-progress, a replica of the Charleyville Cinema), and now on the wide expanse of lawn a game of catch, which included Lewis, who'd skipped up the road wearing the same clothes he'd worn the day before and a catcher's mitt.

"Good morning," she said, standing at the railing.

"Hi, Nora," said Thor before tossing the ball with perfect aim into Lewis's outstretched mitt.

"I'm out," said Thomas, waving his hands as Lewis prepared to throw to him. He was wearing shorts, and as he loped toward the deck and up the stairs, Nora felt a sensation in her low belly that she believed had nothing to do with pregnancy and everything to do with how attractive she found him, skinny, knobby-kneed legs and all.

"Can we go into town?" asked Lewis, when he and Thor, sweaty and smiling, came in an hour later, having stretched their game of catch into a game of "Who can skip the most rocks into the lake?" which moved inland into "Who can hit the mailbox with a rock?" Thor was the victor both times; one of his skips was counted out at twenty-four, and even with a ten-foot-closer handicap, Lewis only hit the mailbox twice. Perched on a wooden stake at the top of the driveway, it was an old metal cylinder. When Thor got done with it, it looked like an old metal cylinder that had been through a hailstorm.

"To see a movie," added Thor.

"*Honey, I Shrunk the Kids*," said Lewis. "It's supposed to be really funny. But we'd go to the arcade first."

"Sure," said Nora. "Do you want a ride?"

"Nah, I'll drive them," said Harry, who'd spent the morning "making some phone calls."

Nora smiled. "So you plan to see Heidi?"

Harry's shrug was exaggerated. "If we feel like a cone before the movie, we might."

"Yeah, a cone," said Thor.

At noon, there were clouds that made a pretty scalloped border alongside the edges of the northern and western horizons. An hour later, the scallops had inflated and darkened, and the breeze that gently ruffled the leaves of the lakeside cottonwood tree had whipped up into a wind that made them shudder.

"Whoa," said Nora. "Looks like we're in for a storm."

When she lived in California, its weather had held few surprises other than more sun or more smog, and she loved this wild part of Minnesota, its winter blizzards and summer storms; she loved how a freezing spring morning could turn into a sixty-degree afternoon with irises and tulips poking through the soil, or how a balmy autumn ablaze in color could turn into a whiteout night of snow flurries.

"I guess we'd better postpone our walk by the Ocean," said Thomas.

"Good," said Nora, easing herself into the part of the massive sectional couch that faced the windows. "Why exercise when you can sit?"

Although she'd only been up and about for several hours, she was already craving a nap.

"Are you all right?" asked Thomas, settling in next to her.

Resting her hands on her belly, she said, "The babies are dancers. Right now they're holding a rhumba contest."

Seconds after Thomas placed his hand next to hers, his eyebrows raised.

"Oh, I felt that."

Nora sighed. "Trust me, I did, too."

She didn't want to complain, even as that's all she wanted to do. She was so tired of the cumbersome weight she carried, so tired of backaches and the heaviness in her legs that made it seem like she was walking through knee-high muddy water, so tired of having to rearrange herself according to how the babies arranged themselves—so she wouldn't have to gulp for breath when they positioned themselves high or wouldn't have the nearly impossible task of getting comfortable when they positioned themselves low, as they were now. And more than anything, she was so tired of being tired.

"How many weeks are you now?"

"Almost thirty-four," said Nora, unable to keep the pride out of her voice.

Thomas whistled. "And you're not on bed rest?"

"Yeah, along with couch rest and lawn-chair rest." Nora tried to sound resigned, but the pride returned. "Did you know that in his career, Dr. Everett has delivered eleven sets of twins and two sets of triplets, and he says out of all of them, I win the Ideal Patient award?"

"I'd expect nothing less," said Thomas and kissed her cheek.

She woke up to a nudging that wasn't from one of the babies' kicks but from Thomas's elbow.

"What?" she said, suffused with drowsiness, but a moment later, hearing a siren, she was suddenly alert, wiping the drool from her mouth. The sky was a color most often seen in soup bowls, a thick pea green. The fir trees swayed in the wind and the branches of the cottonwood tree tossed side to side, like the arms of frenzied fans at a rock concert.

"It's a storm warning," said Nora. "We're supposed to go in the basement."

"Let's get some light in here," said Thomas, flicking on a wall switch.

As they made their way downstairs, lightning cut jagged bolts of white through the sickly sky. Storms always excited Nora, the electricity in the air seeming to spark her own, but she was quickly passing through excitement and into agitation. Thunder didn't crack as much as it exploded, with a boom so loud that Nora reached for Thomas at the same time he reached for her. "I hope Harry and Dad and Lewis aren't caught in this!" she said.

"I'm sure they're fine," said Thomas as the thunder faded into a rumble. "They're probably eating popcorn in the movie theater basement."

The game room was nearly empty, the foosball table having been relocated to Thor's room. Chairs were set up when Silvia taught her music class and pushed to the side when Elise taught dance, and it was in a corner of the room that Nora and Thomas huddled. A long horizontal window on the far wall provided a view of the storm and they stared out mesmerized, as lightning jittered through the sky, followed by a racket of thunder. A siren wailed again, and as the green sky opened up and unleashed a fast and furious rain, Nora's agitation amped up; she felt as if the storm on the outside was gathering inside her.

"Thomas," she whispered, "I don't feel so good."

"Well, you shouldn't be standing," said Thomas. "Let me get you a chair." His voice was so calm and steady that Nora was briefly reassured that of course the strange pulsation in her body was only a transfer of electricity from a thunderstorm, an exaggerated version of the usual hepped-up excitement she felt when Mother Nature threw a tantrum.

There was another great crack of lightning, and in response the big room suddenly went dark.

"Thomas?" said Nora, a flare of fear skittering through her like her own internal lightning bolt.

"Right here, my dear," he said lightly. "I'm right here."

"Thomas, the power's gone out!"

"It appears that way."

"I'm scared!"

"No need, my dear. I'm right here."

"Thomas, can you sing?"

"Sing? I can carry a tune, I guess."

"I can't believe I don't know that about you. I mean, when we were together . . . it seemed we knew everything about each other."

"We're together now."

"You know what I mean," said Nora.

Lightning illuminated the interior of the room in a ghostly light.

"Thomas, I feel like, like things are happening . . . like my weight's shifted. The babies feel much . . . lower."

"On Wisconsin, on—"

"—what!?"

"I'm showing you that I can sing," he said, mock hurt in his voice. "A song I learned cheering for the Badgers in the bleachers at Camp Randall Stadium." He cleared his throat.

"On Wisconsin, On Wisconsin, / Plunge right through that line, / Run the ball clear down the field, boys / Touchdown sure this time! / On Wisconsin, On Wisconsin, / Fight on for her fame, / Fight, Fellows, Fight, Fight, Fight! / We'll win this game!"

Nora made a sound that began like laughter and ended in a yelp. Feeling a gush between her legs, she gasped.

"Thomas . . . I . . . Thomas, my water broke!"

"Well, isn't it lucky I'm here," said Thomas gently, ignoring the alarm that surged through him. "Here for the big day."

"The babies are coming, aren't they?" Nora asked, and her question was answered by a bolt of lightning that flashed not in the sky but in her pelvis.

She cried out, clutching him.

"Okay," said Thomas. "This is what we're going to do. I'm going to call your doctor—"

"—yes, yes, call Dr. Everett!"

"And we'll tell him to meet us at the hospital."

"Yes, yes, let's do that!"

"Do you know the number?" asked Thomas, and as Nora recited it, he went to the wall phone.

Nora did not take it as a good sign when he tamped on the phone's plunger, repeating into the receiver, "Hello? Hello?"

"The phone's not working?" she said, her voice sounding almost giddy. "Of course, the power's out!"

"Nora, don't panic," said Thomas. "Everything'll be fine. I can drive you to the hospital."

"In this? It's a monsoon out there and the hospital's twelve miles away! We'll have to go to the clinic! The clinic in town!"

"Let's go upstairs," said Thomas calmly. "Where there's a little more light."

When the second one came, Nora couldn't deny that what she was feeling was a contraction, and it roared through her body like a train coming off its tracks.

"Ten minutes," said Thomas, who'd been consulting his watch. "Ten minutes from the first one. Plenty of time."

Nora leaned over the kitchen counter, her knuckles white from her grip around its edge.

"Try to breathe into it," said Thomas.

Why hadn't anyone told her about this pain? thought Nora. Sure, she had heard labor stories, but when people had talked about the pain, they certainly hadn't talked about *this* kind of pain. Why didn't anyone tell her it felt like a war was being fought inside her? Why had she been lied to? She never would have wanted a baby if she knew this was what she had to go through to get one! Never mind one baby—three! Oh my God, she was having three! This pain would be tripled, would go on and on until she died from it! Died right here in the lodge's kitchen!

"Help!" She meant to shout, but the word rode weakly on a sharp gasp.

"You're doing fine," said Thomas. "Better than fine."

They both tried to pretend the storm outside was easing up and that they'd soon be in the car and headed to the clinic, but as Nora paced the kitchen, freezing in place when besieged with a contraction, the torrent of wind-whipped rain was unrelenting, pounding against the windows and sliding glass door in diagonal slashes. Nora had told Thomas where in the utility closet to find the flashlights and candles, and circles of light now shone on the ceiling from flashlights propped upright in glasses, and flickering candlelight made the kitchen look almost cozy.

"Thomas, I'm afraid," said Nora.

"Of course you are, darling," said Thomas. "But I'm here and I'm a doctor, remember? I've delivered lots of babies."

"You have?"

"Sure, I almost went into obstetrics," he lied.

"But triplets are higher risk," she said, not telling him anything he didn't already know. "Especially premature ones!"

"Nora, my dear, everything will be fine. You've carried these babies longer than most mothers of triplets do, and they'll have everything they need at the clinic."

"How do you know? It's not the Mayo Clinic—it's just a dinky little small-town clinic!" Her voice raised into a wail of frustration that heightened into a scream of pain as she leaned toward the table, gripping the rungs of a kitchen chair. As the contraction seized her, Thomas looked out the window, whose view was closer to what one might find in a submerged submarine. He could see no landscape—nothing but a green watery darkness. *If this doesn't let up . . . ,* he thought, but before letting fear finish his sentence, he repeated the mantra he used in the hospital when faced with a medical emergency: *Styrke. Fokuser. Pust.* Strength. Focus. Breathe.

Below Nora's moans, the driving rain and a keening whistle of wind filled his ears like white noise. No, white noise soothed a person; this was more a dark gray noise, a deep purple noise that reminded Thomas that if he didn't *styrke, fokusere,* and *puste,* they were, to use American slang, *screwed.*

Harry had dropped Thor and Lewis off at the arcade, explaining that he had business to take care of and he might make it to the movie or he might not. Either way, he'd be at the theater after the show to give them a ride home.

"I know what the name of your business is," said Lewis slyly. "Heidi-at-the-Frostee-Freeze."

"Could be," said Harry, just as slyly.

Thor beat Lewis in three games of foosball, attracting a small group of onlookers who cheered the old guy's prowess, and then as partners, the two took on several different duos, all of which lost.

They played Pac-Man over and over, and when they sat next to each other in simulated race cars, Thor avoided every roadblock, sharp turn, and approaching bad driver, while Lewis crashed not once but four times.

"One day you gotta let me beat you at *something*," said the boy.

A blast of wind grabbed at the door as they left the arcade and banged it against the outside wall.

"Whoa!" said Thor.

The sky was a strange green, and the flag at the post office was a snapping blur of red, white, and blue. Thor and Lewis laughed as they made their way toward the movie theater, the wind shoving them forward.

"Big storm coming!" Lewis shouted, but the wind and a siren drowned out his voice.

Across the street, Monsieur Mel stood in front of the Charleyville Cinema, windmilling his arms, shouting at the line of kids to hurry into the theater.

"We better get inside, too!" shouted Lewis, grabbing his friend's arm. But crossing the street, Thor pulled away.

"Lewis," said Thor, his voice anxious. "Gotta go."

"What?"

"You stay—I gotta go!" shouted Thor, and he was off, loping down Palm Avenue.

By the time he was out of town and on the county road that turned into Lake Road, thunder and lightning took turns filling the sky with sound and fury. When he passed the cabin with the rock garden, rain didn't fall so much as pound down. As Thor neared the gray-shingled house with the German shepherds who liked to run the length of the chain-link fence barking at any passerby (the dogs were nowhere to be seen or heard now), the lights inside it blinked off. He looked back to see that the lit-up cabin he'd just passed was dark, too.

It rained so hard it seemed there was a wall of water in front of him, but Thor kept pushing through that wall, kept running, past lake homes whose order he knew by heart, only now they were blurry, nearly undistinguishable masses. He came to welcome the lightning that lit them up briefly, even though he knew thunder would shortly follow, and the thunder was so loud it sounded like the sky itself was crashing down. His side ached, and once he slipped on the wet gravel and only managed to stop his fall by executing a little hop and then a bigger one, a graceful move from a naturally athletic man.

When he passed the mailbox shaped like a fish (he loved that mailbox), his lungs felt as if they were on fire, but he wasn't far from home now, and he felt a surge of energy that made him speed up. At the same time a surge of electric energy zipped through the sky and the lightning struck an elm tree like an ax, and as it crashed to the ground Thor was caught under it.

He didn't know if he'd been knocked out or not; all he knew was that when he tried to stand up he couldn't, because something seemed to be holding him down. Lying almost sideways but not quite, his left arm splayed behind him, his chin on the gravel, he realized what was pinning him down was a tree, or at least a big branch of one, and he pushed himself up with his right arm—or tried to.

"*Du er okay*," he said to himself. The rain was a constant roar, and he turned his head and again pushed himself with his right arm. Nothing moved or changed other than the sharpening pain in his left shoulder, and he rested his chin on the gravel, panting. After the fifth or sixth failed attempt to lift himself up, Thor began trying to slide himself out from under the heavy branch that blanketed his shoulder and back with wood and leaves. The gravel bit at his face and the palm of his hand, but he kept sliding, inch by inch by inch, with the wind driving the rain sideways into him. He felt a sudden lightness and he wriggled the fingers of his left hand. Now free, he was finally able to push himself up. He did so, staggering as he stood and falling again as his foot got tangled in leaves and branches. Freeing himself again, he began running, cupping his left elbow in his right hand.

He cried out when lightning lit the sky and he saw his own mailbox, the one used as target practice earlier that morning, and he ran up the driveway leading to their cabin, up the deck stairs.

"Nora!" he cried, yanking open the sliding glass door and plunging through the narrow mudroom and into the kitchen.

Thor didn't expect to find her crouched over a kitchen chair moaning—he didn't know what to expect. All he had known was that it was storming and he should be home to protect his daughter.

Startled, Nora abruptly cut off her moaning and said, "Dad!" as Thomas said, "Thor!" adding quickly, "What happened?"

"I . . . my arm . . . Nora!"

Muttering something in Norwegian, Thomas grabbed a dish towel and, holding it under the running tap, asked, "Good God, what's happened to you?"

"Tree fell on me."

Thomas wrung the towel out and held it to the man's bloody face.

"Let me see your arm," he said.

"No!" said Thor, wiggling away from Thomas's administrations. "Nora needs me!"

"Of course I do, Dad," said Nora through gritted teeth. "But where's Harry? Where's Lewis?"

"Town," said Thor. "What's happening?"

Nora's face scrunched up in a grimace, and although she didn't want to scare her dad, she couldn't help the growl of pain that ran up her throat and out her mouth.

"Nora!"

"She's in labor, Thor," said Thomas. "She's going to have the babies soon."

"Here?" said Thor, bewildered. Nora was supposed to have the babies in the hospital.

"Why don't you get out of your wet clothes?" said Thomas gently. "Do you need me to help you?"

"No! Stay with Nora!"

Always a doctor, Thomas called after him to wash his bloody face and hands, and when Thor returned to the kitchen in dry clothes and less blood, he went to his daughter and placed his hand on her shoulder.

"You be okay, Nora."

The laboring mother tried to laugh, but it was laughter laced with hysteria.

"I don't know about that, Dad!"

"The rain's letting up," said Thomas, more hopeful than sure that this was actually the case. Opening drawers, he took a handful of kitchen towels from one. "Thor, help me get Nora to the car. We're going to the clinic."

There were two raincoats on hooks in the mudroom, and Thor grabbed them and an umbrella. The threesome made their way outside, the men flanking Nora who, draped in a leopard-print raincoat whose hood obscured her face, looked like a poorly costumed animal in an elementary school play. The rain had lost its piercing force but the parts of them not covered with rain gear were soaked by the time they'd taken three steps across the deck. Nora welcomed the sensation—would have welcomed blowing snow, hot desert winds, freezing temperatures—anything that shifted her focus, however briefly, from her pain and fear.

"Thor, get in the back with her," said Thomas, when they were at his rental car. "And tell me how to get to the clinic."

"You be with her," said Thor. "I drive." He held out his hand for the keys. "It's okay. I can."

Nora was too deep within herself and what was happening to her body to notice, let alone protest, when Thomas got into the backseat with her and Thor backed the car out of the driveway and onto Lake Road. With the wipers moving like a metronome with overwound pendulums, Thor drove carefully, his back straight as a soldier's, his right hand on the wheel, his left cradled in his lap. He hummed softly and monotonously to himself, for focus, reassurance, and to block out the noises in the backseat and the pain in his left shoulder.

"Thomas! Thomas, oh, God!"

Thor willed himself not to look into the rearview mirror; his job was to get to the clinic and he could allow no distraction in performing his duty.

"You're doing great, Nora," said Thomas, who was half-crouched on the backseat and on the floor, with Nora sprawled out in front of him. The skirt of her dress was pushed up high and she held her hand at her crotch, the way a little girl does when she needs to go to the bathroom.

"Thomas, it's coming! I can feel its head!"

"Here, darling," said Thomas. "Let's get your underpants off." Tugging them down, he couldn't help his gasp.

"What?" screamed Nora. "It's coming, isn't it! Oh, God, get it out!"

"It's time to push," he said, setting one of the kitchen towels underneath her. "So push, Nora. I'll catch her."

Lights from the passing cabins blinked on; electric power had been restored. Thor was not one to put much stock in omens—didn't understand omens, really—but he was heartened by this return to normalcy and felt a ping of tension release itself from his tightly coiled body. Far beyond tightly coiled, Nora's body experienced no relief of tension, and as a crack of thunder reverberated through the air, she screamed, feeling as if she were cracking open herself.

"That's it, Nora, that's it!" said Thomas, his hands cupped and waiting for the emerging head, then shoulders of the baby who would be responsible for an additional charge paid to the car rental company for the extra interior cleanup.

⇛ 22

I T HAD BEEN THEIR YEARS-LONG SECRET, initiated when Thor asked out of the blue on a trip to the grocery store, "Can I drive, Ma?"

"Thor," Ione had said, behind the wheel, "I . . . no, I don't think so."

She glanced at her son and saw the shift of his shoulders, the bow of his head, and the old and very familiar sensation of anger and sadness rose in her. So many things had been taken away from Thor since his accident; why, she thought, take away another?

Driving silently for several blocks, she turned into a Catholic church parking lot, put the gearshift into park, and said, "Okay, son. Drive."

They had exchanged places and Thor sat for a long moment, staring at his fingers curled around the steering wheel. After adjusting the rearview mirror, he offered Ione a smile that was like a gift, put the car into gear, and began driving as expertly as a general's chauffeur. It honestly didn't surprise Ione much; Thor had excellent motor skills and physically was an athletic and agile man.

Any car trip she took with Thor, she let him drive, always making sure he understood that this was a secret privilege, one he was not allowed to share with anyone.

"Not even Nora?" asked Thor.

"Heavens, no," said Ione with a little shiver. Thor had begun driving around the time Nora had begun law school, and Ione did not need to be reminded of the legal ramifications of allowing an unlicensed, uninsured, brain-damaged driver to get behind the wheel. But she loved sitting on the passenger side with her son;

when he drove he was in charge, a position he seldom was privileged to occupy.

Unable to part after their voyage, Ione had brought back home a surprise—Edon—and the couple stood in front of the hospital nursery window, gushing over the tiny babies in pink knitted caps as Patty Jane filled them in on the dramatic tale of their births.

"I should be mad—no, *outraged*—at you for ever allowing such a thing," said Patty Jane, but as she shook her head to emphasize her disapproval, a laugh burbled out of her mouth. "But because Thor knew how to drive, he saved the day. Saved the babies." And then she was crying, and Ione was crying, and a baby in one of the bassinets marked Baby Girl #1–Rolvaag joined in.

Sena was the baby who rebelled against protocol, choosing to have an endocrinologist in a rental car deliver her rather than an obstetrician in a medical facility. Driving up to the clinic, Thor had shouted, "I find someone!" Shoving the gearshift into park, he raced out into the rain, and a moment after the car door slammed, Nora gave a cry and the baby slid into Thomas's hands.

"She's here!" said Thomas, and a surge of adrenaline made him fumble, nearly dropping the baby as he reached for another towel to wrap her in. There was a blue tinge to her color and she was so limp that he was afraid she was dead. Holding the newborn on her side, he cleared fluid out of her mouth with his finger and then rubbed her face with the towel, nearly dropping her again when a cry filled the car and he watched as color came into her tiny face and a blossom of pink spread across her tiny chest.

"Let me hold her!" said Nora, and grabbing at the top of her dress, she pulled hard, buttons scattering like popped corn. "Wait, let me get my bra off!" she said, unfastening the front closure. The volume of her voice was the level of a shout. "I want her to be warm!"

A gust of cool air and rain droplets flew into the car as the back door opened. In a quick and efficient choreography, two people helped Thomas get Nora and the baby out of the car and onto a gurney, rushing her toward the clinic door while Thor ran alongside, holding an umbrella over his daughter and brand-new granddaughter.

Thomas was so fluent in English he could have easily had a side career as a translator. He took pride in the idiosyncratic idioms he had picked up during his years at Madison—"That's a bitch," "Give me a break!" and "He was shit out of luck"—but one expression he hated and hoped he never heard again was "Touch and go." This was what he heard at least a dozen times regarding the condition of the third baby, the one born twenty-nine minutes after the first one and eleven minutes after the second.

Sena—the one Thomas had delivered—weighed four pounds, fourteen ounces, and the second, Grace, weighed an even five, but the third baby, Ulla, weighed only three pounds, eleven ounces, and she was whisked away as soon as her cord was cut. Her very first car ride had been in an ambulance that took her to the hospital, where she spent the night of her birthday, and her second, third, and fourth nights in the neonatal intensive care ward.

Thomas had canceled his flight back to Oslo and telephoned his partners with news that he'd need more time away.

"How much?" asked Dr. Nyberg, who valued routine almost over breathing.

"A week . . . two," said Thomas. "I'm not sure yet; it depends on how things go here."

In the pause it took Dr. Nyberg to consider his very reasoned argument about responsibility to patients, let alone his coworkers, Thomas quickly said, "We'll talk again soon," and hung up.

The dinner party host had a telescope on his rooftop patio and invited his guests to survey the night sky. The stars didn't shine as brightly as those in Charleyville, obscured as they were by the urban lights of the Twin Cities.

"But look at that moon," said Clyde Chuka, during his turn at the telescope. "Gorgeous."

"It's a blue moon," said the host.

"Patty Jane, take a look at this," said Clyde, and when she did, she agreed.

"It's gorgeous."

Neither had any idea of the dramatic weather that roiled through Charleyville earlier that day, nor had either any idea of what had roiled through Nora, and they wouldn't until the following day, when they drove back up north.

All the grand/great/parents/partners were squeezed into the hospital room ("The new mother needs her rest," a good-humored nurse told them, "so I'll be back in ten minutes to throw you out!"), and when Patty Jane told Nora there was a blue moon shining on the triplets' birthday, she said, her smile beatific, "Of course there was."

Sitting next to Thomas, Edon whispered, "*Hva?*"

"*Once in a blue moon* is an expression," the younger man explained. "It's used when something amazing happens."

Days later, sparks flew and saws whined as Clyde worked in the shed. Although Thor's left arm was in a sling, he was able to paint with his right, and they were assisted by Lewis, who was proud that Clyde trusted him to use the spot welder, and by Harry, who had good handwriting.

A wooden sphere, two feet in diameter, was painted a shadowy, cratered blue and etched into it were the words *Blue Moon Lodge*. It was suspended from the outstretched wing of the four-and-a-half-foot loon made from scrap metal and bolted to a sturdy post. On the upper left side of the sign floated a white wooden cloud with three more etched words, so that the sign bore exactly the right name by which Nora had decided to christen their home: "Once in a Blue Moon Lodge."

Thomas had declared his desire to be both the girls' father and Nora's husband in a letter he'd written three and a half weeks after the babies' birth, on the day he returned to his Oslo apartment.

I knew it the moment I caught Sena, he wrote, after he'd written a paragraph about his bumpy flight and the cold reception he'd received from Dr. Nyberg.

> *I thought: It doesn't matter that I wasn't there at their begin-*
> *ning—I was there when she came into the world! And the same with*
> *Grace and Ulla in the delivery room. I was worried my hand might*
> *not ever be ready for surgery after the way you held it, crushing it*
> *with every contraction, but I didn't care: my job was to help you*
> *bring these babies into the world!*
>
> *After their births, and especially when Ulla finally came home,*
> *I thought maybe you didn't need me, what with all your family*
> *around. I think back often to that sweet night when all three of the*
> *girls were sleeping (at the same time!) and we were on the deck*
> *talking, and I was about to tell you, Nora, that I was ready, ready*
> *to be a husband and father, if you'd have me, if the girls would have*
> *me. But then your mother and Clyde came out, and the four of us*
> *gazed at the stars, at Lyra, Sagittarius, and Scorpius.*
>
> *The sky was so bright with stars, Nora, and the night air was so*
> *soft . . . and I could smell you, sitting so close. And you smelled of*
> *milk and lemon, but most of all that undefinable Nora-ness, and*
> *that smell to me was the most beautiful perfume.*
>
> *Remember Odysseus being tied to the mast, his ears plugged*
> *so that he wouldn't be tempted by the siren's call? But what if he*
> *smelled your Nora-ness—how could he resist you?*
>
> *I can't. This is a new life, an unexpected life, but a life I want*
> *more than anything to be mine.*
>
> *Please think over what I've said and telephone me.*
>
> *Your hopeful husband and father of your girls,*
> *Thomas*

Nora didn't need to think over anything, but wanting to give her words the same weight as Thomas's written ones, she took pen to paper.

> *Min elskling,*
> *My T-shirt is wet from the breasts that seem to be like water*

*spigots always turned ON (I know that's kind of gross, but it's my
reality), but I don't yet hear any snuffles or cries from the babies'
room, so I'm writing you. Let me tell you this: even before your
letter, I considered you the girls' father. I knew it might be a fantasy,
and something that was never acknowledged by anyone but me—
let alone legalized—but I always thought, while the babies were
growing inside me, that if I could have chosen their father, their
father would be you.*

*It's easy for women—we get pregnant and there's our indisput-
able proof that we're the mother!—but harder for men, who can't
always know with 100 percent certainty of their patrimony, unless
DNA testing tells you so.*

*Babies are passed to me (what would I do without my support
group?) like footballs, and I nurse them and I burp them. I change
them, I sing to them, I put them to bed for the hour or two that one
or two or all of them will sleep, and then I repeat the routine, but
believe it or not . . . I've had time to think.*

*For the weeks you were here after their birth and so present, so
with me, so with the girls, asking the doctors questions I was afraid
to, holding my hand while I held Grace and you held Sena and we
both looked at Ulla in her incubator . . . well, what is fatherhood but
that?*

*I was so thrilled when I met you in Norway, thinking, Finally!
and then so shocked to realize I was pregnant with triplets
(@&@*&$-!!) and that they weren't yours, weren't biologically
from the man who'd make the perfect father. But you are the perfect
father and that you're willing to be the perfect father . . . Thomas,
how can I tell you all that is in my heart?*

*That you'd consider me for your wife and want to be father to
our girls fills me . . . well, I am so high that I've floated to the moon.
Look out your window and wave to me.*

With things I can't even express, I am yours,
Nora

When she was finished, she placed a long-distance phone call and
screamed into the receiver, "Yes, yes, yes!"

*   *   *

The Once in a Blue Moon Lodge sign welcomed guests on a late August afternoon. Carried along the light breeze that fluttered the ribbons tied around the wedding trellis and made the sign gently sway was a fishy smell from the Ocean and its hem of yellowed foam sloshing along the water's edge. Still, the predicted rain had failed to materialize and the sun shone in a high blue sky, and the wedding guests who gathered on the crest of the lawn complimented the day, the occasion, and a bird's strange serenade.

"That's Lars the Loon," Elise explained to her mother, Marvel. "Ione and Edon named him after an amateur ventriloquist who was at the same party where they first met in Norway."

Bob the Bookseller, sitting on Elise's other side, pressed his shoulder against hers and she pressed hers back.

Patty Jane gifted both brides for whom she served as matron-of-honor with her hairdresser skills, pinning up Nora's dusky blond waves and fluffing up Ione's short snow-white hair. Nora wore a pale blue vintage '50s dress that she and Elise had scored at the Ladies' Aid Consignment Store, a dress whose cut and satin fabric flattered her postpartum body in a way she didn't think possible. At Dayton's Ione found a lavender silk dress that Patty Jane had convinced her to buy, even though it wasn't on sale. Instead of veils, both women wore tiaras of forget-me-nots and white roses that the town florist had constructed to match their bouquets, proving that her shop name, Gladdy's Floral Arts, was no overstatement.

Thor, waiting for them in the kitchen before their bridal march, stood up as Nora and Ione entered, looking for a brief moment like he'd been punched in the gut.

"Nora," he said, dabbing at his eyes with his sleeve. "Ma. Wowie." He solemnly offered his crooked elbows to both women, who took them just as solemnly.

Patty Jane's late sister, Harriet, had traversed a long and torturous road between her first love, who died before their wedding date, and her second. It was her jubilation over a second chance at love that had compelled her to step away from her groom during the nuptials to play a trumpet duet with her niece, Nora.

"I'd love to be able to play Thomas a song," Nora had told her mother, "but I'm not the musician Harriet was. I hardly play my trumpet anymore."

Instead, her brother Harry and her friend Silvia, accompanying themselves on electronic keyboard and guitar, sang a medley, starting off with a jazzy version of the Monkees' "I'm a Believer." As Nora and Thor and Ione processed across the rose petal–strewn deck and down the steps, they switched to Jerome Kern and Ira Gershwin's "Long Ago (and Far Away)" and to the Beach Boys' "God Only Knows" as the trio made their way down the plastic runner (also decorated with rose petals) laid over the lawn and to the trellis where the minister stood. New Charleyville friends and old Minneapolis ones filled the rows of chairs, as well as longtime patrons and employees of Patty Jane's House of Curl, women who'd first met Nora in the beauty salon, when next to her mother's operator's chair she'd sit at a little table, busy with coloring books or styling her dolls' hair.

"Nora's so lovely," whispered Inky Kolstat. "She looks just like Elizabeth Taylor in *Father of the Bride*."

"Except that she doesn't have dark hair and violet eyes," whispered Crabby Bultram back. "She doesn't look like her at all!"

"I believe she's commenting on a shared radiance and hopeful-ness," said Monsieur Mel, who'd been delighted to meet Inky, whose love of movies nearly matched his own.

Admiring the trim figures Ione and Edon cut, Evelyn Bright whispered to Myrna Johnson, "They don't look a day over sixty-five!"

Both brides had agreed to dispense with the old-fashioned custom of having the minister ask, "Who gives away this bride?" Now Nora thought it might have been wise to have given Thor a cue, because he wasn't letting go of her or Ione's crooked arms, even as Thomas and Edon stepped forward.

"Dad," she'd whispered. "Dad, let go. It's okay." He held on tight, until Patty Jane stepped up, carefully lifting his arms so that Nora and Ione could remove theirs.

Nora's sweat glands worked overtime, crescents of darkness growing under her cap sleeves, and one of the babies, being held by Lewis and two high school girls in the back row, wailed during the minister's welcome. Edon nervously flubbed his vows and Ione had a bout of sneezing that required Clyde, standing off to the side, to pass her his handkerchief. Thomas dropped the ring and there was a scramble to find it in the grass, and someone in the small wedding party let loose a fart so noxious that Nora had to will herself not to fan the air with her bouquet. (She never told anyone—not even Thomas—that she was that someone.)

Still, both bridal couples if asked to rate the ceremony on a scale of one to five stars would have said they needed more stars.

Part Three

⇶ 23

1994

P LEASURE. He had felt pleasure in his life, but never in these
daily, incremental doses: passing the coffeepot and the morning paper to Ione; reading aloud to one another editorials,
horoscopes, an unusual obituary; holding her hand while wading
in the Ocean on a summer's day that smelled of pine and wildflow-
ers; sharing a box of Jordan almonds at the Charleyville Cinema;
stooping slightly as Ione straightened his tie or brushed his lapel
as they dressed for church on Sundays. He preferred the English
word to the Norwegian one, *nytelse*; it felt full and soft in his mouth.
Pleasure.

Edon had resigned himself to living out his life in the lonely sar-
cophagus of a marriage that had long ago calcified; he had resigned
himself to loving a son who was only a memory, a blue shadow cast
against his heart. But now, in this unbelievable new life, he was
someone's *darling,* someone's grandfather and BopBop, someone's *Pa.*

When Thor first called him that, he couldn't help the choke in his
throat, the sting of tears in his eyes—and neither could Ione.

"Okay?" Thor had asked, when Ione told him she and Edon were
marrying. "You're with Ma and Ma's Ma, so you are Pa. Ja?"

"*Det ville vaere en aere,*" said Edon. I would be honored.

"Pa, you caught one!"

"I did, didn't I?" said Edon, chuckling as he reeled in his line.

"Too small, though," said Thor, watching as the small perch
flipped back and forth on the line.

"Lucky for you," Edon said to the fish as he released it from the hook and tossed it back in the water.

In the middle of the Ocean, they were in a rowboat. Catching fish was a bonus; the real enjoyment for Edon came simply from being in his stepson's company: in Thor's workroom shed helping him construct his latest birdhouse, in raking leaves with him in the autumn, in playing checkers with him in front of the fire on cold winter nights, in taking a sunset walk with him and Ione along Lake Road. So many moments of ordinary life that filled with a sense of gratefulness and belonging he hadn't felt since Per was alive!

He told Thor things about Per he hadn't thought of in years; he told more stories about his son to his stepson than perhaps he had even told Ione.

"He was popular with the young ladies, and a bit of a rascal, I have to say. One night, Oydis—she was my favorite of all his girlfriends—came storming up to the house, banging on the door calling Per's name, claiming she knew her sister Hella was in there with him. Meanwhile he's sneaking Hella out the back door! Berit and I broke up more than one fight between girls vying for Per's attention!"

Edon described what it was like to watch his son race down a mountain—"He was like a bullet!"—and while he didn't wish harm on Per's competitors, he never minded when they fell; he told how his son would have eaten waffles and cream for every meal if Berit would have let him. He mused how Per might have been an engineer or an inventor had he lived: "That boy took more things apart, and some of them he was even able to put back together!"

Thor's full and quiet attention was a gift: Edon's memories came alive; Per came alive.

"Pa," said Thor now, pointing to the dock where Lewis stood, waving them in.

"Good thing they weren't counting on fish for the birthday dinner tonight," said Edon, regarding the empty bucket.

"Ja," said Thor, picking up the oars. "Good thing."

* * *

In her lifetime, Ione had baked more cakes than she could shake a flour sifter at, but never three at a time, which she was doing the morning of the triplets' fifth birthday. It wasn't the daunting task it would be for nonbakers; they were all simple white sheet cakes, although she had taken color requests as to the buttercream frosting. Sena wanted blue, Grace had asked for yellow, and Ulla wanted pink with purple polka dots.

"Let me taste that," said Edon, watching as Ione dribbled blue food coloring into a small bowl and began mixing it into the frosting.

Ione handed Edon the spoon.

"No," he said. "Put it on your lips and I'll kiss it off." Edon took her in his arms and kissed her.

"Let me see how this one tastes," said Ione, and dipping a finger into another bowl, she swabbed a dab of pink frosting on Edon's lips and pressed her own on top of his.

"MorMor! BopBop!"

Ione and Edon loosened their embrace to regard the owner of the small but indignant voice standing in the kitchen doorway.

"Ulla," said Ione, in a mock strict voice. "Didn't I tell you and your sisters that you had to get out of the kitchen while I make your cakes? I want them to be a surprise."

"I *was* surprised," she said, her smile impish and crooked. "Surprised about you kissing!"

"That's it," said Edon. "Now I'm going to have to get you!"

As he curled his fingers and motored stiff-legged toward the little girl in the monster walk the triplets begged their BopBop daily to assume, Ulla squealed and giggled in equal measure before lurching down the hallway.

It was after the kids' afternoon party that Nora ordered the girls to bed. They did so with minimal complaints, Sena climbing to her top bunk, and Grace and Ulla getting into the bottom bunk, which was a double rather than twin bed.

"Now I know it'll be hard to sleep," said Nora, "but you'll be a lot happier for tonight's party if you do."

"Another party!" said Grace.

"You know that, Gracie," said Sena, leaning over the bed railing. "Tonight's the grown-up party for us."

"Oh yeah," said Grace, her voice dreamy. "I forgot."

"How could you forget more presents?" said Ulla.

"That's right," said their mother. "So be good girls and take a nap so you'll have plenty of energy to open them all."

Leaving the large upstairs bedroom, Nora caught three times more kisses than she threw, and she stood outside the door, which she left open a crack, so as to better eavesdrop. She was quickly rewarded and leaned against the wall, smiling.

"That was the bestest party ever!" said Grace. "I want to play musical chairs *every* day!"

"I liked the beanbag toss," said Sena. "Except when Amanda started crying."

"Amanda's always crying," said Ulla. "And she doesn't like cake! Who doesn't like cake?"

"I *loved* that we had three cakes!" said Grace.

"I *love* birthday parties!" said Ulla. "It was so fun when Uncle Harry made all those balloon animals! I got an elephant!"

"I got an elephant, too," said Sena. "Because that's all Uncle Harry knows how to make."

Ulla chattered on about the party, with waning responses from her sisters.

Grace murmured, "Maybe," when Ulla asked if they didn't think that summertime birthdays were the best of all, "because you get to be outside and it's all sunny and happy," and Sena said, "I don't think it matters," when Ulla offered the opinion that ice cream shouldn't match cake—how chocolate cake goes with vanilla ice cream and how white cake goes with chocolate ice cream.

"And did you see Amber's shoes? I like white shoes, and hers had bows on 'em!"

By the time Ulla was expounding on the game of Pin the Tail on the Donkey and how if she were a donkey she wouldn't want anyone pinning a tail on her, the conversation had narrowed to a monologue, one that Thomas now listened to as well. "Why doesn't the donkey have a tail, anyway? Who took it? Maybe that should be a game—Who Took the Donkey's Tail? A game where you'd have to go to a farm—no, a jungle!—and find out the meanie who took the donkey's tail! I'd play that! Wouldn't you, Sena? . . . Wouldn't you, Grace? . . . Well, I would."

Laughing, the hallway audience of two covered their mouths with their hands, delighted and entertained as only parents can be over the darling geniuses who happen to be their children.

"And why would someone want a donkey's tail, anyway?" continued Ulla, her voice as thoughtful as a young Spinoza. "I'd rather have a pig's tail. They're nice and curly."

Pointing to a roadside drive-in with a sun-blistered sign reading "The Dairy Barn," Lewis asked, "Can we stop there?"

"Already have my blinker on," said Clyde Chuka, turning into the lot.

Scrambling out of the van, Harry said, "We'll go in and order. What do you want, Dad?"

"How about a sundae," said Clyde, leaning on his right hip to better extract his wallet from his left hip pocket.

"No, no, treat's on me," said Harry. "What flavor?"

"Butterscotch," he said and watched as his son raced to the diner with the boy who was like a son.

"I am so glad to be home," said Harry, when they were back in the van with their spoils. "So glad I got to see the face of Kaley."

"Her name was Karlie," said Lewis.

Harry waved his hand. "What's in a name? She was a *babe.*"

"What is with you and girls who work in ice-cream parlors?" asked Clyde, trolling his red plastic spoon along the sticky moat of butterscotch surrounding the mound of ice cream.

"Yeah," said Lewis. "Remember Heidi from the Frostee Freeze?"

"Heidi the Heartbreaker," said Harry, his voice forlorn. "Don't remind me."

Clyde finished his sundae in short order, but Harry and Lewis were still working on the large shakes that could have rightfully been billed as gargantuan.

"So," said Clyde, merging back onto the old county road. "What were we talking about before we were so rudely interrupted by ice cream?"

"The winning painting," said Harry. "Lewis was saying how he didn't like it."

"Oh, yes," said Clyde. Offering a summer arts program at several schools, Clyde had taken Harry and Lewis to an exhibition of his students' work on the Red Lake Indian Reservation. "And why was that, Lewis?"

"I don't think it was very good." He took a long slurp of his shake. "And it made me sad."

"If I agreed with the second part of your sentence—and I do, it made me feel sad, too—then I'd have to disagree with the first part of your sentence."

Exasperated by Clyde's answer, Lewis turned to Harry, stretched out in the seat behind him. "Didn't you think it looked like it was painted by a five-year-old?"

"Quite, quite," said Harry, in a pompous voice, "the technique—primitive indeed. But if art is supposed to make you feel, then, old chap, I'd say it was a very successful piece of art."

Clyde looked in the rearview mirror at his son and winked, saying, "He's got you there, Lewis."

The painting that flummoxed Lewis—and the one winning a blue ribbon in the juried competition—was a self-portrait called *Real Me* and featured a smiley face whose bright yellow color was barely visible under a wash of gray paint.

"But it was so simple," said Lewis, continuing his critique, as they bumped along a potholed road. "A smiley face! You talk so much about technique, Clyde—and there was no technique there!"

"He's got you there, Mr. Chuka," said Harry. "Are you saying in art that feeling is more important than technique?"

"What do you think?" asked Clyde.

Dropping the Thurston Howell accent, Harry leaned forward and said, "In music, I'd have to say technique definitely comes first, and then feeling because I know if I don't practice, the music's shitty."

Harry, who that fall would begin his junior year at UC–Santa

Barbara as a music major, played drums in a jazz band and guitar in an alternative rock band and knew what he was talking about.

"But don't you think you can listen to a very good technician," said Clyde, "and still be unmoved by the music?"

Harry pondered this while he sipped his chocolate shake. "Yeah, but even if you've got all the soul in the world, if you can't play the notes, you can't express the music."

"I would say that's what every artist wants," said Clyde, "that their skill be worthy of what their soul wants to express."

That night, listening to his grandmother snore, Lewis contemplated the conversation they had in the van. Clyde had said that what he liked most about teaching was giving his students the permission to express themselves, because "some people feel they don't deserve what's innate in us—the desire to create, to *make* something."

Was that true? Lewis wondered. What did his mother like to make, besides herself scarce? Or excuses? What was it she felt she didn't deserve to make?

Right now Sal was in Wisconsin—at least that's where she said she was going—with her latest boyfriend, her return date not established. "I'll be back when I'm back," she had told Lewis, while her boyfriend waited in an idling pickup truck outside, its loose muffler rattling its impatience.

A gasp interrupted his grandmother's snore, but it roared back seconds later. Looking at her, Lewis felt a flicker of anger. Asleep more hours than she was awake, what did his grandmother make? Harry's grandmother was a lot older than Lewis's, but Ione made all sorts of things—from the best banana bread and gingerbread cookies in the world, to handmade gifts of hats, mittens, and a sweater that matched one she'd knitted for Thor. And Thor—look at him and his birdhouses! Lewis had spent hours and hours in Thor's workshop, helping him build birdhouses that were, as Clyde called them, "beautiful, functional art."

So many things to make, thought Lewis, staring up at the ceiling, whose water stain looked like a boomerang or a giant lima bean. *Make art, make believe, make certain, make do, make enemies . . .*

Last February, he had advanced to the regionals on his debate team. The night before the competition, after dinner at the Blue Moon (he ate more dinners there than he did at home), Clyde Chuka and Patty Jane walked him home, not because he needed an escort but because they liked to. The night was chalky with gray clouds and ice bordered the edges of the road, and they whispered as they walked, because their regular voices seemed too loud in the still winter air. Nervous about the debate, Lewis confessed to sleeping poorly.

"This is what helps me sometimes," said Patty Jane, whose hand was tucked into the crook of his right arm, Clyde's into his left. "I make lists. Alphabetical lists. About anything. About names— Anastasia, Beatrice, Colleen . . . about cities—Akron, Baltimore, Cincinnati . . . about food—Artichokes, brisket, corn—"

"—brisket?" Lewis asked. "What's brisket?"

He had taken up the habit, not only as an alternative to counting sheep but whenever he wanted to play with a thought or idea. *Make fun, make gravy, make hay, make ice, make jokes, make—k* was hard: he was going to have to punt this one—*make kingdoms, make love, make money (or music, or magic, or movies; m was easy), make noise, make out* (Belinda Fuller's pretty face flashed in his head when he thought of this one), *make pictures, make queries* (his English teacher was fond of the word *query*), *make roads, make sense, make time, make up, make victory, make war, make X-rays* (what else?), *make your best shot* (lame, but it beat *yams*), *make zzzzs . . .*

But Lewis wasn't sleepy.

He stared at his grandmother. While his mother was flashy and liked to be noticed, his grandmother was the opposite, quiet and reserved to the point of apology. But as different as their approaches to life, both of them ultimately seemed to have given up. Lewis knew it had never been easy for them—how many times had Sal told him so, with both his mother and grandmother being abandoned by the rat bastards who'd fathered their children. Still, why would they choose to get stuck the way they had?

Grunting, his grandmother shifted in her sleep.

Maybe it was because they didn't have what Lewis always had, a *belief* in himself. He didn't know where it came from, but he'd always had confidence, impervious to circumstances, a confidence that had bloomed with the help of the people at the lodge, who among the many things they made was a place for him.

"But you have, too, Grandma," Lewis whispered, patting the sleeping woman's stockinged foot. A wave of sadness rose in him, but instead of crashing, it receded as a thought occurred to him.

"Grandma!" he said, "you make me laugh!" It was true, when she was awake she would make little asides, often nearly inaudible, as if she felt they didn't deserve volume, sarcastic one-liners about the television shows they watched, sly ripostes to something Sal or a news commentator said. And inevitably—when he could hear them—they cracked Lewis up.

"And Grandma, that is an awesome thing to make!"

⇉ 24

GRACE AND ULLA WERE IDENTICAL TWINS who'd inherited Nora's blond Nordic looks; by the age of five, they were three inches taller than Sena, who was dark-haired and favored in size her biological father (or as Nora thought of him, the sperm donor in the tent).

"Those two look just like you!" was something not just Nora, but Thomas, heard over and over about Grace and Ulla with the surprised winked addendum, "But that one! Are you sure she's yours?" The thing was, for Thomas the small, dark-haired, blue-eyed eldest triplet was absolutely his. He loved all three girls, with a fullness that sometimes caused him to splay his big hand over his heart, but Sena . . . he had ushered Sena into the world.

"It's not that I love her more than the others," he confessed to Nora several days after their wedding as they'd stood over the three cribs like sentinels. "It's just that . . . she's the one I was there for. The one who went from inside of you and right into my hands."

"Thomas," said Nora, after a silence so long that even the new moon shining a strip of white on the lake wondered if it was time to wane and let the sun come up, "it doesn't matter to me if you love Sena more because . . . well, because I don't think you'd ever show it. That you've married me, that you've agreed these girls are yours, how can I doubt any feeling you have? How can I not think you're a superhero who'll always do right?"

Thomas's arm tightened around her waist. "I'm not a superhero. And I won't always do right. I'll feel good if I do right half the time."

Nora pushed her hip, padded with baby weight, against his.

"Oh, I'll bet you'll do right at least 60 percent of the time."

"I'll try never to play favorites," said Thomas, solemnly.

"How'd I get so lucky?" Nora wondered, but she must have said it out loud because Thomas, looking down at the three bundles sleeping in their cribs, corrected her.

"*We*," he said. "How did we get so lucky."

Luck didn't last when it came to adding to the family. "Why can't I keep your child?" Nora wailed three years into their marriage, after suffering her second miscarriage. "Why do I keep failing you?"

"Failing me?" said Thomas, holding his wife close to him. "How can you ever think you're failing me?"

"But you deserve a child of your own!"

Nora was jostled as Thomas slid upward, resting his back against the pillowed headboard.

"Nora, I *have* three of my own! If one more came from my own sperm, *herlig*—wonderful!—but I don't consider it a necessary credential for being a real father." The tenderness in his voice was darkened with irritation. "Why can't you believe that?" He believed that, but still, holding her as she cried, his wistful thought, *It would have been nice*, brought a tear to his own eye. Impatiently, he thumbed it away. "And didn't I ever tell you?" he said, trying to extricate his arm, numb and prickly from the weight of Nora's head, "that crossed eyes run in my family? And pattern baldness—especially in our women? And don't make me tell you of all my relatives jailed for public lewdness."

After school, the girls got off the school bus the same way they got on; Sena first, Ulla in the middle, and Grace at the end. This was their usual order, the one they fell in naturally, with no thought or preplanning, the one that protected Ulla, if she needed protection. Her walk was pigeon-toed and she limped slightly, favoring her right side. Her left arm and hand were curled and would flail up suddenly, as if she were at a town hall meeting adding an exuberant Aye vote.

According to the pediatric specialists they consulted, her brain function was not affected, and her cerebral palsy was considered mild.

"She'll never be a professional athlete," said one doctor, "but how many of us are? She may tire faster than her sisters, but so what? She'll take a few more naps. If I were you, I wouldn't treat her any differently from the other two. She'll be fine." The doctor had been right about the diagnosis, but not about Ulla tiring faster than her sisters. She was the first one up—occasionally beating the sun—and the first one to decide that daily naps "are for babies, and I'm not a baby."

Sena, by virtue of being the oldest, was the self-proclaimed boss of the trio, but Ulla was the idea girl, the one who could talk the other two into mischief and mayhem. She was the one who kept up the bedtime conversation, even after her sisters had fallen asleep, the one who thought it would be fun to paint their daddy's toenails while he napped on the big couch, the one who taunted their BopBop to be a monster and chase them and when he finally did, arms extended, footsteps heavy, screamed the loudest.

And a week into her career as a kindergartner, she was the one who came home with a note from the teacher:

> *Dear Dr. and Mrs. Strand,*
>
> *I am so excited to have the triplets in my kindergarten class! I look forward to getting to know all three of them as the super children they are! One thing I must bring up, though, is a little incident we had with Ulla and a boy named Noah. I didn't witness the incident, as it took place during recess when the children have the run of the playground, but Noah came up to me crying, claiming that Ulla hit him. Ulla and her sisters claimed that Noah was calling Ulla bad names.*
>
> *She said that she didn't mean to hit him, but that sometimes "my hand flies up by accident and he might have gotten in the way."*
>
> *Dr. and Mrs. Strand, rest assured that I will not tolerate bullying in my class and have had a talk with Noah, and I've sent home a note with him as well. I have also had a talk with Ulla and have told*

her hitting in class is not allowed, and I did not believe her excuse about her hand flying up.

Feel free to contact me with any concerns.

Sincerely,

Ms. Laurie McLaughlin

"Can I go back?" asked Ulla, her blue-green eyes filled with tears she hadn't yet given permission to fall.

"Go back where?" asked Nora.

"Back to kindergarten!" Now the tears were given the signal "Full speed ahead!" and complied, streaming down the little girl's cheeks.

"Oh, Ulla," said Nora, gathering up her daughter in her arms. "Of course you can go back to kindergarten."

"But Teacher doesn't like me! She thinks I'm bad!"

"No, honey, she doesn't think you're bad. She just wants to make sure no one gets hurt in her class. That there's no hitting."

"But that boy made his arm go like this!" Here Ulla demonstrated by flailing her good arm. "He kept doing that and calling me, 'Retard-o, Retard-o!'"

"He did, Mama," said Sena.

After Ulla had handed her mother the note, Nora asked the other girls to leave the room; she wanted a little private time with Ulla. Both Sena and Grace had left the kitchen, but they were pulled back by the invisible towrope of their curiosity and concern and stood in the door's threshold.

"He was mean and had to stop saying those things," said Grace.

"You should write Teacher back and tell her those things!" said Sena.

"That's a good idea," said Nora. "Let's all write a letter to Ms. McLaughlin."

It started out as a serious endeavor, the girls clustered around Nora, watching as she wrote out the date and the words *Dear Ms. McLaughlin* on the pretty stationery Patty Jane and Ione continued to buy even as the world moved toward electronic communication. For the girls' benefit, she read aloud the words she wrote:

"Thank you for telling me about the problem at school today."

"Why are you thanking her?" asked Sena.

"Well, because parents appreciate when teachers let them know what's going on in their classroom."

"This wasn't in the classroom," said Ulla. "This was outside, at recess."

Pressing her lips to stanch her smile, Nora tapped her pen to paper.

"How about this?" she said as she wrote. "*Ulla feels bad about hitting Noah.*"

"No, I don't!"

"Mommy, write that Noah's a big meanie who shouldn't call Ulla names!" said Grace. "No, write to Noah and tell him that!"

"But he can't read!" said Sena.

"But if he could," said Nora, "what would you say to him?"

"That he's a big poopie head!" said Ulla.

The girls laughed.

"A big *stinky* poopie head," said Sena.

"Yeah, Noah," said Grace, "why are you such a big stinky poopie head?"

"Yeah, Noah," said Sena, "why are you such a big stinky *icky* poopie head?"

"Okay, girls," said Nora, remembering how often teachable moments with the trips could turn into a free-for-all.

"No, a big stinky icky *yucky* poopie head!" corrected Ulla and again the girls howled.

"How about if I write this down?" said Nora, and as her pen moved across the page, she said, "*Maybe you're a poopie head because someone's been a poopie head to you.*"

Sensing playtime was over, the girls reluctantly quieted.

"Maybe," said Nora, still writing, "*maybe you say mean things because someone says mean things to you a lot. Maybe you hear mean things more than you hear nice things.*"

"Jeremy told Noah he couldn't sit next to him at Circle," said Sena. "Jeremy said he was saving a place for Liam."

"Is Liam the one with the Ninja Turtles T-shirt?" said Grace. "I like that T-shirt."

"I like the stickers on Amanda's backpack," said Ulla.

"We've got lots of stickers," Sena reminded them. "Let's put 'em on *our* backpacks!"

The letter forgotten, the girls raced off to accessorize their accessories, and Nora sat back in her chair, feeling both exhausted and exhilarated. With triplets, it was an odd but not unusual tandem of emotions.

⇶ 25

THE FAMILY HOME ON NAWADAHA BOULEVARD, in which the original Patty Jane's House of Curl had opened its doors, was now a pied-à-terre, a crash pad for those who'd lived there for decades. After the triplets were born, their grandparents and great-grandparents migrated north to the Once in a Blue Moon Lodge on a more permanent basis rather than a seasonal one. For his bigger pieces, Clyde worked at his studio in Minneapolis, but he found he could build his smaller ones sharing space in Thor's shed. He and Patty Jane attended art and social events at least once a week in the Twin Cities, occasionally spending the night in their old bedroom, but more often than not they made their visits day-trips, not wanting to miss out on the fun, chaos, and life of a household filled with three little girls.

While she still taught her Saturday guitar class at the Blue Moon, Silvia spent the workweek in the Twin Cities, the house's main resident/caretaker. She was employed at a hair salon in the hip Uptown area, but she only worked part-time; her real job, as far as she and Patty Jane were concerned, was finishing her degree in psychology at the University of Minnesota.

"I . . . I can't accept that," Silvia had said several years earlier, when Patty Jane offered to pay for her education. "Once I'm here for a year, I'll get in-state tuition and—"

"—I admire your work ethic, Silvia, but I know you've always wanted to continue your education. And I'd love to invest in it."

"But why?" said Silvia.

"Because the returns are so great—for all involved."

"Psychology!" Harry had said to her over the phone. "Why not major in music?"

"Because I know music. It's people I need to learn more about. Besides, I'll be minoring in musical theater."

"Musical theater?" said Harry, disdain evident in his voice.

"I was in *Oklahoma* and *Guys and Dolls* in high school—have you ever *heard* any of those songs? 'Oh, What a Beautiful Morning'? 'People Will Say We're in Love'? 'Sit Down, You're Rockin' the Boat'? 'Luck Be a—'"

She was interrupted by Harry's loud snore.

After playing together for Nora and Ione's double wedding, a respect for one another's musicality had been forged, and it deepened whenever they jammed together, which was anytime Harry was home on school holidays, first from Braddock and now college. Their friendship had deepened as well, and while music was a constant topic in their long meandering telephone conversations ("Hey, listen to this!" was a common prelude to playing each other pieces of songs they were writing), so were teachers, classes, fellow students, and current romances. Harry fell hard for girls, but their relationships never seemed to last long, and Silvia had been dating a transfer student from Baltimore who was nice enough but didn't like the band Nirvana.

"Then dump him!" said Harry, who personally thought Kurt Cobain was, if not a god, then at least a shaman, and who had called Silvia in tears upon hearing the news of his suicide.

Two boys in Harry's graduating class at Braddock were now professional hockey players, one a New York Ranger, the other a Winnipeg Jet, living the life that headlined in all of their school teammates' dreams, including Harry's. He was a good player—quick and smart on the ice—but he wasn't a great player, and in his senior year when he broke his wrist, Harry had an epiphany: he loved hockey, but he loved music more. The joy of speed or making a great play or dekeing out a goalie mattered, but music mattered more. When he thought how a different injury to his hands could have compromised what he loved most, he decided he didn't want to play college hockey. It freed him up when it came to school selection, and the lure of UC–Santa Barbara's music program as well as shorts and sandals in January made it an easy decision to head west.

He was in two bands, drumming for the school's concert jazz band and pinch-hitting on drums and guitar in the Royal Mongrels, a band he and some dormmates formed. His daily life was infused with music, from theory and composition classes to practice to performances; by his sophomore year, Harry knew that when he was finished with school, he was moving to Los Angeles to play music/ earn a record contract/fill international stadiums with thousands of fans. It was a plan he frequently discussed with Silvia, but by his senior year, a plan once so resolute began to bobble and waver, finally collapsing after his graduation party at the Blue Moon.

Silvia seemed so different to him now. Had she always smelled that good? Had her black hair always been that shiny? And why hadn't he noticed that funny little dimple that appeared under the left corner of her lip when she smiled? Silvia, too, was surprised at the man Harry had become, and their three-year age difference, once seeming like a canyon, had narrowed to a crevasse.

When she played "On His Way," a song she had written in Harry's honor, it immediately replaced Nirvana's "Come as You Are" as his favorite song.

"Why didn't I think of writing you a song when you graduated?" Harry asked later. He and Silvia were in the lodge's basement game room, everyone else having taken off their party hats and gone to bed.

"Well, I wish I could say it was my idea," said Silvia. "But it was your mom's."

"I hope she paid you for it."

"Ha! I'm still trying to figure out how to pay her back for all she's done for me." Flushing at Harry's intent gaze, Silvia strummed the strings of her guitar. "If you had written a song for me, what would it sound like?"

Rising to the challenge, Harry picked up another guitar, and after laying out a melody line, the two began improvising a song celebrating Silvia's psychology degree. The lyrics rhymed *Freud* with *toyed* and *void, Jung* with *clung* and *dung*. It was after Silvia in her honeyed voice had sung, "Is free will really an illusion, Dr. Skinner?" with Harry answering, "If so, do I get to choose what I get for dinner?" that they smiled (Silvia flashing that funny little dimple) and set down their instruments so their arms were free to grab one another.

"I saw that one coming a mile away," said Patty Jane.

"Me, too," said Nora. "Any time Harry mentioned Silvia's name, his voice would change."

"Mom, watch!" said Sena, a request that had been shouted at least a dozen times since the triplets had run out onto the dock. From the narrow sand beach, Nora waved to indicate that yes, she was watching, and Sena dove into the Ocean.

"Grandma, look!" said Grace. She bent over, arms outstretched with biceps touching her ears, but unable or afraid to complete the dive, she jumped in instead.

In the water, Thomas laughed. "Try again, Gracie."

"And when Silvia played that song she wrote for him, uffda!" said Ione. She swatted at a horsefly. "That was a love song if ever I heard one."

Patty Jane laughed. "I had asked her to write him a graduation song. A song about what's next."

"I guess Silvia is," said Nora.

Harry played drums in Vinyl Vortex, a cover band popular in Twin Cities bars and beyond, occasionally traveling for weekend gigs in cities throughout the five-state area ("Bismarck is where it's at!" he wrote on one postcard to Nora, and another to his grandmother read, "Two sold-out shows in Milwaukee!"), but he felt his best music was made as half of a duo. The musical duo Harry and Silvia began to perform their original songs at coffee shop open-mic nights, and after just two performances the manager of Grounds to Arrest gave them a regular slot.

He and Silvia were living in the original House of Curl, and Harry told his mother, "Ma, I love her as much as I love playing music with her. She makes me want to not just be a better musician but to be a better person."

"He found his pilot light," Patty Jane whispered to Clyde Chuka when they, along with Ione and Edon, squeezed around a small wobbly table at Grounds to Arrest and listened to Harry and Silvia harmonize on a song they'd written called "Why Not?"

"Why not jump in even if the water's too cold? Why not do the things we won't regret when we're old?"

Their set was enthusiastically applauded, and not just by the four family members. After they cleared the stage of their amps and guitars, Harry and Silvia joined them at the small wobbly table.

"What's going on?" Patty Jane asked, as the room began to crowd with people.

"It's the Thursday Night Poetry Slam," Harry explained. "Wanna stay for it?"

His parents and grandparents averred that they would.

The emcee, a slight young man with long wavy hair who was wearing what looked like his great-great-grandfather's frock coat, stepped onstage. After nearly hyperventilating during a speech on the power of poetry, he explained that several audience members would be serving as judges.

"Doctors!" yelled the first poet up. "Can you help? Can you write out a prescription to eradicate/erase/expel/excise/alleviate/ameliorate/anesthetize this faulty/fragmented/fatuous/fucked-up body that once knew how to love?"

"Uffda," whispered Ione to Edon.

The judges gave numerical ratings of the performances, and in Patty Jane's opinion it was clear they were easy graders. "Of course," she said, after a morose young woman expounded in jerky rhyme her inability to appreciate appreciation, "maybe I'm just too old to get it."

"Art's supposed to be age-adverse," said Clyde, and Patty Jane leaned to kiss the cheek of her wise man.

They listened to poems about speckled notebooks, a dog named

Tim, soul shrinkage, and "my Mother's toffee bars" (Ione visibly perked up when this title was announced); they listened to poems about loneliness, injustice, and grape popsicles. The Lord Byronesque emcee announced that all the thirteen signed-up poets had spoken but if there were any free spirits out there who'd like to lend their voice to this poetic choir, they were welcome to come onstage now.

There was a long pause, but just as the emcee said, "Well then, judges, let's—" Edon stood up and walked to the stage. As they turned toward one another, Ione's blue eyes were as wide as Patty Jane's hazel-green ones. Harry and Silvia pulverized each other's hand with squeezes.

Clyde Chuka folded his arms across his chest and chuckled.

Taking the mic from the emcee he dwarfed, Edon said, "My woman."

The audience hooted, laughed, and whistled at the tall white-haired man onstage.

"My woman," Edon repeated to the audience, most of which could be his grandchildren or great-grandchildren. "She is the sun. For too long she was eclipsed—at least to me. An eternity I stood, searching the dark skies for her. Dark, cloudy, troubled skies. But now, now she shines full and bright on my world, on me. Shine on, my sun, shine on, my woman, shine on!" He bunched up his lips and nodded once, signaling the poem's end, and walked off the stage. The applause was thunderous. All three judges held up their number-ten placards.

Outside, walking them to their car, Harry asked Edon what inspired him to get up onstage and improvise a love poem to Ione. "Well, it's the anniversary of my son Per's birthday," said Edon. "And Ione has taught me to celebrate it." He beamed at his wife. "I didn't know I was going to do it by making up a poem! But then that young girl—the one with all the rings in her ears—recited that poem about the dead heart."

"Now that was depressing," said Patty Jane.

"That's what I thought," said Edon. "I didn't like that poem, how it sounded as if she had given up on everything. She's too young to have given up on *anything*, especially love."

"Next time I'll get up onstage," said Ione. "And make up a poem about you."

She said something in Norwegian, causing the two of them to laugh and Clyde Chuka to request that they share the joke. "All right," said Edon, and he laughed again. "Ione said she would call her poem 'Eve Was in Her Eden but My Edon's Been in Me.'"

A bell jar of silence clapped over them, tipped over seconds later by a burst of laughter.

"Ione," said Patty Jane, and in her voice there was awe and respect. "I'm shocked."

"It's about time you're on the receiving end," said Ione.

"So you think they're still *doing* it?" Nora asked when Harry, at the Lodge for the weekend, related the story to her.

"Sure sounds like it!"

The two siblings stared at one another before bursting out laughing and kept laughing in between jokes. It was when Nora wondered about their eligibility into the *Guinness Book of World Records* for Oldest Recorded Couple Making Whoopee that Ione entered the kitchen.

Their laughter flash-froze as the emotional temperature of the room plummeted.

"Making whoopee," said Iona, heading toward the coffeemaker. "Isn't that what they used to say on that game show we'd watched together, Nora, that *Newlywed* one?"

Nora nodded, her face hot.

"So will you help me contact those *Guinness* people?" she asked, sitting at the table, coffee cup filled. "That would be quite an honor to be acknowledged by them."

"Grandma, I'm so sorry," said Nora. "We were just—"

"—just goofing off," said Harry, who wore the same flush of embarrassment as his sister. "It was stupid, but we—"

Ione held up a hand. "You don't have to explain anything. I can see where you'd find the subject . . . amusing. Certainly, Edon and I do."

Shame over their grandmother's graciousness made both Nora and Harry offer more apologies and Ione, sipping her coffee, listened as they spoke over one another.

"With you two, I don't have many regrets," she said after the excuses and apologies had finally petered out. "I have had honor— *been* honored—that you have let me into your lives so much, confiding in me, asking my advice. I'm glad you have a mother you can talk to about things you might not want to talk to me about—I've often wondered if *anything* is off limits to Patty Jane! And Harry, I'm sure Clyde also is not afraid to answer any questions of a sex nature."

Taking another sip of coffee, Ione grimaced and said, "This has been in the pot too long. I'll make another."

"Let me," said Nora, as she pushed herself away from the table. Ready to make any kind of amends, she would have regrouted the bathroom tile if Ione asked her. Harry glared at her, thinking the same thing, but not acting as quickly.

Ione laughed, seeing Harry's reaction.

"Ja, sure, when I get started on the subject of sex, suddenly both of you are not so comfortable."

"It . . . it's not that, Grandma," said Harry. "It's just that we—"

Looking to his sister at the counter, he raised his voice. "I'm speaking for the both of us, Nora."

"Please do," said Nora, dumping the remaining bitter coffee into the sink.

Harry reached across the table and took his grandmother's hands.

"It's just . . . well, we're sorry. We don't ever want you thinking that we're making fun of you."

"There's a place for making fun."

She smiled, but there was a glint of tears in her eyes.

"Nora," said Harry, feeling helpless. "She's crying!"

Racing over, Nora squatted next to Ione, wrapping one arm around the old woman.

"Grandma, what's wrong?"

"I'm fine," said Ione, dabbing her eyes. "I just—" She waved her hand, indicating Nora sit back in her chair. When she did, Ione continued. "Since *you* brought the subject of my sex life up, I'm going to tell you some things, not to embarrass you—or me—but, well, who knows, maybe you'll learn something."

Feeling his face heat up again, Harry looked down, finding the salt and pepper shakers suddenly interesting. Nora, on the other hand, could look nowhere but at her grandmother, staring into her eyes as if under a spell.

"Edon and I," began Ione, her own eyes on the wedding band that she twirled around her finger. "We were robbed of years, *decades,* together. No doubt, if we had been together all that time, we would have enjoyed a . . . quite a sex life. We were crazy for one another, and I cannot tell you how much I regretted, no, *mourned* that we did not share our bodies when we first knew each other. I wanted to, I planned to, but then, well . . . then came Berit's big lie that wrecked everything." Her chest rose and lowered in a long sigh. "Now that we're together, why, if I could, I'd light off fireworks every day to celebrate. The wonder of being with my heart's desire again, well, sometimes I still can't believe it. But our bodies aren't what they used to be. We've—"

Her hesitation was long, but Nora and Harry said nothing. "We've tried and have succeeded, at . . . joining them, but Mother Nature hasn't been so . . . so obliging. Why does she turn off the hormones? You would think that she would save the juiciest, lustiest time for old age, when people don't have the worries of pregnancy!" A part of Nora wanted to laugh, but it seemed she had devolved into a primate and was capable of only sitting, hunched, gaping at her grandmother. Her brother, too, stared at Ione in the same chimp-like pose.

"So ja, now Edon and I are trying to make up for lost time with bodies that don't want to cooperate so much. But more than the"— here she panted hard several times, causing both Nora and Harry to gape—"wild sex, we have the closeness, which sometimes can be even more wild. Mostly, we sleep without pajamas so that his skin is always close to mine, and my skin is always close to his."

Both Nora and Harry were open-mouthed, shocked by the candor with which their grandmother addressed a never before discussed topic. Not knowing what to say in the silence they sat in, Harry finally said the word that encapsulated everything that they all were thinking: "Uffda."

➤➤ 26

"H E'S JUST LIKE ME," Ulla said.

Lying on her belly, Grace kept her eyes on the television as she asked, "Who is?"

"Bugs Bunny!"

"How is Bugs Bunny like you?" Sena asked impatiently. "He's a *rabbit*."

The six-year-old girls were sprawled over a pile of pillows, watching a Loony Tunes video their Uncle Harry had given them.

"I know he's a rabbit," said Ulla, "a rabbit who's always got someone after him: Elmer Fudd."

"I don't like Elmer Fudd," said Grace. "Why doesn't he leave Bugs Bunny alone?"

"That's just what I mean!" said Ulla. "Elmer Fudd never leaves him alone! That's why Bugs Bunny and me are so much alike!"

Sena sighed, as she often did when one of her more fanciful sisters said or did something that wasn't clear, that she had to guess at.

"They're cartoons, Ulla, so you can't really be like them." She rolled her eyes, punctuating her argument. "And nobody's after you with a gun."

"I know nobody's after me with a gun!"

"I'd be scared if they were!" said Grace, worried.

"What I mean is"—sitting up, Ulla hugged a pillow to her chest— "is that Elmer Fudd's like my CP! Always bothering me, always after me, never just leaving me alone!" For emphasis, she threw the couch pillow, but at the same time her arm flailed so instead of crashing against the far wall, the pillow flopped to the floor.

"See?" she asked. "See? Elmer Fudd won't even let me throw right!"

Inky Kolstat was not one to resist technology, especially when it allowed her to do more of what she loved, which was to watch old movies. She had been a faithful viewer of whatever late shows or afternoon matinee played these classics on TV, but now with her VCR and the local video store, she could rent *Mildred Pierce* or *It Happened One Night* or *The Maltese Falcon* and watch them at 2 p.m. or a.m.

Breakfasting one morning on black coffee, raisin toast, and *Double Indemnity*, she wondered if life could get any better. The answer was that it couldn't, or at least wouldn't, since the surprised "Oh!" that she expelled was not a comment on the scheming Barbara Stanwyck but a response to a pain that landed like a cleaver in the center of her chest and pitched her forward onto the table. Her neighbor and landlord found her there hours later, when Inky failed to show up for their afternoon cribbage match, and after calling 911, the woman nervously finished the remaining slice of raisin toast.

The House of Curl regulars, who'd made up the majority of attendees, wandered around the vast, parklike Lakewood Cemetery after Inky's brief graveside service.

"I'm surprised there wasn't some kind of reception," said Karen Spaeth.

"Well, you saw the size of her family," said Crabby. "My God, one nephew and one grandniece! At least I can count on my seven brothers and sisters and their pack of kids and grandkids to show up for my funeral! And wouldn't it give my sister-in-law Fern a good excuse to throw a big reception in the fancy house she just loves to show off!" After a moment of silence, Crabby apologized. "God Almighty, that sounded a little harsh, even for me. I'm just . . . sad."

"Me, too," said Ione. "I'll miss her."

Patty Jane's mouth twisted in a funny smile. "Remember that seminar she had on leading men? She and Alva Bundt just about got into a fistfight over who had more sex appeal, Clark Gable or Tyrone Power."

"And Alva gone now, too," said Ione wistfully.

"Ladies, look," said Marvel Stang, stopping in front of an imposing monument. "Mars. That's the candy bar guy."

"There're a lot of dignitaries buried here," said Evelyn Bright. "Politicians, artists, athletes, Charles Lindbergh . . . even Tiny Tim!" They walked a little farther, stopping to read tombstones, until Crabby complained that her feet hurt and Marvel said her hip was acting up.

"Age," said Karen Spaeth, as they headed back to the parking lot. "*Ce n'est pas pour les poules mouillées.*"

When Crabby looked at her, irritated, she translated: "Age isn't for sissies."

"And it's not for *you*, either," said Marvel, as she looked at Patty Jane. "I mean, look at you! We're the same age, and I've got about forty pounds on you, three times the wrinkles, plus my hip aches all the time!"

"Well, I do put in a good walk every day," said Patty Jane. "At least five miles."

"And what about Ione?" Evelyn Bright asked the others. "Honestly, I can't keep up with you, and I'm nine years younger!"

"I like to keep active, too," said Ione with a shrug, feeling like she owed them an apology.

"It isn't fair!" huffed Crabby.

"You're right," said Patty Jane, the group's bad mood settling on her like an acid rain. "It isn't fair. You all know my history—neither of my parents lived to old age, and neither did my sister. But hey, excuse me for beating my genetics."

What went unsaid, and what she'd learned by example from Ione, is that what helped in getting older was not obsessing over it and not complaining about it. She had heard Ione's groans when she got up from a chair and had seen her walk hunched over until her limbs warmed up, but she had never heard Ione complain about stiff joints or sore hips. Patty Jane wasn't especially vain, but she had always liked what she saw in the mirror and had learned that she still liked it, especially when she wasn't wearing her reading glasses and couldn't see in sharp detail the sags and wrinkles.

And as they walked in silence past white monuments and gravestones, Ione didn't express to the group that she and Edon, having lost so many years of being together, had made a vow to turn back the clock, to not get older together, but to get younger together. "Why not?" she had said after relaying this to Patty Jane. "Why not boss Time around for a change?"

When they reached the parking lot, the four Minneapolis residents said their good-byes to the two who had driven down from Charleyville.

"By the way," said Crabby, opening the passenger side door of Evelyn's car, "Inky and Alva didn't argue about Clark Gable and Tyrone Power. They argued about Clark Gable and Ray Milland."

Monsieur Mel, the owner of the Charleyville Cinema, had become the Blue Moon's version of Inky Kolstat, although his seminars on French directors and the auteur movement had a little more scholarship and a lot less gossip than Inky's. He did have what Inky could have only dreamed about: his own theater in which he could screen movies that were the subject of his lectures.

The Once in a Blue Moon Lodge was thriving. Elise's ballroom dancing classes were so popular that she and her two children had relocated from Minneapolis to Charleyville, a move that had made sense when Bob the Bookseller became her dance student, her boyfriend, her fiancé, her husband, and then the father of her third child, a boy named Will.

Vergie Hakkila, another Ocean cabin owner, in her pickling seminars had the personal charisma of a snapping turtle, and in her class evaluations, students wrote things like, "Would it hurt for the teacher to look her students in the eye maybe at least once?" or "Wasn't a laugh riot, but her sauerkraut's dynamite!" Her classes were always booked to capacity, often with return students, who loved the free samples of pungent vegetables Vergie would cheerlessly dole out to demonstrate brine and spice combinations.

Ellen Harug, whom Nora had met the first time she ate at Ma's, taught advanced (Norwegian sweaters), intermediate (hats and mittens), and beginning (scarves) knitting classes, the latter attended by mostly children, including the triplets. Thomas had rigged up a brace that stabilized Ulla's flailing hand, and her stitches were only slightly more uneven or dropped than her sisters'.

Ione and Edon were regular attendees of the Wednesday evening Investment Club meeting helmed by Ellen's husband, Kent, a former insurance man.

"We've got to invest wisely for our old age," Ione joked.

"Ja," said Edon. "Because some day it'll be here."

Lewis's fellow Boy Scouts (Clyde had signed him up and helped out with the troop meetings when he was in town) were the enthusiastic students of Thor's Saturday morning woodworking class, a class that Lewis not only participated in but acted as coteacher of, giving more detailed narration to Thor's demonstrations.

Nora scheduled all the classes and seminars for the lodge, occasionally using the power of her position to launch a class or event that would have special appeal to herself or her children. When the triplets were toddlers, she began the very popular Playtime for Kids and Moms, a twice-weekly class that had the children playing under the supervision of a retired Montessori teacher while the mothers discussed topics ranging from bedwetting, biting, allergy scares, the Atkins Diet versus Weight Watchers, Bill Clinton's and their own husbands' sex appeal, dream analysis (Why did Albert Einstein *and* the Pillsbury Doughboy make frequent appearances in Katy McIntyre's dreams?), and the poisons that threatened everyone and everything—from drinking water to microwavable plastic to toddlers' nonflammable pajamas. When their children started school, the mothers continued to meet, although less frequently, their topics reflecting their life's changes: kids' reading problems, favorite teachers, classroom bullying as well as marital and fertility problems (including Nora, three out of the nine regulars had suffered miscarriages, and Julie Orman had filed for divorce). At one meeting, ground coffee massages were mentioned as a viable cellulite cure; three women tried them later at home but no one noticed a substantial difference in skin texture, although Sheila Walker claimed it made her thighs jittery.

Nora continued to help out friends and family with the odd legal case and had taught a class called Understanding Contracts, but law wasn't a profession that called her, at least not the way it had Brenda Vick, Charleyville's go-to attorney, or her former roommate, Pam Gregory.

"No one wanted to be in Pam's study group because she was always really bossy or always falling asleep," said Nora, as she and Thomas skated around the perimeter of the ice rink they shoveled off the lake every winter. Now Pam was a daily fixture in the news as lead prosecutor in a sensational murder case involving a stockbroker, his mistress who was a congresswoman, and their drug dealer.

"Guess she figured out a way to stay awake," said Thomas.

"I wonder if she's still bossy."

Chuckling, Thomas squeezed his wife's hands; they liked to skate like an old-fashioned pair-skating team, holding each other's crossed-at-the-wrist hands. "You don't wish you had that kind of career?"

For a while, the scrape of their skate blades was the only sound in the cold winter air. "I'm sure her days in court are pretty exciting," said Nora finally. "I probably would have liked that. But all the paperwork, the depositions, the motions leading up to it?" She shook her head. "To me, the excitement-to-tedium ratio was way too low."

They were the only ones left on the rink after their Sunday Skate Night that had been initiated several years earlier. Classical music played through speakers Clyde set up, and for those needing a break from the cold or exercise, hot chocolate and cider were served in the kitchen. Thor was a happy and patient teacher of small children, who waddled and wobbled on their skates. It had become Nora and Thomas's tradition to continue skating after everyone had left, and they loved their private ice time to commune, usually in conversation, but sometimes in silence, under whatever starry, cloud-filled, or moonlit sky the winter night offered.

"I love that you love being a doctor," said Nora. "I hope our girls find the things in life they love to do." Her words streamed out in spurts of vaporous air as she spoke. "I thought—like Pam—that I might love being a lawyer, but I never really did. It took me a while, but I realize I am my mother's daughter. I love what I do here at the Blue Moon, love bringing people together."

Letting go of Nora's hands, Thomas grabbed her in a hug, or tried to, but it was a sudden and awkward choreography that caused Nora to lose her footing, and they both fell in a heap to the ice.

"Smooth move," Nora said, before her husband kissed her.

"AND THIS IS HARRY behind his first drum set," Patty Jane said, explaining each snapshot she set on the tiled table. When she got to one of Harry and Silvia, holding hands and posed for the camera with smiles that dimmed the rest of their features, Estrella leaned forward, staring at the photograph as if it were full of fine print she couldn't quite read.

"It would mean so much if you came to their wedding," Patty Jane said.

Estrella's fingers pushed back strands of black hair that didn't seem streaked so much as beaded with gray. Shaking her head, she said in a light Mexican accent, "I can't. Too much money."

"We'd be happy to get you a plane ticket."

Estrella frowned. "I . . . I don't take charity."

Patty Jane smiled; it wasn't as if she'd thought of everything, but she had thought of *some* things. "It wouldn't cost us any money. Both Clyde and I have lots of frequent-flyer miles. They're ours to give away as we like." Politely listening to Estrella's excuses as to why she couldn't attend her daughter's wedding—it was too hard to get off work; her leg had been bothering her—Patty Jane had to hold up her hand like a traffic cop after Estrella claimed she might have to babysit her grandnephew that same weekend.

"Stop," she said, shaking her head in an attempt to diffuse her anger. "You're telling me that babysitting your grandnephew is more important than being with your daughter on her wedding day?"

Estrella's eyes flashed with anger, but another emotion softened them as they filled with tears. "My . . . at least my grandnephew likes me."

As the crying woman laid her head on the table, Patty Jane scrambled to pick up the remaining photographs, and after she put them back in her purse, she stroked Estrella's back, her voice soft and steady as she offered a litany of comforting words and sounds.

She had told no one she was coming, taking the rental car and explaining to Clyde, who was preparing for another show with Margaret, his Santa Fe art dealer, that she wanted to do a little exploring and would be back later that afternoon. Instead of listening to the radio during the drive to Albuquerque, Patty Jane listened to the sound of her voice (talking out loud helped her think), reassuring herself that she wasn't meddling—that she was merely helping—and whatever the outcome, she'd at least have made the effort.

The look on Silvia's face when she saw her mother and brother (who had bought a ticket as soon as Silvia gave him her wedding date) walk into the Blue Moon's kitchen, and the look on Estrella's face when she watched her daughter proceed down the church aisle on Juan's arm convinced Patty Jane that it was one of her better efforts. In the span of that wedding weekend, Estrella and Silvia got into three arguments (one loud enough to be heard throughout the lodge and possibly across the Ocean), and both cried several times, but that Estrella had shown up was a step. "Where it will lead, I don't know," Silvia told Harry. "But I'm so glad she took it."

"Can Ugly Bart Be Caught?" read the headline of the morning's *Charleyville Chronicle*. It was a question not posed by a disgruntled copywriter publicly goading Sheriff Himmel to find her no-good, alimony-owing ex-husband, but a headline that honored a weekend of fun, festivities, and tourist dollars. The annual Ugly Bart Contest attracted legions of fishermen to cast their lines into the adjoined Mud and Green Lakes and pull up the mythic fifty-pound, one-eyed muskie that legend had skulking in their deep waters.

The triplets—supervised by Patty Jane and Clyde—were at the

nearby park on Guava Avenue, where they bounced around inside an inflatable jump house or had their equilibrium altered on spinning carnival rides. Lewis, who would be entering his senior year in high school that fall, was at the same park with Thor, the two of them trying their luck in games involving good aims and/or reflexes. Ione and Edon were inside the Charleyville Cinema, watching *North by Northwest*, one of the free Alfred Hitchcock movies that Monsieur Mel was playing all day.

Wearing a rose "Bart-oniere," selling for a dollar at Gladdy's Floral Arts, Nora strolled the kiosk-crowded Palm Avenue. "Any surprises?" she asked, leaning into the Charleyville Clinic booth where Thomas and one of his nurses held down the fort, answering questions and giving simple medical tests.

"Couldn't tell you if there were," said Thomas. "Client-patient privacy."

"Would you like to get your blood pressure checked?" asked MaryLynn, the nurse.

"No, thanks," said Nora. "It's bound to soar in the presence of my sexy husband."

"Woman," said Thomas, fanning his face. "Restrain yourself."

Agreeing to meet after Dr. Everett relieved Thomas of his booth duty, Nora browsed in several of the shops offering freebies and/or discounts, and at Bob's Books she took advantage of the buy-one-get-one-half-off sale.

"He's obsessed," said Elise, who was working the register. She nodded at Will, her and Bob's little boy, who sat quietly on the chair by the window, turning the pages of a book about trucks. "Trucks and trains, that's all it takes to make him happy."

As the friends made plans for dinner later in the week, Elise filled the complimentary-with-purchase cloth bag with three novels, a biography, and four chapter books for the girls.

Crossing the street crowded with townies and tourists, Nora dodged a child holding a cone that held less chocolate ice cream than her face, fingers, and the front of her sundress did. With optimism fueled by the wad of tickets she'd bought at the afternoon's raffle drawing, she turned off Palm Avenue, deciding to unload the books in her car so that her arms might be free to accept all and any prizes. She was especially hoping to win the gift certificate for Caroline's Boutique.

Parking was at a premium on Ugly Bart Days, and so she walked two blocks to Carambola Avenue, whose boulevard was lined with black ash trees. A man had just shut the driver's side door of a pickup truck, and as he was crossing the street toward Nora, they both offered smiles—smiles that quickly turned from friendly to frozen.

"Nor-ah?"

Had she been getting her blood pressure checked at that very moment, Thomas might have recommended immediate medical care because surely it shot up past high and into stratospheric.

"Nor-ah, yes? Nor-ah, you me remember? It is so long time!"

Marshaling what saliva was left in her mouth, Nora swallowed. While it hadn't been a recurrent nightmare, it had certainly been a thought that had caused her consternation through the years: what if one day she ran into her children's sperm donor?

"I . . . I . . ."

The compact, dark-haired man bent to pick up the bag that had slipped from Nora's hands. Before replacing the book that had fallen out, he blew imaginary dirt off of it.

"Good as new," he said. "Now for you I carry."

"No, no," she said, grabbing the cloth bag. She looked around, frantic that her interaction with this man might be observed. Her impulse was to run away, but it was an impulse impossible to act on, seeing as she was too stunned to move.

"What are you doing here?!"

The man's expression bore both puzzlement and hurt.

"Why so . . . yelling?" He shrugged. "I . . . I here for the fishing, *naturellement*. For catching the Ugly Bart."

Adrenaline poured through Nora's body as well as her brain, which seemed electrified, sparking and shorting out. *Her town! Her Ugly Bart Days! Her children! Her husband!*

"You . . . ," he said, concerned, "you look . . . not so good." Gesturing toward the curb, he said, "Here, sit."

She shook her head. "I can't." She stepped forward, slightly surprised that her legs were working. She took another step, her pace quickening, another and another. Halfway across the street, she turned around and called out to the perplexed man standing on the corner.

"Bundy's! 9:00 tonight!"

That evening Thomas drove to the lakeside tavern situated between Charleyville and Kanoba Falls.

"It'll be all right, Nora," he said. "Whatever happens, it'll be all right."

Blinking back tears, Nora said, "I can't believe this is happening! Why did I even say anything? Why didn't I keep my big mouth shut?"

She had spent anxious hours debating—whether she should tell Thomas or anyone *anything*, if she should go to the bar or not—but after putting the girls to bed, she had confessed to Thomas the meeting on Carambola Avenue. The color had drained from his face as if a switch had been flipped, and the two stared at one another for a long moment before he pulled Nora tight to him.

"Of course we'll go. We'll go together."

Now as he pulled into Bundy's gravel parking lot, he said, "He might not even show up."

Nora ran her tongue over her dry lips. "Let's turn around. We don't owe him anything."

"If you thought that, you wouldn't have said anything," said Thomas, pulling in between a car with Kansas license plates and a van with South Dakota ones. "But you did, because it's the right thing to do." He took her hand when they were out of the car, and as they walked toward the bar, the cartilage of Nora's knees turned to water.

Facing Clear Lake, Bundy's was a popular gathering spot, but more so with tourists than Charleyville residents, which was why Nora had suggested it as a meeting place. "I don't recognize anyone," Nora whispered as they walked past the deck filled with revelers enjoying the mild summer's night.

"Sweetheart, it wouldn't matter if we did. We're allowed to meet someone at a bar."

"Someone!" said Nora, feeling light-headed.

Inside was slightly less populated than outside, and they settled themselves in a back booth, sitting side by side, both of them facing the entrance. Doreen, a waitress whose bouncy pigtails clashed with her weathered face and cigarette voice, served them beers. Nora had just taken a sip when she heard an accented voice behind them.

"Ah . . . here are you."

She jumped, doing a classic spit take as the man, smelling as if he'd bathed in aftershave, slid into the booth across from them.

"I . . ." He held his hand out to Thomas, looking both friendly and puzzled. "I am Guy."

Shaking his hand, Thomas said, "I am Thomas. Nora's husband."

The French Canadian pondered the information, frowning as if he'd been given directions to a place he hadn't planned on going to.

"Lucky man!" he said finally and held up a finger to summon the waitress.

After Guy was served, they spent several awkward moments, their attention focused on their drinks rather than one another.

Finally, Nora asked, "Are you married?"

Guy flushed and smiled, revealing the chipped front tooth that still hadn't been capped.

"Ah . . . maybe one day."

"Any kids?" said Thomas, and under the table Nora nudged her knee against his.

"Ah . . . none . . . that I know."

He smiled at the old joke but flushed deeper under the intense scrutiny of the party sitting across from him.

"Why . . . why we here?" he asked and Nora felt sympathy, not a flood, but at least a trickle, imagining what ideas this hapless fisherman, reeking of aftershave, his black, oiled hair bearing comb marks, might have had about this particular reunion.

"Guy, look," said Nora, and she felt Thomas's arm slide over the top of the booth and around her shoulder. "You remember that night—that *one* night we spent together?"

Flushing again—the poor man's blood vessels were getting a workout—he stared at his beer and nodded.

"Well, I got pregnant that night."

His head shot up.

"With triplets."

A wide white border encircled the fisherman's pupils and he whispered, "*Mon dieu.*"

He stared at Nora, then Thomas, and his eyes flicked back and forth, back and forth, like a spectator's at a tennis match.

"I . . . I no money."

"We don't want any money," said Thomas. "We just thought you should know."

The French Canadian took a long swallow of beer and wiped the foam, along with sweat, off his upper lip.

"I consider them my children," said Thomas evenly.

"His name's on their birth certificates," said Nora, and a quick shadow of sadness crossed her mind, thinking how much she would have loved his name being on one or two others.

"I asked her to put it on," said Thomas.

Guy wiped the lower part of his face with his hand and Nora noticed the black bristly hairs that sprouted from his knuckles.

"But Nora thought," said Thomas, "or, rather, *we* thought you had a right to know. And while we're at it—we'd like to know about your health history, your family's health—"

"—my people, strong," said Guy, slapping his chest with his palm. "Everybody live long."

"Good to know," said Thomas, nodding.

"*Triplés,*" muttered the fisherman.

Swallowing down a lump that had risen in her throat, Nora said, "If you want to be in their lives, we could figure out some—"

"—*non!*" said Guy, holding his hands up in a don't-shoot gesture. "*Absolument, non!*"

"You don't want to see them or—"

"*Non!* No *infants* for me! *Non!*"

"But what if one day the girls want to—"

Shaking his head with great deliberation, Guy said, "*Non!* I no come back here, never!" and with that pronouncement, he rolled out of the booth like a stuntman.

Nora and Thomas watched as he scrambled across the bar and out the exit, as if dodging bullets. They were silent, staring as if hypnotized by the neon Grain Belt sign blinking above the door. Finally, helpless to do anything with the emotions churning through each of them, they bowed their heads and laughed. Just as it seemed that the laughter had run its course, Nora would snort or Thomas would sigh, setting them off again.

"How are we ever going to tell the girls?" said Nora, giggles stuttering her words.

Thomas hooted.

"*When* are we going to tell the girls?"

As another wave of wild, uncontrollable laughter overtook them, they both hunched over the table, shoulders shaking.

Setting two more glasses of beer in front of the couple, Doreen said, "These are on the house." In her many years of waitressing, she could tell when someone was in need of another drink.

The weekend before she entered third grade, Sena was with her MorMor, packing shampoo, deodorant, and assorted sundries into boxes addressed to Women's Relief and the Red Cross and regaling those around the table with stories of her new cousin.

"She's just so little! And she doesn't have any hair at all, but Silvia says she's not worried. I think she should be—because Rosie is *really* bald. And this is really funny—anytime Grace holds her, she poops! It's like it's automatic. Harry says Grace is like a laxative for Rosie." She looked across the table at Crabby. "Laxatives help you go to the bathroom."

"Thank you, Sena. I believe I'm aware of that."

The girl pulled a wide strip of tape out of a dispenser and smoothed it over a box seam.

"Where'll these go, anyway?"

"Serbia, India, Oklahoma—anywhere," said Myrna Johnson. "That's the sad part—how much help women need *everywhere*."

"It's sad," Ione said to Sena, "but it's true. Women suffer all over the world."

"More than men?" asked Sena.

The Old Bags for Change members exchanged looks before offering a collective nod.

"You see," said Bonnie Winters, reaching for a box of sanitary napkins, "men have *physical* power, and physical power, unfortunately, determines the majority of power."

"It's an imbalance," said Lorraine Hallberg, "an imbalance that doesn't give anyone sure footing."

Evelyn Bright glared at Ione, trying with her eyes to telegraph, *How could you bring your great-granddaughter to this?* but Ione's slight shrug said, *She can handle it.*

And Sena could. Unlike most eight-year-olds, including her sisters, she was interested in the world at large—she *knew* that there was a world at large.

"Can I go?" was a question she'd asked when Ione had made announcements that she was heading down to Minneapolis with Bonnie and Lorraine (Ione was proud of having recruited these Charleyville residents and grateful that they drove) to join the OBFC in a clean-water demonstration or a march at Honeywell protesting weapons of war.

When Ione asked why she wanted to go along, the girl had said, "Because if you're doing it, it must be important."

Now, as they sat in Evelyn's dining room, passing one another bottles and boxes, Sena asked, "Why are we sending this stuff? This shampoo and stuff? Shouldn't we be sending, like, money or food or something they can really use?"

"That's a very good question," said Crabby, trying to shove a box of bath salts into an already overfilled box. "Because these women need money *and* food. But they also need things that make it easier to be themselves."

Taking in Crabby's words, Sena thought for a moment before asking, "What do you mean?"

"She means," said Ione, "that sometimes, when things are really bad—when everything around you seems to have gone crazy—it's nice to have things that help you take care of little things, like keeping clean, like smelling good."

"We give these women some *normalcy*," said Bonnie.

"Pass me those tampons, will you?" Lorraine asked.

"My Aunt Silvia won't need these for a while," said Sena knowingly as she handed the blue box to Lorraine. "Women who nurse their babies often don't get their periods."

Prompted by a conversation they had heard on the school bus and that Ulla repeated to their mother, they had already had "the talk." Sena had further researched the topic by reading and studying the pictures on human reproduction in one of her father's medical books.

When the boxes were all packed, taped up, and addressed, they all thanked Sena for her hard work, with one adding, "You may be just a kid. But you're all right." Later Ione told Sena that she should feel honored because Crabby rarely offered anyone a compliment.

"That was a compliment?" said Sena.

Ione shrugged. "To Crabby it was."

⇶ 28

"TIME'S A LOCOMOTIVE WHEN YOU HAVE KIDS."

It was a resigned statement of fact Patty Jane had used throughout the years, and it was what Nora was thinking as she watched her preteen triplets file into the great room. How was it that they were asking for training bras now when it seemed just last year they were topless, running around in diapers? How was it that these girls, who would yelp with joy when their parents picked them up at nursery school, now wore looks of vague boredom, as if gathering with them was only a step up from waiting for a late bus?

Her nudge to Thomas's side was returned by one to hers, gestures that said both, *We're in this together,* and *Whew—here we go.* What had brought them to this moment was a conversation with Elise, in which the topic of finding the right moment to tell the girls the truth of their patrimony had come up.

"*Now* is the right moment," Elise had said. "They're old enough."

"They're only eleven. Or as they'd say, 'Eleven and a *half.*'"

"Eleven and a half is just a little younger than Jeff," said Elise, who proceeded to remind Nora of her former husband who learned he was adopted the day his parents picked him up from the security office of Gem Discount Store after he'd been arrested for shoplifting a transistor radio. "If this is a blood trait," his father had railed at the seventh grader on the car ride home, "it stops right here. We know nothing of your real parents, but even if one of them was a thief, you're not going to continue the legacy."

"That's one of the reasons—who knows, maybe the biggest one— why Jeff's so screwed up," said Elise.

"My God, who wouldn't be? That's child abuse! What a horrible way to tell someone he's adopted!" Nora's sigh carried a little moan in it. "You know how much they all love their father. When I tell them about the . . . technicality . . . I want to do it in the most loving way I can, when they're ready to hear it."

"Good luck with that."

And so several years after her unasked-for reunion with Guy, Nora thought that the girls were as ready as they'd ever be (even as she wasn't) and had settled them down around her and Thomas on the big sectional couch. After several false starts and an increasingly red face on Nora's part, Ulla finally asked, "Mom, what's your problem? If you've got something to say to us, say it!"

Much to the surprise of the girls, their mother burst into tears.

"Mom, I'm sorry!" said Ulla, who would have sprang up out of her chair if springing had been a little easier for her. Instead, she leaned forward, eyes wide, left arm flailing upward as if to underscore her distress.

The two other girls slid closer to their mother.

"Yeah, Mom," said Sena, "she didn't mean anything."

The lump rising in Grace's throat prevented her from saying anything; often, her reaction to the tears of others was to cry herself.

"Girls," said Thomas, "your mother is just a little . . . scared."

All three sisters thought it, but Sena was the one to ask, "You're not sick, are you, Mom?"

Nora shook her head, and feeling bad about needlessly worrying the girls made her want to cry even harder. But her inner voice hollered at her to *Buck up!* and she took a deep raggedy breath, wiped her eyes, and managed a wan smile.

"I'm not sick. I'm just a little sick-hearted at the story I have to tell you."

Grace started to cry then, not wanting to hear whatever story it was that made her mother feel sick-hearted.

"Is it about Grandma or our Grandpas?" asked Ulla. "Or MorMor and BopBop?"

"No, no," said Nora. "Your grandma and grandpas and MorMor and BopBop are all fine—this is a story about our little family—"

"—is it Dad then?" asked Sena.

"No, Dad's fine, too." She looked at Thomas. "Aren't you, Thomas?"

"Yes," he said, nodding at each of his daughters. "I'm fine, too."

"Then what is it?" said Ulla, more impatient than distressed.

Nora's smile was wider, and for an unhinged moment she thought she was going to erupt into a fit of nervous giggles. She pressed her lips together and stared at Thor's latest birdhouse displayed on the mantelpiece. Having honored the local architecture with birdhouses modeled after everything from the Frostee Freeze to the Charleyville Cinema, Thor was now working on replicas of the great buildings of the world; displayed on the mantelpiece was a rendering of the Colosseum, complete with a gladiator and lion he had fashioned out of empty thread spools and clothespins. Seeing it, the frenzied flashes of Nora's emotional circuitboard calmed.

"All right." She looked evenly at each girl. "What I have to tell you might seem like a pretty big thing, but it's really just a little-bitty thing."

As she began her story, the triplets sat still as statuary, up until the part about having sex in the tent with a Canadian fisherman, at which point they all crumbled.

"Mom—ewwww!"

"Why are you telling us this?"

"Mom, stop! This is gross!"

Once order was restored, Nora dropped the bombshell.

"The thing of it is," she said with a warble in her voice, "that *one* time, that one time that I had too much to drink and had sex with a near-stranger, is the time that you were all conceived."

Thomas would ask Nora later if she noticed how the color hadn't drained from the girls' faces so much as *evaporated*—and all at the same time.

They sat in stunned silence, until Sena cried out, "But Dad is our dad!" and Grace trumpeted her, "Yeah, Mom, Daddy's our dad!"

"You're right about that," Thomas said solemnly. "I'm your dad, as real a dad as I could be."

"Except you're not!" said Ulla, her voice cracking with anger. "Not according to what Mom just said!"

She burst into tears, followed by her sisters, followed by Nora. Feeling he could easily join the cry fest, Thomas recited to himself his mantra: *Styrke. Fokuser. Pust.* Strength. Focus. Breathe.

"I am and always will be your father," he said in a voice that dared them to question otherwise. "Your mother and I met and fell in love before we knew she was pregnant. I was at your births—you've heard that story—I assisted Dr. Everett in bringing you, Grace, and you, Ulla into the world, and Sena, I delivered you. I couldn't love you any more if you were biologically mine."

"But how do you *know* that?" asked Ulla.

Thomas shrugged. "Because my heart's all filled up with my love for you three."

After inhaling a choppy breath, Grace said, "And Mom."

"My wife-heart is filled up with love for her," Thomas said, solemnly. "My daughters-heart is filled up with my love for you."

"So I'll bet you've been extra sad when Mom lost those other babies," said Ulla.

The girls had learned of Nora's miscarriages several years earlier, when they came home from school, saying that an older girl on the bus had been talking about her aunt's miscarriage. They had asked, "What's a miscarriage?" Nora had told them about her own, about how three different times the beginnings of babies growing inside her weren't ready to grow further and came out of her body. That had been a rough afternoon, full of tears and questions.

"They came out of your *vagina*?" said Sena, who was always the first to use more clinical terminology. "Little babies?"

"Yes to the first part," said Nora, "and no to the second. It was just . . . blood."

"Were they boys or girls?" Grace asked.

"Way too early to tell."

"Did you do something wrong to make them not stay inside you?" asked Ulla.

Here Nora had blinked back tears and shook her head and said, "I don't think so. I hope not."

It was Grace who'd wrapped her mother in a hug and said, "It must have been so hard for you, Mommy. So hard for Daddy." Both Sena and Ulla were first taken aback and then shamed by Grace's ability to step outside what was most important—their own feelings—to consider their mother and father's, but following her example they, too, gathered around Nora offering her their own arms and consoling words.

But the news of their mother's eggs colluding with sperm other than their father's affected them far more than the miscarriages, and the girls' nightly bedtime conference was heated. "It changes everything!" Ulla had wailed dramatically, to which after a thoughtful moment Grace said, "Well, it changes some things, but not *everything*," and Sena said, "Yeah, but at least you guys look like Dad could be your dad. I must take after *him*!" She said the word *him* with vitriol before bursting into what had been burst into throughout the evening: tears.

It was Sena, however, who came to accept the news the easiest and worked hard on her sisters to accept it as well. "Because, look," she had said a week later, when they were still picking up shrapnel from the dropped bombshell, "Dad's been there from the very beginning. What if Mom had been raped?"

"Sena!" Grace had said, shocked.

"Well, what if she had? And what if she'd gotten pregnant by the rapist—would you think a part of you was missing because you didn't know your rapist dad? Would you want to try to find your rapist dad?"

"Stop saying those words, Sena!" said Ulla. "I don't even want to think about stuff like rapist dads!"

"I'm just trying to point out there are all sorts of . . . scenarios. I mean, who knows? Maybe Dad's sperm—because you know he and Mom had sex before they were married—maybe Dad's sperm somehow snuck into Mom's eggs, the ones that were already fertilized by the Canadian guy! So maybe we've got some of his traits, too!"

"Now that's just ridiculous," said Ulla, even though she wasn't a hundred percent sure that it was. "Once an egg's fertilized, it's not like it leaves a window open for other sperm to come in."

"It's not like a fertilized egg *has* a window," said Grace, with a little scoff.

"Like I said, there are all kinds of scenarios we could think of, but big deal! We've got a real dad who's been with us from the very start of our lives! And I'm not gonna feel bad—or make him feel bad—by being bothered by a bunch of crap that doesn't even matter!"

A week later, Ulla watched as Harry stood at the door that led out of the Blue Moon's game room, offering words of encouragement to the departing students. The Saturday Afternoon Group Guitar was a long-standing and popular class that of late had been focusing on songwriting, as many of its nine students wanted to write or already wrote their own music.

"So next week we get the preview?" asked Carole Williamson, Charleyville's librarian who was forever grateful that she had stuck to her New Year's resolution five years ago to take up the guitar.

"Yup," said Harry. "If we don't chicken out."

He and Silvia had been writing a new musical and had promised their students a special sneak preview.

"Why would you chicken out?" asked Ulla.

"Uh, maybe because of what happened with our first one?" said Harry.

"I loved *Zombie Heaven!*"

"Unfortunately, dear Ulla," said her uncle, "that was not a sentiment shared by the public at large."

"*Zombie Heaven* more accurately should be called *Zombie Hell*," noted one Twin Cities theater critic, while another wrote, "Rather than being entertained by zombies in this misbegotten musical, I felt like one." Its reception had shocked Harry more than it did Silvia. They had been commissioned by a small theater to write the script and music, based on an idea by the producer who insisted that zombies sell. The contract gave him final say over content, jettisoning in Silvia's estimation several of their best songs and scenes.

"What did we expect?" Silvia asked Harry. "First we said yes to an idea we weren't that crazy about, and then we gave up all control. Next time, we'll do it differently."

"The public at large was wrong," said Ulla now. "Your music's awesome. *All* of it."

"You might be a little biased," said Silvia, folding up a music stand.

The perks of being related to Harry and Silvia were many, especially when it came to their musical education. They taught Sena and Grace piano and Ulla voice and took the triplets to big arenas to rock out to Bruce Springsteen or U2; to smaller venues where they were introduced to blues, bluegrass, zydeco, or gospel; to theaters where they fell in love with Rafiki in *The Lion King* and hissed at Miss Hannigan in *Annie*. Ulla was allowed to audit their lodge classes whenever she wanted, and she was not above taking advantage of her privileged position, bragging to their devoted students that she'd already heard some of their new songs.

After Carole left, Harry announced he was off to the rink. "Unless you need more help?"

It was a bright winter's day, and most of the family had convened on the shoveled-off rink on the Ocean.

"Go, go," said Silvia. "And make sure Rosie's warm enough, will you?"

Ulla was happy for the rare chance to be alone with Silvia. She was the triplets' favorite aunt, and would have been their favorite aunt even if she weren't their only one. Silvia had asked them to be flower girls ("Aren't we kind of old?" eight-year-old Sena had asked, having just seen some videos of weddings gone awry whose flower girls all looked to Sena to be around three). A year later, when she had presented them with their cousin Rosie, it only upped their devotion.

As Ulla helped Silvia put away the folding chairs that had been arranged in a circle, she said, "You know what made me first realize what a good songwriter you were? When you made up the 'Lars the Loon' song for us."

Silvia laughed. "I totally forgot about that song."

"Not me!" said Ulla, and she began to sing. "'Boo hoo, I can't coo, and I can't trill like a whip-poor-will. / But ya gotta dig this far-out tune that comes outta this crazy loon!' We *loved* that song!"

"I remember anytime I babysat, it was the only way to get you guys to sleep. Or at least *you* to sleep."

"You said in today's class that you and Harry write songs differently."

"Umm hmm," said Silvia as she sat next to Ulla on the bench of the electric keyboard.

"And that all sorts of things can inspire a song."

Silvia nodded. "In the case of 'Lars the Loon,' I remember him warbling like crazy one night, and I imagined he was trying to convince a lady friend that no, he didn't sound *loco*."

"So ideas can come to you in all sorts of ways?"

Again, Silvia nodded. "You heard Harry say how sometimes he dreams the tune of a song."

"Which is almost as crazy as how he says he can see colors in music." Ulla's arm flailed up as if to underscore her words. "The dreams I have—the ones I remember at least—never have music in them."

"Are you writing songs, Ulla?" asked Silvia.

"I don't know what I'm doing." Reaching into the pocket of her jeans, Ulla pulled out a crumpled piece of paper.

"I write a lot of stuff. Stories, poems—at least I think they're poems. But I think this one is a song. This weird melody keeps going through my head every time I hear it."

Silvia smoothed the paper on her thigh and read the first line: "Dads, guess what—I've got two. There's one who loves me, drives me to school, makes me toast. / Then there's the other, who's nothing more than a ghost." When she finished reading it, Silvia lifted the piano's fallboard and asked Ulla to hum her weird melody, and echoing Ulla's notes on the keys, Silvia played the sad, sad song.

Part Four

⇶ 29

"I T ALL HAPPENED SO FAST," said the woman sporting a fading black eye and a jaunty straw hat. "One minute we were all having a gay old time and the next minute—kaboom!—pandemonium!"

Patty Jane's daily walks were sacrosanct, a time for her to exercise body, mind, and soul, and when the approaching car had tooted its horn as she strode along Lake Road and into town, she ignored it. When it tooted again, she was ready to holler something obscene, but the driver pulled to the side of the road, rolled down her window, and frantically waved her over. "I was just on my way to see you and your family," she said. "I was there!"

Her words were a forceful magnet, and Patty Jane, a mere paperclip, was yanked toward them. She opened the passenger door of the SUV and got in, pushing aside with her feet a litter of maps, cassette tapes, and a crumpled fast-food bag.

"What can you tell me?" Patty Jane said, but seeing the woman's face sag, she added, "I'm sorry, I didn't mean to sound so harsh. It's just that"—Patty Jane fanned her own face—"whew!"

"I know," said the woman, the wattle under her chin trembling as she shook her head.

She introduced herself as Genevieve, but added, "You can call me Gen," and proceeded to tell her version of a story Patty Jane already knew. "It's the nightmare I'm still hoping I'll wake up from. And it was supposed to be such a happy occasion, celebrating our book club's thirtieth year together!" The woman's eyes brimmed with tears, but Patty Jane's, depleted for now, did not.

"I . . . I just wanted you to know how grateful we are . . . and how sorry." The woman's chin quivered. "Everyone else flew back home—we're so traumatized. I'm one of those babies who's afraid to fly, so I drove. It's really a great way to see the country. Joanie had joined me on the trip out, but—"

Patty Jane reached for the woman's hand. "Please," she said, just in case the woman hadn't understood the physical prompt to get back to the story. "Please—tell me everything."

And so Genevieve Wozniak, from Paducah, Kentucky, did.

"The Ladies' Reading and Drinking Club was a joke name. We just thought it made us sound British—or like one of those special clubs they have in those Ivy League schools." She told Patty Jane how the book club had decided to vacation on a Minnesota lake after reading Sinclair Lewis's *Main Street*. "See, every summer we've taken a vacation that's tied to a book we've read, although one year we read both *Hawaii* and *Bonjour Tristesse* and then we wind up going to Ohio because we'd read *Raintree County*! Our choices are more based on what's feasible money-wise than exotic-wise. Of course, how would I have gotten to Hawaii if I don't fly? So, anyway, this year, Pam Harte said her brother had a lake cabin we could stay in, and well, that was that. I can't say a lot of our vacation is centered around the book, although we did take a day-trip to—oh, where was Sinclair Lewis from?"

"Sauk Centre," said Patty Jane, trying to keep out of her voice her impatience over the woman's meandering narrative. She had of course heard from the sheriff; from Gil Wilbers who was fishing on the north cove; and from several people who had lakeshore homes; but she hadn't heard from anyone who was *in* the accident.

The Ladies' Reading and Drinking Club had cocktails on the cruising pontoon boat that belonged to Pam's brother, but no one was drunk. "Except for Donna, who's just gone through a very painful divorce and needed a little relief. And besides, what if we were? Pam was driving the boat, and the strongest thing she drinks is Diet Coke! We were just enjoying being out on the water, watching that gorgeous sunset."

They were on their way back to shore, only fifty yards from the floating dock, when the accident occurred, when the lone fisherman still out on the lake and later identified as Homer Jensen from

Bemidji, apparently suffered a heart attack and lost control of his motorboat, which plowed into the pontoon, sending six of its ten occupants into the waters of Petal Lake. "I was one of the lucky ones who wasn't thrown off," said Gen, "but I got this black eye and dislocated my shoulder. And I can't say *that* was fun, but after it was popped back in, no problem-o!"

All safe boaters, they had worn life jackets, at least at the beginning of the boat ride. "But then Sally, who was a cheerleader at Western Kentucky, decides to show us some old cheers and her life jacket gets in the way, so she takes it off, and Jean and Donna join her because they were cheerleaders too, although only just in high school, and I doubt Donna was even varsity. Anyway, we were all laughing and clapping along as they led us in cheers—and then, kaboom! Of the six thrown off the boat, they were the three who didn't have life jackets. The ones your husband rescued."

Patty Jane remained upright, but inside she felt all curled up, like an animal fending off predators.

"He got to Sally first—she was the one yelling the loudest, I guess, and he pulled her to our boat, which was still floating, and then he got Jean aboard, and then everyone's shouting, 'Where's Donna, where's Donna?' and he kept diving in and diving, and meanwhile Donna's got ahold of a part of that fisherman's boat who plowed into us, only nobody knows that—it's dusk by now and hard to see—and, well, she paddled herself safely to shore. By then a couple of boats came out to help us . . . but your husband . . . he didn't come up."

"No, he didn't," said Patty Jane, slumping under a grief heavy as armor.

"It . . . it was a nice article they had about him in the newspaper. Those birdhouses he made were really something."

"Yes," said Patty Jane. "Yes, they were."

Late-morning sun streamed through the two stained glass windows of St. Stephen's, the small white clapboard church that served the faithful Lutherans of Charleyville. With posture so straight it seemed a salute, Edon delivered the first eulogy, one he had Thomas go over and over for any errors in English.

"There is a phrase that begins 'Never in my wildest dreams,' and it is the phrase that begins this eulogy," said Edon. "Never in my wildest dreams did I ever imagine I would have the privilege of being Thor Rolvaag's stepfather. Of course, I wish the honor had occurred much earlier in life, but we are greedy about the good things, aren't we?

"I cannot express the gratitude for the twelve years I got to hear Thor address me as 'Pa.'

"I have heard stories of his youth, of his vigor and intelligence and curiosity, but I met him long after the accident that changed him. The Thor I knew still had vigor—Was any man as strong and agile as he was?—and he also had great kindness, a loyalty, a stalwart heart. If he loved you, he *loved* you. It was easy for me—when he understood that I loved his mother, he knew he loved me. As simple as that.

"My dear wife, Ione, has shared with me many stories of Thor's youth, and I feel so close to the five-year-old boy who led his mother by the hand to the neighbor's peony bushes and directed her to put her face in the blossoms and 'Smell,' because that was his birthday present to her. I feel so close to the excited architecture student showing his mother a model of a house he had designed for her—'And one we'll build after I make my millions designing skyscrapers!'

"Of course that boy and young man and all his tremendous potential was so greatly missed, but tempering that loss was the man we got. The man whose great gentleness was his great strength. The man who would sit quietly and listen. The man who knew how to literally jump for joy.

"Thor and I used to speak in Norwegian—he never forgot his first language—and in one of our last conversations, I remember him saying to me, *'Jeg er glad du er med mora mi. Hun er glad. Vil du gå til Frostee Freeze for en chocolate malt?'*

"This translates to, 'I am glad you are with my mother. She is happy. Do you want to go to the Frostee Freeze for a chocolate malt?'

"He knew, more than anyone, what was important.

"Thor, *god reise. Jeg elsker deg.*"

* * *

When it was Nora's turn, she stood behind the dais and shuffled her papers, scratched her jaw, fiddled with the microphone, and willed her knees to stop shaking. When she couldn't figure out any more busywork, she looked up at the congregation. Seeing the faces in every filled pew, all air escaped from her, and she had to remind herself she'd been breathing all her life; surely it couldn't be that hard to inhale and exhale?

Twelve-year-old Ulla's arm flailed up. Later, Lewis would tell her he was powerless to stop the impulse that made him clench his fist and raise his arm, shouting, "To Thor!" His gesture and words were mimicked by family members and quickly picked up by everyone else. "To Thor!" resonated through the small church, and all tension was released from Nora's body (so much so that for a moment, she thought she might have peed herself), and she began to speak.

"My dad, Thor Rolvaag, had two lives, one before his accident and one after. My grandmother and mother are the only people in this church who knew the before-Thor; Grandma remembers the baby born with white blond hair whose eyes one admiring nurse said were blue as sapphires.

"He was an athlete at an early age; he could scale monkey bars when he was a toddler, and on Field Days at school he always came home with the most medals. He was a practical joker, a free spirit, a tenderhearted boy, but when his father died, he began to put up defenses."

Ione and Patty Jane had shared many reminiscences, but neither had wanted to hear the eulogy in advance and looking up now, Nora met the eyes of her grandmother, her own asking the question, *Is this okay?* The depth of the hush in the sanctuary matched the depth of emotion that played across Ione's face, and after she nodded, Nora looked at her mother, who managed through teary eyes to wink.

"If anyone could help knock down those defenses," she continued, "it was my mother, Patty Jane. She's told me stories of a twenty-two-year-old Thor who couldn't get on a bus, couldn't walk into a store, couldn't do anything without women—and occasionally men—craning their necks to get a better look at him. He was embarrassed by the attention his looks gave him, so of course my mother had to tease him, and she says he began to learn how to laugh at himself. They laughed a lot. They held hands when they ice-skated together, and he'd declare every egg Patty Jane scrambled or every can of tomato soup she heated the best thing he'd ever eaten. She knew he was lying, but he believed in her, and Patty Jane believed in him."

Turning the page, Nora sighed.

"Fate took him away before my parents celebrated their first anniversary and didn't bring him back until almost fifteen years later, and all of us had to learn how to fit this new, strange man into our lives. His brain was damaged but not his heart; in fact, his heart got bigger and bigger and more open and loving, and all of us were made better by his love.

"I was. I was made better by his love. When I was a fourteen-year-old and met the father I'd yearned for all those years, I was shocked and scared. *No*, I thought. *I don't want a weirdo father like this!*

"Eventually I wised up. It took a lot of time, but the faked feelings I forced gradually became real.

"He could read my crazy teenaged moods and somehow knew what I needed to get out of them—a wild snowball fight, a skate down at the park, a bike ride along the creek, or just having me sit by him as he made his birdhouses.

"Thor Rolvaag was my hero, and every day, in small openhearted ways, he lived heroically. Sometimes he did big heroic things, like help Thomas and me bring our daughters into the world, and on the last day of his life, he saved the lives of others.

"Three days ago, Thor had set off after supper on his bicycle, riding out to Petal Lake to deliver a birdhouse he'd made for a client. He'd swum out to the floating dock. We can only surmise that he just wanted to witness the beauty of that summer evening. He loved sunsets; he'd sit and watch them with the same intensity he watched the Stanley Cup finals, and we like to think he was admiring that sunset when all went wrong out on the lake.

"We're so proud that he saved those lives, so proud that, thinking there was someone else still underwater, he kept trying to find her.

"'Amazing Grace' is the name of a song, and it's also a description of what fueled Thor's life. He was lost, he was found, he was blind . . . and he made all of us see.

"I am so honored to be his daughter, to be a part of the world Thor Rolvaag made better."

Everyone in the church inhaled, the sentence sitting for a while in their chests. Their exhale was the musicians' cue, and as they stood, Harry felt his whole body tremble, the way it had several years earlier in that same church, when he'd married Silvia.

Thor had been so proud to be a member of the wedding party, and thinking of him standing so solemnly by the same altar, Harry thought, *I'm going to lose it.* As they walked to the microphone, Silvia kept squeezing his hand, a Morse code of reassurance, and when she picked up her guitar, he was ready to sing to his wife's harmony the song Nora had just quoted.

⇉ 30

PATTY JANE REMEMBERED hearing Queen Elizabeth describe a tough time facing the royal family as an *annus horribilis,* and Thor's death marked for her the beginning of the same thing. But instead of choosing Latin, Patty Jane described the past year as "absolutely shitcrapulous."

It was a calendar listing one terrible thing after another. In August, Thor had died. In September, the whole world was changed by 9/11. In October, her friend Paige Larkin found out she had bladder cancer ("What'd I ever do to my bladder?" she asked Patty Jane, in a conversation that lurched from moans of despair to howls of laughter); the day before Thanksgiving, Dixie Anderson, her employee from the very beginning, suffered a stroke so severe that she had to be moved to a nursing home; and in December, the always smiling Karen Spaeth, who for decades had taught French to hundreds of House of Curl, Etc. students, swallowed a bottle of tranquilizers and never woke up. She left behind a note, but its terse "*Je suis desoleé,*" only added to the shocking mystery a suicide often is. After the funeral, Joyce, a fellow Francophile who'd traveled abroad with Karen, told Patty Jane that Mademoiselle Spaeth had suffered from depression all her life.

This news stunned Patty Jane. "But she always . . . she always seemed so happy!"

"That's how she wanted to be perceived," said Joyce. "She put tremendous effort into seeming to be happy."

*   *   *

On the anniversary of Thor's death, the family had gathered around a campfire, passing stories and sticks for roasting marshmallows. Log after log was thrown onto the fire, the sky was a jeweler's black velvet backdrop to millions of diamonds, and yawns grew contagious. In pairs or trios, people headed off to bed.

Patty Jane jabbed at the fire with a stick and a sputter of sparks rose in protest.

"And then in January, remember we heard Reese had died?"

Reese had been Harriet's beloved husband who long ago had moved to Florida with his new wife, who had sent word of his passing.

"Ja," said Ione, "but at least he had a heart attack on a golf course and not shoveling snow."

Patty Jane considered this for a moment. "I don't know . . . I don't think you really care about the weather when you're having a heart attack."

"Well, wouldn't you rather go in shorts and a T-shirt than in long underwear and a parka?"

The two women laughed softly, inspiring Lars the Loon to add his two cents' worth.

Thor's death had done what time seemed powerless to do: it made Ione *old*. They were all worried about her, this vital woman whose daily bath seemed to be in the Fountain of Youth; overnight, she was tiny and frail, her bright blue eyes leeched of color. September 11 had exacerbated her decline, at first, but then it helped to stop it. Her great-granddaughters had tromped into the kitchen after school in early October, and Ione heard the banging of cupboard doors as they foraged for food.

"Jake says we should just bomb them all," said Ulla. "Show them what it feels like!"

"Noah says his cousin just joined the army," said Sena. "He said if there's a war on terrorism, he wants to be a part of it!"

"I just don't feel safe anymore," said Grace.

*   *   *

In their pillow talk that evening, Ione had recounted the triplets' conversation. "It was a kick to the pants, Edon: I'm still here! Is it helping anyone when I act half-dead? Is it helping you? Or the rest of the family? Is it helping our poor world that needs all the help it can get?"

The next morning the triplets came into a kitchen that smelled of something it hadn't smelled of in a long time, Ione's baking—a luscious, fragrant blueberry coffee cake.

"MorMor!" said Sena. "You're back!"

She was, and not just as a great-grandmother. Claiming the world needed a recommitted Old Bags for Change more than ever, she made phone calls to Crabby and Evelyn Bright.

"I can't tell you how happy I was when you came back," Patty Jane said now, prodding the fire again with her stick. "We were so worried about you."

"I was worried, too," said Ione, slowly nodding. "Especially because it took me so long to remember something I learned long ago—that the only thing to help the hurting is to do something." Pulling her light sweater around her shoulders, she stared at the fire. "But we're not done with the year yet. In January . . . January was when Minna finally died. And Marvel's husband!"

"*And* the woman we owe this all to," said Patty Jane as her arm swept the air.

"Good old Nellie," said Ione. "I'll miss all that money." Nellie had settled into her family's old Brooklyn brownstone, and every year at Christmas Ione mailed her a big tin of gingerbread cookies, and every year Nellie would reciprocate by sending Ione a card with a crisp two-dollar bill tucked inside.

"Now there was a true eccentric," said Patty Jane. "Lucky for us."

"And then, in February," said Ione, getting back to the summary of the year's events, "you married Clyde Chuka! That was a bright spot."

"We had to do something to offset all this deluge of crappy shit."

Ione chuckled. "Only you would get married to offset crappy shit."

It had been a spontaneous courthouse ceremony in nearby Brainerd held on a February day that pelted sleet and icy winds at anyone brave or dumb enough to venture outside. They had told no one and giggled like eloping teenagers, so much so that the presiding judge, in a perpetually convivial mood now that his retirement was only a week away, joined in. Clyde's braid was silver; the judge's crew cut was white, and without its dye job, Patty Jane's hair would have been a color somewhere in between. Yet surrendering to spasms of laughter, the trio had to start the brief ceremony and stop and start again, feeling punch drunk on love punch.

Although Nora grumbled about how "you'd think my only mother would invite her only daughter to her wedding," no one was really upset over the method Patty Jane and Clyde had chosen to finally tie the knot in the long and deeply interwoven threads of their love.

"You used to joke," said Ione now, "that the reason you never divorced Thor is that you didn't want to lose me as a mother-in-law." In the dark, Patty Jane nodded and Ione reached for her hand and said, "You never will."

Like a bartender announcing last call, Lars the Loon sent out a tired warble that sounded across the lake waters.

"And in March," said Ione. "In March, Elise threw that big birthday party for Nora."

Patty Jane's smile gleamed in the firelight. "She was so surprised. And then I got to go to Prague with Clyde."

"And then remember, on Per's birthday at our little gold cake party, Harry and Silvia announced they were pregnant again."

"And then their musical opened!"

"And Sena went to the state finals for History Day."

After agreeing that for a bad year, it did have some pretty good things happen, too, Patty Jane, her knees creaking, stood up, and, pressing her palms at the small of her back, she arched her back. "I'm bushed."

"Me, too," said Ione, and holding out her hand, she said, "Help me up."

⇶ 31

CLYDE HAD LONG AGO shared his curriculum vitae with his son, Harry: he had done his one semester of college at the U, but the long 7 a.m. walks across the bridge from the West Bank to the East Bank campus in a winter that dipped the windchill into the minus-thirty range had not only nearly frozen him but convinced him that college wasn't for him after all; he already knew what he wanted to do and now was the time to do it. He worked as a fry cook at the Red Rooster Diner in downtown Minneapolis, earning enough money to cover his rent and bills. When the restaurant burned down (not because of any careless cooking on his part, but because of a shorted-out wire in the tail of the signature Red Rooster sign), he worked as a delivery man for both a Chinese restaurant and an appliance store, a security guard in a condemned office building ("I got ideas for some of my darker pieces there"), an assemblyman in a photo-processing factory, and a cashier at Dale's Superette. By the time he became a manicurist at Patty Jane's House of Curl, he'd already made dozens of sculptures.

"And that's the key, son; no matter what your circumstances, you can do what it is you really want to do. I didn't care that I was a fry cook or a cashier—I was, more importantly, a sculptor. I was making my art in a little apartment that always smelled of the fried Spam that was a part of my next-door neighbor's daily diet, and I was happy. Don't worry about the piddly little jobs you might have to take to support yourself: just keep making what you love. You might get lucky like me and the making starts making money, so you can forget about the piddly little jobs!"

Harry thought of his words as the band began playing the overture and sent a telepathic thank-you to his father, sitting rows and rows ahead of him and Silvia in the theater.

"I thought I felt something," said Clyde later, when Harry told him of this. "But I thought it was just gas." In truth, no one could have been prouder of Harry and Silvia than Clyde, unless it was Patty Jane. If pride were a sin, everyone in row eight, seats five through sixteen, which also included Nora, Thomas, Ione, Edon, the triplets, Lewis, and Silvia's mother and brother, was a serious trespasser.

Harry squeezed his cowriter's hand and Silvia squeezed back. While she was as excited as Harry, she had an extra concern he would never fully understand: would she leak through her black silk shirt? She was *fairly confident* she had pumped enough milk for Soren, their ten-month-old son, but fairly confident left room for error. The baby and Rosie, his four-year-old sister, were in the hotel suite with Cecile, their babysitter, and Silvia blinked back tears, remembering how Rosie prompted by Cecile had called out to her parents, "Break a leg!" All thoughts fled when the notes they had written rose up from the orchestra pit; the couple took a deep breath as the overture began.

Silvia had professed a good-natured jealousy over her husband's strange ability to see color in music, and now as the light, sprightly notes that were cheer and good humor suddenly turned jazzy, Harry saw the colors change: yellow into blue as a saxophonist pushed himself into the trumpeter's solo and the guitarist asserted herself—it was as if the three instrumentalists were in a game of tag, with the rest of the orchestra urging them on, and then blue darkened into a deep purple, the drum and bass beats heavy, the piano being played as if the fingers on its keys were weighted. Melancholy filled the theater, music of loss and loneliness and romance, and out of that, as the curtain rose, came lightness again, this time from both the spotlight shining on the man onstage, playing the violin and the lilting music he was making.

There hadn't been a lot of enthusiasm when Harry and Silvia first mentioned their project to theater backers in the Twin Cities (especially those who had seen *Zombie Heaven*).

"Ole Bull, who the hell is Ole Bull?"

"He was a famous Norwegian violinist and composer," Harry would answer, and Silvia (who'd asked Harry the same question when, strolling through Loring Park, Harry had pointed out a statue of the man to her), added, "The 1800s version of a rock star." Throughout their pitches, they learned to invert the two sentences so that the rock star part (people warmed up to those words) came first.

It wasn't until *Bull!* broke all box-office records of a small, experimental theater in St. Paul that investor interest began, and after a year and a half of negotiations and rewrites and replacement casting (although the deal had been contingent on keeping Roy Schaubel, the local actor to play the lead), *Bull!* opened on Broadway. "It's destined for the Great White Way!" Nora had said after seeing its initial opening, and she liked to remind others, with a happy smugness, of her prediction.

In the final act, after the character Ole Bull played "Saeterjentens Sondag" on a mountaintop and the curtain closed, the wave of applause built, lifting people out of their seats and shouting, "Bravo! Bravo!" as the cast took their bows. When Roy Schaubel took his, the applause was immense—Clyde Chuka understood the adjective *thunderous* because, really, it seemed he stood in the middle of a storm—and was even more amplified when the calls for "Author! Author!" brought his son and Silvia to the stage.

Patty Jane reached over, caressing her husband's face with her palm.

"You're crying," she said, and he turned to her, kissing her quickly.

"So are you," he said, tasting salt.

Bob allowed a crate filled with stuffed animals in the children's area, but the toys were not for sale, a concession only for the whiniest kids who couldn't be placated by the store's source of entertainment and edification: books.

"He thought he was a big sellout when I finally talked him into these 'dumb' mugs and T-shirts, " said Elise to Nora, pointing to the shelf where they were displayed.

"It's a bookstore," said Bob. "Why can't a bookstore just sell books?"

"It can, honey," said Elise, kissing her husband's cheek. "If we don't ever want to get a second car."

"Bob," said Ulla, behind the cash register, "Mrs. Kipper wants to know if we got the latest Jack Reacher book."

"I'll check in the back," said Bob. He wagged his finger at Elise and Nora. "Now, you two—don't go crazy at Caroline's."

"I'm only going to spend what we made last month from selling those dumb mugs and T-shirts," said Elise. "Which was a *fortune*." The two middle-aged women, with plans to take advantage of a rare sale at the ritzy boutique, left the store giggling, leaving Ulla behind the register, shaking her head at how "people could be so immature."

Grace earned her mad money from babysitting and had a dedicated clientele that occasionally fought amongst itself for her services. Sena made chocolate dip cones and malts at the Frostee Freeze, which now, thanks to a building addition and better insulation, was open year-round. Ulla felt sorry for her sisters and their plebeian tastes; she worked in a place of ideas and knowledge. "Today a tourist from Missouri and I discussed Jane Austen," Ulla told her sisters one night, in a high British accent. "She prefers *Pride and Prejudice* while I shall always be partial to *Emma*."

"Well, today," said Sena, trying but failing to match Ulla's accent, "a customer and I discussed whether she should get sprinkles or crushed peanuts on her cone."

"And today," said Grace, who was also talented with accents and now sounded like a member of British royalty, "little Mathias McCleary told me he wished I was his Mummy!"

"No," said Sena, her accent forgotten. "Did he really?"

"He says his mom never colors with him," said Grace. "And we color together all the time. Mathias is a coloring fiend."

It wasn't that Ulla had been the most prodigious reader of the three; that award would have gone to Sena, who'd pore over a cereal box with the same intensity she gave to a textbook, and who read every article in the *New England Journal of Medicine*, which her father subscribed to. She herself was partial to thrillers and the many magazines that featured boy bands, cable TV stars, and promises of clearer complexions on their covers, while Grace's tastes ran to romance or "sigh and cry books," as Sena called them.

Ulla was fidgety on her first day—a hot June afternoon that was more conducive to lounging on a boat or beach towel than in a bookstore—and when Bob disappeared in the back office, she wandered over to the Staff Summer Picks shelf. In handwriting as pretty as invitation calligraphy, a bookseller named Lois wrote, "Lose yourself in James Michener's big wide worlds!" Three fat books—*Hawaii, Space,* and *The Drifters*—were stacked above the recommendation, and Ulla was paging through the third one, when Bob said, "Lois is nuts about Michener."

Startled, Ulla's arm jerked upward and she dropped the book. Silently, she cursed her CP, aka Elmer Fudd, her nemesis, and bending to pick up the book, she said, "Sorry, I didn't hear you."

"*My* apologies. For sneaking up on you." Bob lifted a foot. "It's these felt slippers. Elise threatens to burn them, but I think they're an important part of my earnest bookseller uniform."

Knowing Bob was trying to be funny, Ulla laughed.

"You're welcome to recommend any of your favorite books," said Bob. "We find customers are always interested in what the bookseller likes."

Feeling herself flush, Ulla said, "Well, I'm not exactly a bookseller."

"You're working here, aren't you?" Bob held out his arms in an expansive gesture.

"What I mean is, I probably haven't read a lot of books your customers would be interested in."

"*Our* customers," said Bob. "Now that you're a part of Bob's Books, they're your customers, too." He nodded at the book Ulla had replaced on the shelf. "And if you're looking for something to read right this minute, why not check out *The Drifters* and see what you think? Lois would be thrilled to know you were reading one of her recommendations."

"Okay," said Ulla, although the size of the book, even in paperback, was daunting. Later that day, she felt an odd sense of pride, ringing up her first sale.

"Kent'll read one," said Ellen Harug, handing Ulla two mysteries. "And I'll read one. Then we'll switch and talk about them both over a beer at Skippy's. Nice ritual, eh?"

She sold five more books on her first day and each sale came with a conversation initiated by the customer, each one interesting to Ulla because none of them began with an adult's usual question to a teenager about whether or not she was enjoying the summer or what grade she was going into. Instead, Kay Frentz, the pharmacist, when picking up a copy of *Joy of Cooking*, joked about how she could read a prescription better than a recipe; when Ulla was ringing up a book called *Dude, Where's My Country?* Sheriff Himmel told her the secret to a happy marriage was "giving your partner what she wants instead of what you think she wants." "I learned long ago Claire prefers a book to a bouquet," he said, watching as Ulla wrapped, somewhat clumsily, the book in complimentary gift paper. "So she gets a new one every month."

Now, after working at Bob's for nearly six months, Ulla had acquired a serious reading habit, as well as customers who'd become book buddies. After her mother and Elise left the store, she picked up the copy of *A Good Man Is Hard to Find* stashed under the register and settled into chapter five. The way Flannery O'Connor wrote comforted her, showed her that most people, in one way or another, were beset by some type of burden like her CP.

Ulla's parents thought she would be the tough one to shepherd through teendom. Like her sisters—like any teenager—she had to deal with raging hormones and acne and unwelcoming cliques and unrequited crushes, but Ulla also had to deal with all of those things while dealing with her uninvited sidekick, Elmer Fudd. Sena and Grace were vigilant henchmen, ready to do battle with anyone who teased or bullied her, but Ulla's good humor and quick wit went a long way in her self-defense, so much so that her parents (and grandparents and great-grandparents) thought that as uninvited as Fudd was, Ulla had accepted his presence and was determined that *she* was in charge, not him.

Several years earlier, at a middle school soccer game in which Nora mistook Ulla's spectator-boredom with anger over not being able to play herself, the girl delivered what Nora described to Thomas that evening as Ulla's "Definition of Self."

"Mom," Ulla had said, the word more a rebuke than an address. "Once I tell you I'm all right, you don't have to keep asking. *I'm all right*, okay?"

"It's just that you seem so . . . ansty."

"Because I'm bored! Because soccer's stupid!"

A faint smile on her face, Nora nodded, but Ulla was not fooled by the sincerity of either the smile or the nod. "Mom, please—you've got that pity look on your face."

"I do not, I—"

"—that" (Ulla's voice rose into a whine) "'I'm so sorry Ulla can't run fast enough or gracefully enough to play sports. It's so unfair that she has to sit in the bleachers while her sisters get to race around, doing important things like scoring goals.'"

Nora's smile widened, this time with sincerity.

"Well, goals are sort of important when you're playing soccer."

Ulla rolled her eyes.

"*If* you're a soccer fan, which I am *not*. I only come to these stupid games because you think it's important I support my sisters—like I don't support my sisters!—but, really, Mom, the simple truth is: *I think the game of soccer is boring!*"

Nora's attention was diverted by Grace's well-placed kick, which sent the ball to a teammate right in front of the net.

"Go, Tigers!" she cried, and when the opponent's goalie stopped the ball, she sat down and smiled sheepishly. "Sorry."

"Mom, don't be sorry. I'm glad you like to watch Sena and Grace run around banging their heads against a ball. I'm glad Dad feels bad when he has to work and miss a soccer game. I'm glad you guys are so supportive. Just like *I* am when I watch Sena play hockey or Grace play volleyball—sports that aren't stupid! Am I sorry that Fudd won't let me play them? Sure, but sorry enough that it's going to wreck my life? No!"

From their vantage point at the top of the bleachers (Ulla's preferred seating, the better from which to ogle any cute boys in attendance), they had a big wide view of not just the game (and guys) but the autumn day in all its October splendor, the bright blue sky, the gold and garnet jewels that were worn by the trees across the playing field.

Nora poured herself a cup of coffee from the thermos, not yet totally convinced by Ulla's argument. "Honey, we've always told you that if things get to bother you too much and you don't want to talk to any of us, you can always talk to a professional."

"Yes, you have always told me that, about a million times." The girl sighed and stared off at the playing field for a long moment. "And maybe someday, if I feel like I need it, I will. But right now, I don't."

"Ulla, honey, I know how strong you are. But unfortunately, *especially* now that you're a teenager, things are going to get even rougher and it might be—"

Cheers rose up from the bleachers across the field as the opposing team scored.

"—it might be a perfect time for you to talk to a professional who can—"

"—I believe," said Ulla in a southern drawl, "that what we have here is a failure to communicate." A good mimic, she had a large repertoire of lines from the old movies she and Grace liked to watch in the Teen Cine Club, the bimonthly screenings Monsieur Mel held to expose the town's youth to something other than what he called "the trash that passes for art and/or entertainment these days."

"So I'm going to try and spell it out for you, Mother." She puffed up her cheeks and exhaled air and when she began to talk, she leaned forward, not looking at Nora, but at the game in which she had no interest. "There are a lot of weird things about being a triplet, and here's a couple of them. I am not Sena. I am not Grace. I am Ulla. Like, 'Duh,' right? But because Grace and I are identical—except for Fudd, of course—I can see myself, my outside self, anytime I look at her. So I know I'm tall and blond and pretty—not to brag, but those are facts, Mom. And I also get to see how I'd be without Fudd. And do I wish my outsides totally matched Grace's? Sure, I'd be stupid *not* to. But I'm also not stupid enough to wreck my life because they don't. People've got all sorts of things to bring them down, big stuff, not-so-big stuff, and sometimes they even make up stuff to bring them down! Why would I want to do that? Why don't I just deal with what I've got, which is an unbelievable oversupply in the brains, looks, and charm department!"

Nora pressed her lips together and blinked.

"I know you and Dad feel bad for me but, really, Fudd could have screwed me up a lot more than he has, so why don't you just forgive him?"

"Forgive Fudd?" asked Nora in a small voice.

"Yeah. Like I'm trying to. I'm not saying I'm jumping up and down that he's here—and at least I *can* jump up and down, Mom—but the fact is, he *is* here, and who knows, maybe in some weird way he's added to all the things that make me so wonderful."

"Oh, honey, I—"

Another cheer rose up as Sena lunged forward, her head making contact with the ball flying through the air and redirecting it toward the goal.

Ulla sighed. "Dumb game. I get a headache just watching it."

⇛ 32

S PENDING A WEEK IN LOS ANGELES, readying the West Coast premiere of *Bull!* Harry and Silvia left their children at the lodge, which according to Rosie was even better than Disneyland.

Patty Jane laughed when she expressed this to her.

"Why's that, Rosie-Posey?"

Because you call me names like that, she might have said, had she been able to articulate the many ways she was made to feel so cherished. "Because I caught two fish with Grandpa!" she said instead. "Because the malts at the Frostee Freeze are so good! And because I love my cousins!"

"Your cousins love you, too," said Patty Jane.

They were sitting on the deck, playing with the old troll dolls that had been handed down from Nora's toy box and into the triplets'. Thor had long ago built a castle birdhouse complete with a surrounding blue plywood moat, dark alligator shadows painted onto it, and Rosie had concocted a long and involved story line for the trolls, who were its royal denizens.

Resuming play, Patty Jane said in a creaky old voice (her doll was the wicked witch), "Tell you what, little princess: I'll give you a pot of gold for one of those cousins!"

"No way!" said Rosie, in the high voice she had assumed for her character. Doll in hand, she raced it (bumping the side of her hand along the deck floor) toward the magic castle. "And you can't come in here either, you mean old witch!"

Patty Jane did her best evil cackle. "You haven't seen the last of me!"

Setting her doll inside the castle, Rosie said, "The princess wants to take a nap now. Do you have a favorite cousin?"

Patty Jane smiled at the sharp turns a child's conversation can take. "You know what, pumpkin? I don't have any cousins."

"That's sad."

Patty Jane nodded in agreement.

"I like my cousins the same," said Rosie. "But for different reasons." She lay on her side facing her grandmother, head supported by her propped-up arm. Assuming the same position, facing her granddaughter, Patty Jane felt the sun-warmed wood on her bare legs and arms.

"I like Ulla because she's funny and Sena because she's teaching me how to play Sudoku—it's hard!—and Grace because she reads all my favorite books to me. And I'm glad she's not sick."

"Not sick? What do you mean, honey, 'not sick'?"

The little girl's face flushed. "That's what she told me last night when she was throwing up."

"Grace was throwing up?" It wasn't as if Patty Jane knew everything that went on with the lodge's inhabitants, but she usually was aware if someone was sick.

Rosie's flush deepened. "I don't think I was supposed to tell."

"No, no, I think it's good that you're telling me," said Patty Jane, as a prickle of fear jigged through her.

"I had to go to the bathroom *bad*," said Rosie. "I don't go in my pants like Soren still does sometimes."

Patty Jane said nothing in defense of her toddler grandson but instead nodded, urging her on.

"And I ran up from the fire—'member we were all around the campfire after supper? I *love* that. Anyway, I forget there's a bathroom right by the kitchen, so I ran upstairs to the bathroom by my room, and that's when I heard someone throwing up in there, and I knocked on the door because I really had to go and because I wanted to know if the person inside was okay, too, and then I heard a flush and then Grace came out, and she said hi and I said, 'Are you sick?' and she said she just got the flu for a little bit but she thought she was fine now and not to say anything because she didn't want anyone to worry about something dumb like that, and did I want her to read me *The Secret Garden* later? and I said sure, and then I had to run into the bathroom so I wouldn't pee in my pants."

Staring at her grandmother's face, she teared up.

"Am I in trouble?"

Patty Jane picked up her troll doll and in her witch's voice said, "You're always in trouble with me, Princess!"

Leaping to her feet, Rosie said, "You can't catch me, mean old witch!" and Patty Jane took the invitation, although her leap was more of a stagger as she grabbed the deck's banister and pulled herself up, proceeding to chase (or amble quickly after) her granddaughter toward the lake.

Later she recited Rosie's words to Nora.

"It might not be anything, but don't you think she's been looking a little . . . peaked lately?"

"Thomas said the same thing last night," said Nora, "only he said 'gaunt,' and I laughed and said, 'Well, she is a long-distance runner' and—" A little sob escaped her. "Oh, Mom, you don't think she's making herself throw up, do you?" She didn't listen for whatever answer Patty Jane might give, continuing a barrage of questions: "But wouldn't her sisters tell me if she were? She's already thin: why would she think she had to do that? How long do you think she's been doing it for? Is she bulimic? Or anorexic? Oh, Mom!"

"Well, I just think it's silly," sniffed Crabby Bultram. "In our day, we'd never do anything like that."

A car honked, and she and the small crowd raised their hands in acknowledgment.

"Crabby, this goes back to Roman times," said Elise. "They even had public vomitoriums!"

"Romans, schmomans," muttered Crabby and waved her cane. "Set up my chair, will you, Elise?"

"Get a job!" yelled a man slowly driving by in an SUV.

The group responded, as they did to all hecklers, by giving the peace sign.

"Fuck you!" shouted the man.

"Why do people get so mad at peace?" asked Sena. It was a baffling and never-answered question.

The Lake Street/Marshall Avenue Bridge Peace Vigil had been a long-standing Wednesday date on Ione's and the other Old Bags for Change members' calendar, but lately, because of pesky and increasing health and energy concerns of hers and Edon's, Ione now managed to join her fellow demonstrators only sporadically, and only if she could hitch a ride down to the Cities. She rarely drove in the day and had given up night driving altogether when she began to feel she was at the helm of a bad carnival ride.

Elise had been up for a day trip—it gave her a good excuse to stop in and see her widowed mother. And because she was not scheduled to work at the Frostee Freeze that summer's day, Sena joined them, the threesome making the drive from Charleyville to Minneapolis.

While not officially confirmed (there were others whose hair had gone gray or white), it was fairly obvious that Ione and Crabby were the eldest assembled on the bridge, protesting the war in Iraq that none of them had believed was necessary, let alone legal—a war that was supposed to have been over in a matter of weeks, a war that to those carrying signs every Wednesday on the bridge was fomenting more terrorism rather than stopping it.

Crabby would have been happy to stay in her little brick bungalow, watching the many cooking and home decor shows that cable television had brought into her life (and that intruded on her own cooking and household maintenance), but she was willing to forgo the battle between Iron Chefs or a lesson on how to turn her bathroom into a spa to take a stand with her friend Ione, who, since Evelyn had moved to Des Moines to be near her daughter, was the only other original Old Bag for Change.

To maximize being seen during rush-hour traffic, the vigil began at five, but now at several minutes past six the group of nearly fifty was dispersing, and Ione, Sena, Crabby, and Elise walked toward the Minneapolis side of the bridge spanning the Mississippi. They waved to fellow demonstrators going east toward St. Paul, accepted a flyer from one of them about an upcoming Peace Strategy potluck, and signed a get-well card to a longtime demonstrator who was recuperating from a bout of pneumonia. All vigil business finished, they had settled into a conversation about Grace.

"I'd be happy to talk to her," said Elise, who had her own history as an emotional binge eater (although she joked she'd never had the stomach for throwing up afterward), "if you thought it would do any good."

Sena, who was not afraid to express an opinion, was quiet. Having racked her brain figuring out ways to help her sister, she was willing to listen to what the older and (maybe) wiser people had to say.

"*Takk*, Elise, I'll let you know. But right now Grace feels enough people are talking to her, that we're ganging up on her in fact. Last night, she had a fit after Nora made her sit at the table long after dinner was done. 'Mom,' she practically screamed, 'I told you I wasn't going to throw up anymore—don't you trust me?'" Even though it was a balmy summer's evening, Ione shivered and looked at her great-granddaughter. "I hope I'm not betraying any confidences."

Sena shrugged. "It's not like Grace hasn't betrayed some things," she said. Even though it was true, she immediately felt disloyal for saying it.

"Anyway," Ione continued, "she told Thomas and Nora she'd never do it again, but can we believe her?"

"Is she seeing a professional?" asked Elise.

Ione nodded, at the question and at a protestor passing by.

"Silvia gave us some names of her classmates who are working in that field." She turned to Crabby and said, "That's Harry's wife. She majored in psychology."

"You don't have to yell, I'm not *that* deaf," said Crabby. "And of course I know who Silvia is and what she went to school for, although why she never decided to use that degree is beyond—"

Rolling her eyes, Ione turned to Elise. "Anyway, a friend of hers has a practice not that far away. In Little Falls, I think."

"She should talk to a dentist, too," said Crabby. "A dentist would tell her how she'll puke off all the enamel on her teeth if she keeps it up. Better yet, have her talk to a bunch of starving kids in Africa who never get enough in their stomachs to throw anything up."

"*En, to, tre, fire, fem, seks . . . ,*" counted Ione in Norwegian so that she wouldn't—peace vigil or not—sock Crabby in her big fat mouth. "*Sju, åtte, ni, ti.*"

Sena, her teeth clenched, said, "It's not that simple."

"Nothing is," said Crabby. "That's the problem. We complicate everything. What that girl needs is a good, firm—"

"Losers!" shouted a man in the passenger seat of a commercial van whose side panel read Leo's Pest Control. "Get a job!"

His voice was drowned out by another driver's, who shouted, "I'm with ya! Bring our troops home!"

When the triplets piled into the double bed, as was their nighttime gossip/discussion/confession ritual, the tone of the conversation, after they'd found out about Grace, was much different from usual.

"I can't believe you've been barfing all this time and we didn't even know it!" said Ulla.

"It wasn't *all this time,*" Grace had said, her voice weakened from having just finished yet another cry marathon. "It was only a couple of months."

"Only a *couple of months*?" said Sena, scooting herself up against the headboard. "You were throwing up multiple times a day for only a couple of months? Grace, what is wrong with you?"

Nora and Thomas had told their daughters to be extra sensitive with Grace, but stupid was stupid, and they had to call their sister on it.

"And don't start crying again," warned Ulla, lying on her side, her head propped up with her good, steady arm. "Just start explaining."

It had all started, Grace began, when Caleb Williamson broke up with her before Christmas. Sena made a mental note that "only a couple of months" was a little longer, considering it was now the middle of summer.

"Remember?" said Grace, wiping the tears that ignored Ulla's admonition. "He broke up with me right before Snow Dance?" Snow Dance was a semi-formal dance for which Grace had already, under her MorMor's tutelage, sewn a semi-formal dress.

"I remember," said Ulla. "What a jerk. That was such a pretty dress."

"Still," said Sena. "You said you were going to break up with him anyway."

"But *after* Snow Dance. I'd really wanted to go to Snow Dance." She sighed in the dramatic way reserved for teenaged girls and said, "You know *why* he broke up with me?"

"You said *he* said it was because he wanted more space," said Sena.

"Yeah," said Ulla. "But the real reason was because he was seeing some girl in Nisswa, right?"

Deflated that her sisters were able to answer her question—she did, after all, tell them *almost* everything—Grace nodded. "And even though I was going to break up with him—I mean, Ulla, you were right—he is *so* boring, but still . . . *so* cute. Anyway, remember when we played Nisswa in hockey—not your team, Sena, the guys— and Janie Chisholm pointed out that really pretty girl in the stands and told me she was the girl Caleb was with now?"

"Oh yeah," said Ulla. "I do remember that. But I don't think she was that pretty. She had like really nasty teeth."

Grace allowed herself a small laugh. "She was sitting across the rink. There's no way you could have seen her teeth."

"I saw her when I went to the bathroom. She was at the concession stand, tearing apart a jumbo hot dog with those god-awful, yellow, pointy snaggle teeth."

Grace chuckled and Sena silently thanked Ulla for always finding a way to make someone laugh who needed it.

"I wish," said Grace. "But the truth is, I did see her at the concession stand. Only she was ordering, like, a Diet Coke or something, and she was *beautiful*, like a model. And I thought, of course, Caleb would pick someone like her over someone like me, and I just kept thinking and thinking about that. And the next night I didn't go with you to Spanish Club. Instead I snuck a whole bunch of leftover Christmas cookies from the freezer and ate them all in the bathroom, and then I felt so sick I made myself throw them all up!"

"What kind of Christmas cookies?" asked Ulla. "The candy cane ones?"

"Oh, I love those," said Grace, turning to look at her sister. "But no, these were the shortbread ones."

"Could we please stay on track?" said Sena. "So that started it?"

Grace, sitting with her knees hugged to her chest, nodded. "Eating whatever I wanted made me feel good."

"But you've always eaten whatever you want!" said Ulla. "We all have!"

That was true, and their examples had been Ione, Patty Jane, and Nora, who, as far as the triplets knew, had never dieted; had never even talked about dieting; and ate what they wanted, when they wanted, the simple secret being, of course, that then they stopped.

"Yeah, but I've never eaten a whole tin of MorMor's cookies," Sena pointed out.

"A couple of days later, when I babysat at the Mullins?" said Grace, now in full confession mode. "I had two bowls of cereal with Nicky and Casey—you know how they always get cereal before they go to bed—and then I ate some strawberry ice cream and almost a whole bag of Cheese Doodles and then threw it all up!"

"But didn't that, like, gross you out?" asked Ulla.

Grace, her face solemn, looked at her sister for a long moment.

"At first it seemed kind of fun. Like I was getting away with something." Her chin trembled. "Then it . . . then it was just harder and harder to stop. I mean, I didn't even have to pig out—I'd throw up after lunch at school, and lots of times at home after dinner, even though I was so scared of getting caught."

"Well, now that you have," said Sena, "are you going to stop?"

"I guess so."

"You *guess* so?" said Ulla. "Grace, of course you've got to stop. Didn't you ever hear of Amanda Martin's cousin in California? She nearly died from anorexia."

"I don't have anorexia," said Grace. "I just . . . it's just so hard with you guys."

The look Sena and Ulla exchanged was full of question, confusion, and outrage.

"What's that supposed to mean?" said Ulla.

Grace picked at her thumb cuticle.

"You guys are so perfect!"

"*What?!*"

Sena, you're so smart, and Ulla, you're so funny, and I'm—"

"—you're Grace!" said Sena. "You're our wonderful Gracie, and there's no such thing as perfect!"

"Well, speak for yourself," said Ulla.

The mood was lightened for a moment, until the persistent crying virus struck again, starting with Grace and quickly spreading to the other two.

⫸ 33

Patty Jane's parents had sent their girls to Sunday School but rarely made it into a church's pew themselves, Sabbath mornings reserved for sleeping in, almost always hungover. The aunt who Patty Jane and Harriet briefly lived with after Elmo's and Anna's death was a dedicated Jehovah's Witness, but her redeeming love for God was nontransferable to the two teenaged girls who'd infringed upon and upended her dry, rigid life.

If an attendance card had been issued by Kind Savior's Lutheran Church, Ione's would have been crowded with stars. After Thor's disappearance, when she'd moved in with the young family her son had abandoned, she issued invitations to Patty Jane and Harriet, wanting to share the solace and hope she received there as a worshipper. "You two go ahead," Patty Jane would answer. "If God wants to find me or the baby, he knows where we are." Later her tone became a little less belligerent, but her disinterest in church attendance did not soften. *If I want to find God, I don't need to look for him in a church* was Patty Jane's thought, and certainly she did find peace and serenity in her long daily walks, especially the ones that took her into the woods and along the river, and now around the Ocean.

She hadn't objected when Nora's religious instruction as a child was under the purview of Ione; Nora willingly attended both Sunday School and, later, church with her grandmother, and Patty Jane certainly didn't object when Harry chose to do the same thing years later. Clyde Chuka hadn't minded either, believing that Harry was getting a well-rounded religious education, especially as he schooled the boy in lessons he'd been taught by his grandmother about the Great Spirit.

If asked what his own religion was, Clyde said, "I believe in nature and people and art, and I also believe in mystery." Patty Jane thought that pretty well defined her own belief system, although she would have added *and the holiness of chocolate*.

But now, in the small sanctuary of St. Stephen's Lutheran, Patty Jane found herself kneeling, her hands propped on top of the pew in front of her. The church hadn't been a destination, but after the long walk into town had failed to lighten her heavy heart, she impulsively pushed its heavy front handle, a little surprised when the door opened. It was a Tuesday morning, and she went inside. *Please God, please make him be all right. Please let him be all right.* Her head resting on her folded hands, thumbs positioned on the sides of her nose and pressing into her eye sockets, this was the prayer that ran over and over in her head in a loop.

"It's not a death sentence," Paige Larkin said during Patty Jane's panicked telephone call telling her of Clyde's diagnosis. "Look at me. I just passed my third annual physical with flying cancer-free colors."

"Thomas said the same thing," said Patty Jane. "Well, about it not being a death sentence. Not about the flying fucking cancer-free colors."

Paige laughed. "Feel free to embellish."

It was a long chatty phone call; Paige was at her daughter's vacation home in Palm Springs and had just come off the golf course where she'd bogeyed the third hole and birdied the fifth.

"It would probably impress me," said Patty Jane, "if I knew anything about golf."

"Which I can't believe you don't. You love walking! Plus you get to hit things with a club!"

"Ralph doesn't get enough grief teaching middle school science," his wife, Bernie, liked to tease. "Oh, *no*. He's got to spend his summers teaching driver's ed."

Grace hadn't had Mr. Lawson as a teacher and he was taciturn during her lessons, offering nothing more than instruction. But with Sena, who'd been one of his star students, he couldn't help but engage in conversation about astronomy, about prairie grasses, about the feasibility of heating winter roads with solar panels—the girl was not shy about asking questions and positing opinions—and more than once, Mr. Lawson forgot to tell her to turn right or take a left at the stoplight.

Armed with permits, the fifteen-year-old girls volunteered their driving services to anyone needing them.

"MorMor, just think," said Sena. "Next summer I can drive us to Minneapolis for the Wednesday night protests!"

"Uffda, surely the war will be over by then," said Ione.

When Grace or Sena was successful in talking Nora into letting them drive her to the grocery store or Patty Jane to the post office, Ulla often went along, assuming the role of backseat driver, a role she excelled at: "Geez, Grace, can you brake any harder? I just about got whiplash!" or "Sena, you do realize, don't you, that stop signs mean 'Stop' and not 'Slow down and breeze through'?"

One evening, after accompanying Grace on her drive to her babysitting job, Thomas told Ulla, "You know, you might be able to drive, too."

"I don't think so, Dad."

It was just the two of them on the drive home, and Ulla had moved up to the front seat.

"We can have special adjustments made to a car," said Thomas.

"Dad, don't you think I know that?"

Thomas might have scolded her for the tone of her voice if he didn't understand the frustration that fueled it.

"Of course I know you know that. But," he said, wandering into a familiar zone of *Do I push or do I pull back?* "knowing that, doesn't it make you want to learn to drive?"

Fudd shot her arm up and her hand banged on the car roof.

"Hey, if you left a dent, I'm taking it out of your allowance." It was the perfect thing to say, and Ulla's tears remained on the verge, instead of spilling over. Thomas felt himself melt in his daughter's smile.

"You know what, Dad? If I can drive with Fudd—if I pass whatever test they give people with an uncontrollable arm—maybe I will learn to drive . . . someday. I'll drive a big old adapted Cadillac—no, a Rolls-Royce. But until then, I'm happy having people chauffeur me." She made a graceful swoop with her right arm. "Drive on, Jeeves!"

"I'm a cue ball," said Clyde, after he had Patty Jane shave off the thin straggles of remaining hair.

"And a more handsome cue ball I couldn't imagine," said Patty Jane, trying not to cry as she swept up the last valiant strands and threw them in the trash. His beautiful long silver braid, which she had cut off when he'd begun chemo, was tucked away in the back of her sweater drawer.

"Why do you keep it there?" he asked one day, sitting on the bed.

"It's so beautiful, I couldn't bear to throw it out," said Patty Jane.

"No, I meant why do you keep it *there*? In with your sweaters. I really think my braid would be much more comfortable in, oh, maybe your sexy lingerie drawer."

Patty Jane laughed. "I don't have a sexy lingerie drawer."

"Any lingerie you wear is sexy," said Clyde, pulling her toward him.

While Thomas agreed that Clyde could get excellent treatment at the clinic ("After all, I am a partner there"), he nevertheless recommended a medical school friend of his, a urology oncologist who practiced at the University of Minnesota. When they came down for treatments, he and Patty Jane stayed in their old bedroom at the original House of Curl, which was a comfort to its current occupants, Harry and his family.

A fight between the triplets over clothes or boys or some such weighted topic made escape an irresistible temptation to Nora, and she had seized it, hitching a ride to Minneapolis with her mother and Clyde. After a family dinner, the grandparents agreed to watch Rosie and Soren, and Nora, Harry, Silvia, and Lewis nursed beers at the Come Right Inn, an old tavern whose bar stools were bright red around the edges and a duller pink in their worn centers, and whose neon beer signs were dimmed by dust. They had chosen the place not for its atmosphere, which had sagged into seediness, but for its history. It was the bar where Nora and Harry's Aunt Harriet had been introduced to the fine art of drinking to obliteration by Merry Chuka, Clyde's mother, and where the finally sober Harriet, along with Clyde, spotted the long-missing Thor.

"Dad says it was in this booth," said Harry, his tone reverent, "that that crazy Temple Curry and Thor were sitting. Dad said he didn't recognize him—his hair had been dyed black—but Harriet did."

Nora nodded as a shiver spasmed up her back.

"It's so strange, isn't it? To think of your dad, my dad, our aunt, and your Grandma Chuka all being in this place?"

"It gives me goose flesh," said Silvia, holding out her arm. "Look."

"To all of them," said Harry, and they clinked their glasses. "To everyone in our crazy family."

"Including you, Lewis," said Nora. "What a nice surprise to see you."

Completing his master's degree in architecture at the U, Lewis lived in the Twin Cities and saw Harry and Silvia often, but school and work didn't allow for as many trips to the Blue Moon as they would all have liked.

"I thought Clyde looked good," Lewis said to Harry, immediately tearing up.

"You think so?" asked Harry.

Lewis's head bobbed in a nod as he collected himself.

"Sorry," he said finally, bringing his hands to his eyes and swiping them dry. "It's just that . . . well, you all know what Clyde means to me."

"And we all know what you mean to him," said Harry.

A man wearing safety glasses and whose overhanging gut stretched tight the purple fabric of his Vikings jersey stood at the jukebox, punching buttons, and "The Circle Game" filled the air.

"*Oh, come on,*" said Nora. "Now *I'm* going to cry."

Silvia laughed. "Never would I have pegged that guy to play Joni Mitchell."

"Maybe he punched the wrong button," said Lewis.

"He gets three songs for a quarter," said Harry. "If the next one is Janis Ian, then we'll know we definitely misjudged him."

"I love that you know who Janis Ian is," said Nora and clinked her brother's glass again. They sat listening to Joni's clear and mellow voice sing about seasons going round and round, followed by her "Blue." The booth's vinyl seat was thin and lumpy, and Nora thought of all the family backsides that might have had a part in flattening its cushion.

"Hey," said Lewis, "we were starting to cheer up, remember?"

"Sorry," said Harry. "It's just hard . . . thinking of my dad."

"Let me offer a toast before I start bawling like a baby again." Lewis held up his beer glass. "To Clyde and Thor—the two men who changed my life."

"Thor would have been so proud that you're becoming what he wanted to be," said Nora.

"To architects," said Harry, and they all clinked glasses again.

"Only problem is," said Lewis, "all my designs look like birdhouses."

They laughed then, and again when the Vikings fan's third song came on. It was "Poetry Man" by Phoebe Snow.

"Good God," said Nora. "This guy's going way back. He's playing all the songs my girlfriends and I used to cry to when we got ignored by boys."

"I can't imagine you getting ignored by boys," said Silvia. She swallowed the last inch of her beer and said, "Speaking of boys—and girls—I think I'll go home and make sure the kids aren't driving your parents crazy."

Harry rose but Silvia waved at him to sit.

"You stay here. Drive home with Nora."

"I'll walk you out," said Lewis. "I should get home, too—I've got to hand in a model of a solar-powered, all-natural-materials condominium tomorrow."

"How's it going?" asked Harry.

"Great," said Lewis, "except that it looks just like a—"

"—birdhouse," chorused the others.

After they left, the siblings discussed the progress of *Sacagawea* (Silvia and Harry's new musical) and laughed as the buddy of the Joni Mitchell fan played his own, slightly less sensitive three-quarter lineup of AC/DC, Twisted Sister, and ZZ Top. Finally, Harry, rubbing his forehead, said, "I couldn't believe I held it together when Lewis lost it . . . but really, Nora, I just . . . I don't know what I'll do if Pop doesn't make it."

"I know. But Thomas says the prognosis is really good."

"Say that again."

"Thomas says the prognosis is really good."

"Thanks," said Harry, raising his head and offering Nora a smile. "Keep reminding me of that."

"I'll call or text you every day."

"It took you long enough to join the modern world."

"The girls forced my hand. When they got cell phones, I realized in a hurry that they'll answer a text a lot faster than a phone message."

"Well, you can text me every day . . . or you could just yell across the lake."

Ready to take another sip of beer, Nora set her glass down.

"What's that supposed to mean?"

"It means that Silvia and I put a bid on Mac and Marlys's house."

The long-established Charleyville barbering couple was leaving the Ocean for the real one their Florida condominium faced.

"Harry, I'm thrilled!" The siblings leaned forward, grasping each other's arms. That Nora's glass was tipped over and a stream of beer made its way to the drop-off at the table's edge was nothing the bartender hadn't seen dozens—no, hundreds—of times before.

⇛ 34

READING THE LETTER, Patty Jane chuckled.

"What's so funny?" asked Ione.

"Remember how at Christmas brunch I was griping about how no one sends Christmas cards anymore?"

Ione shook her head. "We used to get so many! Remember how Thor loved going to the mailbox?"

"Well, I guess Lewis was paying attention. He wrote me a newsletter."

"Read it to me."

After taking a sip of coffee, Patty Jane cleared her throat and with a flourish snapped the paper.

Dear Loved Ones,

Quiet isn't something you get a lot in this place, but my cellmate's asleep so at least I don't hear his snoring and his nightmare cries of "Duck!" or "Lillian!" I would have written in time for you to get this at Christmas, but I just got out of Solitary yesterday, and they don't give you pencils or paper there, figuring we're all MacGyver types who could either draw our way out or melt down the graphite and fashion a weapon . . . or a toxic gas. I liked Solitary, though: it gave me time to think. First on my mind is turning my life around. Why waste my time in petty larceny when I can get a job on Wall Street?

My wives tell me all is going well (that is, as long as they don't find out about one another!). Gina is expecting her fourth baby (thank God for those conjugal visits!); Tabitha's appeal looks

promising; and Britney is ready to release a new album. I love her so
much, but why must she torture me in those flamboyant videos?

Uh-oh, the guard we call Sadisto is walking the halls, nightstick
in hand, so I'd better sign off before my skull gets bashed.

Wishing you a belated Merry Christmas and a crime-free
New Year,

Lewis aka Convict #77153

Ione responded with her usual "Uffda" followed by a wistful, "He was such a good friend to Thor."

"And Thor was a good friend to him, *and* an inspiration. He'll have his master's in architecture this spring!"

"It's funny, isn't it? The way the world works."

After pondering that thought for a long moment, Ione yawned, her jaw crackling. "I'm off to bed. Good night."

Watching her, Patty Jane thought that from the back Ione could have been mistaken for a woman decades younger; she was slim and straight-backed. From the front, it was obvious she was old—as soon as one's hair grayed or turned white, age was obvious—but still, if anyone had flouted time's cruelty, it was Ione.

Folding up Lewis's letter, Patty Jane held it to her heart for a moment. That he, after hearing her complain about getting so few boastful Christmas newsletters, would write a parody of the ones she claimed to miss . . . well, it touched her. Her Christmas holiday couldn't have been better, and had she written her own newsletter about it, it would have been one its recipient would crumple up and toss into the wastebasket, grousing that nobody's family is *that* happy. When mothers were asked about their kids, Patty Jane had heard responses ranging from a teary "Don't ask!" to a wide-eyed "Fantastic!" During some of Nora's teenage years, she had only been able to muster up a wan "Okay" to the question, but now, if asked, her honest answer would have been that her children were flourishing.

Sacagawea was having its premiere in a few months in Minneapolis, and Harry and Silvia were now spending the majority of their time in the house they had bought across the lake, so she saw a lot of Rosie and Soren, her grandchildren who'd taken cute to the heights only grandchildren can take it. After much cajoling on Nora's part, Thomas had finally agreed to take Elise's ballroom dance class, and although the box step and waltz didn't do much for him, he'd turned into a Latin dance fiend, cha-cha and rhumba-ing with Nora every weekend at Schmitz's Supper Club on Clear Lake.

And the triplets! The triplets were thriving! Ulla had a boyfriend, something she'd once confessed to Patty Jane during a walk that she wasn't sure she'd ever have. "I mean, sure, a lot of guys like me because of my personality—which you think would be sort of *important*—but I don't know of any who want to deal with Mr. Fudd." But it turned out that there was another kind of chemistry going on between Ulla and Drew Emory, her science lab partner, who whispered to her one afternoon, "If this strip changes color, how about you go out with me?"

They were testing acidity with their homemade pH paper.

"Of course, it'll change color," said Ulla. "It's lemon juice!" She looked at Drew, her eyes wide. "Wait a second, did you just ask me out?"

Sena was a scholastic whiz kid and an athlete who'd made her varsity hockey team as a freshman. Grace was thin, but a normal thin as far as Patty Jane could tell. She seemed as happy as her sisters, who seemed as happy as fifteen-year-old girls in the throes of being fifteen could be. As their grandmother, Patty Jane could tolerate, was even entertained by, their drama much more than she could have been as their mother. But Nora handled everything with fairly good humor, and when she couldn't, Thomas could.

God bless Thomas, thought Patty Jane, and although it wasn't often she asked God to bless anyone or anything (it seemed presumptuous: He/She should know whom to bless!), the words felt right. And God bless Silvia. She couldn't have ordered better in-laws.

"Well, you look awfully . . . beatific," said Clyde Chuka, padding into the kitchen in his slippers and robe.

"*Beatific.* I like that word. And I guess I am."

"Before I make my Dagwood sandwich from all the leftovers," said Clyde, whose bald head still had the power of startling Patty Jane, "tell me why."

Sitting next to her, he took her hands in his.

"I just read Lewis's faux-Christmas newsletter to Ione. We had a good laugh."

Clyde smiled. "Good old Lewis."

"And I'm just sitting here right now . . . feeling so gifted."

"So you're not mad I gave you a toaster?"

Patty Jane laughed. "You know what I mean."

Taking her hands to his mouth, Clyde kissed them. "I do."

The outside thermometer registered minus seven degrees, and after a failed rabbit chase, a dog limped on nearly frozen paws down Lake Road to his home. At Skippy's, a fight broke out between a man who'd just signed his divorce papers and another man who'd just lost his job; in Kanoba Falls, the forty-seven-year-old mayor, whose wife giggled under the covers after having just put on a sheer nightgown and her diaphragm, collapsed dead on the bathroom floor; and in Baxter, a mother with a split lip and ribs that hurt when she breathed loaded her five kids into a station wagon she wasn't sure would start, hoping she would be at least two hundred miles away before her husband got home from the night shift.

There were bigger, greater, unimaginable troubles in their borders and beyond, but the bitter wind that blew snow into jagged drifts couldn't penetrate the walls of the Once in a Blue Moon Lodge, where inside at the kitchen table two people sat holding hands.

⇶ 35

THROUGHOUT THE DECADES, appliances, wallpaper, cupboards, backsplashes, and even the houses in which they were situated had come and gone, but from childhoods spanning Nora's, Harry's, Lewis's, and now the triplets', Ione was a fixture in their favorite hangout, the kitchen. After-school clubs, sports, and jobs meant it was rare that the triplets were in the kitchen together, but today they all rushed in, tromping snow from their boots, their laughter and chatter flying through the room like confetti.

"Valentine cookies!" said Sena. "And they're shaped like hearts!" Ulla opened the refrigerator door to get the milk, Grace grabbed glasses, and Sena brought the platter of cookies to the table, where it served as a quickly disappearing centerpiece. Grace, Ione noticed, didn't keep up with her sisters' consumption, eating only a bite of a cookie (when would Ione stop noticing how much the girl ate?) but helped herself to a banana from the fruit bowl.

"So, what are you guys doing for Valentine's Day?" she asked, pulling down the peel.

"We haven't made any plans yet," said Ione, as Edon said, "Probably sit and stare at the beauty that is your great-grandmother."

"Guess who's the romantic in that relationship," said Ulla.

Hearing the conversation as she entered the kitchen, Nora greeted the girls. Addressing her grandparents, she said, "You sure you don't want to join us at Schmitz's?"

"No, we'll figure something out," said Ione. "I think I'll make omelets—Edon's favorite, spinach and cheese—and Edon can make the toast and we'll have a nice cozy dinner by the fire."

"And maybe roll up the rug and dance the night away," said Edon, to which Sena said, "Roll up the rug?" which launched a story about how when they were young and danced to phonograph records, the room's rug would be rolled up for a better dancing surface.

"What kind of dances did you do?" asked Ulla. "The Jitterbug? The Charleston?"

"All of those," said Edon. "But with your grandmother, I liked the waltzes best. The ones where I could hold her tight." This elicited sounds of both delight and lasciviousness from the triplets, and an "Awww" from Nora.

"What about you, Mom?" asked Grace. "What kind of dances did you do when you were young?"

"*Were* young?" said Nora with mock outrage. "*Still* young. And tonight your dad and I will be samba-ing and tangoing and scorching up the floor while we're doing it!"

"Scorching up the floor?" said Ulla, as the triplets laughed. "Give us a break!"

Before she and Thomas left the house, Nora modeled the red silk dress she bought at Caroline's, twirling the skirt to show how dance-friendly it was.

"You look great, Mom," said Grace. "Your waist looks so tiny!"

"I'll have to fight off all the men trying to cut in," said Thomas, handsome in his suit and holiday-appropriate tie patterned with red and pink hearts.

On their way to the supper club, Nora and Thomas dropped off the triplets at the high school for an all-grades dance. Alone at the lodge, Edon added another log to the fire and Ione put in the mixtape CD Harry had made for her; the two nonagenarians met in each other's open arms and began swaying to Fred Astaire singing "Cheek to Cheek" and continued to sway as Frank Sinatra sang "I've Got You Under My Skin," Peggy Lee sang "Fever," and Dean Martin sang "That's Amore." Edon's knees wouldn't allow any fancy steps, and their dancing was confined to swaying, Ione's bony cheek pressed against Edon's bony chest. When they decided Tony Bennett wouldn't mind if they sat down rather than dance/sway to "Exactly Like You," they retired to the gigantic couch, their gaze, when it wasn't on one another, on the crackling fire.

"Remember our first dance at Guri's house?" Ione asked.

Edon shook his head. "No, what happened?" He offered a smile that still bore most of his real teeth. "Of course, I do. *Det var natten som lyste opp himmelen min.*"

"It was the night that lit up my sky, too," said Ione. Her sigh was filled with contentment. "And remember when we danced at that little cantina in Acapulco?"

"Ione, I remember every single dance I've ever been lucky enough to dance with you."

Ione's sigh now was one of contentment laced with sadness. "We're so lucky to remember things. Sometimes it doesn't seem fair, how lucky I've been. How lucky *we've* been."

"Ja, but remember, we had all those years when we weren't so lucky. When we were apart."

A little shiver rippled through her shoulders. "*That* I don't care to remember at all."

"I do," said Edon. "Remembering all the . . . darkness . . . makes me appreciate the light even more." Staring into the fire, he rubbed his jawline with his hand. "The bad luck of our being apart might have lasted longer, but the good luck of our being together, well, it has made *everything* good."

"Ja, maybe the bad luck was our road that led to the good!"

Edon nodded, contemplating this for a moment. "Still . . . I wouldn't have minded a detour."

At Schmitz's, the band was taking a break and the sweaty quartet of Nora, Thomas, Elise, and Bob was splitting a bottle of champagne when Nora's phone rang, and because they were all parents, no one was offended when she checked it. Seeing who it was, Nora mouthed, "My mother." Into the phone she said, "Hi, Mom. Everything all right?" Hearing her mother's response, she rose, nodding to the others. In the lounge area of the ladies' room, she sat on a tufted velveteen chair in front of a vanity that spanned the length of the room.

"I just talked to Ione," said Patty Jane. "Sounds like they're having a pretty romantic Valentine's Day. So I thought I'd call my kids to make sure it's unanimous."

"Harry and Silvia were going to join us," said Nora, "but they decided to stay in and watch a movie with the kids." She paused for a moment. "*Wussies.*"

Mimicking a favorite expression of the triplets, Patty Jane said, "*Totally.*"

"So how are you and Clyde celebrating?"

"Well, we're at the gallery right now. It's quite a party; there're some people in costumes—there's even a Cupid running around. I'm in the ladies' lounge—"

"—I am, too!"

"And there's a big crowd of art lovers fawning over Clyde, so yes, we're having a good time. And we'll be having dinner at the Top of the Mark."

"Ooh, swanky."

"*And* the gallery owner is buying!"

"Better yet. So Clyde's feeling okay?"

"He's feeling great. Michael—he owns the gallery—was a little shocked when he saw him without his beautiful braid, but I have to say, hair or no hair, Clyde Chuka is one handsome muchacho."

"It's a shame you're so bored with him."

"Isn't it? So how'd the girls look for the dance?"

"They all wore jeans. As Ulla said, 'It's not a big-deal dance, just a stupid all-grades dance.' But you should see me in my new red silk dress, and Thomas is wearing the Valentine's tie I gave him. And we've danced to every song the band's played. I tell you, Ma, Thomas has turned into a dancing machine."

"Good old Elise," said Patty Jane.

"I know. I've told her her dance classes have done more for couples than any marriage counselor could."

Patty Jane chuckled. "Remember when she and Thor got up

onstage with those dancers—that Felipe and Vanessa, or whatever their names were?"

Regarding her mirrored reflection, Nora shrugged one shoulder to better hold the phone and rummaged in her purse for lipstick. "Elise says it was the night that changed her life."

There was a long pause, long enough for Nora to ask her mother if she was all right.

"I'm fine," she said, although her voice was thick with emotion. "Someone just came in wearing a rainbow-colored wig!"

"Well, you are in San Francisco."

Patty Jane sniffed. "It just . . . it just made me remember when Crabby wore a wig like that. A rainbow-colored clown wig."

"Hmm," said Nora, frowning. "Somehow I can't see that."

"When I took Harriet out wig shopping, when she was losing her hair to chemo, well, when we came back, everyone in the shop wore a wig or a silly hat. I can't remember what everyone had on, but I do remember Millie was in a black Cleopatra wig, Paige was wearing a pirate's hat, and Crabby had on this big goofy rainbow clown wig! All to make Harriet feel better. Well," said Patty Jane, breaking the brief silence that rested between them, "I should get back to the party and my dashing bald artist. Give my love to all."

Patty Jane was not the only one journeying down Memory Lane, although Ione's trip took place while she was sleeping. After a vivid dream replayed the night of Thor's return to his family, she woke up with a start, staring up at the bedroom ceiling for a long while, until she realized that, yes, it was her bedroom ceiling at the lodge she was staring at, and she was not in the living room of the house on Nawadaha when that crazed Temple Curry sat with her muddy shoes on Patty Jane's coffee table, gleefully relaying the story of Thor's disappearance. The dream hadn't veered from the memory that had been seared into Ione's head that long-ago rainy night, except that Thor wasn't the pale, broken man Temple had hidden away for years, but the energetic, handsome young man he'd been before that fateful night.

"Edon?" she whispered, and after waiting a few moments, listening to his steady breaths, she was glad she hadn't awakened him. His warm body next to hers was a calming reassurance, but apparently not enough to ease her back into sleep, and after lying in bed watching the minutes flick on the digital clock, she quietly got out of bed and made her way down the hallway. The lodge tsked and murmured like a kindly but exasperated housemother who knows that one of her charges is up and about when she should be in bed.

Hanging from its ear/strap on a kitchen chair was Ulla's Bugs Bunny purse (designed and sewn by Grace, it was supposed to protect her from Mr. Fudd), and on the table Sena had unceremoniously left the silk rose a freshman boy had presented her, a boy whose affection sophomore Sena did not reciprocate.

Ione and Edon had still been up when the triplets were dropped off by a friend's parent and when Thomas and Nora returned, and they'd been treated to a recap of both groups' outings.

She considering making a cup of warm milk, but the clatter of newly made ice tumbling in the freezer startled her, and she left the kitchen empty-handed.

The fire had long been put out, but Ione could still feel its lingering warmth as she entered the moonlit great room. Snow was falling and she settled herself into a pillowy corner of the sectional closest to the windows to watch, and its lazy, meandering descent worked like a soporific on Ione, who was soon softly snoring.

"Are you sure?" said Berit, wielding a pair of scissors over Ione's head.

"Absolutely!" said Ione. "We are modern and adventurous women!"

She squeezed her stuffed bear BoBo tighter as the scissor blades snipped and swirls of her honey hair fell to the floor.

Olaf was in the dream that followed, Olaf trying to hide his excitement when telling his young wife he'd been hired by the Fresh N' Pure Dairy.

"I work delivering milk for two, three years," he said in the English he always had trouble with. "Then to management. And one day, I own the company!"

His blue eyes had sparkled; earnest and diligent, Olaf didn't often allow himself the fanciful ideas that made for sparkling eyes, and Ione felt a rush of tenderness for this man who'd saved her, who'd taken her away from her atrophied life in Norway.

It seemed the right time, while they were enjoying their after-dinner black coffee there at the small square kitchen table draped in gingham oil cloth, to tell her husband something that might keep that sparkle going.

"Olaf," she said, suddenly shy. "Olaf, jeg er . . . I think that . . . Olaf, I am having a baby."

His eyes rounded and his mouth dropped open. He scratched behind his right ear, the O of his mouth stretching into a smile. "Are you for certain?" he asked, his voice a hoarse whisper.

Ione nodded. "Ja."

It took Olaf two seconds—no more than three—to leap from his chair and envelop Ione in his arms, and time seemed to stop in their embrace, but of course it didn't, their coffee cooling and their next-door neighbor calling up from his backyard for Olaf to hurry up for their scheduled game of horseshoes.

Featuring Harriet and her old friends Gudrun Mueller and Minna Czelski, her third dream did not, like the others, replay a real scene from Ione's life.

"Ione," Harriet said, as her fingers strummed her harp strings. "Did you know Minna never learned how to play an instrument?"

"Too bad," said Gudrun. "The flügelhorn has given me much joy." She tapped her fingers on the valves before playing a few bars of a vaguely familiar song.

"I wish I played an instrument. I always wanted to," said Minna, who looked as she had in her forties, when her auburn hair was styled in a flip, and she was partial to tight cardigan sweaters that she didn't button all the way up and the occasional toke of marijuana from her son Dennis's stash. "But I have a tin ear."

Plucking out the tune "Inka Dinka Doo," Harriet said, "No one has a tin ear."

"No one except me," said Minna, pulling back a shank of her hair to reveal a shiny ear that was indeed tin.

Gudrun amped up the volume of her song and Ione snorted a laugh.

The sound of her own laugh woke her up, and once again it took her a long moment to figure out where she was. It was still snowing, but the speed and volume of the flakes had increased, meaning that Sena would accept a cash payment from her sisters for the shoveling they were all tasked to do but that Grace and Ulla were not above using bribes to escape.

Hoisting herself off the couch, her knees creaking as if they needed oiling, Ione padded back to her bedroom, her brain still clouded with dream images, especially the spectacle of Minna's big tin ear and Gudrun playing the flügelhorn.

Oh, thought Ione, feeling a little zip of pleasure. *I remember the song Gudrun was playing! It was the theme song from* Green Acres! She smiled, remembering too how watching the program, she and Nora would sing along, and she whispered now, "The Chores! The Stores! Fresh Air! Times Square!"

Edon murmured when she slid into bed next to him.

"What did you say, my love?" she whispered, pulling over her shoulder the patchwork quilt she'd made decades ago.

A low snore was his answer, and she snuggled up to him.

Wanting to share her dreams but not wanting to wake him, she moved her lips, her whisper so faint it was inaudible. "I dreamed of the night Thor was brought back to us. Uffda, Edon, it was so real. That awful woman, Temple Curry." Her neck creaked in rhythm as she shook her head back and forth. "After that I dreamed of Berit and me bobbing our hair—that was the day we met, remember? Then I dreamed of Olaf and the night I told him I was pregnant. It was all so real! Just as it happened!" A swell of emotion filled her chest. "Then I dreamed of Harriet and Gudrun and Minna, only Minna was much younger. Gudrun wasn't; but she always seemed old, even when she wasn't."

The light in the bedroom was gray and seemed fuzzy, as if it had texture. Over her husband's shoulder, she saw the number on the clock, 4:03, and she read it as both a time and a date.

"Look, Edon," she said, her whisper louder. "It's time to celebrate! I have to make a gold cake!"

➤➤ 36

EDON'S WALKS TO THE BATHROOM were long and belabored, but he was too stubborn to "pee in a pot," as Ione had suggested. Of the mind that one concession led to another and that it wasn't that far a leap from a chamber pot to a catheter, Edon didn't fight the infirmities of age as much as he ignored them. If his bladder had shrunk to the size of an acorn and he had to take several slow nocturnal strolls to relieve himself, so be it.

In his youth, whiskers sprung up like a lush lawn on his face and both an a.m. and p.m. shave were necessary; now it was only every couple of days he scraped a razor along his wattled jawline and under the space between his nose and mouth (which, in his estimation, had gotten a lot longer). Still, after he brushed his teeth (twelve of which were still his), he always slapped on aftershave; he liked the little astringent jolt it gave him, and Ione loved its bayberry smell, calling it his "Edonaroma."

Now he inhaled one of his favorite smells in the world—brewing coffee. He never appeared at a breakfast table disheveled or in a ratty robe that gaped open in places he didn't want gaped at, always dressing for the day. He'd pulled on his pants and was buttoning his shirt when he said to the still slumbering lump in bed, "Ione, darling. Coffee's on."

Having spent far too many days apart, they liked to begin and end each day together.

"Darling, *våkn opp.*"

She didn't stir and so he raised his voice.

"Ione, wake up, dear. Let's get our coffee."

285

Still getting no response, he went to her bedside and softly shook her shoulder.

"You are really in dreamland, ja?" he said, slowly positioning himself on the bed next to her so he could kiss her cheek. "I hope those dreams are—"

His lips on her cheek met an odd coolness and his heart flipped in his chest.

"Ione?" He shook her gently. "Ione?" He shook her with more force. "Ione!"

He wasn't aware of the volume of his voice, wasn't aware of much of anything but his cool-to-the-touch wife who wasn't waking up for her morning coffee. But Nora, passing in the hallway, heard his anguished cry. Racing into their room, she stopped suddenly, standing frozen like a dog who knows she'll get shocked if she crosses the invisible electric fence. A rational part of Nora understood that, barring her own unexpected demise, she would one day have to face the loss of her grandmother, but the irrational part of her believed that Ione was invincible and would outlive everybody.

"No," she whispered, staring at Edon holding a limp and lifeless Ione—it was a physical impossibility that Ione be limp and lifeless— and softly keening her name over and over.

I'm dreaming, Nora told herself. *I'll wake up and she'll be in the kitchen, frosting cinnamon rolls.*

"Ione!" cried Edon, rocking his wife in his arms. "Ione!"

It was then that the electric fence was turned off and Nora was able to step forward, step forward to comfort Edon, step forward to a life without Ione.

Everyone in the family was bereft, but no one more so than Edon . . . unless it was Patty Jane. After they got the news, she and Clyde left San Francisco and on the plane Patty Jane wouldn't let go of his hand. "She wasn't just my mother-in-law," she told him. "She was my mother, my sister, and my best friend, all rolled into one."

The flight attendant, who couldn't help eavesdropping, was completing the last leg of a flight that had left Japan hours earlier and thoughtfully served them a tea she had picked up at her favorite shop in Tokyo, a tea that guaranteed peace and serenity. (She herself drank it to help her deal with a pilot husband who more and more was flying away from her.)

At home, Patty Jane collapsed into Nora's arms and continued collapsing into whomever's arms were available. "I should have been home! I should have been here for her!"

"Ma," Nora pointed out. "We were all here; there was nothing *we* could do."

"That's right," said Thomas, who as a doctor spoke on some authority. "It was her time, Patty Jane."

"I don't want it to be her time!" her voice was as sorrowful and petulant as her grandson Soren's upon discovering, when they were watching *Bambi* on one of their movie nights together, that Bambi's mother was not coming back. She tried not to cry in front of Edon, whose sadness was so forceful a presence that it seemed he had shrunk under its weight.

He shuffled instead of walked and picked at the food set before him.

"BopBop, you've got to eat," said Grace, repeating the words that had so often been directed at her. "How about I make you some rømmegrøt?"

Welcoming apprentice cooks in the kitchen, Ione had taught her great-granddaughters a lot over the years, but Grace was the only one who had mastered making the sweet cream porridge, probably because she was the only one of the triplets who liked it.

But Edon loved it, and the bowls Grace set before him were finished.

"It's almost as good as Ione's," he'd say, his tears adding salt to the flavor.

Over and over, Edon recounted their last day together: how he had pressed the heart-shaped cookie cutter into the dough Ione had rolled out, how when they had the house to themselves they had cut a rug and danced. He recounted how, when the triplets returned from their dance, Ione laughed and joked with them, and he recalled the conversation they'd had with Nora and Thomas about the good food served at the Supper Club.

"And then we went to bed," he said, his voice weak and rusty.

"I'm sure I must have gotten up to the biffy—Ione tells me I get up at least three times a night, but I never remember doing it." Hearing himself refer to her in the present tense, his voice caught. "What I do remember, though, is Ione saying that it was my son Per's birthday, but I must have dreamt that, because why would she say that?"

"Right," said Patty Jane, who through the years had eaten many of the gold cakes Ione made in honor of Per's birthday. "It's in April, right?"

Edon wobbled his head up and down. "Ja. April third."

"I don't know how long he can last," Thomas had whispered to Nora once they'd helped the bereaved man into bed after Ione's funeral service. He hadn't had the energy or desire to acknowledge the many people at the church or those who came to the Blue Moon afterward for a reception.

"BopBop, I made MorMor's sandbakkels," Sena said, holding out a tray.

"She would have loved that," Edon said in his weakened voice but waved his hand at her offering.

Thomas was right, but it didn't take a medical degree to see that Edon had lost the will to live, or at least to live in a world without Ione. Two and a half weeks after Ione died in her sleep, so did the man who'd been her first and last love.

⇛ 37

"**B**YE, NANA!" shouted Rosie.

"Bye, Nana!" echoed her brother, Soren.

After waving to her grandchildren, Estrella pointed and frowned, letting it be known that the silliness of extended good-byes was over and she had to attend to the business of walking through the security gate.

"It gets harder and harder to say good-bye," Silvia told Harry, her voice thick. That Estrella was back in her life to say good-bye—let alone "hello" or "I love you"—could still floor her.

When the kids fell asleep, Harry and Silvia went to the extravagant multileveled deck that faced the Ocean and that they were forever grateful Mac and Marlys had built. It was a cool spring evening, and they wore jackets as they reclined on lawn furniture that had only recently been liberated from the storage shed. The sky was black and offered a starry spectacle, and Harry and Silvia were content to do nothing more taxing than stare up at it.

"I am so exhausted," said Silvia. "I feel like I've run a couple of marathons."

Harry smiled in the dark. "But you're glad she came."

"And glad she's gone."

They both chuckled.

"But she has gotten so much better," said Silvia. "When she asks me to play my guitar—ay. She never used to be interested in my music."

"What a loss for her," said Harry, reaching over the chair's plastic armrest to take his wife's hand.

"And wasn't that great when she made tamales with the kids?"

"They loved that. I can't tell you how many hours I spent in the kitchen with Grandma. She'd always pull up a stool and I'd stand next to her, rolling out piecrusts or sprinkling sugar on dough . . ." Harry's voice wavered before trailing off, and a long moment passed before he spoke again.

"You know I never met my real grandmothers; both had died before I was born."

"What were their names again?" asked Silvia.

"Anna was Patty Jane's mom, and Merry was Clyde's," he said. "They both sure had their problems . . . but Ione . . ." A ragged gasp rose in his throat and he sighed it out. "Ione was the best grandmother I could have ever imagined. The very best. I still can't believe she's gone. Can't believe Edon's gone, too."

"Ja," said Silvia, and as foreign as the word once was to her ears as well as her lips, it was now a word that came naturally, paying homage to those gone and those here in this Nordic family in which she was fully immersed.

Monsieur Mel devoted a whole weekend to Ione and Edon, titled "Scandinavian Legends," and his program guide included these notes:

In Ninotchka *we see a rare comic side of Greta Garbo, and it is delightful!* Autumn Sonata *features two Bergmans—the great actress Ingrid and the great director Ingmar! Also in this movie is the lovely Liv Ullmann, who costars with the taciturn Max von Sydow in* The Emigrants. *In* Spellbound, *once again the lovely Ingrid keeps us enraptured. (And Gregory Peck! I don't know what his ancestry is, but there's something about his body type that reminds me of Edon!) I hope in seeing these wonderful motion pictures, you will be reminded of two Scandinavians who walked in our midst and gave Charleyville a bit of needed continental flair! Ione and Edon often had date nights here at the cinema, and despite their age, I do believe they were two of the most young-at-heart people I've ever met. I shall miss them!*

*   *   *

Before a Wednesday night peace vigil on the bridge, Sena and Elise stopped in to see Crabby Bultram, who tearfully said she would no longer be joining the others there.

"I'm too old and too tired," she said. "With Ione gone, I don't see the point of Old Bags for Change. In fact, this old bag doesn't feel the point of much of anything."

Nora and Patty Jane got up early one Saturday morning, attempting to wake up the family with the aroma of fresh-baked cinnamon rolls, but they hadn't thought to have Ione write down the recipe she had in her head, instead using one they'd found in a cookbook. The pastries might have been enjoyed by another family, but not theirs; they lacked the ineffable Ioneness, and what was meant to be a cheery breakfast tribute was not: paper napkins were used to wipe away tears more than crumbs.

The one thing that helped the family in their sadness was that they had one another. But grief can manage to worm its way into even the tightest huddle, and Grace, not knowing how to deal with her sense of loss, started to b&p again, which in her mind, sounded much better than *binge and purge*.

Sena and Grace spent the morning of their sixteenth birthday taking their driver's license tests, and when they returned home, their mood was not especially festive.

"Oh, no, did you flunk?" asked Ulla, as her sisters clomped into the kitchen.

"I passed," said Sena.

"So did I," said Grace.

"They had a huge argument about who should drive home," said Nora, shaking her head as she sat down at the table. "So I didn't let either one of them."

"And she won't let me take the car now to drive over to Amanda's house," said Grace.

"Why should she?" asked Sena. "Why should you get to drive over to Amanda's instead of me getting to drive to the clinic to show Dad my new license?"

"New *temporary* license," said Grace. "It's just a stupid piece of paper—it's not like the license we'll get in the mail."

"Oh, you mean the one we'll get with the picture on it?" asked Sena, her voice mewling with sarcasm. "The one you put on so much makeup for that you'll probably have to retake it because it doesn't even look like you?"

By now the girls were out of the kitchen, but their argument continued in the hallway.

"Just because I take a little effort in my appearance," said Grace.

"Just because you act like getting your picture taken for your license is the same as a *Vogue* photo shoot!"

When their voices had blurred into incomprehension, Nora, still shaking her head, said, "That's what I've been putting up with all morning." Noticing the book splayed under Ulla's folded arms, she asked, "Hey, are you planning to bake something?"

Fudd threw up Ulla's arm.

"Yeah, maybe a *cake*! Maybe a *birthday* cake since no one else around here seems to be making one!"

"Ulla, I was—"

"—I mean, I know MorMor always made our cakes, and you probably don't want to be bothered making three like she did, but still, I would have thought someone around here would have made some kind of effort!"

Pushing herself away from the table, she lurched toward the hallway, crying, but Ulla's misdirected misery (Patty Jane was picking up specialty cakes they'd ordered from the bakery), along with the girls' bickering, was not a leash connected to Nora, pulling her up and after them, but rather a tether, tying her to the chair from which she seemed incapable of moving.

⇶ 38

THE GIRLS' SOUR SIXTEENTH didn't end the day after their birthday, or after a week, or even months, stretching on into November and looking as if it might be a description of their entire sixteenth year. Certainly they had fought in the past, but their fights then were like sun showers that burst open and quickly evaporated, whereas now a storm cloud simmered over them and their all-for-one Three Musketeers ethos had shriveled into a miserly one-for-one credo.

They all busied themselves with sports and activities. Sena had switched to goaltending on both her soccer and hockey teams, patrolling the net the way a determined bouncer guards the door of an exclusive club. Grace played soccer and volleyball. After-school activities (Ulla was in the drama club and Sena was president of Concerned Students, a group whose mission statement said simply, "We *can* change the world!"), music lessons, and work took up more hours, so that to Nora, it seemed like family time was something now measured in seconds.

"Well, at least we've got today," said Patty Jane, cutting open a paper grocery bag.

"Yeah, only on Thanksgiving when everything's closed can I be sure we'll all be together," said Nora. "Doesn't that pan have a lid?"

"That's how Ione always made it," said Patty Jane, tucking in the corners. "It's supposed to cook it better." Nora opened the oven door as Patty Jane hefted the speckled roasting pan holding the twenty-three-pound turkey tented under a brown grocery bag.

"We'll take it off during the last half-hour or so," said Patty Jane.

"Then the turkey'll get nice and golden." She wiped her hands on the apron that had been Ione's and said, "We don't have to do anything for a couple hours. Want to take a walk?"

As they turned onto Lake Road, the November air was sharp with cold, but a rosy sunrise softened the eastern sky. "It's so beautiful!" said Nora, even as she slapped her upper arms to generate heat that needed to be generated.

"Sunrise walks are my favorite," said Patty Jane. "Unless it's sunset ones. Or ones Ulla takes with me."

"Oh, Ma," said Nora, the exuberance of being outside and greeting the morning suddenly deflating. "What's the matter with my girls?"

"The same thing that's the matter with all of us," said Patty Jane, tucking her hand in the crook of her daughter's elbow. "We're all at sea. All at sea without our captain, Ione."

"Grandma, the captain?" said Nora, surprised. "No, *you're* the captain."

Patty Jane's smile was wistful. "I suppose we're all captains . . . but Ione was the captain who'd been in the water the longest. She's the one I could always go to when I got off course."

"I felt that same way about her. And I feel the same way about you."

"And your daughters feel the same way about you."

"Do you think? Oh, I hope so. But lately, I just feel so . . . hopeless. It's been, what? seven months, eight, since Grandma and Edon died, and afterward, well, remember how we were all so kind and tender toward one another? What happened? Shouldn't we all be doing at least a little better? I feel like I don't know how to help my girls feel better!"

"That's the hard thing—well, one of the hard things about being a mother—when you realize that it's not always in your power to make your children feel better." The past week of below-freezing temperatures had turned the lake water to ice, and the two women stopped to admire it's mirror-smooth surface. "Thor would have been out on that," said Patty Jane. "Out on that ice with his hockey stick, shooting pucks."

"He would have loved that Harry lives right across the Ocean now. They'd be having one-on-one games every day."

The two women continued walking as the pink horizon faded and diamonds of sunshine glinted through the tree line.

"I just didn't expect this *unraveling*," said Nora. "I mean, I thought if anything, the girls would pull together, not apart."

"Maybe it's something they have to go through. Maybe it's because they've always been so close and they're realizing that they're separate people and they have to figure out how to handle things by themselves . . . and not always as a team."

"I don't know . . ." said Nora, unconvinced.

"I don't know either," admitted Patty Jane. "I'm just throwing things out."

They sang "Be Present at Our Table, Lord," the hymn that Anna and Harriet had harmonized to when Patty Jane was a child, the hymn that was now sung in three-part harmony by Harry, Silvia, and Ulla.

It was halfway through the meal, before everyone was stuffed with stuffing, et cetera, that Clyde stood and palmed a hand over the inch or so of hair that had grown back. "You've all heard that my mother didn't think much of Thanksgiving," he said, in what had become his annual speech. "'Sure, those damn pilgrims were grateful we shared our food with them, but not grateful enough to stop taking our land, to stop slaughtering us!'" He smiled at those around the table. "But me, I love Thanksgiving; it's an official day to be grateful. Not that we need an official day to be grateful—in fact, I think it's healthy to practice gratitude every day—but it's a day to enjoy all our bounty and express that thanks to everyone." He raised his water glass in a toast. "Okay, you all know what comes next."

From a bowl that was passed around the table, everyone picked a folded piece of paper and, as tradition had it, Patty Jane unfolded hers first. "Silvia," she said, reading the name on the paper. "Well, I'm grateful that my son was smart enough to find the most fantastic woman to be his wife *and* musical partner, and the mother of my grandchildren, and of course, my most beloved daughter-in-law."

Pressing her palms together at her chest, her fingertips touching her chin, Silvia smiled.

"And I'm also grateful that she's given up knitting." Silvia had taken Knitting II and gifted Patty Jane with the class project—a misshapen hat made of yarn the unfortunate mustard color of infant poop.

"No more grateful than Harry," said Silvia. "I was threatening to knit him a sweater."

Thomas's paper read "Lewis."

"I'm grateful that Lewis, now in his capacity as a licensed architect, designed a beautiful addition for our clinic . . . and I'm grateful for his big 'friends and family' discount."

That was how the tradition worked: a sincere expression of gratitude for the person and, for leavening purposes, a lighter one.

Harry was grateful for his father's latest scan, which showed no cancer. "And I'm really grateful that he's not making that carbonated swill anymore." Clyde had made a big batch of root beer that past summer, and at his Suds Party those who weren't driven away by the smell emanating from the opened bottles were by the taste.

The turns continued, eliciting "Awwwws" and dabbed-at eyes and laughter, and they were nearly all the way around the table when Ulla unfolded her square and said, "I've got Sena." She was the only triplet to have gotten one of her sister's names and sat for a while, studying the name on the paper.

"I know how lucky I am to—"

"—no, you're supposed to start with 'I'm grateful for,'" said Rosie, a stickler for the rules.

Fudd threw Ulla's arm up—it was why she sat at the end of the table or at the end of an aisle, not wanting to bean anyone. She smiled at her cousin and told her she was right.

"Okay, then . . . I'm grateful that Sena's my sister . . . and I'm grateful Grace is my sister." The words came slowly but were followed by ones that came out in a torrent. "Because I love them so much and need them so much and I miss them so much when we're fighting,

and I know it's hard because MorMor and BopBop aren't here anymore and we're all so sad, and I didn't mean it, Sena, when I said you
have the soul of a snail, and Grace, I didn't mean it when I said it's
good you don't have a mind of your own because you wouldn't know
how to use it anyway, and I'm sorry for all those other mean things—"

She didn't get to continue, both Sena and Grace having practically
upended their chairs in their rush to get to her, wailing their own
apologies as they enveloped each other.

"Hey," said Rosie. "What about the funny part? She forgot to tell
the funny part."

Nora resisted the urge to stand outside the triplets' closed door
eavesdropping, only wanting to know they were having what once
had been commonplace but had been rare of late: a marathon gabfest.

Emerging from the bathroom, Thomas looked at her, shrugging
his shoulders in question.sti

Waving her fists in victory as she tiptoed down the hallway toward
him, she mouthed, "They're talking!'

It was a relief and a joy for the sisters to do so, and after their
giggly gossip session, which included a ranking on looks, brains, and
personality of virtually every boy and a few girls in their junior class,
Grace leaned back against a pillow, sated from laughing, and said,
"You guys, let's promise never, *ever* to fight again."

"I don't think we were exactly fighting," said Sena.

"Yeah, we were," said Ulla. "Just because we weren't screaming
at each other and throwing things around doesn't mean we weren't
fighting."

Grace nodded. "We were fighting in the meaner way—by ignoring
each other."

Sena was confident in her point of view, but that didn't mean
she couldn't consider others'. "You're right," she said. "Being ignored
makes you feel so . . . inconsequential. And what's weird is that we
all could make each other feel that way. What's the matter with us?"

"What *was*," corrected Ulla. "'Cause we're not going to be like
anymore, right?"

Her sisters agreed that they absolutely were not.

"Because MorMor would have hated that."

"And BopBop, too," said Grace softly, and the air seemed suddenly misted with sadness, and they leaned into one another, seeking protection.

After a long moment, Sena said, "Do you know I talk to them?"

"You do?" said both Grace and Ulla in unison, surprised. Their sister was the no-nonsense, fact-based pragmatist of the trio.

"It's not like I expect an answer or anything, it just . . . well, it makes me feel a little less lonely."

"What do you talk to them about?" asked Ulla.

"Oh, anything I would have talked to them about when they were here. Stuff about school, friends, you know. Normal stuff."

"That's the thing I miss so much," said Grace. "Just being able to sit with MorMor and tell her normal stuff. She always acted like our normal stuff was so *interesting*."

"Maybe I'll start talking to her, too," said Ulla. "Tell her all my deep, dirty secrets."

"Nah, we've got each other for that," said Sena. "Right, Grace?"

"Right."

But her renewed b&p habit was one secret Grace was not willing to tell. It tickled her, in a perverse way, to know that she was still able to get away with something she had promised she'd never do again. Besides, it wasn't as if she were doing it as much as she had done before; she'd lost only two pounds. It was easy to sit around the dinner table without running to the bathroom because she wasn't around the dinner table all that often, thanks to her sports schedule and her popularity as a babysitter. Mrs. McCleary was teaching three nights a week at the community college in Brainerd; Mr. McCleary usually watched the kids, but as he was away on a long business trip, Grace was recruited.

Unlike babysitters who set the kids in front of the TV so that they could wile away the hours online or on the phone, Grace was engaged, coloring with Mathias and Melanie and reading them stacks of picture books, and the kids rewarded her for it, going to bed easily. It was then that Grace would unpack the junk food she'd brought in her backpack or troll the kitchen, eating spoonfuls of ice cream, forkfuls of cold casserole. She'd given the kids Cheerios for their bedtime snack and now stood before the cupboard studying the other boxes of bright and sugary cereal, knowing that a bowl out of each one wouldn't be missed. It was after her fifth, when her stomach pressed hard against the waistband of her jeans, that she performed the *p* part of her routine.

The bathroom was too close to the kids' rooms, and so, always sly and mindful of being caught, Grace purged in the kitchen, and when she was finished, she ran water in the sink as the garbage disposal obliterated her vomit. She proceeded to clean up the rest of the evidence—put the boxes back in the cupboard and the milk in the refrigerator, and wash her spoon and bowl. Now after the nearly frenzied excitement of eating and the nasty but satisfying purge, calm descended and she curled up on the couch to begin her history homework, which was to write a book report on a biography of Che Guevara that she was only two chapters into. She didn't know until the next day that Mathias had gotten out of bed to share the exciting news that his loose tooth had felt "extra loosey" but had instead stopped in the kitchen doorway to see her stooped over the sink throwing up.

"Hey, Mom," Grace had said, getting into the front seat of the van after soccer practice.

Her mother didn't return the greeting. Instead, her voice choked as she said, "Mrs. McCleary phoned me this afternoon."

⇶ 39

WHILE THEY SPOKE, their guitars perched on their laps as easily as house cats and were picked up when they played a line of a song or a chorus. To the teenager's question, "Who inspires you, like, musically?" Silvia had said simply, "Life." Harry's answers tended to be a little more expansive. "My Aunt Harriet. She died before I was born, but throughout my life I've heard stories about her musicality—she had almost a savant talent at whatever instrument she chose to play. My mother has told me she chose to play the trumpet and harp because they were the instruments of angels and Louie Armstrong, which she considered one in the same." He looked at his audience. "Any of you ever heard of Louis Armstrong?"

One girl raised her hand. "He sang that song about a wonderful world. My grandpa plays it all the time."

"Oh," said Harry, "what does your grandfather play?"

"Uh . . . his CD player." The girl flushed as everyone laughed at the joke she had unintentionally made.

"That song," said Harry, "was in fact one of my aunt's favorite songs. She played it at her wedding . . . on the trumpet."

"She played the trumpet at her *wedding*?" asked a girl named Olivia.

Harry nodded. "So did Grace's mom. Right there in the middle of the ceremony, the two of them played 'What a Wonderful World.'"

"That just seems *weird*."

The room was small enough so everyone heard the girl's snippy comment.

Grace shrugged. She had been both embarrassed and thrilled that her aunt and uncle had come to speak to them. Usually they had nutritionists or women who'd successfully been in recovery for years. But she didn't like when Harry had shifted the attention toward her and that everyone was looking at her, expecting her to answer Olivia, the meanest girl in the whole facility.

"I . . ." Her heart beat in her chest and unconsciously she began to twirl a strand of her hair. "I . . ." She looked up at Silvia, and the expression on her aunt's face was a silent cheer and she let it lift her. "I think it's pretty cool, actually," she said, pulling her finger out of her hair and turning to Olivia.

"Yeah," said Jana, whose own hair was thin and, in some places on her scalp, missing. "If I ever get married, I'd want to do something like that. Something special to celebrate, instead of just standing around in a lame white dress."

Through the murmur of voices, Silvia's louder one said, "That's what I love about music. It has so many purposes. You can celebrate with it, cry with it, be inspired by it, get mad with it—"

"—give us an example!" said Molly, who always wanted to play the flute but whose mother said she would pay for dance lessons or music lessons but not both.

"Okay," said Harry after he and Silvia conferred for a moment. "This is from our musical *Sacagawea*. Remember, the story about the native woman who leads Lewis and Clark on their expedition? This song's called 'Who's in Charge.'" The girls laughed as they sang the Lewis and Clark duet, which was full of bluster and braggadocio.

Next, Silvia, in a warm but plaintive voice sang "Little One," which Sacagawea sings to the baby she delivers en route. When she was finished, several girls wiped tears from their eyes. But not Olivia, Silvia noticed.

"We are so proud of you," Harry said, as they walked to the parking lot.

"What for?" asked Grace.

"For being here."

"Only people who are in trouble are here."

"People in trouble who are smart enough to get help," said Silvia.

Her arm was around Grace, and she was relieved that she felt more skin than bone.

"Or people whose *parents* are smart enough to get them help."

Silvia smiled and squeezed her niece's shoulder; she thought it was a good sign that the usually acquiescent Grace dared to be a little lippy.

"I hope we didn't embarrass you too much," said Harry.

"No, you guys were great," she said, her voice breaking. "You're the ones who should be embarrassed of *me.*"

Harry put down the guitar cases so he could join in the hug.

"I just feel so stupid that I even have to be here! I just miss all of you guys so much!"

"We miss you, too," said Silvia. "And we're all rooting for you."

GRACE'S GRADUATION SPEECH FROM SARA'S PLACE

It seems weird, after all I've been through, that I use a food analogy to describe emotions, but here goes: it's like my feelings are stacked up in a sundae glass, the tall parfait ones they use at the Frostee Freeze. On the bottom is a pool of rhubarb sauce. That's my shame. Some chopped-up hazelnuts are on top of it: that's my embarrassment. My sadness is that big scoop of maple nut ice cream. (I hate all those things—rhubarb sauce, hazelnuts, and maple nut ice cream—yuk!) But wait, the sundae gets better, because on top of the maple nut ice cream is about an inch of hot fudge, followed by a scoop of pecan praline ice cream, an inch of butter-scotch sauce, a scoop of chocolate chip, a big swirl of whipped cream, and a cherry on top. What these yummy ingredients stand for are a lot of things that begin with self: self-acceptance, self-love, self-awareness, self-confidence, and on top of all that, strength and a little bit of pride. And I'm not worried that the icky stuff's buried underneath—it's all in the parfait glass so nothing's hidden and I know it's there. But I also know that I don't have to keep digging at it with my spoon.

I was more mad at my mom and dad than I've ever been mad at anyone when they made me come here to Sara's Place. I thought I was doing fine. I mean, sure, I'd broken my promise and was back to throwing up, but this time I was a lot smarter about not getting caught. Except

I did. And I was hoping to get as skinny as I had gotten the first time because I still hated the way I looked. That's one of the things I learned here: that you can be blind to seeing yourself as you really are. And not just on the outside.

It was really weird sleeping in a room without my sisters. I think I cried myself to sleep for about two weeks (in the back of my mind, I was thinking how much I'd lose in water weight!), wanting so much to be piled in Ulla's bed, all of us laughing and talking and sharing our secrets.

I learned here, though, that I didn't share enough of them—my secrets. I didn't share how losing my MorMor took me back to feeling not as good as them, or anyone. My roommate, Taylor, had a sign on her bulletin board written by one of the Roosevelt presidents, the one who started all those national parks: "Comparison is the thief of joy."

This place is practically wallpapered in quotes, but that's the one that's stuck with me most because it's so true. How much time did I waste comparing myself to my sisters, my friends, to athletes I'd compete against, to models I'd see in magazines? What my counselors showed me is that the one thing I can do better than anyone else is to be myself.

"The grass is always greener on the other side," Liza said in group therapy, "but we don't know if it's because of good gardening or overuse of pesticides!"

"Better yet," said Margo, "just worry about your own yard. Don't worry about the greenest grass—plant a flower garden, plant a rock garden! Build a tree fort!"

So that's what I'm doing, concentrating on my own backyard, weeding, planting, and pruning. It scares me a little to think about how I'll be once I leave this place, but mostly I'm excited. Excited to be me in the world, and not being sorry about it!

It was always a lot easier for me to see the good in everybody but myself. To all the girls here who thought we had to waste away to be noticed: thanks for all your help, and I wish for you what I wish for me: knowing that just as we are, we're enough. Thanks to all my counselors who held my hand physically and emotionally and even spiritually. I can't say that I'm happy about my bulimia, but I am happy that it brought me to a place like this where I learned so much.

When I leave today, it won't surprise me if my family and I go out to celebrate. And if we do, I'll order what I want to eat—maybe an ice-cream sundae, ha ha—and when I'm done, I won't be scared and panicky, wondering where I can throw it all up. But if I am—because, like Liza says, "Prepare for backsliding"—I've got a new tool kit filled with tools that'll help me build myself up and not tear myself down.

Thank you.

"Look, you're on the front page," said Ulla.

"Let me see that," said Grace.

"Sure pays to have your sister be editor of the school newspaper," said Ulla, jabbing a straw into her open milk carton.

"Talk to the sports editor," said Sena. "He's the one who thought it was such a great picture."

"It is pretty good," said Grace, picking up the newly released issue of the *Charleyville High Clarion*. "It looks like I'm running so fast."

"You *were* running fast," said Sena. "You won the race, remember?"

"Like it says in the headline," said Ulla, pointing. "'Charleyville Senior Takes First Place in Crow Wing County Classic. Brainerd's Rowena Mua Takes Second.'"

"I can't believe I beat Rowena," said Grace of her longtime rival. "She's like mega-fast."

"And you're mega-*mega*-fast," said Ulla.

"Nice article," said Mitchell Wagenstein, setting his lunch tray next to Sena's and sitting down.

"Yeah," said Meghan Pearson, his girlfriend and a force on the soccer team that Grace had quit, deciding to concentrate on sports she really enjoyed rather than those she thought she should play. "But are you sure you're still not hurling? Because you're still skinny."

Three voices rose in protest—Ulla's, Sena's, and Mitchell's—but Grace raised a hand, silencing them, and smiled at Meghan, who as a midfielder was known for her chippy, selfish play.

"Still not hurling," she said and knocked on the tabletop, even though it was laminate and not wood.

"But I am," said Ulla. "Only I don't have to stick my finger down my throat to do it: I only have to listen to the stupid stuff you say." She pretended to gag. "Automatic projectile vomiting."

The triplets watched as an insulted Meghan flounced away, followed by Mitchell, after he'd given them a shrug of apology.

"What a bitch," said Ulla.

"Don't say that word," said Grace. "It's so demeaning."

"But she is!"

"I get what you're saying," said Sena, who was proud of, but still
getting used to, the new Grace who spoke her mind without apology.
"But, Ulla, it is kind of sexist."

"Is *witch,* too, then? Which Meghan definitely is." Ulla considered
the gelatinous mound of chow mein on her plate, on Fridays considered the lesser evil of the other lunch offering, tuna noodle surprise.
"How about *asswipe?* Does that fit your politically correct names to
call someone, or does it defame toilet paper?" Her sisters laughed.

"No," said Sena, "*asswipe* works."

⇥ 40

"Time's a—"

"—I know, I know—a locomotive when you have kids," said Nora, finishing her mother's oft-repeated adage.

"Actually," said Patty Jane, perturbed that her daughter found her words so predictable. "Actually, I was going to say, 'Thyme's a seasoning I enjoy using.'"

The two women stared at one another for a second before they laughed. "How do you feel about parsley and sage?" said Nora, and looking out the kitchen window she added, "Okay, they've pulled the car up. Let's make a run for it."

It was the fifth of June, the day of the triplets' high school graduation ceremony, and while the morning had started off with the appearance of a glorious, here-I-am sun, pushy clouds had thrown a gray tarp over it, and now in the early afternoon the tarp had sprung a leak. A big leak: this was no mere shower but a downpour. With raincoats held overhead, they raced to the car and scrambled inside. Thomas turned to his wife and said, "It reminds me of the day they were born." They weren't in a rental car, of course, and Thor wasn't behind the steering wheel, of course, and Nora wasn't doubled over with contractions that more aptly should have been called "organ-squeezing-death-grips," but Nora could remember it all as if it were yesterday, which of course it was not.

"Where did the years go?" she asked as Thomas turned onto Lake Road.

"Where they all go," said Patty Jane from the backseat. "Into our memories, into the past, lickety-split."

"I think you need to turn on the radio, Thomas," said Clyde. "And find some rock 'n' roll, will you? We need it."

Of their class of 103 students, Sena was named valedictorian and thus was tapped to give a speech at the graduation ceremony. "You've got to help me," she'd told Grace. "Help me write a speech like the one you gave at Sara's Place."

Grace was flattered that Sena, the A-plus-in-every-subject, wanted her help.

"Just talk about how you really feel," she said, "and get Ulla to help you with the jokes."

In the auditorium, which had hastily been adorned with twined crepe paper and the balloons the junior decorating committee had planned on tying to the football field's goalposts, Sena gave the kind of speech given by thousands of valedictorians across the country, filled with uplifting "Today is the first day of the rest of your life" quotes and speckled with a few (thanks to Ulla) laughs. It was only at the end, when her confident delivery faltered, that Sena looked at her family, at who was there and who was missing.

"As all of you know, I am one of triplets," she said, and despite the quiver in her voice, she kept going. "And so I speak for my sisters, too, when I mention some very important people in our lives who are no longer with us: our Grandpa Thor, our Great-grandmother MorMor, and our Great-grandfather BopBop. I could drone on and on about the things we learned from them—their young spirits, their energy, and their readiness to try new things are but a few. In fact, I could drone on about all the things we've learned from our family who's here tonight. But all of their actions spoke—and still speak—so much louder than words. And to you, fellow graduates, I offer a translation—as well as a challenge—of what their actions so often say: *Let's go!*"

*　*　*

The Ocean had not yet warmed to its full summer temperature, but Patty Jane and Nora only planned to stay on its surface, in the paddleboat. Clouds hid most of the stars, allowing only a pale moonlight, but the rain had stopped hours earlier and the air felt fresh and scrubbed. They pedaled hard enough to propel themselves forward but with more a meandering pace than a speedy one. In the cup holders were plastic glasses of champagne left over from the graduation toast given that night at dinner.

"What are we going to do when they leave in the fall?"

"Damn," said Patty Jane, reaching for her glass. "I knew we were going to get morose."

"I'm not morose. I'm just wondering." Nora sighed. "Noah Peterson's mother told me that he's taking a gap year. Why can't the triplets take a gap year?"

"And do what?"

"And stay home!"

"That would only postpone their leaving. Why don't you celebrate their independent spirits the way I celebrated yours? I was *thrilled* when you left for Berkeley."

"You were?"

"Sure," said Patty Jane. They were both whispering, not wanting their voices to carry over the lake. "After I stopped crying . . . around the middle of your sophomore year."

Nora's laugh was soft. "But I came back."

"And maybe the girls will. Or at least two of them. Maybe one. Or maybe none."

"Mom!" said Nora and took a big swig of champagne.

"But that'll be fine—if they're fine. If they're happy and thriving and excited about their lives, you'll be happy, too, wherever they are."

Lars the Loon—or one of his progeny, they couldn't be sure—warbled a "Where are you?" cry and a moment later his mate answered with a melancholy yodel. The two women paddled as the last traces of Lars's beseeching call faded, content to listen for a long while to the swish-swish of the water churning under their pedals.

"I hope Drew will be okay," said Nora finally.

The girls were back at the high school for the all-night party, and Ulla had announced at dinner that her goals were to stay up all night, win at least three prizes ("They're giving away all sorts of cool stuff, including an iPod *and* a twenty-dollar gift certificate to Candy Town!"), and to break up with her boyfriend.

"Don't you think that's kind of harsh?" Grace had asked. "Breaking up with him at our graduation party?"

"Graduation means moving on," said Ulla. "And I need to move on from him."

"Especially since he and Amanda were at last week's Teen Cine club together," said Sena, if not helpfully, then factually.

In a house on the other shore, lights flicked on and off, on and off, and on again. They turned to see a light in the lodge blink on and off in the same rhythm. Harry and Silvia and the kids had been over for the graduation dinner, and as was their tradition, they signaled (it was more fun than telephoning) when they got home.

"Guess we should get back, too," said Patty Jane. "I promised Clyde a massage before he went to bed." A massage therapist from a fancy Minneapolis spa had given a two-day seminar at the Blue Moon, and Clyde was reaping the benefits of Patty Jane's attendance.

"Thomas is probably already in bed, reading Sena's speech. He's got a copy of the one Grace gave at Sara's Place, and I can't tell you how many times he's read that one."

"Those girls can sure give some great speeches."

"With Ulla's help, they *and* Ulla will remind you. In fact, Ulla informed me that she hopes her sisters will return the favor and help her out when she writes her speech . . . her Presidential inaugural speech."

"I'd vote for her," said Patty Jane.

The clouds had parted and the moon lit a shimmery path across the lake.

"If I had been valedictorian—of course, my graduating class was over seven hundred, and so—"

Patty Jane's hoot cut short her daughter's words.

"I didn't mean it like that!" said Nora, laughing. "I'm sure Sena would have been valedictorian of any size class—of a class of seven *thousand.* What I was going to say is, if I'd been valedictorian, I might have quoted you in my speech."

"Oh yeah? What have I said that's speech worthy?"

"Ma, come on, you've got a whole repertoire. This is one that left a real impression: 'Life can be a ballroom dance, and it can be full of shit. Your job in both cases is to watch where you step.'"

"That would have gone over real well in a high school auditorium," said Patty Jane. "I think I like Sena's message better."

"Which one?"

"The one that she said she'd learned from Ione and Edon and Thor. From all of us. The one that's really the one sane response to life's invitations."

A flare of flame shot up from the strip of sandy beach, and approaching the dock the women could see that neither of their husbands was in bed, waiting for a massage or rereading a speech, but instead building a fire in the pit.

"Hope they brought marshmallows," said Patty Jane, and smiling at her daughter as they pedaled faster through the dark water, she said, "Let's go!"

EPILOGUE

D<small>R. EVERETT</small> retired from his medical practice when he was seventy, and Thomas plans to do the same. What's unbelievable is that seventy is not that far off; those hazy, distant hills of old age are suddenly in much sharper focus, and we're no longer allowed to amble on the road that leads to them. What we find ourselves on now is a moving walkway, like the kind they have in airports, and ambling is impossible.

I can still hear the squeak of Magic Markers on posterboard as Ione, in her nineties, wrote out a Stop the War sign; I turn away from my computer and look out the window to watch my mother shoot hoops with her grandson, Soren. Sure, age is all in the mind, but it's supported immeasurably by a body that can still do things. Thomas and I continue burning up the dance floor, our samba steps leaving behind trails of charred wood and ashes. Patty Jane puts in a daily five-mile walk and is not bothered by her slower pace, claiming it helps her to better commune with nature, plus her shoes last longer. Clyde is still sculpting and has said it's his dream to die with blowtorch in hand.

"Well, that'll take care of cremation expenses," said Patty Jane.

Speaking of cremation (Ulla's taught me about segues), we all went to Norway to throw the ashes of our loved ones into Lake Tinnsjø. Cleaning out their bedroom, Patty Jane had found the program from Ione's funeral in Edon's nightstand, and on the front of it, in faint spidery handwriting, something in Norwegian. Thomas translated it: "I want to go back home with you, my darling, to the country where we found each other twice." The girls had been promised a trip to celebrate their high school graduation/eighteenth birthday, and although Sena lobbied hard for a work vacation in Alaska, counting endangered caribou or some such thing, Norway had the most votes.

We walked the same path we'd long ago walked with Edon, and I noted how different it was in the summer.

"Ja," said Thomas. "It was cold and icy when we were here, and Nora and I slipped and slid, trying to keep up with Edon."

"That man could *move*," I said.

"He sure could," said Clyde Chuka. "Remember, Thomas, when he first came to the lodge and we took him for a walk around the lake? We could barely keep up!"

"Soren, don't!" said Rosie. "Mom, Soren's stepping on the back of my shoes!"

"Well, don't walk so slow!" said the little boy.

Patty Jane smiled. "You're just like BopBop, aren't you sweetheart?"

I pointed across the lake.

"Edon told us that's where the Norwegian resistance blew up a plant where Nazis were trying to build a bomb. What was it called again, Thomas?"

"Operation Gunnerside."

"Grace!" said Ulla. "We saw that movie!"

"Oh my god!" said Grace. "Yes! *The Heroes of Telemark!*"

I told them how Edon had mentioned the same movie, and Grace explained how the leading man was the father of Michael Douglas. "I don't think he's as cute as his dad," said Ulla. "But he's a good actor. Monsieur Mel showed some of his movies—*Wall Street, Basic Instinct*—"

Sena cleared her throat, silencing her sister.

"Sorry," said Ulla. "I guess I'm just a little nervous."

"We all are, honey," I said, as Thomas took the plastic bag out of his sport coat pocket. It had seemed ignoble to carry some of Ione's, Edon's, and Thor's last remains in a sealable plastic bag (we had taken Ione's locket containing a pinch of Dad's ashes), but we had opted for practicality over style.

"Someone should invent that," Ulla had said, "a bag for ashes. You know, something classy. Maybe leather."

"Leather's not classy," said Sena, who'd long ago committed animal rights to her long list of causes.

In two rented vans, we had all driven to the house Edon had long ago sold, but no one answered the door when we knocked.

"They're on holiday!" an inquisitive neighbor shouted from her front yard.

"I'm sure it's all different inside anyhow," I said, both disappointed and relieved. I pointed to the front windows, whose shades were pulled. "Berit's Hardanger curtains used to hang there. Ione said she hated to admit it, but they were far beyond her capabilities."

Sena sniffed dismissively. "Nothing was beyond MorMor's capabilities."

At the lakeshore, as Patty Jane doled out tiny piles of ash into everyone's hand, Harry began singing, "Oh, Ole," from their musical, a mournful yet beautiful ballad that always brought the house down. The assemblage joined in; the *Ole* and *Sacagawea* sound tracks were ones played so often in the lodge that everyone had memorized every single song:

How do I say good-bye,
Good-bye to this life I've led?
How do I set down my bow,
Put my violin to bed?
When there's still so much music to make,
Melodious, divine,
The heavenly choir might be that,
But this earthly one's been mine.

As Ione would have said, "Uffda."

Fat clouds loitered in the blue sky, their edges turning to gauze, and on that sunny Norwegian afternoon, I felt my mother's shoulder press against my own as the singing continued: "The heavenly choir might be that, but this earthly one's been mine." The words trailed off, the silence of the group broken by Harry who shouted, "Good-bye, MorMor! Good-bye, BopBop! Good-bye, Thor!" as he flung a mist of grit into the water.

This led to a chorus of good-byes as everyone pitched and lobbed Ione and Edon and Thor into the waters of Lake Tinnsjø. Grace would later claim that it was because everyone was standing so close and that Ulla had jostled her; whatever her excuse, the end result was that her toss lost its accuracy, flinging up and sideways, pelting Patty Jane's chest.

"Oh, Grandma, I'm so sorry!" she said.

"Don't be," she said, laughing. "It's perfect. It's just perfect."

Brushing the shadow of ash off her white blouse, she held her hand to her heart.

"I don't know why you all had to be so obvious," she said, looking to the sky. "It's not as if you weren't already there."

That moment was pretty hard to top, but later that night it was, when I presented the girls with their copies of the family history I'd been laboring over. "*Once in a Blue Moon*," said Sena, reading the cover page I'd hired Katelyn, Elise's artistic daughter, to design. "Oh, Mommy, I love it!"

Sena hadn't called me "Mommy" in at least a decade, and the address was like a little gift.

As the proprietor of the B&B in Drangedal served us waffles and fresh strawberries in a dining room decorated with portraits of JFK, Stein Eriksen, and ABBA, we read aloud the stories, and before the girls went up to their room, I accepted long, hard hugs from each of them.

"I'm so glad to be in this family!" Sena said.

"I wouldn't want to be in any other!" said Grace.

Before she bent down to embrace me, Fudd flew up Ulla's arm. "I like that we're so strange!" she said.

*   *   *

In the fall, all three did leave and I did cry—hard—for four nights, after which I cried less hard for about five more. Then I sniffled, and after that my sinuses cleared.

At the end of that summer, Paige Larkin died, not from a recurrence of cancer: while visiting her daughter in Palm Springs, she was hit by a limousine running a red light on El Paseo Drive. A couple of weeks later, Myrna Johnson succumbed to a virulent case of food poisoning.

"I'm so glad I sold the House of Curl, Etc.," my mother said. "It would have been so hard running it without any of the old regulars."

"Crabby's still around," I reminded her.

Patty Jane smiled. "Do you know she was always my biggest tipper?"

My childhood home by Minnehaha Falls remains in the family, and in fact Grace lives there now with a couple of friends she met at the U. She has a degree in social work and is a counselor in a facility similar to Sara's Place. I'll have a new title this spring—the mother of the bride—when she marries Leo del Vecchio. His name sounds like he's an Italian movie star, but Leo's an Iron Range kid, having grown up outside Duluth. What's really exotic about him is that he's getting his master's of divinity degree.

"Oh, so you're going to make candy?" said Patty Jane when Grace brought him home for the first time.

"There is sweetness in my calling," Leo said solemnly, "but my hope is to fill cavities, not cause them."

Silence filled the room before Grace burst out laughing.

"Ha, ha—he got you, Grandma."

That afternoon, using Ione's recipe for nougat fudge, we all made divinity together.

Sena's on the Galapagos Islands, studying sea urchins. In the summer after her freshman year at Tufts, she crewed on a Greenpeace boat, and every summer since she has traveled to some far-flung locale where she studies endangered rain forest habitats or warming ocean currents or changes in bird migration. Her goal is to preserve and protect our planet. Its loftiness doesn't surprise her sisters. "If anyone can do it," they both agree, "it's Sena."

Ulla, parlaying the love of literature ignited by her tenure at Bob's Books, went to St. John's College in Santa Fe. She stayed there after graduation and by day is working in Margaret Arlen's art gallery. ("Hey," she'd told Clyde, who'd arranged the job for her, "what are strings for but to be pulled?") By night, she performs with a comedy improvisational troupe. During one show, Fudd was particularly acting up, causing Ulla to face the audience and in a deep voice intone, "Pay no attention to the man behind the curtain." Thinking fast (which I guess is the point of improv), another actor pretended to be pushing the buttons and pulling the levers that controlled Ulla's movements. This led to a wildly spastic dance that the whole troupe entered into. We in the audience howled.

Harry and his family are regular visitors to New Mexico, visiting Silvia's mother Estrella ("She's mellowed so much I hardly recognize her," Silvia told me), and her brother Juan, who has taught Rosie and Soren how to ride horses. As an added bonus, they get to spend time with Ulla. Lewis joined them during their last visit, after which Ulla sent me a text: "Dinner after show with H, S & Lewis. Loads o fun."

I didn't put much meaning into it at the time, but it seems that reunion has led Lewis and my youngest daughter to forge a mutual admiration society. She'll be his date tonight when we all go to the premiere of *Frida!*—Harry and Silvia's new musical about the Mexican artist. Before we meet the playwrights at the theater, we gather at the house on Nawadaha and the air is filled with the spice of excitement and perfume.

"Thanks so much!" says Sena, home from her island study. "This is the first dress I've worn in months!"

Thinking they'd be perfect to wear to *Frida!* Ulla has gifted her sisters with embroidered dresses she bought at a flea market in Santa Fe.

"And you look great in it," says Grace, "especially with that tan."

"Your accessory's not so bad either," says Ulla, throwing an approving nod toward Leo, elegant in a navy pinstriped suit.

Leo blushes and smooths the lapels. "It's my roommate's. He just bought it for his new job."

Grace laughs. "Tell them what he majored in."

"Mortuary science."

It's a cold windy night, and as we walk to the cars, I see Lewis drape a protective arm around Ulla.

"Will wonders never cease?" I say under my breath, but under my breath is loud enough for Thomas to hear, and as he takes my arm, he whispers, "I hope not."

ACKNOWLEDGMENTS

Big thanks to the University of Minnesota Press, including Emily Hamilton, Rachel Moeller, Daniel Ochsner, Kristian Tvedten, Maggie Sattler, Jeff Moen, Shelby Schirmer, Heather Skinner, Laura Westlund, and Matt Smiley. And to Erik Anderson—*tusen takk* for your enthusiasm, for asking the right questions, and for the lavender-infused French toast.

I don't know if it's the winters, the latitude, or the fumes from church basement hotdishes, but the State of Minnesota lures a lot of writers and artists into its lake-filled borders, and I feel lucky to live among people so passionate about the arts.

Thanks to Louisa Castner for her copyediting expertise; thanks to Sheila de Chantal, whose love of books and libraries inspired the peerless Wine and Words; to Twin Cities book maven Pamela Klinger Horn; and to the Loft Literary Center. Thanks to all the booksellers whose support of *Patty Jane's House of Curl* thrilled a first-time novelist; special thanks to Sally Smith of the late and lamented A Woman's Place in Salt Lake City. Thanks to the theaters and venues that have granted my extrovert side a stage, particularly Kristin Van Loon and the fabulous one-of-a-kind Bryant Lake Bowl.

As always, I am grateful to my friends and family, with whom I laugh and solve the world's problems, borrow money from, and love. To Charles: you're not an officer but you're the most gentlemanly gentleman I know, and your kindness and good humor increase my serotonin levels daily.

Finally, to the memory of Julio, our handsome, elegant, softest-fur-ever dog, who for years accompanied me on long walks along the river during which I could ponder and puzzle out whatever book I was working on and where he could gambol like a lamb and sniff out the earth's great mysteries.

ONCE IN A BLUE MOON LODGE
READER'S GUIDE

1. *Once in a Blue Moon Lodge* is a sequel to *Patty Jane's House of Curl*, although it's not necessary to have read the first book to follow the story of the second. Have you ever read a sequel you enjoyed more than the book that inspired it?

2. As a senior citizen, Ione is moved to start a group working for social justice called Old Bags for Change. Do you have a particular cause that inspires you to invest time and action?

3. There are several main characters in this book. Whose story resonates most with you and why?

4. Why do you think Ione hid such a big part of her life history for so long? Have you ever heard a story or learned a secret about a relative or friend that has surprised or shocked you?

5. Ione describes Berit as not being satisfied with the many gifts she had. Do you think a person like Berit suffers as a result of her own behavior toward others?

6. Nora's heritage is Norwegian, and she visits Norway for the first time as an adult. If your ancestors came from another country or countries, have you visited those places or met distant relatives?

7. Nora escapes to Minnesota's north woods and gets more than the rest and renewal she was seeking. Is there a choice you've made that has altered the course you thought you'd mapped out for yourself?

8. Because of a loyalty she feels toward her deceased husband, Nellie hasn't moved out of the lodge, even though she closes it down for business. Have you ever regretted—or been happy about—something you have done out of loyalty for someone?

9. Nellie's a real eccentric. Is there someone in your own life who could be described this way?

10. Why do you think Ione is willing to risk so much to let her son feel what he rarely feels: competent and in control? Describe something your mother did to support you, or something you've done to help someone feel confident and independent.

11. Silvia accepts Patty Jane's impulsive invitation to leave New Mexico and come to Minnesota. Neither of them imagines that one day they will be in-laws! Have you ever invited someone to do something and then been surprised by the unexpected results?

12. Silvia and Harry find success in making music together. If you could share a dream career with a partner, spouse, or friend, what would it be?

13. Thor and Clyde Chuka are important role models for Harry and Lewis. How does each man influence these boys?

14. Lewis is inspired by all the creativity of the people who live at the lodge. How do you fulfill your need to make something?

15. If you were hired to teach a class or a seminar at the Blue Moon Lodge, what would you teach?

16. When she feels the triplets are old enough to understand, Nora tells them about their father. Do you think she should have told them earlier, later, or not at all? Some people believe secrets are ultimately harmful, but others believe they can protect us or the people we love. What do you think?

17. Age doesn't slow down Ione or Patty Jane; it seems to affect some of their friends much more. Do you know someone who has stayed youthful in mind, body, or spirit, and how have they done that?

18. The Once in a Blue Moon Lodge is a sanctuary for its inhabitants. Is there a special place that serves that purpose for you?

19. Ulla has a strong sense of self and won't allow "Elmer Fudd," (her cerebral palsy) to define who she is. Despite her physical challenges, she is often able to navigate smoothly through life's difficult moments, while her sister Grace experiences more complications with her problems. What are the personal characteristics of each of the three sisters that helps them deal with the relationships and the surprises in their lives?

20. If you could ask the author a question, what would it be?

LORNA LANDVIK is the author of eleven novels, including the best-selling *Patty Jane's House of Curl, Angry Housewives Eating Bon Bons,* and *Best to Laugh* (Minnesota, 2014). She has performed stand-up and improvisational comedy around the country and is a public speaker, playwright, and actor, most recently in her one-woman, all-improvised show *Party in the Rec Room.* She lives in Minneapolis.